Stephen Crane

Pictures of War

Stephen Crane

Pictures of War

ISBN/EAN: 9783337009243

Printed in Europe, USA, Canada, Australia, Japan

Cover: Foto ©Andreas Hilbeck / pixelio.de

More available books at **www.hansebooks.com**

PICTURES OF WAR

BY

STEPHEN CRANE

AUTHOR OF "THE OPEN BOAT," ETC.

LONDON
WILLIAM HEINEMANN
1898

Contents

An Appreciation

ALL men are aware of antagonism and desire, or at the least are conscious, even in the nursery, that their hearts are the destined theatres of these emotions; all have felt or heard of their violence; all know that, unlike other emotions, these must often be translated into the glittering drama of decisive speech and deed ; all, in short, expect to be lovers, and peer at the possibility of fighting. And yet how hard it is for the tried to compare notes, for the untried to anticipate experience ! Love and war have been the themes of song and story in every language since the beginning of the world, love-making and fighting the supreme romances of most men and most nations; but any one man knows little enough of either beyond the remembered record of his own chances and achievements, and knows still less whither to turn in order to learn more. We resent this ignorance as a slur on our manhood, and snatch at every chance of dispelling it. And at first, in the scientific "climate" of our time, we are disposed to ask for documents: for love-letters, and letters written from the field of battle. These we imagine, if collected and classified, might supply the evidence for an induction. But on second thoughts, we remember that such love-letters as have been published are, for the most part, not nearer to life than romantic literature, but farther removed from it by many stages: that they are feeble echoes of conventional art—not immediate reflections, but blurred impressions of used plates carelessly copied from meretricious paintings. And so it is with the evidence at first hand upon war. The letters and journals of soldiers and subordinate officers in the field are often of a more pathetic interest than most love-letters; but to the searcher after truth they are still disappointing, for they deal almost exclusively with matters beyond the possibilities of the writer's acquaintance. They are all of surmises—of what dear ones are doing at home, or of the enemy's intentions and the general's plans for outwitting him: they reflect the writer's love and professional ambition, but hardly ever the new things he has heard and seen and felt. And when they attempt these things they sink to the level of the love-letters, and become mere repetitions of accepted form.

I can remember one letter from an English private, describing an engagement in which some eighty men were killed and wounded out of a force of eight thousand: he wrote of comrades in his own battalion "falling like sheep," and gave no clue to the country in which he served. It might have been in Siberia or the Sahara, against savages or civilised troops; you could glean nothing except that he had listened to patriotic songs in music halls at home. Perhaps the most intimate love-letters and battle-letters never get printed at all. But, as it is, you cannot generalise from collections of documents as you can from collections of ferns and beetles: there is not, and there never can be, a science of the perceptions and emotions which thrill young lovers and recruits.

The modern soldier is a little less laconic than his mediæval forebear. Indeed he could hardly surpass the tantalising reserve of, say, Thomas Denyes, a gentleman who fights at Towton, and sums up the carnage of thirty-eight thousand men in a single sentence : "Oure Soveraign Lord hath wonne the feld."* But it is astonishing to note how little even the modern soldier manages to say. He receives rude and swift answers in the field to the questions that haunted his boyish dreams, but he keeps the secret with masonic self-possession.

Marbot's *Memoirs* and, in a lesser degree, Tomkinson's *Diary of a Cavalry Officer*, are both admirable as personal accounts of the Peninsular Campaign, but the warfare they describe is almost as obsolete as that of the Roses, and, even if it were not so, they scarcely attempt the recreation of intense moments by the revelation of their imprint on the minds that endured them. And, on the score of art and of reticence, one is glad that they do not. Their authors were gallant soldiers waging war in fact, and not artists reproducing it in fiction. They satisfy the special curiosity of men interested in strategy and tactics, not the universal curiosity of Man the potential Combatant. He is fascinated by the picturesque and emotional aspects of battle, and the experts tell him little of either. To gratify that curiosity you must turn from the Soldier to the Artist, who is trained both to see and tell, or inspired, even without seeing, to divine what things have been and must be. Some may rebel against accepting his evidence, since it is impossible to prove the truth of his report. But it is equally impossible

* Review of the Paston Letters, *Saturday Review*, November 3c, 1895.

to prove the beauty of his accomplishment. Yet
both are patent to every one capable of accepting
truth or beauty, and by a surer warrant than any
chance coincidence of individual experience and
taste.

Mr. Stephen Crane, the author of *The Red Badge
of Courage* (London : Heinemann), is a great artist,
with something new to say, and consequently, with
a new way of saying it.   His theme, indeed, is an old
one, but old themes re-handled anew in the light of
novel experience, are the stuff out of which masterpieces are made, and in *The Red Badge of Courage*
Mr. Crane has surely contrived a master-piece. He
writes of war—the ominous and alluring possibility
for every man, since the heir of all the ages has won
and must keep his inheritance by secular combat.
The conditions of the age-long contention have
changed and will change, but its certainty is coeval
with progress : so long as there are things worth
fighting for fighting will last, and the fashion of
fighting will change under the reciprocal stresses
of rival inventions. Hence its double interest of
abiding necessity and ceaseless variation. Of all
these variations the most marked has followed,
within the memory of most of us, upon the adoption
of long-range weapons of precision, and continues to
develop, under our eyes, with the development of
rapidity in firing. And yet with the exception of
Zola's *La Débâcle*, no considerable attempt has been
made to portray war under its new conditions. The
old stories are less trustworthy than ever as guides
to the experiences which a man may expect in
battle, and to the emotions which those experiences
are likely to arouse. No doubt the prime factors
in the personal problem—the chances of death and

mutilation — continue to be about the same. In these respects it matters little whether you are pierced by a bullet at two thousand yards or stabbed at hands' play with a dagger. We know that the most appalling death-rolls of recent campaigns have been more than equalled in ancient warfare; and, apart from history, it is clear that, unless one side runs away, neither can win save by the infliction of decisive losses. But although these personal risks continue to be essentially the same, the picturesque and emotional aspects of war are completely altered by every change in the shape and circumstance of imminent death. And these are the fit materials for literature—the things which even dull men remember with the undying imagination of poets, but which, for lack of the writer's art, they cannot communicate. The sights flashed indelibly on the retina of the eye; the sounds that after long silences suddenly cipher; the stenches that sicken in after-life at any chance allusion to decay; or, stirred by these, the storms of passions that force yells of defiance out of inarticulate clowns; the winds of fear that sweep by night along prostrate ranks, with the acceleration of trains and the noise as of a whole town waking from nightmare with stertorous, indrawn gasps—these colossal facts of the senses and the soul are the only colours in which the very image of war can be painted. Mr. Crane has composed his palette with these colours, and has painted a picture that challenges comparison with the most vivid scenes of Tolstoï's *La Guerre et la Paix* or of Zola's *La Débâcle*. This is unstinted praise, but I feel bound to give it after reading the book twice and comparing it with Zola's Sédan and Tolstoï's account of Rostow's squadron for the first time under fire. Indeed, I think that Mr. Crane's picture of war is more complete than Tolstoï's, more true than Zola's. Rostow's sensations are conveyed by Tolstoï with touches more subtile than any to be found even in his *Sébastopol*, but they make but a brief passage in a long book, much else of which is devoted to the theory that Napoleon and his marshals were mere waifs on a tide of humanity, or to the analysis of divers characters exposed to civilian experiences. Zola, on the other hand, compiles an accurate catalogue of almost all that is terrible and nauseating in war; but it is his own catalogue of facts made in cold blood, and not the procession of flashing images shot through the senses into one brain, and fluctuating there with its rhythm of exaltation and fatigue. *La Débâcle* gives the whole truth, the truth of science, as it is observed by a shrewd intellect, but not the truth of experience as it is felt in fragments magnified or diminished in accordance with the patient's mood. The terrible things in war are not always terrible; the nauseating things do not always sicken. On the contrary, it is even these which sometimes lift the soul to heights from which they become invisible. And, again, at other times, it is the little miseries of most ignoble insignificance which fret through the last fibres of endurance.

Mr. Crane, for his distinction, has hit on a new device, or at least on one which has never been used before with such consistency and effect. In order to show the features of modern war, he takes a subject—a youth with a peculiar temperament, capable of exaltation and yet morbidly sensitive. Then he traces the successive impressions made on such a temperament, from minute to minute, during two days of heavy fighting. He stages the drama of war, so to speak, within the mind of one man, and then admits you as to a theatre. You may, if you please, object that this youth is unlike most other young men who serve in the ranks, and that the same events would have impressed the average man differently; but you are convinced that this man's soul is truly drawn, and that the impressions made in it are faithfully rendered. The youth's temperament is merely the medium which the artist has chosen: that it is exceptionally plastic makes but for the deeper incision of his work. It follows from Mr. Crane's method that he creates by his art even such a first-hand report of war as we seek in vain among the journals and letters of soldiers. But the book is not written in the form of an autobiography: the author narrates. He is therefore at liberty to give scenery and action, down to the slightest gestures and outward signs of inward elation or suffering, and he does this with the vigour and terseness of a master. Had he put his descriptions of scenery and his atmospheric effects, or his reports of overheard conversations, into the mouth of his youth, their very excellence would have belied all likelihood. Yet in all his descriptions and all his reports he confines himself only to such things as that youth heard and saw, and, of these, only to such as influenced his emotions. By this compromise he combines the strength and truth of a monodrama with the directness and colour of the best narrative prose. The monodrama suffices for the lyrical emotion of Tennyson's *Maud*; but in Browning's *Martin Relph* you feel the constraint of a form which in his *Ring and the Book* entails repetition often intolerable.

Mr. Crane discovers his youth, Henry Fleming,

in a phase of disillusion. It is some monotonous months since boyish "visions of broken-bladed glory" impelled him to enlist in the Northern Army towards the middle of the American war. That impulse is admirably given: "One night as he lay in bed, the winds had carried to him the clangouring of the church bells, as some enthusiast jerked the rope frantically to tell the twisted news of a great battle. This voice of the people rejoicing in the night had made him shiver in a prolonged ecstasy of excitement. Later he had gone down to his mother's room, and had spoken thus: 'Ma, I'm going to enlist.' 'Henry, don't you be a fool,' his mother had replied. She had then covered her face with the quilt. There was an end to the matter for that night." But the next morning he enlists. He is impatient of the homely injunctions given him in place of the heroic speech he expects in accordance with a tawdry convention, and so departs, with a "vague feeling of relief." But, looking back from the gate, he sees his mother "kneeling among the potato parings. Her brown face upraised and stained with tears, her spare form quivering." Since then the army has done "little but sit still and try to keep warm" till he has "grown to regard himself merely as a part of a vast blue demonstration." In the sick languor of this waiting, he begins to suspect his courage, and lies awake by night through hours of morbid introspection. He tries "to prove to himself mathematically that he would not run from a battle"; he constantly leads the conversation round to the problem of courage in order to gauge the confidence of his messmates.

"How do you know you won't run when the time comes?" asked the youth. "Run?" said the loud one, "run?—of course not!" He laughed. "Well," continued the youth, "lots of good-a-'nough men have thought they was going to do great things before the fight, but when the time come they skedaddled." "Oh, that's all true, I s'pose," replied the other, "but I'm not going to skedaddle. The man that bets on my running will lose his money, that's all." He nodded confidently.

The youth is a "mental outcast" among his comrades, "wrestling with his personal problem," and sweating as he listens to the muttered scoring of a card game, his eyes fixed on the "red, shivering reflection of a fire." Every day they drill; every night they watch the red camp-fires of the enemy on the far shore of a river, eating their hearts out. At last they march: "In the gloom before the break of the day their uniforms glowed a deep purple blue. From across the river the red eyes were still peering. In the eastern sky there was a yellow patch, like a rug laid for the feet of the coming sun; and against it, black and pattern-like, loomed the gigantic figure of the colonel on a gigantic horse." The book is full of such vivid impressions, half of sense and half of imagination: The columns as they marched "were like two serpents crawling from the cavern of night." But the march, which, in his boyish imagination, should have led forthwith into melodramatic action, is but the precursor of other marches. After days of weariness and nights of discomfort, at last, as in life, without preface, and in a lull of the mind's anxiety, the long-dreaded and long-expected is suddenly and smoothly in process of accomplishment: "One grey morning he was kicked on the leg by the tall soldier, and then, before he was entirely awake, he found himself running down a wood road in the midst of men who were panting with the first effects of speed. His canteen banged rhythmically upon his thigh, and his haversack bobbed softly. His musket bounced a trifle from his shoulder at each stride and made his cap feel uncertain upon his head." From this moment, reached on the thirtieth page, the drama races through another hundred and sixty pages to the end of the book, and to read those pages is in itself an experience of breathless, lambent, detonating life. So brilliant and detached are the images evoked that, like illuminated bodies actually seen, they leave their fever-bright phantasms floating before the brain. You may shut the book, but you still see the battle-flags "jerked about madly in the smoke," or sinking with "dying gestures of despair," the men "dropping here and there like bundles"; the captain shot dead with "an astonished and sorrowful look as if he thought some friend had done him an ill turn"; and the litter of corpses, "twisted in fantastic contortions," as if "they had fallen from some great height, dumped out upon the ground from the sky." The book is full of sensuous impressions that leap out from the picture: of gestures, attitudes, grimaces, that flash into portentous definition, like faces from the climbing clouds of nightmare. It leaves the imagination bounded with a "dense wall of smoke, furiously slit and slashed by the knife-like fire from the rifles." It leaves, in short, such indelible traces as are left by the actual experience of war. The picture shows grisly shadows and vermilion splashes, but, as in the vast drama it reflects so truly, these features, though insistent, are small in size, and are lost in the immensity of the theatre. The tranquil forest stands around; the "fairy-blue of the sky" is over it all. And, as in the actual experience of war, the impressions which

these startling features inflict, though acute, are
localised and not too deep : are as it were mere pin-
pricks, or, at worst, clean cuts from a lancet in a
body thrilled with currents of physical excitement
and sopped with anæsthetics of emotion. Here is
the author's description of a forlorn hope :—

As the regiment swung from its position out into a cleared
space the woods and thickets before it awakened. Yellow
flames leaped toward it from many directions. The line
swung straight for a moment. Then the right wing swung
forward ; it in turn was surpassed by the left. Afterward
the centre careered to the front until the regiment was a
wedge-shaped mass . . . . the men, pitching forward insanely, had burst into cheerings, mob-like and barbaric, but
tuned in strange keys that can arouse the dullard and the
stoic . . . . There was the delirium that encounters despair
and death, and is heedless and blind to odds . . . . Presently
the straining pace ate up the energies of the men. As if by
agreement, the leaders began to slacken their speed. The
volleys directed against them had a seeming wind-like effect.
The regiment snorted and blew. Among some stolid trees it
began to falter and hesitate . . . . The youth had a vague
belief that he had run miles, and he thought, in a way, that
he was now in some new and unknown land . . . .

The charge withers away, and the lieutenant, the
youth, and his friend run forward to rally the
regiment.

In front of the colours three men began to bawl, "Come on !
Come on !" They danced and gyrated like tortured savages.
The flag, obedient to these appeals, bended its glittering form
and swept toward them. The men wavered in indecision for a
moment, and then with a long wailful cry the dilapidated regiment surged forward and began its new journey. Over the
field went the scurrying mass. It was a handful of men
splattered into the faces of the enemy. Toward it instantly
sprang the yellow tongues. A vast quantity of blue smoke
hung before them. A mighty banging made ears valueless.
The youth ran like a madman to reach the woods before a

bullet could discover him. He ducked his head low, like a
football player. In his haste his eyes almost closed, and the
scene was a wild blur. Pulsating saliva stood at the corner
of his mouth. Within him, as he hurled forward, was born a
love, a despairing fondness for this flag that was near him.
It was a creation of beauty and invulnerability. It was a
goddess radiant, that bended its form with an imperious
gesture to him. It was a woman, red and white, hating and
loving, that called him with the voice of his hopes. Because
no harm could come to it he endowed it with power. He
kept near, as if it could be a saver of lives, and an imploring
cry went from his mind.

This passage directly challenges comparison with
Zola's scene, in which the lieutenant and the old
tradition, of an invincible Frenchman overrunning
the world "between his bottle and his girl," expire
together among the morsels of a bullet-eaten flag.
Mr. Crane has probably read *La Débâcle*, and wittingly
threw down his glove. One can only say that he is
justified of his courage.

 Mr. Crane's method, when dealing with things
seen and heard, is akin to Zola's : he omits nothing
and extenuates nothing, save the actual blasphemy
and obscenity of a soldier's oaths. These he indi-
cates, sufficiently for any purpose of art, by brief
allusions to their vigour and variety. Even Zola
has rarely surpassed the appalling realism of Jim
Conklin's death in Chapter X. Indeed, there is
little to criticise in Mr. Crane's observation, except
an undue subordination of the shrill cry of bullets
to the sharp crashing of rifles. He omits the long
chromatic whine defining its invisible arc in the air,
and the fretful snatch a few feet from the listener's
head. In addition to this gift of observation, Mr.
Crane has at command the imaginative phrase. The
firing follows a retreat as with "yellings of eager

metallic hounds"; the men at their mechanic loading and firing are like "fiends jigging heavily in
the smoke"; in a lull before the attack "there
passed slowly the intense moments that precede the
tempest"; then, after single shots, "the battle roar
settled to a rolling thunder, which was a single long
explosion." And, as I have said, when Mr. Crane
deals with things felt he gives a truer report than
Zola. He postulates his hero's temperament—a day-
dreamer given over to morbid self-analysis who
enlists, not from any deep-seated belief in the holi-
ness of fighting for his country, but in hasty pursuit
of a vanishing ambition. This choice enables Mr.
Crane to double his picturesque advantage with an
ethical advantage equally great. Not only is his
youth, like the sufferer in *The Fall of the House of
Usher*, supersensitive to every pin-prick of sensation: he is also a delicate meter of emotion and
fancy. In such a nature the waves of feeling take
exaggerated curves, and hallucination haunts the
brain. Thus, when awaiting the first attack, his
mind is thronged with vivid images of a circus he
had seen as a boy: it is there in definite detail, even
as the Apothecary's shop usurps Romeo's mind at
the crisis of his fate. And thus also, like Herodotus'
Aristodemus, he vacillates between cowardice and
heroism. Nothing could well be more subtile than
his self-deception and that sudden enlightenment which leads him to "throw aside his mental
pamphlets on the philosophy of the retreated and
rules for the guidance of the damned." His soul is
of that kind which, "sick with self-love," can only
be saved "so as by fire"; and it is saved when the
battle-bond of brotherhood is born within it, and is
found plainly of deeper import than the cause for

which he and his comrades fight, even as that cause is loftier than his personal ambition.   By his choice of a hero Mr. Crane displays in the same work a pageant of the senses and a tragedy of the soul.

But he does not obtrude his moral.   The "tall soldier" and the lieutenant are brave and content throughout, the one by custom as a veteran, the other by constitution as a hero.   But the two boys, the youth and his friend, "the loud soldier," are at first querulous braggarts, but at the last they are transmuted by danger until either might truly say—

" We have proved we have hearts in a cause, we are noble still,
    And myself have awaked, as it seems, to the better mind ;
    It is better to fight for the good than to rail at the ill ;
    I have felt with my native land, I am one with my kind,
    I embrace the purpose of God, and the doom assigned."

Let no man cast a stone of contempt at these two lads during their earlier weakness until he has fully gauged the jarring discordance of battle.   To be jostled on a platform when you have lost your luggage and missed your train on an errand of vital importance gives a truer pre-taste of war than any field-day ;   yet many a well-disciplined man will denounce the universe upon slighter provocation. It is enough that these two were boys and that they became men.

Yet must it be said that this youth's emotional experience was singular.   In a battle there are a few physical cowards, abjects born with defective circulations who, literally, turn blue at the approach of danger, and a few on whom danger acts like the keen, rare atmosphere of snow-clad peaks.   But between these extremes come many to whom danger is as strong wine, with the multitude which gladly accepts the "iron laws of tradition" and finds welcome support in "a moving box." To this youth, as the cool dawn of his first day's fighting changed by infinitesimal gradations to a feverish noon, the whole evolution pointed to "a trap"; but I have seen another youth under like circumstances toss a pumpkin into the air and spit it on his sword. To this youth the very landscape was filled with "the stealthy approach of death." You are convinced by the author's art that it was so to this man. But to others, as the clamour increases, it is as if the serenity of the morning had taken refuge in their brains. This man "stumbles over the stones as he runs breathlessly forward"; another realises for the first time how right it is to be adroit even in running. The movement of his body becomes an art, which is not self-conscious, since its whole intention is to impress others within the limits of a modest decorum. We know that both love and courage teach this mastery over the details of living. You can tell from the way one woman, out of all the myriads, walks down Piccadilly, that she is at last aware of love. And you can tell from the way a man enters a surgery or runs toward a firing-line that he, too, realises how wholly the justification of any one life lies in its perfect adjustment to others. The woman in love, the man in battle, may each say, for their moment, with the artist, "I was made perfect too." They also are of the few to whom "God whispers in the ear."

But had Mr. Crane taken an average man he would have written an ordinary story, whereas he has written one which is certain to last. It is glorious to see his youth discover courage in the bed-rock of primeval antagonism after the collapse of his tinsel bravado; it is something higher to see him raise upon that rock the temple of resignation. Mr. Crane, as an artist, achieves by his singleness of purpose a truer and completer picture of war than either Tolstoï, bent also upon proving the insignificance of heroes, or Zola, bent also upon prophesying the regeneration of France. That is much; but it is more that his work of art, when completed, chimes with the universal experience of mankind; that his heroes find in their extreme danger, if not confidence in their leaders and conviction in their cause, at least the conviction that most men do what they can or, at most, what they must. We have few good accounts of battles—many of shipwrecks; and we know that, just as the storm rises, so does the commonplace captain show as a god, and the hysterical passenger as a cheerful heroine.

It is but a further step to recognise all life for a battle and this earth for a vessel lost in space. We may then infer that virtues easy in moments of distress may be useful also in everyday experience.

GEORGE WYNDHAM.

The
Red Badge of Courage

CHAPTER I

THE cold passed reluctantly from the earth, and the retiring fogs revealed an army stretched out on the hills, resting. As the landscape changed from brown to green, the army awakened, and began to tremble with eagerness at the noise of rumours. It cast its eyes upon the roads, which were growing from long troughs of liquid mud to proper thoroughfares. A river, amber-tinted in the shadow of its banks, purled at the army's feet; and at night, when the stream had become of a sorrowful blackness, one could see across it the red, eye-like gleam of hostile camp-fires set in the low brows of distant hills.

Once a certain tall soldier developed virtues and went resolutely to wash a shirt. He came flying back from a brook waving his garment banner-like. He was swelled with a tale he had heard from a reliable friend, who had heard it from a truthful cavalryman, who had heard it from his trustworthy

*

A

brother, one of the orderlies at division headquarters. He adopted the important air of a herald in red and gold.

"We're goin' t' move t' morrah—sure," he said pompously to a group in the company street. "We're goin' 'way up the river, cut across, an' come around in behint 'em."

To his attentive audience he drew a loud and elaborate plan of a very brilliant campaign. When he had finished, the blue-clothed men scattered into small arguing groups between the rows of squat brown huts. A negro teamster who had been dancing upon a cracker-box with the hilarious encouragement of twoscore soldiers was deserted. He sat mournfully down. Smoke drifted lazily from a multitude of quaint chimneys.

"It's a lie! that's all it is—a thunderin' lie!" said another private loudly. His smooth face was flushed, and his hands were thrust sulkily into his trousers' pockets. He took the matter as an affront to him. "I don't believe the derned old army's ever going to move. We're set. I've got ready to move eight times in the last two weeks, and we ain't moved yet."

The tall soldier felt called upon to defend the truth of a rumour he himself had introduced. He and the loud one came near to fighting over it.

A corporal began to swear before the assemblage. He had just put a costly board floor in his house, he said. During the early spring he had refrained from adding extensively to the comfort of his environment, because he had felt that the army might start on the march at any moment. Of late, however, he had been impressed that they were in a sort of eternal camp.

Many of the men engaged in a spirited debate. One outlined in a peculiarly lucid manner all the plans of the commanding general. He was opposed by men who advocated that there were other plans of campaign. They clamoured at each other, numbers making futile bids for the popular attention. Meanwhile, the soldier who had fetched the rumour bustled about with much importance. He was continually assailed by questions.

"What's up, Jim?"

"Th' army's goin' t' move."

"Ah, what yeh talkin' about? How yeh know it is?"

"Well, yeh kin b'lieve me er not, jest as yeh like. I don't care a hang."

There was much food for thought in the manner in which he replied. He came near to convincing them by disdaining to produce proofs. They grew much excited over it.

There was a youthful private who listened with eager ears to the words of the tall soldier and to the varied comments of his comrades. After receiving a fill of discussions concerning marches and attacks, he went to his hut and crawled through an intricate hole that served it as a door. He wished to be alone with some new thoughts that had lately come to him.

He lay down on a wide bank that stretched across the end of the room. In the other end, cracker-boxes were made to serve as furniture. They were grouped about the fireplace. A picture from an illustrated weekly was upon the log walls, and three rifles were paralleled on pegs. Equipments hung on handy projections, and some tin dishes lay upon a small pile of firewood. A folded tent was serving as a roof. The sunlight, without, beating upon it, made it glow a light yellow shade. A small window shot an oblique square of whiter light upon the cluttered floor. The smoke from the fire at times neglected the clay chimney and wreathed into the room, and this flimsy chimney of clay and sticks made endless threats to set ablaze the whole establishment.

The youth was in a little trance of astonishment. So they were at last going to fight. On the morrow, perhaps, there would be a battle, and he would be in it. For a time he was obliged to labour to make himself believe. He could not accept with assurance an omen that he was about to mingle in one of those great affairs of the earth.

He had, of course, dreamed of battles all his life— of vague and bloody conflicts that had thrilled him with their sweep and fire. In visions he had seen himself in many struggles. He had imagined peoples secure in the shadow of his eagle-eyed prowess. But awake he had regarded battles as crimson blotches on the pages of the past. He had put them as things of the bygone with his thought-images of heavy crowns and high castles. There was a portion of the world's history which he had regarded as the time of wars, but it, he thought, had been long gone over the horizon and had disappeared for ever.

From his home. his youthful eyes had looked upon the war in his own country with distrust. It must be some sort of a play affair. He had long despaired of witnessing a Greek-like struggle. Such would be no more, he had said. Men were better, or more timid. Secular and religious education had effaced the throat-grappling instinct, or else firm finance held in check the passions.

He had burned several times to enlist. Tales of great movements shook theland. They might not be distinctly Homeric, but there seemed to be much glory in them. He had read of marches, sieges, conflicts, and he had longed to see it all. His busy mind had drawn for him large pictures extravagant in colour, lurid with breathless deeds.

But his mother had discouraged him. She had affected to look with some contempt upon the quality of his war ardour and patriotism. She could calmly seat herself, and with no apparent difficulty give him many hundreds of reasons why he was of vastly more importance on the farm than on the field of battle. She had had certain ways of expression that told him that her statements on the subject came from a deep conviction. Moreover, on her side, was his belief that her ethical motive in the argument was impregnable.

At last, however, he had made firm rebellion against this yellow light thrown upon the colour of his ambitions. The newspapers, the gossip of the village, his own picturings, had aroused him to an uncheckable degree. They were in truth fighting finely down there. Almost every day the newspapers printed accounts of a decisive victory.

One night, as he lay in bed, the winds had carried to him the clangouring of the church bell, as some enthusiast jerked the rope frantically to tell the twisted news of a great battle. This voice of the people rejoicing in the night had made him shiver in a prolonged ecstasy of excitement. Later he had gone down to his mother's room and had spoken thus: "Ma, I'm going to enlist."

"Henry, don't you be a fool," his mother had replied. She had then covered her face with the quilt. There was an end to the matter for that night.

Nevertheless, the next morning he had gone to a town that was near his mother's farm and had enlisted in a company that was forming there. When he had returned home his mother was milking the brindle cow. Four others stood waiting. "Ma, I've enlisted," he had said to her diffidently. There was a short silence. "The Lord's will be done, Henry," she had finally replied, and had then continued to milk the brindle cow.

When he had stood in the doorway with his soldier's clothes on his back, and with the light of excitement and expectancy in his eyes almost defeating the glow of regret for the home bonds, he had seen two tears leaving their trails on his mother's scarred cheeks.

Still, she had disappointed him by saying nothing whatever about returning with his shield or on it.

He had privately primed himself for a beautiful scene. He had prepared certain sentences which he thought could be used with touching effect. But her words destroyed his plans. She had doggedly peeled potatoes, and addressed him as follows: "You watch out, Henry, an' take good care of yerself in this here fighting business—you watch out, an' take good care of yerself. Don't go a-thinkin' you can lick the hull rebel army at the start, because yeh can't. Yer jest one little feller amongst a hull lot of others, and yeh've got to keep quiet an' do what they tell yeh. I know how you are, Henry.

"I've knet yeh eight pair of socks, Henry; and I've put in all yer best shirts, because I want my boy to be jest as warm and comf'able as anybody in the army. Whenever they get holes in 'em, I want yeh to send 'em right-away back to me, so's I kin dern 'em.

"An' allus be careful an' choose yer comp'ny. There's lots of bad men in the army, Henry. The army makes 'em wild, and they like nothing better than the job of leading off a young feller like you, as ain't never been away from home much, and has allus had a mother, an' a-learning 'em to drink and swear. Keep clear of them folks, Henry. I don't want yeh to ever do anything, Henry, that yeh would be 'shamed to let me know about. Jest think as if I was a-watchin' yeh. If yeh keep that in yer mind allus, I guess yeh'll come out about right.

"Yeh must allus remember yer father, too, child, an' remember he never drunk a drop of licker in his life, and seldom swore a cross oath.

"I don't know what else to tell yeh, Henry, excepting that yeh must never do no shirking, child, on my account. If so be a time comes when yeh have to be kilt or do a mean thing, why, Henry, don't think of anything 'cept what's right, because there's many a woman has to bear up 'ginst sech things these times, and the Lord 'll take keer of us all.

"Don't forgit about the socks and the shirts, child; and I've put a cup of blackberry jam with yer bundle, because I know yeh like it above all things. Good-bye, Henry. Watch out, and be a good boy."

He had, of course, been impatient under the ordeal of this speech. It had not been quite what he expected, and he had borne it with an air of irritation. He departed feeling vague relief.

Still, when he had looked back from the gate, he had seen his mother kneeling among the potato parings. Her brown face, upraised, was stained with tears, and her spare form was quivering. He bowed his head and went on, feeling suddenly ashamed of his purposes.

From his home he had gone.to the seminary to bid adieu to many schoolmates. They had thronged about him with wonder and admiration. He had felt the gulf now between them, and had swelled with calm pride. He and some of his fellows who had donned blue were quite overwhelmed with privileges for all of one afternoon, and it had been a very delicious thing. They had strutted.

A certain light-haired girl had made vivacious

fun at his martial spirit; but there was another and darker girl whom he had gazed at steadfastly, and he thought she grew demure and sad at sight of his blue and brass. As he had walked down the path between the rows of oaks, he had turned his head and detected her at a window watching his departure. As he perceived her, she had immediately begun to stare up through the high tree branches at the sky. He had seen a good deal of flurry and haste in her movement as she changed her attitude. He often thought of it.

On the way to Washington his spirit had soared. The regiment was fed and caressed at station after station until the youth had believed that he must be a hero. There was a lavish expenditure of bread and cold meats, coffee, and pickles and cheese. As he basked in the smiles of the girls, and was patted and complimented by the old men, he had felt growing within him the strength to do mighty deeds of arms.

After complicated journeyings with many pauses, there had come months of monotonous life in a camp. He had had the belief that real war was a series of death struggles, with small time in between for sleep and meals; but since his regiment had come to the field the army had done little but sit still and try to keep warm.

He was brought then gradually back to his old ideas. Greek-like struggles would be no more. Men were better, or more timid. Secular and religious education had effaced the throat-grappling instinct, or else firm finance held in check the passions.

He had grown to regard himself merely as a

part of a vast blue demonstration. His province was to look out, as far as he could, for his personal comfort. For recreation he could twiddle his thumbs and speculate on the thoughts which must agitate the minds of the generals. Also, he was drilled and drilled and reviewed, and drilled and drilled and reviewed.

The only foes he had seen were some pickets along the river bank. They were a sun-tanned, philosophical lot, who sometimes shot reflectively at the blue pickets. When reproached for this afterwards, they usually expressed sorrow, and swore by their gods that the guns had exploded without their permission. The youth, on guard duty one night, conversed across the stream with one of them. He was a slightly ragged man, who spat skilfully between his shoes, and possessed a great fund of bland and infantile assurance. The youth liked him personally.

"Yank," the other had informed him, "yer a right dum good feller." This sentiment, floating to him upon the still air, had made him temporarily regret war.

Various veterans had told him tales. Some talked of grey, bewhiskered hordes who were advancing with relentless curses, and chewing tobacco with unspeakable valour—tremendous bodies of fierce soldiery who were sweeping along like the Huns. Others spoke of tattered and eternally hungry men who fired despondent powders. "They'll charge through hell's fire an' brimstone t' git a holt on a haversack, an' sech stomachs ain't a-lastin' long," he was told. From the stories, the youth imagined the red, live bones sticking out through slits in the faded uniforms.

Still, he could not put a whole faith in veterans' tales, for recruits were their prey. They talked much of smoke, fire, and blood, but he could not tell how much might be lies. They persistently yelled "Fresh fish!" at him, and were in nowise to be trusted.

However, he perceived now that it did not greatly matter what kind of soldiers he was going to fight, so long as they fought, which fact no one disputed. There was a more serious problem. He lay in his bunk pondering upon it. He tried to mathematically prove to himself that he would not run from a battle.

Previously he had never felt obliged to wrestle too seriously with this question. In his life he had taken certain things for granted, never challenging his belief in ultimate success, and bothering little about means and roads. But here he was confronted with a thing of moment. It had suddenly appeared to him that perhaps in a battle he might run. He was forced to admit that as far as war was concerned he knew nothing of himself.

A sufficient time before he would have allowed the problem to kick its heels at the outer portals of his mind, but now he felt compelled to give serious attention to it.

A little panic-fear grew in his mind. As his imagination went forward to a fight, he saw hideous possibilities. He contemplated the lurking menaces of the future, and failed in an effort to see himself standing stoutly in the midst of them. He recalled his visions of broken-bladed glory, but in the shadow of the impending tumult he suspected them to be impossible pictures.

He sprang from the bunk and began to pace nervously to and fro. "Good Lord, what's th' matter with me?" he said aloud.

He felt that in this crisis his laws of life were useless. Whatever he had learned of himself was here of no avail. He was an unknown quantity. He saw that he would again be obliged to experiment as he had in early youth. He must accumulate information of himself, and meanwhile he resolved to remain close upon his guard lest those qualities of which he knew nothing should everlastingly disgrace him. "Good Lord!" he repeated in dismay.

After a time the tall soldier slid dexterously through the hole. The loud private followed. They were wrangling.

"That's all right," said the tall soldier as he entered. He waved his hand expressively. "You can believe me or not, jest as you like. All you've got to do is to sit down and wait as quiet as you can. Then pretty soon you'll find out I was right."

His comrade grunted stubbornly. For a moment he seemed to be searching for a formidable reply. Finally he said, "Well, you don't know everything in the world, do you?"

"Didn't say I knew everything in the world," retorted the other sharply. He began to stow various articles snugly into his knapsack.

The youth, pausing in his nervous walk, looked down at the busy figure. "Going to be a battle sure, is there, Jim?" he asked.

"Of course there is," replied the tall soldier. "Of course there is. You jest wait 'til to-morrow, and you'll see one of the biggest battles ever was. You jest wait."

"Thunder!" said the youth.

"Oh, you'll see fighting this time, my boy, what'll be regular out-and-out fighting," added the tall soldier, with the air of a man who is about to exhibit a battle for the benefit of his friends.

"Huh!" said the loud one from a corner.

"Well," remarked the youth, "like as not this story 'll turn out jest like them others did."

"Not much it won't," replied the tall soldier, exasperated. "Not much it won't. Didn't the cavalry all start this morning?" He glared about him. No one denied his statement. "The cavalry started this morning," he continued. "They say there ain't hardly any cavalry left in camp. They're going to Richmond, or some place, while we fight all the Johnnies. It's some dodge like that. The regiment's got orders, too. A feller what seen 'em go to headquarters told me a little while ago. And they're raising blazes all over camp—anybody can see that."

"Shucks!" said the loud one.

The youth remained silent for a time. At last he spoke to the tall soldier. "Jim!"

"What?"

"How do you think the reg'ment 'll do?"

"Oh, they'll fight all right, I guess, after they once get into it," said the other, with cold judgment. He made a fine use of the third person. "There's been heaps of fun poked at 'em because they're new, of course, and all that; but they'll fight all right, I guess."

"Think any of the boys 'll run?" persisted the youth.

"Oh, there may be a few of 'em run, but there's them kind in every regiment, 'specially when they first goes under fire," said the other in a tolerant way. "Of course it might happen that the hull kit-and-boodle might start and run, if some big fighting came first-off, and then again they might stay and fight like fun. But you can't bet on nothing. Of course they ain't never been under fire yet, and it ain't likely they'll lick the hull rebel army all-to-oncet the first time; but I think they'll fight better than some, if worse than others. That's the way I figger. They call the reg'ment 'Fresh fish' and everything; but the boys come of good stock, and most of 'em 'll fight like sin after they oncet git shootin'," he added, with a mighty emphasis on the last four words.

"Oh, you think you know——" began the loud soldier with scorn.

The other turned savagely upon him. They had a rapid altercation, in which they fastened upon each other various strange epithets.

The youth at last interrupted them. "Did you ever think you might run yourself, Jim?" he asked. On concluding the sentence he laughed as if he had meant to aim a joke. The loud soldier also giggled.

The tall private waved his hand. "Well," said he profoundly, "I've thought it might get too hot for Jim Conklin in some of them scrimmages, and if a whole lot of boys started and run, why, I s'pose I'd start and run. And if I once started to run, I'd run like the devil, and no mistake. But if everybody was a-standing and a-fighting, why, I'd stand and fight. Be jiminey, I would. I'll bet on it."

"Huh!" said the loud one.

The youth of this tale felt gratitude for these words of his comrade. He had feared that all of the untried men possessed a great and correct confidence. He now was in a measure reassured.

CHAPTER II

THE next morning the youth discovered that his tall comrade had been the fast-flying messenger of a mistake. There was much scoffing at the latter by those who had yesterday been firm adherents of his views, and there was even a little sneering by men who had never believed the rumour. The tall one fought with a man from Chatfield Corners and beat him severely.

The youth felt, however, that his problem was in nowise lifted from him. There was, on the contrary, an irritating prolongation. The tale had created in him a great concern for himself. Now, with the new-born question in his mind, he was compelled to sink back into his old place as part of a blue demonstration.

For days he made ceaseless calculations, but they were all wondrously unsatisfactory. He found that he could establish nothing. He finally concluded that the only way to prove himself was to go into the blaze, and then figuratively to watch his legs to discover their merits and faults. He reluctantly admitted that he could not sit still and with a mental slate and pencil derive an answer. To gain it, he must have blaze, blood, and danger, even as a chemist requires this, that, and the other. So he fretted for an opportunity.

Meanwhile he continually tried to measure himself by his comrades. The tall soldier, for one, gave him some assurance. This man's serene unconcern dealt him a measure of confidence, for he had known him since childhood, and from his intimate knowledge he did not see how he could be capable of anything that was beyond him, the youth. Still, he thought that his comrade might be mistaken about himself. Or, on the other hand, he might be a man heretofore doomed to peace and obscurity, but, in reality, made to shine in war.

The youth would have liked to have discovered another who suspected himself. A sympathetic comparison of mental notes would have been a joy to him.

He occasionally tried to fathom a comrade with seductive sentences. He looked about to find men in the proper mood. All attempts failed to bring forth any statement which looked in any way like a confession to those doubts which he privately acknowledged in himself. He was afraid to make an open declaration of his concern, because he dreaded to place some unscrupulous confidant upon the high plane of the unconfessed from which elevation he could be derided.

In regard to his companions his mind wavered between two opinions, according to his mood. Sometimes he inclined to believing them all heroes. In fact, he usually admitted in secret the superior development of the higher qualities in others. He could conceive of men going very insignificantly about the world bearing a load of courage unseen; and although he had known many of his comrades through boyhood, he began to fear that his judgment of them had been blind. Then, in other moments, he flouted these theories, and assured himself that his fellows were all privately wondering and quaking.

His emotions made him feel strange in the presence of men who talked excitedly of a prospective battle as of a drama they were about to witness, with nothing but eagerness and curiosity apparent in their faces. It was often that he suspected them to be liars.

He did not pass such thoughts without severe condemnation of himself. He dinned reproaches at times. He was convicted by himself of many shameful crimes against the gods of traditions.

In his great anxiety his heart was continually clamouring at what he considered the intolerable slowness of the generals. They seemed content to perch tranquilly on the river bank, and leave him bowed down by the weight of a great problem. He wanted it settled forthwith. He could not long bear such a load, he said. Sometimes his anger at the commanders reached an acute stage, and he grumbled about the camp like a veteran.

One morning, however, he found himself in the ranks of his prepared regiment. The men were whispering speculations, and recounting the old rumours. In the gloom before the break of the day their uniforms glowed a deep purple hue. From across the river the red eyes were still peering. In the eastern sky there was a yellow patch, like a rug laid for the feet of the coming sun ; and against it, black and pattern-like, loomed the gigantic figure of the colonel on a gigantic horse.

From off in the darkness came the trampling of feet. The youth could occasionally see dark shadows that moved like monsters. The regiment stood at rest for what seemed a long time. The youth grew impatient. It was unendurable the way these affairs were managed. He wondered how long they were to be kept waiting.

As he looked all about him and pondered upon the mystic gloom, he began to believe that at any moment the ominous distance might he aflare, and the rolling crashes of an engagement come to his ears. Staring once at the red eyes across the river, he conceived them to be growing larger, as the orbs of a row of dragons advancing. He turned toward the colonel and saw him lift his gigantic arm and calmly stroke his moustache.

At last he heard from along the road at the foot of the hill the clatter of a horse's galloping hoofs. It must be the coming of orders. He bent forward, scarce breathing. The exciting clickety-click, as it grew louder and louder, seemed to be beating upon his soul. Presently a horseman with jangling equipment drew rein before the colonel of the regiment. The two held a short, sharp-worded conversation. The men in the foremost ranks craned their necks.

As the horseman wheeled his animal and galloped

away he turned to shout over his shoulder, "Don't forget that box of cigars!" The colonel mumbled in reply. The youth wondered what a box of cigars had to do with war.

A moment later the regiment went swinging off into the darkness. It was now like one of those moving monsters wending with many feet. The air was heavy, and cold with dew. A mass of wet grass, marched upon, rustled like silk.

There was an occasional flash and glimmer of steel from the backs of all these huge crawling reptiles. From the road came creakings and grumblings as some surly guns were dragged away.

The men stumbled along, still muttering speculations. There was a subdued debate. Once a man fell down, and as he reached for his rifle a comrade, unseeing, trod upon his hand. He of the injured fingers swore bitterly and aloud. A low, tittering laugh went among his fellows.

Presently they passed into a roadway and marched forward with easy strides. A dark regiment moved before them, and from behind also came the tinkle of equipments on the bodies of marching men.

The rushing yellow of the developing day went on behind their backs. When the sun-rays at last struck full and mellowingly upon the earth, the youth saw that the landscape was streaked with two long, thin, black columns which disappeared on the brow of a hill in front, and rearward vanished in a wood. They were like two serpents crawling from the cavern of the night.

The river was not in view. The tall soldier burst

into praises of what he thought to be his powers of perception.

Some of the tall one's companions cried with emphasis that they, too, had evolved the same thing, and they congratulated themselves upon it. But there were others who said that the tall one's plan was not the true one at all. They persisted with other theories. There was a vigorous discussion.

The youth took no part in them. As he walked along in careless line, he was engaged with his own eternal debate. He could not hinder himself from dwelling upon it. He was despondent and sullen, and threw shifting glances about him. He looked ahead, often expecting to hear from the advance the rattle of firing.

But the long serpents crawled slowly from hill to hill without bluster of smoke. A dun-coloured cloud of dust floated away to the right. The sky overhead was of a fairy blue.

The youth studied the faces of his companions, ever on the watch to detect kindred emotions. He suffered disappointment. Some ardour of the air which was causing the veteran commands to move with glee—almost with song—had infected the new regiment. The men began to speak of victory as of a thing they knew. Also, the tall soldier received his vindication. They were certainly going to come around in behind the enemy. They expressed commiseration for that part of the army which had been left upon the river bank, felicitating themselves upon being a part of a blasting host.

The youth, considering himself as separated from the others, was saddened by the blithe and merry speeches that went from rank to rank. The company wags all made their best endeavours. The regiment tramped to the tune of laughter.

The blatant soldier often convulsed whole files by his biting sarcasms aimed at the tall one.

And it was not long before all the men seemed to forget their mission. Whole brigades grinned in unison, and regiments laughed.

A rather fat soldier attempted to pilfer a horse from a door-yard. He planned to load his knapsack upon it. He was escaping with his prize when a young girl rushed from the house and grabbed the animal's mane. There followed a wrangle. The young girl, with pink cheeks and shining eyes, stood like a dauntless statue.

The observant regiment, standing at rest in the roadway, whooped at once, and entered whole-souled upon the side of the maiden. The men became so engrossed in this affair that they entirely ceased to remember their own large war. They jeered the piratical private, and called attention to various defects in his personal appearance; and they were wildly enthusiastic in support of the young girl.

To her, from some distance, came bold advice, "Hit him with a stick."

There were crows and catcalls showered upon him when he retreated without the horse. The regiment rejoiced at his downfall. Loud and vociferous congratulations were showered upon the maiden, who stood panting and regarding the troops with defiance.

At nightfall the column broke into regimental pieces, and the fragments went into the fields to camp. Tents sprang up like strange plants. Camp fires, like red, peculiar blossoms, dotted the night.

The youth kept from intercourse with his companions as much as circumstances would allow him. In the evening he wandered a few paces into the gloom. From this little distance the many fires, with the black forms of men passing to and fro before the crimson rays, made weird and satanic effects.

He lay down in the grass. The blades pressed tenderly against his cheek. The moon had been lighted and was hung in a tree-top. The liquid stillness of the night enveloping him made him feel vast pity for himself. There was a caress in the soft winds; and the whole mood of the darkness, he thought, was one of sympathy for himself in his distress.

He wished, without reserve, that he was at home again, making the endless rounds from the house to the barn, from the barn to the fields, from the fields to the barn, from the barn to the house. He remembered he had often cursed the brindle cow and her mates, and had sometimes flung milking-stools. But, from his present point of view, there was a halo of happiness about each of their heads, and he would have sacrificed all the brass buttons on the continent to have been enabled to return to them. He told himself that he was not formed for a soldier. And he mused seriously upon the radical differences between himself and those men who were dodging imp-like around the fires.

As he mused thus he heard the rustle of grass, and, upon turning his head, discovered the loud soldier. He called out, "Oh, Wilson!"

The latter approached and looked down. "Why, hello, Henry; is it you? What you doing here?"

"Oh, thinking," said the youth.

The other sat down and carefully lighted his pipe. "You're getting blue, my boy. You're looking thundering peeked. What the dickens is wrong with you?"

"Oh, nothing," said the youth.

The loud soldier launched then into the subject of the anticipated fight. "Oh, we've got 'em now!" As he spoke his boyish face was wreathed in a glee-ful smile, and his voice had an exultant ring. "We've got 'em now. At last, by the eternal thunders, we'll lick 'em good!"

"If the truth was known," he added more soberly, "*they've* licked *us* about every clip up to now; but this time—this time, we'll lick 'em good!"

"I thought you was objecting to this march a little while ago," said the youth coldly.

"Oh, it wasn't that," explained the other. "I don't mind marching if there's going to be fighting at the end of it. What I hate is this getting moved here and moved there, with no good coming of it, as far as I can see, excepting sore feet and damned short rations."

"Well, Jim Conklin says we'll get a plenty of fighting this time."

"He's right for once, I guess, though I can't see how it come. This time we're in for a big battle, and we've got the best end of it, certain sure. Gee rod! how we will thump 'em!"

He arose and began to pace to and fro excitedly. The thrill of his enthusiasm made him walk with an elastic step. He was sprightly, vigorous, fiery in his belief in success. He looked into the future with clear, proud eye, and he swore with the air of an old soldier.

The youth watched him for a moment in silence. When he finally spoke his voice was as bitter as dregs. "Oh, you're going to do great things, I s'pose!"

The loud soldier blew a thoughtful cloud of smoke from his pipe. "Oh, I don't know," he remarked with dignity; "I don't know. I s'pose I'll do as well as the rest. I'm going to try like thunder." He evidently complimented himself upon the modesty of this statement.

"How do you know you won't run when the time comes?" asked the youth.

"Run?" said the loud one; "run?—of course not!" He laughed.

"Well," continued the youth, "lots of good-a-'nough men have thought they was going to do great things before the fight, but when the time come they skedaddled."

"Oh, that's all true, I s'pose," replied the other; "but I'm not going to skedaddle. The man that bets on my running will lose his money, that's all." He nodded confidently.

"Oh, shucks!" said the youth. "You ain't the bravest man in the world, are you?"

"No, I ain't," exclaimed the loud soldier indignantly; "and I didn't say I was the bravest man in the world, neither. I said I was going to do my share of fighting—that's what I said. And I am, too. Who are you, anyhow? You talk as if you thought you was Napoleon Bonaparte." He glared at the youth for a moment, and then strode away.

The youth called in a savage voice after his comrade: "Well, you needn't git mad about it!" But the other continued on his way and made no reply.

He felt alone in space when his injured comrade had disappeared. His failure to discover any mite of resemblance in their view points made him more miserable than before. No one seemed to be wrestling with such a terrific personal problem. He was a mental outcast.

He went slowly to his tent and stretched himself on a blanket by the side of the snoring tall soldier. In the darkness he saw visions of a thousand-tongued fear that would babble at his back and cause him to flee, while others were going coolly about their country's business. He admitted that he would not be able to cope with this monster. He felt that every nerve in his body would be an ear to hear the voices, while other men would remain stolid and deaf.

And as he sweated with the pain of these thoughts, he could hear low, serene sentences.

"I'll bid five." "Make it six." "Seven." "Seven
goes."

He stared at the red, shivering reflection of a
fire on the white wall of his tent until, exhausted
and ill from the monotony of his suffering, he fell
asleep.

CHAPTER III

WHEN another night came the columns, changed
to purple streaks, filed across two pontoon bridges.
A glaring fire wine-tinted the waters of the river.
Its rays, shining upon the moving masses of troops,
brought forth here and there sudden gleams of
silver or gold. Upon the other shore a dark and
mysterious range of hills was curved against the
sky. The insect voices of the night sang solemnly.

After this crossing the youth assured himself
that at any moment they might be suddenly and fear-
fully assaulted from the caves of the lowering woods.
He kept his eyes watchfully upon the darkness.

But his regiment went unmolested to a camping-
place, and its soldiers slept the brave sleep of
wearied men. In the morning they were routed
out with early energy, and hustled along a narrow
road that led deep into the forest.

It was during this rapid march that the regiment
lost many of the marks of a new command.

The men had begun to count the miles upon
their fingers, and they grew tired. "Sore feet
an' damned short rations, that's all," said the loud
soldier. There was perspiration and grumblings.
After a time they began to shed their knapsacks.

Some tossed them unconcernedly down; others hid them carefully, asserting their plans to return for them at some convenient time. Men extricated themselves from thick shirts. Presently few carried anything but their necessary clothing, blankets, haversacks, canteens, and arms and ammunition. " You can now eat and shoot," said the tall soldier to the youth. " That's all you want to do."

There was sudden change from the ponderous infantry of theory to the light and speedy infantry of practice. The regiment, relieved of a burden, received a new impetus. But there was much loss of valuable knapsacks, and, on the whole, very good shirts.

But the regiment was not yet veteran-like in appearance. Veteran regiments in the army were likely to be very small aggregations of men. Once, when the command had first come to the field, some perambulating veterans, noting the length of their column, had accosted them thus: " Hey, fellers, what brigade is that? " And when the men had replied that they formed a regiment and not a brigade, the older soldiers had laughed, and said, " O Gawd ! "

Also, there was too great a similarity in the hats. The hats of a regiment should properly represent the history of headgear for a period of years. And, moreover, there were no letters of faded gold speaking from the colours. They were new and beautiful, and the colour-bearer habitually oiled the pole.

Presently the army again sat down to think. The odour of the peaceful pines was in the men's nostrils. The sound of monotonous axe-blows rang through the forest; and the insects, nodding upon their perches, crooned like old women. The youth returned to his theory of a blue demonstration.

One grey dawn, however, he was kicked in the leg by the tall soldier, and then, before he was entirely awake, he found himself running down a wood road in the midst of men who were panting from the first effects of speed. His canteen banged rhythmically upon his thigh, and his haversack bobbed softly. His musket bounced a trifle from his shoulder at each stride and made his cap feel uncertain upon his head.

He could hear the men whisper jerky sentences: " Say—what's all this — about? " " What th' thunder—we—skedaddlin' this way fer? " " Billie —keep off m' feet. Yeh run—like a cow." And the loud soldier's shrill voice could be heard: "What th' devil they in sich a hurry for? "

The youth thought the damp fog of early morning moved from the rush of a great body of troops. From the distance came a sudden spatter of firing.

He was bewildered. As he ran with his comrades he strenuously tried to think, but all he knew was that if he fell down those coming behind would tread upon him. All his faculties seemed to be needed to guide him over and past obstructions. He felt carried along by a mob.

The sun spread disclosing rays, and, one by one, regiments burst into view like armed men just born of the earth. The youth perceived that the time had come. He was about to be measured. For a moment he felt in the face of his great trial like a babe, and the flesh over his heart seemed very thin. He seized time to look about him calculatingly.

But he instantly saw that it would be impossible for him to escape from the regiment. It inclosed him. And there were iron laws of tradition and law on four sides. He was in a moving box.

As he perceived this fact it occurred to him that he had never wished to come to the war. He had not enlisted of his free will. He had been dragged by the merciless government. And now they were taking him out to be slaughtered.

The regiment slid down a bank and wallowed across a little stream. The mournful current moved slowly on, and from the water, shaded black, some white bubble eyes looked at the men.

As they climbed the hill on the farther side artillery began to boom. Here the youth forgot many things as he felt a sudden impulse of curiosity. He scrambled up the bank with a speed that could not be exceeded by a bloodthirsty man.

He expected a battle scene.

There were some little fields girted and squeezed by a forest. Spread over the grass and in among the tree trunks he could see knots and waving lines of skirmishers, who were running hither and thither and firing at the landscape. A dark battle line lay upon a sunstruck clearing that gleamed orange colour. A flag fluttered.

Other regiments floundered up the bank. The brigade was formed in line of battle, and after a pause started slowly through the woods in the rear of the receding skirmishers, who were continually melting into the scene to appear again farther on. They were always busy as bees, deeply absorbed in their little combats.

The youth tried to observe everything. He did not use care to avoid trees and branches, and his forgotten feet were constantly knocking against stones or getting entangled in briers. He was aware that these battalions with their commotions were woven red and startling into the gentle fabric of softened greens and browns. It looked to be a wrong place for a battlefield.

The skirmishers in advance fascinated him. Their shots into thickets and at distant and prominent trees spoke to him of tragedies—hidden, mysterious, solemn.

Once the line encountered the body of a dead soldier. He lay upon his back staring at the sky. He was dressed in an awkward suit of yellowish brown. The youth could see that the soles of his shoes had been worn to the thinness of writing paper, and from a great rent in one the dead foot projected piteously. And it was as if fate had betrayed the soldier. In death it exposed to his enemies that poverty which in life he had perhaps concealed from his friends.

The ranks opened covertly to avoid the corpse. The invulnerable dead man forced a way for himself. The youth looked keenly at the ashen face. The wind raised the tawny beard. It moved as if a hand were stroking it. He vaguely desired to walk around and around the body and stare;

the impulse of the living to try to read in dead eyes the answer to the Question.

During the march the ardour which the youth had acquired when out of view of the field rapidly faded to nothing. His curiosity was quite easily satisfied. If an intense scene had caught him with its wild swing as he came to the top of the bank, he might have gone roaring on. This advance upon Nature was too calm. He had opportunity to reflect. He had time in which to wonder about himself, and to attempt to probe his sensations.

Absurd ideas took hold upon him. He thought that he did not relish the landscape. It threatened him. A coldness swept over his back, and it is true that his trousers felt to him that they were no fit for his legs at all.

A house standing placidly in distant fields had to him an ominous look. The shadows of the woods were formidable. He was certain that in this vista there lurked fierce-eyed hosts. The swift thought came to him that the generals did not know what they were about. It was all a trap. Suddenly those close forests would bristle with rifle barrels. Iron-like brigades would appear in the rear. They were all going to be sacrificed. The generals were stupids. The enemy would presently swallow the whole command. He glared about him, expecting to see the stealthy approach of his death.

He thought that he must break from the ranks and harangue his comrades. They must not all

*

C

be killed like pigs; and he was sure it would come to pass unless they were informed of these dangers. The generals were idiots to send them marching into a regular pen. There was but one pair of eyes in the corps. He would step forth and make a speech. Shrill and passionate words came to his lips.

The line, broken into moving fragments by the ground, went calmly on through fields and woods. The youth looked at the men nearest him, and saw, for the most part, expressions of deep interest, as if they were investigating something that had fascinated them. One or two stepped with over-valiant airs, as if they were already plunged into war. Others walked as upon thin ice. The greater part of the untested men appeared quiet and absorbed. They were going to look at war, the red animal—war, the blood-swollen god. And they were deeply engrossed in this march.

As he looked the youth gripped his outcry at his throat. He saw that even if the men were tottering with fear they would laugh at his warning. They would jeer him, and, if practicable, pelt him with missiles. Admitting that he might be wrong, a frenzied declamation of the kind would turn him into a worm.

He assumed, then, the demeanour of one who knows that he is doomed alone to unwritten responsibilities. He lagged, with tragic glances at the sky.

He was surprised presently by the young lieutenant of his company, who began heartily to beat him with a sword, calling out in a loud and insolent voice: "Come, young man, get up into ranks there. No skulking 'll do here." He mended his pace with suitable haste. And he hated the lieutenant, who had no appreciation of fine minds. He was a mere brute.

After a time the brigade was halted in the cathedral light of a forest. The busy skirmishers were still popping. Through the aisles of the wood could be seen the floating smoke from their rifles. Sometimes it went up in little balls, white and compact.

During this halt many men in the regiment began erecting tiny hills in front of them. They used stones, sticks, earth, and anything they thought might turn a bullet. Some built comparatively large ones, while others seemed content with little ones.

This procedure caused a discussion among the men. Some wished to fight like duellists, believing it to be correct to stand erect and be, from their feet to their foreheads, a mark. They said they scorned the devices of the cautious. But the others scoffed in reply, and pointed to the veterans on the flanks who were digging at the ground like terriers. In a short time there was quite a barricade along the regimental fronts. Directly, however, they were ordered to withdraw from that place.

This astounded the youth. He forgot his stewing over the advance movement. "Well, then, what did they march us out here for?" he demanded of the tall soldier. The latter with calm faith began a heavy explanation, although he had been compelled to leave a little protection of stones and dirt to which he had devoted much care and skill.

When the regiment was aligned in another position, each man's regard for his safety caused another line of small intrenchments. They ate their noon meal behind a third one. They were moved from this one also. They were marched from place to place with apparent aimlessness.

The youth had been taught that a man became another thing in a battle. He saw his salvation in such a change. Hence this waiting was an ordeal to him. He was in a fever of impatience. He considered that there was denoted a lack of purpose on the part of the generals. He began to complain to the tall soldier. "I can't stand this much longer," he cried. "I don't see what good it does to make us wear out our legs for nothin'." He wished to return to camp, knowing that this affair was a blue demonstration; or else to go into a battle and discover that he had been a fool in his doubts, and was, in truth, a man of traditional courage. The strain of present circumstances he felt to be intolerable.

The philosophical tall soldier measured a sandwich of cracker and pork, and swallowed it in a nonchalant manner. "Oh, I suppose we must go reconnoitring around the country jest to keep 'em from getting too close, or to develop 'em, or something."

"Huh!" said the loud soldier.

"Well," cried the youth, still fidgeting, "I'd rather do anything''most than go tramping 'round

the country all day doing no good to nobody and
jest tiring ourselves out."

"So would I," said the loud soldier. "It ain't
right. I tell you if anybody with any sense was
a-runnin' this army it——"

"Oh, shut up!" roared the tall private. "You
little fool. You little damn' cuss. You ain't had
that there coat and them pants on for six months,
and yet you talk as if——"

"Well, I wanta do some fighting anyway," interrupted the other. "I didn't come here to walk. I
could 'ave walked to home—'round an' 'round the
barn, if I jest wanted to walk."

The tall one, red-faced, swallowed another sandwich as if taking poison in despair.

But gradually, as he chewed, his face became
again quiet and contented. He could not rage in
fierce argument in the presence of such sandwiches.
During his meals he always wore an air of blissful
contemplation of the food he had swallowed. His
spirit seemed then to be communing with the viands.

He accepted new environment and circumstance
with great coolness, eating from his haversack at
every opportunity. On the march he went along
with the stride of a hunter, objecting to neither gait
nor distance. And he had not raised his voice when
he had been ordered away from three little protec-
tive piles of earth and stone, each of which had been
an engineering feat worthy of being made sacred to
the name of his grandmother.

In the afternoon the regiment went out over the
same ground it had taken in the morning. The

landscape then ceased to threaten the youth. He had been close to it, and become familiar with it.

When, however, they began to pass into a new region his old fears of stupidity and incompetence reassailed him, but this time he doggedly let them babble. He was occupied with his problem, and in his desperation he concluded that the stupidity did not greatly matter.

Once he thought he had concluded that it would be better to get killed directly and end his troubles. Regarding death thus out of the corner of his eye, he conceived it to be nothing but rest, and he was filled with a momentary astonishment that he should have made an extraordinary commotion over the mere matter of getting killed. He would die; he would go to some place where he would be understood. It was useless to expect appreciation of his profound and fine senses from such men as the lieutenant. He must look to the grave for comprehension.

The skirmish fire increased to a long clattering sound. With it was mingled far-away cheering. A battery spoke.

Directly the youth would see the skirmishers running. They were pursued by the sound of musketry fire. After a time the hot, dangerous flashes of the rifles were visible. Smoke clouds went slowly and insolently across the fields like observant phantoms. The din became crescendo, like the roar of an oncoming train.

A brigade ahead of them and on the right went into action with a rending roar. It was as if it had exploded. And thereafter it lay stretched in the distance behind a long grey wall, that one was obliged to look twice at to make sure that it was smoke.

The youth, forgetting his neat plan of getting killed, gazed spellbound. His eyes grew wide and busy with the action of the scene. His mouth was a little ways open.

Of a sudden he felt a heavy and sad hand laid upon his shoulder. Awakening from his trance of observation, he turned and beheld the loud soldier.

"It's my first and last battle, old boy," said the latter, with intense gloom. He was quite pale, and his girlish lip was trembling.

"Eh?" murmured the youth in great astonishment.

"It's my first and last battle, old boy," continued the loud soldier. "Something tells me——"

"What?"

"I'm a gone coon this first time, and—and I w-want you to take these here things—to—my folks." He ended in a quavering sob of pity for himself. He handed the youth a little packet done up in a yellow envelope.

"Why, what the devil——" began the youth again.

But the other gave him a glance as from the depths of a tomb, and raised his limp hand in a prophetic manner and turned away.

CHAPTER IV

THE brigade was halted in the fringe of a grove. The men crouched among the trees and pointed their restless guns out at the fields. They tried to look beyond the smoke.

Out of this haze they could see running men. Some shouted information and gestured as they hurried.

The men of the new regiment watched and listened eagerly, while their tongues ran on in gossip of the battle. They mouthed rumours that had flown like birds out of the unknown.

"They say Perry has been driven in with big loss."

"Yes, Carrott went t' th' hospital. He said he was sick. That smart lieutenant is commanding 'G' Company. Th' boys say they won't be under Carrott no more if they all have t' desert. They allus knew he was a——"

"Hannises' batt'ry is took."

"It ain't either. I saw Hannises' batt'ry off on th' left not more'n fifteen minutes ago."

"Well——"

"Th' general, he ses he is goin' t' take th' hull command of th' 304th when we go inteh action, an' then he ses we'll do sech fightin' as never another one reg'ment done."

"They say we're catchin' it over on th' left. They say th' enemy driv' our line inteh a devil of a swamp an' took Hannises' batt'ry."

"No sech thing. Hannises' batt'ry was 'long here 'bout a minute ago."

"That young Hasbrouck, he makes a good off'cer. He ain't afraid 'a nothin'."

"I met one of th' 148th Maine boys, an' he ses his brigade fit th' hull rebel army fer four hours over on th' turnpike road an' killed about five thousand of 'em. He ses one more sech fight as that an' th' war 'll be over."

"Bill wasn't scared either. No, sir! It wasn't that. Bill ain't a-gittin' scared easy. He was jest mad, that's what he was. When that feller trod on his hand, he up an' sed that he was willin' t' give his hand t' his country, but he be dumbed if he was goin' t' have every dumb bushwhacker in th' kentry walkin' 'round on it. So he went t' th' hospital disregardless of th' fight. Three fingers was crunched. Th' dern doctor wanted t' amputate 'm, an' Bill, he raised a heluva row, I hear. He's a funny feller."

The din in front swelled to a tremendous chorus. The youth and his fellows were frozen to silence. They could see a flag that tossed in the smoke angrily. Near it were the blurred and agitated forms of troops. There came a turbulent stream of men across the fields. A battery changing position at a frantic gallop scattered the stragglers right and left.

A shell screaming like a storm banshee went over the huddled heads of the reserves. It landed in the grove, and, exploding redly, flung the brown earth. There was a little shower of pine needles.

Bullets began to whistle among the branches and nip at the trees. Twigs and leaves came sailing down. It was as if a thousand axes, wee and invisible, were being wielded. Many of the men were constantly dodging and ducking their heads.

The lieutenant of the youth's company was shot in the hand. He began to swear so wondrously, that a nervous laugh went along the regimental line. The officer's profanity sounded conventional. It relieved the tightened senses of the new men. It was as if he had hit his fingers with a tack-hammer at home.

He held the wounded member carefully away from his side, so that the blood would not drip upon his trousers.

The captain of the company, tucking his sword under his arm, produced a handkerchief and began to bind with it the lieutenant's wound. And they disputed as to how the binding should be done.

The battle-flag in the distance jerked about madly. It seemed to be struggling to free itself from an agony. The billowing smoke was filled with horizontal flashes.

Men running swiftly emerged from it. They grew in numbers until it was seen that the whole command was fleeing. The flag suddenly sank down as if dying. Its motion as it fell was a gesture of despair.

Wild yells came from behind the walls of smoke. A sketch in grey and red dissolved into a mob-like body of men who galloped like wild horses.

The veteran regiments on the right and left of the 304th immediately began to jeer. With the passionate song of the bullets and the banshee shrieks of shells were mingled loud catcalls and bits of facetious advice concerning places of safety.

But the new regiment was breathless with horror. "Gawd! Saunders's got crushed!" whispered the man at the youth's elbow. They shrank back and crouched as if compelled to await a flood.

The youth shot a swift glance along the blue ranks of the regiment. The profiles were motionless, carven; and afterward he remembered that the colour-sergeant was standing with his legs apart, as if he expected to be pushed to the ground.

The following throng went whirling around the flank. Here and there were officers carried along on the stream like exasperated chips. They were striking about them with their swords and with their left fists, punching every head they could reach. They cursed like highwaymen.

A mounted officer displayed the furious anger of a spoiled child. He raged with his head, his arms, and his legs.

Another, the commander of the brigade, was galloping about bawling. His hat was gone, and his clothes were awry. He resembled a man who has come from bed to go to a fire. The hoofs of his horse often threatened the heads of the running men, but they scampered with singular fortune. In this rush they were apparently all deaf and blind. They heeded not the largest and longest of the oaths that were thrown at them from all directions.

Frequently over this tumult could be heard the grim jokes of the critical veterans; but the retreating men apparently were not even conscious of the presence of an audience.

The battle reflection that shone for an instant in the faces on the mad current made the youth feel that forceful hands from heaven would not have been able to have held him in place if he could have got intelligent control of his legs.

There was an appalling imprint upon these faces. The struggle in the smoke had pictured an exaggeration of itself on the bleached cheeks and in the eyes wild with one desire.

The sight of this stampede exerted a flood-like force that seemed able to drag sticks and stones and men from the ground. They of the reserves had to hold on. They grew pale and firm, and red and quaking.

The youth achieved one little thought in the midst of this chaos. The composite monster which had caused the other troops to flee had not then appeared. He resolved to get a view of it, and then, he thought he might very likely run better than the best of them.

CHAPTER V

THERE were moments of waiting. The youth thought of the village street at home before the arrival of the circus parade on a day in the spring. He remembered how he had stood, a small, thrillful boy, prepared to follow the dingy lady upon the white horse, or the band in its faded chariot. He saw the yellow road, the lines of expectant people, and the sober houses. He particularly remembered an old fellow who used to sit upon a cracker-box in front of the store and feign to despise such exhibitions. A thousand details of colour and form surged in his mind. The old fellow upon the cracker-box appeared in middle prominence.

Some one cried, " Here they come ! "

There was rustling and muttering among the men. They displayed a feverish desire to have every possible cartridge ready to their hands. The boxes were pulled around into various positions, and adjusted with great care. It was as if seven hundred new bonnets were being tried on.

The tall soldier, having prepared his rifle, produced a red handkerchief of some kind. He was engaged in knitting it about his throat with exquisite attention to its position, when the cry was repeated up and down the line in a muffled roar of sound.

"Here they come! Here they come!" Gun-locks clicked.

Across the smoke-infested fields came a brown swarm of running men who were giving shrill yells. They came on, stooping and swinging their rifles at all angles. A flag, tilted forward, sped near the front.

As he caught sight of them, the youth was momentarily startled by a thought that perhaps his gun was not loaded. He stood trying to rally his faltering intellect so that he might recollect the moment when he had loaded, but he could not.

A hatless general pulled his dripping horse to a stand near the colonel of the 304th. He shook his fist in the other's face. "You've got to hold 'em back!" he shouted savagely; "you've got to hold 'em back!"

In his agitation the colonel began to stammer. "A-all r-right, general, all right, by Gawd! We-we'll do our—we-we'll d-d-do—do our best, general." The general made a passionate gesture and galloped away. The colonel, perchance to relieve his feelings, began to scold like a wet parrot. The youth, turning swiftly to make sure that the rear was unmolested, saw the commander regarding his men in a highly resentful manner, as if he regretted above everything his association with them.

The man at the youth's elbow was mumbling, as if to himself, "Oh, we're in for it now! oh, we're in for it now!"

The captain of the company had been pacing excitedly to and fro in the rear. He coaxed in schoolmistress fashion, as to a congregation of boys with primers. His talk was an endless repetition. "Reserve your fire, boys—don't shoot till I tell you—save your fire—wait till they get close up—don't be damned fools——"

Perspiration streamed down the youth's face, which was soiled like that of a weeping urchin. He frequently, with a nervous movement, wiped his eyes with his coat-sleeve. His mouth was still a little ways open.

He got the one glance at the foe-swarming field in front of him, and instantly ceased to debate the question of his piece being loaded. Before he was ready to begin—before he had announced to himself that he was about to fight—he threw the obedient, well-balanced rifle into position, and fired a first wild shot. Directly he was working at his weapon like an automatic affair.

He suddenly lost concern for himself, and forgot to look at a menacing fate. He became not a man but a member. He felt that something of which he was a part—a regiment, an army, a cause, or a country—was in a crisis. He was welded into a common personality which was dominated by a single desire. For some moments he could not flee, no more than a little finger can commit a revolution from a hand.

If he had thought the regiment was about to be annihilated, perhaps he could have amputated himself from it. But its noise gave him assurance.

The regiment was like a firework that, once ignited, proceeds superior to circumstances until its blazing vitality fades. It wheezed and banged with a mighty power. He pictured the ground before it as strewn with the discomfited.

There was a consciousness always of the presence of his comrades about him. He felt the subtle battle brotherhood more potent even than the cause for which they were fighting. It was a mysterious fraternity born of the smoke and danger of death.

He was at a task. He was like a carpenter who has made many boxes, making still another box, only there was furious haste in his movements. He, in his thought, was careering off in other places, even as the carpenter who, as he works, whistles and thinks of his friend or his enemy, his home or a saloon. And these jolted dreams were never perfect to him afterward, but remained a mass of blurred shapes.

Presently he began to feel the effects of the war atmosphere—a blistering sweat, a sensation that his eyeballs were about to crack like hot stones. A burning roar filled his ears.

Following this came a red rage. He developed the acute exasperation of a pestered animal, a well-meaning cow worried by dogs. He had a mad feeling against his rifle, which could only be used against one life at a time. He wished to rush forward and strangle with his fingers. He craved a power that would enable him to make a world-sweeping gesture and brush all back. His impotency appeared to him, and made his rage into that of a driven beast.

Buried in the smoke of many rifles, his anger was directed not so much against the men whom he knew were rushing toward him, as against the swirling battle phantoms which were choking him, stuffing their smoke robes down his parched throat. He fought frantically for respite for his senses, for air, as a babe being smothered attacks the deadly blankets.

There was a blaré of heated rage mingled with a certain expression of intentness on all faces. Many of the men were making low-toned noises with their mouths, and these subdued cheers, snarls, imprecations, prayers, made a wild, barbaric song that went as an undercurrent of sound, strange and chant-like, with the resounding chords of the war march. The man at the youth's elbow was babbling. In it there was something soft and tender, like the monologue of a babe. The tall soldier was swearing in a loud voice. From his lips came a black procession of curious oaths. Of a sudden another broke out in a querulous way, like a man who has mislaid his hat. "Well, why don't they support us? Why don't they send supports? Do they think——"

The youth in his battle sleep heard this as one who dozes hears.

There was a singular absence of heroic poses. The men, bending and surging in their haste and rage, were in every impossible attitude. The steel ramrods clanked and clanged with incessant din as the men pounded them furiously into the hot rifle-barrels. The flaps of the cartridge-boxes were all unfastened, and bobbed idiotically with each movement. The rifles, once loaded, were jerked to the shoulder and fired without apparent aim into the smoke or at one of the blurred and shifting forms which upon the field before the regiment had been growing larger and larger, like puppets under a magician's hand.

The officers, at their intervals, rearward, neglected to stand in picturesque attitudes. They were bobbing to and fro, roaring directions and encouragements. The dimensions of their howls were extraordinary. They expended their lungs with prodigal wills. And often they nearly stood upon their heads in their anxiety to observe the enemy on the other side of the tumbling smoke.

The lieutenant of the youth's company had encountered a soldier who had fled screaming at the first volley of his comrades. Behind the lines these two were acting a little isolated scene. The man was blubbering and staring with sheep-like eyes at the lieutenant, who had seized him by the collar and was pommeling him. He drove him back into the ranks with many blows. The soldier went mechanically, dully, with his animal-like eyes upon the officer. Perhaps there was to him a divinity expressed in the voice of the other—stern, hard, with no reflection of fear in it. He tried to reload his gun, but his shaking hands prevented. The lieutenant was obliged to assist him.

The men dropped here and there like bundles. The captain of the youth's company had been killed in an early part of the action. His body lay stretched out in the position of a tired man resting, but upon his face there was an astonished and sorrowful look, as if he thought some friend had done him an ill turn. The babbling man was grazed by a shot that made the blood stream widely down his face. He clapped both hands to his head. "Oh!" he said, and ran. Another grunted suddenly as if he had been struck by a club in the stomach. He sat down and gazed ruefully. In his eyes there was mute, indefinite reproach. Farther up the line a man, standing behind a tree, had had his knee-joint splintered by a ball. Immediately he had dropped his rifle and gripped the tree with both arms. And there he remained, clinging desperately and crying for assistance, that he might withdraw his hold upon the tree.

At last an exultant yell went along the quivering line. The firing dwindled from an uproar to a last vindictive popping. As the smoke slowly eddied away, the youth saw that the charge had been repulsed. The enemy were scattered into reluctant groups. He saw a man climb to the top of the fence, straddle the rail, and fire a parting shot. The waves had receded, leaving bits of dark débris upon the ground.

Some in the regiment began to whoop frenziedly. Many were silent. Apparently they were trying to contemplate themselves.

After the fever had left his veins, the youth thought that at last he was going to suffocate. He became aware of the foul atmosphere in which he had been struggling. He was grimy and dripping like a labourer in a foundry. He grasped his canteen and took a long swallow of the warmed water.

A sentence with variations went up and down the line. "Well, we've helt 'em back. We've helt 'em back; derned if we haven't." The men said it blissfully, leering at each other with dirty smiles.

The youth turned to look behind him and off to the right and off to the left. He experienced the joy of a man who at last finds leisure in which to look about him.

Under foot there were a few ghastly forms motionless. They lay twisted in fantastic contortions. Arms were bent and heads were turned in incredible ways. It seemed that the dead men must have fallen from some great height to get into such positions. They looked to be dumped out upon the ground from the sky.

From a position in the rear of the grove a battery was throwing shells over it. The flash of the guns startled the youth at first. He thought they were aimed directly at him. Through the trees he watched the black figures of the gunners as they worked swiftly and intently. Their labour seemed a complicated thing. He wondered how they could remember its formula in the midst of confusion.

The guns squatted in a row like savage chiefs. They argued with abrupt violence. It was a grim pow-wow. Their busy servants ran hither and thither.

A small procession of wounded men were going

drearily toward the rear. It was a flow of blood from the torn body of the brigade.

To the right and to the left were the dark lines of other troops. Far in front he thought he could see lighter masses protruding in points from the forest. They were suggestive of unnumbered thousands.

Once he saw a tiny battery go dashing along the line of the horizon. The tiny riders were beating the tiny horses.

From a sloping hill came the sound of cheerings and clashes. Smoke welled slowly through the leaves.

Batteries were speaking with thunderous oratorical effort. Here and there were flags, the red in the stripes dominating. They splashed bits of warm colour upon the dark lines of troops.

The youth felt the old thrill at the sight of the emblem. They were like beautiful birds strangely undaunted in a storm.

As he listened to the din from the hillside, to a deep pulsating thunder that came from afar to the left, and to the lesser clamours which came from many directions, it occurred to him that they were fighting, too, over there, and over there, and over there. Heretofore he had supposed that all the battle was directly under his nose.

As he gazed around him the youth felt a flash of astonishment at the blue, pure sky and the sun gleamings on the trees and fields. It was surprising that Nature had gone tranquilly on with her golden process in the midst of so much devilment.

CHAPTER VI

THE youth awakened slowly. He came gradually
back to a position from which he could regard himself. For moments he had been scrutinising his
person in a dazed way as if he had never before
seen himself. Then he picked up his cap from the
ground. He wriggled in his jacket to make a more
comfortable fit, and kneeling, relaced his shoe. He
thoughtfully mopped his reeking features.

So it was all over at last! The supreme trial had
been passed. The red, formidable difficulties of war
had been vanquished.

He went into an ecstasy of self-satisfaction. He
had the most delightful sensations of his life.
Standing as if apart from himself, he viewed that
last scene. He perceived that the man who had
fought thus was magnificent.

He felt that he was a fine fellow. He saw himself
even with those ideals which he had considered as
far beyond him. He smiled in deep gratification.

Upon his fellows he beamed tenderness and good
will. "Gee! ain't it hot, hey?" he said affably to
a man who was polishing his streaming face with his
coat-sleeves.

"You bet!" said the other, grinning sociably.

"I never seen sech dumb hotness." He sprawled out luxuriously on the ground. "Gee, yes! An' I hope we don't have no more fightin' till a week from Monday."

There were some handshakings and deep speeches with men whose features were familiar, but with whom the youth now felt the bonds of tied hearts. He helped a cursing comrade to bind up a wound of the shin.

But, of a sudden, cries of amazement broke out along the ranks of the new regiment. "Here they come ag'in! Here they come ag'in!" The man who had sprawled upon the ground started up and said, "Gosh!"

The youth turned quick eyes upon the field. He discerned forms begin to swell in masses out of a distant wood. He again saw the tilted flag speeding forward.

The shells which had ceased to trouble the regiment for a time came swirling again, and exploded in the grass or among the leaves of the trees. They looked to be strange war flowers bursting into fierce bloom.

The men groaned. The lustre faded from their eyes. Their smudged countenances now expressed a profound dejection. They moved their stiffened bodies slowly, and watched in sullen mood the frantic approach of the enemy. The slaves toiling in the temple of this god began to feel rebellion at his harsh tasks.

They fretted and complained each to each. "Oh, say, this is too much of a good thing! Why can't somebody send us supports?"

"We ain't never goin' to stand this second banging. I didn't come here to fight the hull damn' rebel army."

There was one who raised a doleful cry. "I wish Bill Smithers had trod on my hand, insteader me treddin' on his'n." The sore joints of the regiment creaked as it painfully floundered into position to repulse.

The youth stared. Surely, he thought, this impossible thing was not about to happen. He waited as if he expected the enemy to suddenly stop, apologise, and retire bowing. It was all a mistake.

But the firing began somewhere on the regimental line and ripped along in both directions. The level sheets of flame developed great clouds of smoke that tumbled and tossed in the mild wind near the ground for a moment, and then rolled through the ranks as through a gate. The clouds were tinged an earth-like yellow in the sun-rays and in the shadow were a sorry blue. The flag was sometimes eaten and lost in this mass of vapour, but more often it projected, sun-touched, resplendent.

Into the youth's eyes there came a look that one can see in the orbs of a jaded horse. His neck was quivering with nervous weakness, and the muscles of his arms felt numb and bloodless. His hands, too, seemed large and awkward, as if he was wearing invisible mittens. And there was a great uncertainty about his knee-joints.

The words that comrades had uttered previous to the firing began to recur to him. "Oh, say, this is too much of a good thing! What do they take us for—why don't they send supports? I didn't come here to fight the hull damned rebel army."

He began to exaggerate the endurance, the skill, and the valour of those who were coming. Himself reeling from exhaustion, he was astonished beyond measure at such persistency. They must be machines of steel. It was very gloomy struggling against such affairs, wound up, perhaps, to fight until sundown.

He slowly lifted his rifle and, catching a glimpse of the thickspread field, he blazed at a cantering cluster. He stopped then and began to peer as best he could through the smoke. He caught changing views of the ground covered with men, who were all running like pursued imps, and yelling.

To the youth it was an onslaught of redoubtable dragons. He became like the man who lost his legs at the approach of the red and green monster. He waited in a sort of a horrified, listening attitude. He seemed to shut his eyes and wait to be gobbled.

A man near him, who up to this time had been working feverishly at his rifle, suddenly stopped and ran with howls. A lad whose face had borne an expression of exalted courage, the majesty of he who dares give his life, was, at an instant, smitten abject. He blanched like one who has come to the edge of a cliff at midnight and is suddenly made aware. There was a revelation. He, too, threw down his gun and fled. There was no shame in his face. He ran like a rabbit.

Others began to scamper away through the smoke. The youth turned his head, shaken from his trance by this movement as if the regiment was leaving him behind. He saw the few fleeting forms.

He yelled then with fright and swung about. For a moment, in the great clamour, he was like a proverbial chicken. He lost the direction of safety. Destruction threatened him from all points.

Directly he began to speed toward the rear in great leaps. His rifle and cap were gone. His unbuttoned coat bulged in the wind. The flap of his cartridge-box bobbed wildly, and his canteen, by its slender cord, swung out behind. On his face was all the horror of those things which he imagined.

The lieutenant sprang forward bawling. The youth saw his features wrathfully red, and saw him make a dab with his sword. His one thought of the incident was that the lieutenant was a peculiar creature to feel interested in such matters upon this occasion.

He ran like a blind man. Two or three times he fell down. Once he knocked his shoulder so heavily against a tree that he went headlong.

Since he had turned his back upon the fight, his fears had been wondrously magnified. Death about to thrust him between the shoulder blades was far more dreadful than death about to smite him between the eyes. When he thought of it later, he conceived the impression that it is better to view the appalling than to be merely within hearing. The noises of the battle were like stones; he believed himself liable to be crushed.

As he ran on he mingled with others. He dimly

saw men on his right and on his left, and he heard
footsteps behind him. He thought that all the regiment was fleeing, pursued by these ominous crashes.

In his flight the sound of these following footsteps
gave him his one meagre relief. He felt vaguely
that death must make a first choice of the men who
were nearest; the initial morsels for the dragons
would be then those who were following him. So
he displayed the zeal of an insane sprinter in his
purpose to keep them in the rear. There was a
race.

As he, leading, went across a little field he found
himself in a region of shells. They hurtled over his
head with long wild screams. As he listened, he imagined them to have rows of cruel teeth that grinned
at him. Once one lit before him, and the livid lightning of the explosion effectually barred the way in
his chosen direction. He grovelled on the ground,
and then springing up, went careering off through
some bushes.

He experienced a thrill of amazement when he
came within view of a battery in action. The men
there seemed to be in conventional moods, altogether
unaware of the impending annihilation. The battery
was disputing with a distant antagonist, and the
gunners were wrapped in admiration of their shooting. They were continually bending in coaxing
postures over the guns. They seemed to be patting
them on the back, and encouraging them with
words. The guns, stolid and undaunted, spoke with
dogged valour.

The precise gunners were coolly enthusiastic.

They lifted their eyes every chance to the smoke-wreathed hillock from whence the hostile battery addressed them. The youth pitied them as he ran. Methodical idiots! Machine-like fools! The refined joy of planting shells in the midst of the other battery's formation would appear a little thing when the infantry came swooping out of the woods.

The face of a youthful rider, who was jerking his frantic horse with an abandon of temper he might display in a placid barn-yard, was impressed deeply upon his mind. He knew that he looked upon a man who would presently be dead.

Too, he felt a pity for the guns, standing, six good comrades, in a bold row.

He saw a brigade going to the relief of its pestered fellows. He scrambled upon a wee hill and watched it sweeping finely, keeping formation in difficult places. The blue of the line was crusted with steel colour, and the brilliant flags projected. Officers were shouting.

This sight also filled him with wonder. The brigade was hurrying briskly to be gulped into the infernal mouths of the war god. What manner of men were they, anyhow? Ah, it was some wondrous breed! Or else they didn't comprehend—the fools.

A furious order caused commotion in the artillery. An officer on a bounding horse made maniacal motions with his arms. The teams went swinging up from the rear, the guns were whirled about, and the battery scampered away. The cannon, with their noses poked slantingly at the ground, grunted and grumbled like stout men, brave, but with objections to hurry.

The youth went on, moderating his pace since he had left the place of noises.

Later he came upon a general of division seated upon a horse that pricked its ears in an interested way at the battle. There was a great gleaming of yellow and patent leather about the saddle and bridle. The quiet man astride looked mouse-coloured upon such a splendid charger.

A jingling staff was galloping hither and thither. Sometimes the general was surrounded by horsemen, and at other times he was quite alone. He looked to be much harassed. He had the appearance of a business man whose market is swinging up and down.

The youth went slinking around this spot. He went as near as he dared, trying to overhear words. Perhaps the general, unable to comprehend chaos, might call upon him for information. And he could tell him. He knew all concerning it. Of a surety the force was in a fix, and any fool could see that if they did not retreat while they had opportunity— why——

He felt that he would like to thrash the general, or at least approach and tell him in plain words exactly what he thought him to be. It was criminal to stay calmly in one spot and make no effort to stay destruction. He loitered in a fever of eagerness for the division commander to apply to him.

As he warily moved about, he heard the general

call out irritably: "Tompkins, go over an' see Taylor, and tell him not t' be in such an all-fired hurry; tell him t' halt his brigade in th' edge of th' woods; tell him t' detach a reg'ment—say I think the centre 'll break if we don't help it out some; tell him t' hurry up."

A slim youth on a fine chestnut horse caught these swift words from the mouth of his superior. He made his horse bound into a gallop almost from a walk in his haste to go upon his mission. There was a cloud of dust.

A moment later the youth saw the general bounce excitedly in his saddle.

"Yes, by heavens, they have!" The officer leaned forward. His face was aflame with excitement. "Yes, by heavens, they've held 'im! They've held 'im!"

He began to blithely roar at his staff: "We'll wallop 'im now. We'll wallop 'im now. We've got 'em sure." He turned suddenly upon an aid: "Here —you—Jones—quick—ride after Tompkins—see Taylor—tell him t' go in—everlastingly—like blazes —anything."

As another officer sped his horse after the first messenger, the general beamed upon the earth like a sun. In his eyes was a desire to chant a pæan. He kept repeating, "They've held 'em, by heavens!"

His excitement made his horse plunge, and he merrily kicked and swore at it. He held a little carnival of joy on horseback.

CHAPTER VII

THE youth cringed as if discovered in a crime. By heavens, they had won after all! The imbecile line had remained and become victors. He could hear cheering.

He lifted himself upon his toes and looked in the direction of the fight. A yellow fog lay wallowing on the tree-tops. From beneath it came the clatter of musketry. Hoarse cries told of an advance.

He turned away amazed and angry. He felt that he had been wronged.

He had fled, he told himself, because annihilation approached. He had done a good part in saving himself, who was a little piece of the army. He had considered the time, he said, to be one in which it was the duty of every little piece to rescue itself if possible. Later the officers could fit the little pieces together again, and make a battle front. If none of the little pieces were wise enough to save themselves from the flurry of death at such a time, why, then, where would be the army? It was all plain that he had proceeded according to very correct and commendable rules. His actions had been sagacious things. They had been full of strategy. They were the work of a master's legs.

Thoughts of his comrades came to him. The

brittle blue line had withstood the blows and won. He grew bitter over it. It seemed that the blind ignorance and stupidity of those little pieces had betrayed him. He had been overturned and crushed by their lack of sense in holding the position, when intelligent deliberation would have convinced them that it was impossible. He, the enlightened man who looks afar in the dark, had fled because of his superior perceptions and knowledge. He felt a great anger against his comrades. He knew it could be proved that they had been fools.

He wondered what they would remark when later he appeared in camp. His mind heard howls of derision. Their density would not enable them to understand his sharper point of view.

He began to pity himself acutely. He was ill used. He was trodden beneath the feet of an iron injustice. He had proceeded with wisdom and from the most righteous motives under heaven's blue, only to be frustrated by hateful circumstances.

A dull, animal-like rebellion against his fellows, war in the abstract, and fate grew within him. He shambled along with bowed head, his brain in a tumult of agony and despair. When he looked loweringly up, quivering at each sound, his eyes had the expression of those of a criminal who thinks his guilt and his punishment great, and knows that he can find no words.

He went from the fields into a thick wood, as if resolved to bury himself. He wished to get out of hearing of the crackling shots which were to him like voices.

The ground was cluttered with vines and bushes, and the trees grew close, and spread out like bouquets. He was obliged to force his way with much noise. The creepers, catching against his legs, cried out harshly as their sprays were torn from the barks of trees. The swishing saplings tried to make known his presence to the world. He could not conciliate the forest. As he made his way, it was always calling out protestations. When he separated embraces of trees and vines, the disturbed foliages waved their arms and turned their face leaves toward him. He dreaded lest these noisy motions and cries should bring men to look at him. So he went far, seeking dark and intricate places.

After a time the sound of musketry grew faint, and the cannon boomed in the distance. The sun, suddenly apparent, blazed among the trees. The insects were making rhythmical noises. They seemed to be grinding their teeth in unison. A woodpecker stuck his impudent head around the side of a tree. A bird flew on light-hearted wing.

Off was the rumble of death. It seemed now that Nature had no ears.

This landscape gave him assurance. A fair field holding life. It was the religion of peace. It would die if its timid eyes were compelled to see blood. He conceived Nature to be a woman with a deep aversion to tragedy.

He threw a pine cone at a jovial squirrel, and he ran with chattering fear. High in a tree-top he stopped, and, poking his head cautiously from behind a branch, looked down with an air of trepidation.

The youth felt triumphant at this exhibition. There was the law, he said. Nature had given him a sign. The squirrel, immediately upon recognising danger, had taken to his legs without ado. He did not stand stolidly baring his furry belly to the missile, and die with an upward glance at the sympathetic heavens. On the contrary, he had fled as fast as his legs could carry him; and he was but an ordinary squirrel, too—doubtless no philosopher of his race. The youth wended, feeling that Nature was of his mind. She re-enforced his argument with proofs that lived where the sun shone.

Once he found himself almost into a swamp. He was obliged to walk upon bog tufts, and watch his feet to keep from the oily mire. Pausing at one time to look about him he saw, out at some black water, a small animal pounce in and emerge directly with a gleaming fish.

The youth went again into the deep thickets. The brushed branches made a noise that drowned the sounds of cannon. He walked on, going from obscurity into promises of a greater obscurity.

At length he reached a place where the high arching boughs made a chapel. He softly pushed the green doors aside and entered. Pine needles were a gentle brown carpet. There was a religious half light.

Near the threshold he stopped, horror-stricken at the sight of a thing.

He was being looked at by a dead man, who was seated with his back against a column-like tree. The corpse was dressed in a uniform that once had been blue, but was now faded to a melancholy shade of green. The eyes, staring at the youth, had changed to the dull hue to be seen on the side of a dead fish. The mouth was open. Its red had changed to an appalling yellow. Over the grey skin of the face ran little ants. One was trundling some sort of a bundle along the upper lip.

The youth gave a shriek as he confronted the thing. He was for moments turned to stone before it. He remained staring into the liquid-looking eyes. The dead man and the living man exchanged a long look. Then the youth cautiously put one hand behind him and brought it against a tree. Leaning upon this he retreated, step by step, with his face still toward the thing. He feared that if he turned his back the body might spring up and stealthily pursue him.

The branches, pushing against him, threatened to throw him over upon it. His unguided feet, too, caught aggravatingly in brambles; and with it all he received a subtle suggestion to touch the corpse. As he thought of his hand upon it he shuddered profoundly.

At last he burst the bonds which had fastened him to the spot and fled, unheeding the underbrush. He was pursued by a sight of the black ants swarming greedily upon the grey face, and venturing horribly near to the eyes.

After a time he paused, and, breathless and panting, listened.   He imagined some strange voice would come from the dead throat and squawk after him in horrible menaces.

The trees about the portal of the chapel moved soughingly in a soft wind.   A sad silence was upon the little guarding edifice.

CHAPTER VIII

The trees began softly to sing a hymn of twilight. The sun sank until slanted bronze rays struck the forest. There was a lull in the noises of insects, as if they had bowed their beaks and were making a devotional pause. There was silence, save for the chanted chorus of the trees.

Then, upon this stillness, there suddenly broke a tremendous clangour of sounds. A crimson roar came from the distance.

The youth stopped. He was transfixed by this terrific medley of all noises. It was as if worlds were being rended. There was the ripping sound of musketry, and the breaking crash of the artillery.

His mind flew in all directions. He conceived the two armies to be at each other, panther fashion. He listened for a time. Then he began to run in the direction of the battle. He saw that it was an ironical thing for him to be running thus toward that which he had been at such pains to avoid. But he said, in substance, to himself that if the earth and the moon were about to clash, many persons would doubtless plan to get upon the roofs to witness the collision.

As he ran, he became aware that the forest had

stopped its music, as if at last becoming capable of hearing the foreign sounds. The trees hushed and stood motionless. Everything seemed to be listening to the crackle and clatter and ear-shaking thunder. The chorus pealed over the still earth.

It suddenly occurred to the youth that the fight in which he had been was, after all, but perfunctory popping. In the hearing of this present din he was doubtful if he had seen real battle scenes. This uproar explained a celestial battle; it was tumbling hordes a-struggle in the air.

Reflecting, he saw a sort of a humour in the point of view of himself and his fellows during the late encounter. They had taken themselves and the enemy very seriously, and had imagined that they were deciding the war. Individuals must have supposed that they were cutting the letters of their names deep into everlasting tablets of brass, or enshrining their reputations for ever in the hearts of their countrymen, while, as to fact, the affair would appear in printed reports under a meek and immaterial title. But he saw that it was good, else, he said, in battle every one would surely run save forlorn hopes and their ilk.

He went rapidly on. He wished to come to the edge of the forest that he might peer out.

As he hastened, there passed through his mind pictures of stupendous conflicts. His accumulated thought upon such subjects was used to form scenes. The noise was as the voice of an eloquent being, describing.

Sometimes the brambles formed chains, and tried

to hold him back. Trees, confronting him, stretched out their arms and forbade him to pass. After its previous hostility, this new resistance of the forest filled him with a fine bitterness. It seemed that Nature could not be quite ready to kill him.

But he obstinately took roundabout ways, and presently he was where he could see long grey walls of vapour where lay battle lines. The voices of cannon shook him. The musketry sounded in long irregular surges that played havoc with his ears. He stood regardant for a moment. His eyes had an awestruck expression. He gawked in the direction of the fight.

Presently he proceeded again on his forward way. The battle was like the grinding of an immense and terrible machine to him. Its complexities and powers its grim processes, fascinated him. He must go close and see it produce corpses.

He came to a fence and clambered over it. On the far side the ground was littered with clothes and guns. A newspaper, folded up, lay in the dirt. A dead soldier was stretched with his face hidden in his arm. Farther off there was a group of four or five corpses keeping mournful company. A hot sun had blazed upon the spot.

In this place the youth felt that he was an invader. This forgotten part of the battle-ground was owned by the dead men, and he hurried, in the vague apprehension that one of the swollen forms would rise and tell him to begone.

He came finally to a road from which he could see in the distance dark and agitated bodies of troops, smoke-fringed. In the lane was a blood-stained crowd streaming to the rear. The wounded men were cursing, groaning, and wailing. In the air, always, was a mighty swell of sound that it seemed could sway the earth. With the courageous words of the artillery and the spiteful sentences of the musketry mingled red cheers. And from this region of noises came the steady current of the maimed.

One of the wounded men had a shoeful of blood. He hopped like a schoolboy in a game. He was laughing hysterically.

One was swearing that he had been shot in the arm through the commanding general's mismanagement of the army. One was marching with an air imitative of some sublime drum-major. Upon his features was an unholy mixture of merriment and agony. As he marched, he sang a bit of doggerel in a high and quavering voice:

> "Sing a song 'a vic'try,
> A pocketful 'a bullets,
> Five an' twenty dead men
> Baked in a—pie."

Parts of the procession limped and staggered to this tune.

Another had the grey seal of death already upon his face. His lips were curled in hard lines, and his teeth were clinched. His hands were bloody from where he had pressed them upon his wound. He seemed to be awaiting the moment when he should pitch headlong. He stalked like the spectre

of a soldier, his eyes burning with the power of a
stare into the unknown.

There were some who proceeded sullenly, full of
anger at their wounds, and ready to turn upon anything as an obscure cause.

An officer was carried along by two privates. He
was peevish. "Don't joggle so, Johnson, yeh fool,"
he cried. "Think m' leg is made of iron? If yeh
can't carry me decent, put me down, an' let some
one else do it."

He bellowed at the tottering crowd who blocked
the quick march of his bearers. "Say, make way
there, can't yeh? Make way, dickens take it all."

They sulkily parted and went to the roadsides.
As he was carried past they made pert remarks to
him. When he raged in reply and threatened them,
they told him to be damned.

The shoulder of one of the tramping bearers
knocked heavily against the spectral soldier who
was staring into the unknown.

The youth joined this crowd and marched along
with it. The torn bodies expressed the awful
machinery in which the men had been entangled.

Orderlies and couriers occasionally broke through
the throng in the roadway, scattering wounded men
right and left, galloping on followed by howls. The
melancholy march was continually disturbed by the
messengers, and sometimes by bustling batteries
that came swinging and thumping down upon them,
the officers shouting orders to clear the way.

There was a tattered man, fouled with dust, blood,
and powder stain from hair to shoes, who trudged

quietly at the youth's side. He was listening with eagerness and much humility to the lurid descriptions of a bearded sergeant. His lean features wore an expression of awe and admiration. He was like a listener in a country store to wondrous tales told among the sugar barrels. He eyed the story-teller with unspeakable wonder. His mouth was agape in yokel fashion.

The sergeant, taking note of this, gave pause to his elaborate history while he administered a sardonic comment. "Be keerful, honey, you'll be a-ketchin' flies," he said.

The tattered man shrank back abashed.

After a time he began to sidle near to the youth, and in a different way try to make him a friend. His voice was gentle as a girl's voice, and his eyes were pleading. The youth saw with surprise that the soldier had two wounds, one in the head, bound with a blood-soaked rag, and the other in the arm, making that member dangle like a broken bough.

After they had walked together for some time the tattered man mustered sufficient courage to speak. "Was pretty good fight, wa'n't it?" he timidly said. The youth, deep in thought, glanced up at the bloody and grim figure with its lamb-like eyes. "What?"

"Was pretty good fight, wa'n't it?"

"Yes," said the youth shortly. He quickened his pace.

But the other hobbled industriously after him. There was an air of apology in his manner, but he evidently thought that he needed only to talk for a time, and the youth would perceive that he was a good fellow.

"Was pretty good fight, wa'n't it?" he began in a small voice, and then he achieved the fortitude to continue. "Dern me if I ever see fellers fight so. Laws, how they did fight! I knowed th' boys 'd like when they onct got square at it. Th' boys ain't had no fair chanct up t' now, but this time they showed what they was. I knowed it 'd turn out this way. Yeh can't lick them boys. No, sir! They're fighters, they be."

He breathed a deep breath of humble admiration. He had looked at the youth for encouragement several times. He received none, but gradually he seemed to get absorbed in his subject.

"I was talkin' 'cross pickets with a boy from Georgie, onct, an' that boy, he ses, 'Your fellers 'll all run like hell when they onct hearn a gun,' he ses. 'Mebbe they will,' I ses, 'but I don't b'lieve none of it,' I ses; 'an' b'jiminey,' I ses back t' 'um, 'mebbe your fellers 'll all run like hell when they onct hearn a gun,' I ses. He larfed. Well, they didn't run t' day, did they, hey? No, sir! They fit, an' fit, an' fit."

His homely face was suffused with a light of love for the army which was to him all things beautiful and powerful.

After a time he turned to the youth. "Where yeh hit, ol' boy?" he asked in a brotherly tone.

The youth felt instant panic at this question, although at first its full import was not borne in upon him.

" What ? " he asked.

" Where yeh hit ? " repeated the tattered man.

" Why," began the youth, " I—I—that is—why—I——"

He turned away suddenly and slid through the crowd. His brow was heavily flushed, and his fingers were picking nervously at one of his buttons. He bent his head and fastened his eyes studiously upon the button as if it were a little problem.

The tattered man looked after him in astonishment.

CHAPTER IX

THE youth fell back in the procession until the tattered soldier was not in sight. Then he started to walk on with the others.

But he was amid wounds. The mob of men was bleeding. Because of the tattered soldier's question he now felt that his shame could be viewed. He was continually casting sidelong glances to see if the men were contemplating the letters of guilt he felt burned into his brow.

At times he regarded the wounded soldiers in an envious way. He conceived persons with torn bodies to be peculiarly happy. He wished that he, too, had a wound, a red badge of courage.

The spectral soldier was at his side like a stalking reproach. The man's eyes were still fixed in a stare into the unknown. His grey, appalling face had attracted attention in the crowd, and men, slowing to his dreary pace, were walking with him. They were discussing his plight, questioning him, and giving him advice. In a dogged way he repelled them, signing to them to go on and leave him alone. The shadows of his face were deepening, and his tight lips seemed holding in check the moan of great despair. There could be seen a certain stiffness in the movements of his body, as if he were taking infinite care not to arouse the passion of his wounds. As he went on he seemed always looking for a place, like one who goes to choose a grave.

Something in the gesture of the man as he waved the bloody and pitying soldiers away made the youth start as if bitten. He yelled in horror. Tottering forward he laid a quivering hand upon the man's arm. As the latter slowly turned his wax-like features toward him, the youth screamed—

"Gawd! Jim Conklin!"

The tall soldier made a little commonplace smile. "Hello, Henry," he said.

The youth swayed on his legs and glared strangely. He stuttered and stammered. "Oh, Jim—oh, Jim—oh, Jim——"

The tall soldier held out his gory hand. There was a curious red and black combination of new blood and old blood upon it. "Where yeh been, Henry?" he asked. He continued in a monotonous voice, "I thought mebbe yeh got keeled over. There's been thunder t' pay t'-day. I was worryin' about it a good deal."

The youth still lamented. "Oh, Jim—oh, Jim—oh, Jim——"

"Yeh know," said the tall soldier, "I was out there." He made a careful gesture. "An', Lord, what a circus! An', b'jiminey, I got shot—I got shot. Yes, b'jiminey, I got shot." He reiterated this fact in a bewildered way, as if he did not know how it came about.

The youth put forth anxious arms to assist him,

but the tall soldier went firmly on as if propelled. Since the youth's arrival as a guardian for his friend, the other wounded men had ceased to display much interest. They occupied themselves again in dragging their own tragedies toward the rear.

Suddenly, as the two friends marched on, the tall soldier seemed to be overcome by a terror. His face turned to a semblance of grey paste. He clutched the youth's arm and looked all about him, as if dreading to be overheard. Then he began to speak in a shaking whisper—

"I tell yeh what I'm 'fraid of, Henry—I'll tell yeh what I'm 'fraid of. I'm 'fraid I'll fall down—an' then yeh know—them damned artillery waggons —they like as not 'll run over me. That's what I'm 'fraid of——"

The youth cried out to him hysterically, "I'll take care of yeh, Jim!—I'll take care of yeh! I swear t' Gawd I will!"

"Sure—will yeh, Henry?" the tall soldier beseeched.

"Yes—yes—I tell yeh—I'll take care of yeh, Jim!" protested the youth. He could not speak accurately because of the gulpings in his throat.

But the tall soldier continued to beg in a lowly way. He now hung babe-like to the youth's arm. His eyes rolled in the wildness of his terror. "I was allus a good friend t' yeh, wa'n't I, Henry? I've allus been a pretty good feller, ain't I? An' it ain't much t' ask, is it? Jest t' pull me along outer th' road? I'd do it fer you, wouldn't I, Henry?"

He paused in piteous anxiety to await his friend's reply.

The youth had reached an anguish where the sobs scorched him. He strove to express his loyalty, but he could only make fantastic gestures.

However, the tall soldier seemed suddenly to forget all those fears. He became again the grim, stalking spectre of a soldier. He went stonily forward. The youth wished his friend to lean upon him, but the other always shook his head and strangely protested. "No—no—no—leave me be—leave me be——"

His look was fixed again upon the unknown. He moved with mysterious purpose, and all of the youth's offers he brushed aside. "No—no—leave me be—leave me be——"

The youth had to follow.

Presently the latter heard a voice talking softly near his shoulder. Turning, he saw that it belonged to the tattered soldier. "Ye'd better take 'im outa th' road, pardner. There's a batt'ry comin' helitywhoop down th' road an' he'll git runned over. He's a goner anyhow in about five minutes—yeh kin see that. Ye'd better take 'im outa th' road. Where th' blazes does he git his stren'th from?"

"Lord knows!" cried the youth. He was shaking his hands helplessly.

He ran forward presently and grasped the tall soldier by the arm. "Jim! Jim!" he coaxed, "come with me."

The tall soldier weakly tried to wrench himself free. "Huh," he said vacantly. He stared at the youth for a moment.   At last he spoke as if dimly comprehending.   "Oh! Inteh th' fields?   Oh!"

He started blindly through the grass.

The youth turned once to look at the lashing riders and jouncing guns of the battery.   He was startled from this view by a shrill outcry from the tattered man.

"Gawd!   He's runnin'!"

Turning his head swiftly, the youth saw his friend running in a staggering and stumbling way toward a little clump of bushes.   His heart seemed to wrench itself almost free from his body at this sight.   He made a noise of pain.   He and the tattered man began a pursuit.   There was a singular race.

When he overtook the tall soldier he began to plead with all the words he could find.   "Jim— Jim—what are you doing?—what makes you do this way?—you'll hurt yerself."

The same purpose was in the tall soldier's face. He protested in a dulled way, keeping his eyes fastened on the mystic place of his intentions. "No—no—don't tech me—leave me be—leave me be——"

The youth, aghast and filled with wonder at the tall soldier, began quaveringly to question him. "Where yeh goin', Jim?   What you thinking about? Where you going?   Tell me, won't you, Jim?"

The tall soldier faced about as upon relentless pursuers.   In his eyes there was a great appeal. "Leave me be, can't yeh?   Leave me be fer a minnit."

The youth recoiled. "Why, Jim," he said, in a dazed way, "what's the matter with you?"

The tall soldier turned and, lurching dangerously, went on. The youth and the tattered soldier followed, sneaking as if whipped, feeling unable to face the stricken man if he should again confront them. They began to have thoughts of a solemn ceremony. There was something rite-like in these movements of the doomed soldier. And there was a resemblance in him to a devotee of a mad religion, blood-sucking, muscle-wrenching, bone-crushing. They were awed and afraid. They hung back lest he have at command a dreadful weapon.

At last they saw him stop and stand motionless. Hastening up, they perceived that his face wore an expression telling that he had at last found the place for which he had struggled. His spare figure was erect; his bloody hands were quietly at his side. He was waiting with patience for something that he had come to meet. He was at the rendezvous. They paused and stood, expectant.

There was a silence.

Finally, the chest of the doomed soldier began to heave with a strained motion. It increased in violence until it was as if an animal was within, and was kicking and tumbling furiously to be free.

This spectacle of gradual strangulation made the youth writhe, and once, as his friend rolled his eyes, he saw something in them that made him sink wailing to the ground. He raised his voice in a last supreme call.

"Jim—Jim—Jim——"

The tall soldier opened his lips and spoke. He made a gesture. "Leave me be—don't tech me—leave me be——"

There was another silence while he waited.

Suddenly his form stiffened and straightened. Then it was shaken by a prolonged ague. He stared into space. To the two watchers there was a curious and profound dignity in the firm lines of his awful face.

He was invaded by a creeping strangeness that slowly enveloped him. For a moment the tremor of his legs caused him to dance a sort of hideous hornpipe. His arms beat wildly about his head in expression of imp-like enthusiasm.

His tall figure stretched itself to its full height. There was a slight rending sound. Then it began to swing forward, slow and straight, in the manner of a falling tree. A swift muscular contortion made the left shoulder strike the ground first.

The body seemed to bounce a little way from the earth. "God!" said the tattered soldier.

The youth had watched, spellbound, this ceremony at the place of meeting. His face had been twisted into an expression of every agony he had imagined for his friend.

He now sprang to his feet and, going closer, gazed upon the paste-like face. The mouth was open, and the teeth showed in a laugh.

As the flap of the blue jacket fell away from the body, he could see that the side looked as if it had been chewed by wolves.

The youth turned, with sudden, livid rage, toward the battlefield. He shook his fist. He seemed about to deliver a philippic.

"Hell——"

The red sun was pasted in the sky like a wafer.

CHAPTER X

The tattered man stood musing.

"Well, he was reg'lar jim-dandy fer nerve, wa'n't he," said he finally, in a little awestruck voice. "A reg'lar jim-dandy." He thoughtfully poked one of the docile hands with his foot. "I wonner where he got 'is stren'th from? I never seen a man do like that before. It was a funny thing. Well, he was a reg'lar jim-dandy."

The youth desired to screech out his grief. He was stabbed, but his tongue lay dead in the tomb of his mouth. He threw himself again upon the ground and began to brood.

The tattered man stood musing.

"Look-a-here, pardner," he said after a time. He regarded the corpse as he spoke. "He's up an' gone, ain't 'e, an' we might as well begin t' look out fer ol' number one. This here thing is all over. He's up an' gone, ain't 'e? An' he's all right here. Nobody won't bother 'im. An' I must say I ain't enjoying any great health m'self these days."

The youth, awakened by the tattered soldier's tone, looked quickly up. He saw that he was swinging uncertainly on his legs, and that his face had turned to a shade of blue.

"Good Lord!" he cried, "you ain't goin' t'—not you, too."

The tattered man waved his hand. "Nary die," he said. "All I want is some pea soup an' a good bed. Some pea soup," he repeated dreamfully.

The youth arose from the ground. "I wonder where he came from. I left him over there." He pointed. "And now I find 'im here. And he was coming from over there, too." He indicated a new direction. They both turned toward the body as if to ask of it a question.

"Well," at length spoke the tattered man, "there ain't no use in our stayin' here an' tryin' t' ask him anything."

The youth nodded an assent wearily. They both turned to gaze for a moment at the corpse.

The youth murmured something.

"Well, he was a jim-dandy, wa'n't he?" said the tattered man as if in response.

They turned their backs upon it and started away. For a time they stole softly, treading with their toes. It remained laughing there in the grass.

"I'm commencin' t' feel pretty bad," said the tattered man, suddenly breaking one of his little silences. "I'm commencin' t' feel pretty damn' bad."

The youth groaned. "O Lord!" He wondered if he was to be the tortured witness of another grim encounter.

But his companion waved his hand reassuringly. "Oh, I'm not goin' t' die yit! There too much dependin' on me fer me t' die yit. No, sir! Nary die! I *can't!* Ye'd oughta see th' swad a' chil'ren I've got, an' all like that."

The youth, glancing at his companion, could see by the shadow of a smile that he was making some kind of fun.

As they plodded on the tattered soldier continued to talk. "Besides, if I died, I wouldn't die th' way that feller did. That was th' funniest thing. I'd jest flop down, I would. I never seen a feller die th' way that feller did.

"Yeh know Tom Jamison, he lives next door t' me up home. He's a nice feller, he is, an' we was allus good friends. Smart, too. Smart as a steel trap. Well, when we was a-fightin' this atternoon, all-of-a-sudden he begin t' rip up an' cuss an' beller at me. 'Yer shot, yeh blamed infernal!'—he swear horrible—he ses t' me. I put up m' hand t' m' head, an' when I looked at m' fingers, I seen, sure 'nough, I was shot. I give a holler an' begin t' run, but b'fore I could git away another one hit me in th' arm an' whirl' me clean 'round. I got skeared when they was all a-shootin' b'hind me, an' I run t' beat all, but I cotch it pretty bad. I've an idee I'd a' been fightin' yit if 'twasn't fer Tom Jamison."

Then he made a calm announcement: "There's two of 'em—little ones—but they're beginnin' t' have fun with me now. I don't b'lieve I kin walk much furder."

They went slowly on in silence. "Yeh look pretty peek-ed yerself," said the tattered man at last. "I bet yeh've got a worser one than yeh think. Ye'd better take keer of yer hurt. It

don't do t' let sech things go. It might be inside
mostly, an' them plays thunder. Where is it
located?" But he continued his harangue without waiting for a reply. "I see 'a feller git hit
plum in th' head when my reg'ment was a-standin'
at ease onct. An' everybody yelled out to 'im:
'Hurt, John? Are yeh hurt much?' 'No,' ses
he. He looked kinder surprised, an' he went on
tellin' 'em how he felt. He sed he didn't feel
nothin'. But, by dad, th' first thing that feller
knowed he was dead. Yes, he was dead—stone
dead. So, yeh wanta watch out. Yeh might have
some queer kind 'a hurt yerself. Yeh can't never
tell. Where is your'n located?"

The youth had been wriggling since the introduction of this topic. He now gave a cry of exasperation, and made a furious motion with his
hand. "Oh, don't bother me!" he said. He was
enraged against the tattered man, and could have
strangled him. His companions seemed ever to
play intolerable parts. They were ever upraising the
ghost of shame on the stick of their curiosity. He
turned toward the tattered man as one at bay. "Now,
don't bother me," he repeated with desperate menace.

"Well, Lord knows I don't wanta bother anybody," said the other. There was a little accent of
despair in his voice as he replied, "Lord knows
I've gota 'nough m' own t' tend to."

The youth, who had been holding a bitter debate
with himself, and casting glances of hatred and contempt at the tattered man, here spoke in a hard
voice. "Good-bye," he said.

The tattered man looked at him in gaping amazement. "Why — why, pardner, where yeh goin'?" he asked unsteadily. The youth, looking at him, could see that he, too, like that other one, was beginning to act dumb and animal-like. His thoughts seemed to be floundering about in his head. "Now — now — look — a — here, you Tom Jamison—now—I won't have this—this here won't do. Where—where yeh goin'?"

The youth pointed vaguely. "Over there," he replied.

"Well, now look — a — here — now," said the tattered man, rambling on in idiot fashion. His head was hanging forward, and his words were slurred. "This thing won't do, now, Tom Jamison. It won't do. I know yeh, yeh pig-headed devil. Yeh wanta go trompin' off with a bad hurt. It ain't right—now—Tom Jamison—it ain't. Yeh wanta leave me take keer of yeh, Tom Jamison. It ain't—right—it ain't—fer yeh t' go—trompin' off —with a bad hurt—it ain't—ain't—ain't right—it ain t."

In reply the youth climbed a fence and started away. He could hear the tattered man bleating plaintively.

Once he faced about angrily. "What?"

"Look—a—here, now, Tom Jamison—now—it ain't——"

The youth went on. Turning at a distance he saw the tattered man wandering about helplessly in the field.

He now thought that he wished he was dead.

He believed that he envied those men whose bodies lay strewn over the grass of the fields and on the fallen leaves of the forest.

The simple questions of the tattered man had been knife thrusts to him. They asserted a society that probes pitilessly at secrets until all is apparent. His late companion's chance persistency made him feel that he could not keep his crime concealed in his bosom. It was sure to be brought plain by one of those arrows which cloud the air and are constantly pricking, discovering, proclaiming those things which are willed to be for ever hidden. He admitted that he could not defend himself against this agency. It was not within the power of vigilance.

CHAPTER XI

He became aware that the furnace roar of the battle was growing louder. Great brown clouds had floated to the still heights of air before him. The noise, too, was approaching. The woods filtered men, and the fields became dotted.

As he rounded a hillock, he perceived that the roadway was now a crying mass of waggons, teams, and men. From the heaving tangle issued exhortations, commands, imprecations. Fear was sweeping it all along. The cracking whips bit, and horses plunged and tugged. The white-topped waggons strained and stumbled in their exertions like fat sheep.

The youth felt comforted in a measure by this sight. They were all retreating. Perhaps, then, he was not so bad after all. He seated himself and watched the terror-stricken waggons. They fled like soft, ungainly animals. All the roarers and lashers served to help him to magnify the dangers and horrors of the engagement that he might try to prove to himself that the thing with which men could charge him was in truth a symmetrical act. There was an amount of pleasure to him in watching the wild march of this vindication.

Presently the calm head of a forward-going column of infantry appeared in the road. It came swiftly on. Avoiding the obstructions gave it the sinuous movement of a serpent. The men at the head butted mules with their musket stocks. They prodded teamsters indifferent to all howls. The men forced their way through parts of the dense mass by strength. The blunt head of the column pushed. The raving teamsters swore many strange oaths.

The commands to make way had the ring of a great importance in them. The men were going forward to the heart of the din. They were to confront the eager rush of the enemy. They felt the pride of their onward movement when the remainder of the army seemed trying to dribble down this road. They tumbled teams about with a fine feeling that it was no matter so long as their column got to the front in time. This importance made their faces grave and stern. And the backs of the officers were very rigid.

As the youth looked at them the black weight of his woe returned to him. He felt that he was regarding a procession of chosen beings. The separation was as great to him as if they had marched with weapons of flame and banners of sunlight. He could never be like them. He could have wept in his longings.

He searched about in his mind for an adequate malediction for the indefinite cause, the thing upon which men turn the words of final blame. It—whatever it was—was responsible for him, he said. There lay the fault.

The haste of the column to reach the battle seemed to the forlorn young man to be something much finer than stout fighting. Heroes, he thought, could find excuses in that long seething lane. They could retire with perfect self-respect and make excuses to the stars.

He wondered what those men had eaten that they could be in such haste to force their way to grim chances of death. As he watched, his envy grew until he thought that he wished to change lives with one of them. He would have liked to have used a tremendous force, he said, throw off himself and become a better. Swift pictures of himself, apart, yet in himself, came to him—a blue desperate figure leading lurid charges with one knee forward and a broken blade high—a blue, determined figure standing before a crimson and steel assault, getting calmly killed on a high place before the eyes of all. He thought of the magnificent pathos of his dead body.

These thoughts uplifted him. He felt the quiver of war desire. In his ears he heard the ring of victory. He knew the frenzy of a rapid successful charge. The music of the trampling feet, the sharp voices, the clanking arms of the column near him, made him soar on the red wings of war. For a few moments he was sublime.

He thought that he was about to start for the front. Indeed, he saw a picture of himself, dust-stained, haggard, panting, flying to the front at the proper moment to seize and throttle the dark, leering witch of calamity.

Then the difficulties of the thing began to drag at him. He hesitated, balancing awkwardly on one foot.

He had no rifle; he could not fight with his hands, said he resentfully to his plan. Well, rifles could be had for the picking. They were extraordinarily profuse.

Also, he continued, it would be a miracle if he found his regiment. Well, he could fight with any regiment.

He started forward slowly. He stepped as if he expected to tread upon some explosive thing. Doubts and he were struggling.

He would truly be a worm if any of his comrades should see him returning thus, the marks of his flight upon him. There was a reply that the intent fighters did not care for what happened rearward, saving that no hostile bayonets appeared there. In the battle-blur his face would, in a way, be hidden, like the face of a cowled man.

But then he said that his tireless fate would bring forth, when the strife lulled for a moment, a man to ask of him an explanation. In imagination he felt the scrutiny of his companions as he painfully laboured through some lies.

Eventually, his courage expended itself upon these objections. The debates drained him of his fire.

He was not cast down by this defeat of his plan, for, upon studying the affair carefully, he could not but admit that the objections were very formidable.

Furthermore, various ailments had begun to cry

out. In their presence he could not persist in flying high with the wings of war; they rendered it almost impossible for him to see himself in a heroic light. He tumbled headlong.

He discovered that he had a scorching thirst. His face was so dry and grimy that he thought he could feel his skin crackle. Each bone of his body had an ache in it, and seemingly threatened to break with each movement. His feet were like two sores. Also, his body was calling for food. It was more powerful than a direct hunger. There was a dull, weight-like feeling in his stomach, and, when he tried to walk, his head swayed and he tottered. He could not see with distinctness. Small patches of green mist floated before his vision.

While he had been tossed by many emotions, he had not been aware of ailments. Now they beset him and made clamour. As he was at last compelled to pay attention to them, his capacity for self-hate was multiplied. In despair, he declared that he was not like those others. He now conceded it to be impossible that he should ever become a hero. He was a craven loon. Those pictures of glory were piteous things. He groaned from his heart and went staggering off.

A certain moth-like quality within him kept him in the vicinity of the battle. He had a great desire to see, and to get news. He wished to know who was winning.

He told himself that, despite his unprecedented suffering, he had never lost his greed for a victory, yet, he said, in a half-apologetic manner to his conscience, he could not but know that a defeat for the army this time might mean many favourable things for him.   The blows of the enemy would splinter. regiments into fragments.   Thus, many men of courage, he considered, would be obliged to desert the colours and scurry like chickens.   He would appear as one of them. They would be sullen brothers in distress, and he could then easily believe he had not run any farther or faster than they.   And if he himself could believe in his virtuous perfection, he conceived that there would be small trouble in convincing all others.

He said, as if in excuse for this hope, that previously the army had encountered great defeats, and in a few months had shaken off all blood and tradition of them, emerging as bright and valiant as a new one; thrusting out of sight the memory of disaster, and appearing with the valour and confidence of unconquered legions.   The shrilling voices of the people at home would pipe dismally for a time, but various generals were usually compelled to listen to these ditties.   He of course felt no compunctions for proposing a general as a sacrifice.   He could not tell who the chosen for the barbs might be, so he could centre no direct sympathy upon him.   The people were afar, and he did not conceive public opinion to be accurate at long range.   It was quite probable they would hit the wrong man, who, after he had recovered from his amazement, would perhaps spend the rest of his days in writing replies to the songs of his alleged failure. It would be very unfortunate, no doubt, but in this case a general was of no consequence to the youth.

In a defeat there would be a roundabout vindication of himself. He thought it would prove, in a manner, that he had fled early because of his superior powers of perception. A serious prophet upon predicting a flood should be the first man to climb a tree. This would demonstrate that he was indeed a seer.

A moral vindication was regarded by the youth as a very important thing. Without salve, he could not, he thought, wear the sore badge of his dishonour through life. With his heart continually assuring him that he was despicable, he could not exist without making it, through his actions, apparent to all men.

If the army had gone gloriously on he would be lost. If the din meant that now his army's flags were tilted forward he was a condemned wretch. He would be compelled to doom himself to isolation. If the men were advancing, their indifferent feet were trampling upon his chances for a successful life.

As these thoughts went rapidly through his mind, he turned upon them and tried to thrust them away. He denounced himself as a villain. He said that he was the most unutterably selfish man in existence. His mind pictured the soldiers who would place their defiant bodies before the spear of the yelling battle fiend; and as he saw their dripping corpses on an imagined field, he said that he was their murderer.

*

Again he thought that he wished he was dead. He believed that he envied a corpse. Thinking of the slain, he achieved a great contempt for some of them, as if they were guilty for thus becoming lifeless. They might have been killed by lucky chances, he said, before they had had opportunities to flee, or before they had been really tested. Yet they would receive laurels from tradition. He cried out bitterly that their crowns were stolen, and their robes of glorious memories were shams. However, he still said that it was a great pity he was not as they.

A defeat of the army had suggested itself to him as a means of escape from the consequences of his fall. He considered now, however, that it was useless to think of such a possibility. His education had been that success for that mighty blue machine was certain ; that it would make victories as a contrivance turns out buttons. He presently discarded all his speculations in the other direction. He returned to the creed of soldiers.

When he perceived again that it was not possible for the army to be defeated, he tried to bethink him of a fine tale which he could take back to his regiment, and with it turn the expected shafts of derision.

But, as he mortally feared these shafts, it became impossible for him to invent a tale he felt he could trust. He experimented with many schemes, but threw them aside, one by one, as flimsy. He was quick to see vulnerable places in them all.

Furthermore, he was much afraid that some arrow of scorn might lay him mentally low before he could raise his protecting tale.

He imagined the whole regiment saying, " Where's Henry Fleming ? He run, didn't 'e ? Oh, my ! " He recalled various persons who would be quite sure to leave him no peace about it. They would doubtless question him with sneers, and laugh at his stammering hesitation. In the next engagement they would try to keep watch of him to discover when he would run.

Wherever he went in camp, he would encounter insolent and lingeringly-cruel stares. As he imagined himself passing near a crowd of comrades, he could hear some one say, " There he goes ! "

Then, as if the heads were moved by one muscle, all the faces were turned toward him with wide, derisive grins. He seemed to hear some one make a humorous remark in a low tone. At it the others all crowed and cackled. He was a slang phrase.

THE column that had butted stoutly at the obstacles in the roadway was barely out of the youth's sight before he saw dark waves of men come sweeping out of the woods and down through the fields. He knew at once that the steel fibres had been washed from their hearts. They were bursting from their coats and their equipments as from entanglements. They charged down upon him like terrified buffaloes.

Behind them blue smoke curled and clouded above the tree-tops, and through the thickets he could sometimes see a distant pink glare. The voices of the cannon were clamouring in interminable chorus.

The youth was horror-stricken. He stared in agony and amazement. He forgot that he was engaged in combating the universe. He threw aside his mental pamphlets on the philosophy of the retreated and rules for the guidance of the damned.

The fight was lost. The dragons were coming with invincible strides. The army, helpless in the matted thickets and blinded by the overhanging night, was going to be swallowed. War, the red animal war, the blood-swollen god, would have bloated fill.

Within him something bade to cry out. He had the impulse to make a rallying speech, to sing a battle hymn, but he could only get his tongue to call into the air, "Why—why—what—what's th' matter?"

Soon he was in the midst of them. They were leaping and scampering all about him. Their blanched faces shone in the dusk. They seemed, for the most part, to be very burly men. The youth turned from one to another of them as they galloped along. His incoherent questions were lost. They were heedless of his appeals. They did not seem to see him.

They sometimes gabbled insanely. One huge man was asking of the sky, "Say, where de plank road? Where de plank road?" It was as if he had lost a child. He wept in his pain and dismay.

Presently, men were running hither and thither in all ways. The artillery booming, forward, rearward, and on the flanks, made jumble of ideas of direction. Landmarks had vanished into the gathered gloom. The youth began to imagine that he had got into the centre of the tremendous quarrel, and he could perceive no way out of it. From the mouths of the fleeing men came a thousand wild questions, but no one made answers.

The youth, after rushing about and throwing interrogations at the heedless bands of retreating infantry, finally clutched a man by the arm. They swung around face to face.

"Why—why——" stammered the youth, struggling with his balking tongue.

The man screamed, "Let go me! Let go me!" His face was livid, and his eyes were rolling uncontrolled. He was heaving and panting. He still grasped his rifle, perhaps having forgotten to release his hold upon it. He tugged frantically, and the youth, being compelled to lean forward, was dragged several paces.

"Let go me! Let go me!"

"Why—why——" stuttered the youth.

"Well, then!" bawled the man in a lurid rage. He adroitly and fiercely swung his rifle. It crushed upon the youth's head. The man ran on.

The youth's fingers had turned to paste upon the other's arm. The energy was smitten from his muscles. He saw the flaming wings of lightning flash before his vision. There was a deafening rumble of thunder within his head.

Suddenly his legs seemed to die. He sank writhing to the ground. He tried to arise. In his efforts against the numbing pain he was like a man wrestling with a creature of the air.

There was a sinister struggle.

Sometimes he would achieve a position half erect, battle with the air for a moment, and then fall again, grabbing at the grass. His face was of a clammy pallor. Deep groans were wrenched from him.

At last, with a twisting movement, he got upon his hands and knees, and from thence, like a babe trying to walk, to his feet. Pressing his hands to his temples, he went lurching over the grass.

He fought an intense battle with his body. His dulled senses wished him to swoon, and he opposed them stubbornly, his mind portraying unknown dangers and mutilations if he should fall upon the field. He went tall soldier fashion. He imagined secluded spots where he could fall and be unmolested. To search for one he strove against the tide of his pain.

Once he put his hand to the top of his head and timidly touched the wound. The scratching pain of the contact made him draw a long breath through his clenched teeth. His fingers were dabbled with blood. He regarded them with a fixed stare.

Around him he could hear the grumble of jolted cannon as the scurrying horses were lashed toward the front. Once, a young officer on a besplashed charger nearly ran him down. He turned and watched the mass of guns, men, and horses sweeping in a wide curve toward a gap in a fence. The officer was making excited motions with a gauntleted hand. The guns followed the teams with an air of unwillingness, of being dragged by the heels.

Some officers of the scattered infantry were cursing and railing like fishwives. Their scolding voices could be heard above the din. Into the unspeakable jumble in the roadway rode a squadron of cavalry. The faded yellow of their facings shone bravely. There was a mighty altercation.

The artillery were assembling as if for a conference.

The blue haze of evening was upon the field. The lines of forest were long purple shadows. One cloud lay along the western sky partly smothering the red.

As the youth left the scene behind him, he heard the guns suddenly roar out. He imagined them shaking in black rage. They belched and howled like brass devils guarding a gate. The soft air was filled with the tremendous remonstrance. With it came the shattering peal of opposing infantry. Turning to look behind him, he could see sheets of orange light illumine the shadowy distance. There were subtle and sudden lightnings in the far air. At times he thought he could see heaving masses of men.

He hurried on in the dusk. The day had faded until he could barely distinguish place for his feet. The purple darkness was filled with men who lectured and jabbered. Sometimes he could see them gesticulating against the blue and sombre sky. There seemed to be a great ruck of men and munitions spread about in the forest and in the fields.

The little narrow roadway now lay lifeless. There were overturned waggons like sun-dried boulders. The bed of the former torrent was choked with the bodies of horses and splintered parts of war machines.

It had come to pass that his wound pained him but little. He was afraid to move rapidly, however, for a dread of disturbing it. He held his head very still, and took many precautions against stumbling. He was filled with anxiety, and his face was pinched and drawn in anticipation of the pain of any sudden mistake of his feet in the gloom.

His thoughts, as he walked, fixed intently upon

his hurt. There was a cool, liquid feeling about it, and he imagined blood moving slowly down under his hair. His head seemed swollen to a size that made him think his neck to be inadequate.

The new silence of his wound made much worriment. The little blistering voices of pain that had called out from his scalp were, he thought, definite in their expression of danger. By them he believed that he could measure his plight. But when they remained ominously silent he became frightened, and imagined terrible fingers that clutched into his brain.

Amid it he began to reflect upon various incidents and conditions of the past. He bethought him of certain meals his mother had cooked at home, in which those dishes of which he was particularly fond had occupied prominent positions. He saw the spread table. The pine walls of the kitchen were glowing in the warm light from the stove. Too, he remembered how he and his companions used to go from the school-house to the bank of a shaded pool. He saw his clothes in disorderly array upon the grass of the bank. He felt the swash of the fragrant water upon his body. The leaves of the overhanging maple rustled with melody in the wind of youthful summer.

He was overcome presently by a dragging weariness. His head hung forward and his shoulders were stooped as if he were bearing a great bundle. His feet shuffled along the ground.

He held continuous arguments as to whether he should lie down and sleep at some near spot, or force himself on until he reached a certain haven.

He often tried to dismiss the question, but his body persisted in rebellion, and his senses nagged at him like pampered babies.

At last he heard a cheery voice near his shoulder: " Yeh seem t' be in a pretty bad way, boy ? "

The youth did not look up, but he assented with thick tongue. " Uh ! "

The owner of the cheery voice took him firmly by the arm. " Well," he said, with a round laugh, "I'm goin' your way. Th' hull gang is goin' your way. An' I guess I kin give yeh a lift." They began to walk like a drunken man and his friend.

As they went along, the man questioned the youth, and assisted him with the replies, like one manipulating the mind of a child. Sometimes he interjected anecdotes. " What reg'ment do yeh b'long teh ? Eh ? What's that ? Th' 304th N' York ? Why, what corps is that in ? Oh, it is ? Why, I thought they wasn't engaged t'-day—they're 'way over in th' centre. Oh, they was, eh ? Well, pretty nearly everybody got their share 'a fightin' t'-day. By dad, I give myself up fer dead any number 'a times. There was shootin' here an' shootin' there, an' hollerin' here an' hollerin' there, in th' damn' darkness, until I couldn't tell t' save m' soul which side I was on. Sometimes I thought I was sure 'nough from Ohier, an' other times I could 'a swore I was from th' bitter end of Florida. It was th' most mixed up dern thing I ever see. An' these here hull woods is a reg'lar mess. It'll be a miracle if we find our reg'ments t'-night. Pretty soon, though, we'll meet a - plenty of guards an' provost-guards, an' one thing an' another. Ho! there they go with an off'cer, I guess. Look at his hand a-draggin'. He's got all th' war he wants, I bet. He won't be talkin' so big about his reputation an' all when they go t' sawin' off his leg. Poor feller! My brother's got whiskers jest like that. How did yeh git 'way over here, anyhow? Your reg'ment is a long way from here, ain't it? Well, I guess we can find it. Yeh know there was a boy killed in my comp'ny t'-day that I thought th' world an' all of. Jack was a nice feller. By ginger, it hurt like thunder t' see ol' Jack jest git knocked flat. We was a-standin' purty peaceable fer a spell, 'though there was men runnin' ev'ry way all 'round us, an' while we was a-standin' like that, 'long come a big fat feller. He began t' peck at Jack's elbow, an' he ses, 'Say, where's th' road t' th' river?' An' Jack, he never paid no attention, an' th' feller kept on a-peckin' at his elbow an' sayin', 'Say, where's th' road t' th' river?' Jack was a-lookin' ahead all th' time tryin' t' see th' Johnnies comin' through th' woods, an' he never paid no attention t' this big fat feller fer a long time, but at last he turned 'round an' he ses, 'Ah, go t' hell an' find th' road t' th' river!' An' jest then a shot slapped him bang on th' side th' head. He was a sergeant, too. Them was his last words. Thunder, I wish we was sure 'a findin' our reg'ments t'-night. It's goin' t' be long huntin'. But I guess we kin do it."

In the search which followed, the man of the cheery voice seemed to the youth to possess a wand of a magic kind. He threaded the mazes of the tangled forest with a strange fortune. In encounters with guards and patrols he displayed the keenness of a detective and the valour of a gamin. Obstacles fell before him and became of assistance. The youth, with his chin still on his breast, stood woodenly by while his companion beat ways and means out of sullen things.

The forest seemed a vast hive of men buzzing about in frantic circles, but the cheery man conducted the youth without mistakes, until at last he began to chuckle with glee and self - satisfaction. "Ah, there yeh are! See that fire?"

The youth nodded stupidly.

"Well, there's where your reg'ment is. An' now good-bye, ol' boy, good luck t' yeh."

A warm and strong hand clasped the youth's languid fingers for an instant, and then he heard a cheerful and audacious whistling as the man strode away. As he who had so befriended him was thus passing out of his life, it suddenly occurred to the youth that he had not once seen his face.

CHAPTER XIII

THE youth went slowly toward the fire indicated by his departed friend. As he reeled, he bethought him of the welcome his comrades would give him. He had a conviction that he would soon feel in his sore heart the barbed missiles of ridicule. He had no strength to invent a tale; he would be a soft target.

He made vague plans to go off into the deeper darkness and hide, but they were all destroyed by the voices of exhaustion and pain from his body. His ailments, clamouring, forced him to seek the place of food and rest, at whatever cost.

He swung unsteadily toward the fire. He could see the forms of men throwing black shadows in the red light, and as he went nearer it became known to him in some way that the ground was strewn with sleeping men.

Of a sudden he confronted a black and monstrous figure. A rifle barrel caught some glinting beams. "Halt! halt!" He was dismayed for a moment, but he presently thought that he recognised the nervous voice. As he stood tottering before the rifle barrel, he called out, "Why, hello, Wilson, you—you here?"

The rifle was lowered to a position of caution, and the loud soldier came slowly forward. He peered into the youth's face. "That you, Henry?"

"Yes, it's—it's me."

"Well, well, ol' boy," said the other, "by ginger, I'm glad t' see yeh! I give yeh up fer a goner. I thought you was dead sure enough." There was husky emotion in his voice.

The youth found that now he could barely stand upon his feet. There was a sudden sinking of his forces. He thought he must hasten to produce his tale to protect him from the missiles already at the lips of his redoubtable comrades. So, staggering before the loud soldier, he began, "Yes, yes. I've —I've had an awful time. I've been all over. 'Way over on th' right. Ter'ble fightin' over there. I had an awful time. I got separated from the reg'- ment. Over on th' right I got shot. In th' head. I never see sech fightin'. Awful time. I don't see how I could 'a got separated from th' reg'ment. I got shot, too."

His friend had stepped forward quickly. "What? Got shot? Why didn't yeh say so first? Poor ol' boy, we must—hol' on a minnit; what am I doin'? I'll call Simpson."

Another figure at that moment loomed in the gloom. They could see that it was the corporal. "Who yeh talkin' to, Wilson?" he demanded. His voice was anger-toned. "Who yeh talkin' to? Yeh th' derndest sentinel—why—hello, Henry, you here? Why, I thought you was dead four hours ago! Great Jerusalem, they keep turnin' up every ten minutes or so! We thought we'd lost forty-two men by straight count, but if they keep on a-comin' this way, we'll git th' comp'ny all back by mornin' yit. Where was yeh?"

"Over on th' right. I got separated——" began the youth with considerable glibness.

But his friend had interrupted hastily. "Yes, an' he got shot in th' head, an' he's in a fix, an' we must see t' him right away." He rested his rifle in the hollow of his left arm and his right around the youth's shoulder.

"Gee, it must hurt like thunder!" he said.

The youth leaned heavily upon his friend. "Yes, it hurts—hurts a good deal," he replied. There was a faltering in his voice.

"Oh," said the corporal. He linked his arm in the youth's and drew him forward. "Come on, Henry. I'll take keer 'a yeh."

As they went on together the loud private called out after them, "Put 'im t' sleep in my blanket, Simpson. An'—hol' on a minnit—here's my canteen. It's full 'a coffee. Look at his head by th' fire an' see how it looks. Maybe it's a pretty bad un. When I git relieved in a couple 'a minnits, I'll be over an' see t' him."

The youth's senses were so deadened that his friend's voice sounded from afar, and he could scarcely feel the pressure of the corporal's arm. He submitted passively to the latter's directing strength. His head was in the old manner hanging forward upon his breast. His knees wobbled.

The corporal led him into the glare of the fire.

"Now, Henry," he said, "let's have look at yer ol'
head."

The youth sat down obediently, and the corporal,
laying aside his rifle, began to fumble in the bushy
hair of his comrade. He was obliged to turn the
other's head so that the full flush of the fire-light
would beam upon it. He puckered his mouth with
a critical air. He drew back his lips and whistled
through his teeth when his fingers came in contact
with the splashed blood and the rare wound.

"Ah, here we are!" he said. He awkwardly made
further investigations. "Jest as I thought," he
added presently. "Yeh've been grazed by a ball.
It's raised a queer lump jest as if some feller had
lammed yeh on th' head with a club. It stopped
a-bleedin' long time ago. Th' most about it is, that
in th' mornin' yeh'll feel that a number ten hat
wouldn't fit yeh. An' your head 'll be all het up an'
feel as dry as burnt pork. An' yeh may git a lot 'a
other sicknesses, too, by mornin'. Yeh can't never
tell. Still, I don't much think so. It's jest a damn'
good belt on th' head, and nothin' more. Now,
you jest sit here an' don't move, while I go rout
out th' relief. Then I'll send Wilson t' take keer 'a
yeh."

The corporal went away. The youth remained on
the ground like a parcel. He stared with a vacant
look into the fire.

After a time he aroused, for some part, and the
things about him began to take form. He saw that
the ground in the deep shadows was cluttered
with men, sprawling in every conceivable posture.

Glancing narrowly into the more distant darkness, he caught occasional glimpses of visages that loomed pallid and ghostly, lit with a phosphorescent glow. These faces expressed in their lines the deep stupor of the tired soldiers. They made them appear like men drunk with wine. This bit of forest might have appeared to an ethereal wanderer as the scene of the result of some frightful debauch.

On the other side of the fire the youth observed an officer asleep, seated bolt upright, with his back against a tree. There was something perilous in his position. Badgered by dreams, perhaps, he swayed with little bounces and starts, like an old, toddy-stricken grandfather in a chimney corner. Dust and stains were upon his face. His lower jaw hung down, as if lacking strength to assume its normal position. He was the picture of an exhausted soldier after a feast of war.

He had evidently gone to sleep with his sword in his arms. These two had slumbered in an embrace, but the weapon had been allowed in time to fall unheeded to the ground. The brass-mounted hilt lay in contact with some parts of the fire.

Within the gleam of rose and orange light from the burning sticks were other soldiers, snoring and heaving, or lying death-like in slumber. A few pairs of legs were stuck forth, rigid and straight. The shoes displayed the mud or dust of marches, and bits of rounded trousers, protruding from the blankets, showed rents and tears from hurried pitchings through the dense brambles.

The fire crackled musically. From it swelled

light smoke.   Overhead the foliage moved softly. The leaves, with their faces turned toward the blaze, were coloured shifting hues of silver, often edged with red.   Far off to the right, through a window in the forest, could be seen a handful of stars lying, like glittering pebbles, on the black level of the night.

Occasionally, in this low-arched hall, a soldier would arouse and turn his body to a new position, the experience of his sleep having taught him of uneven and objectionable places upon the ground under him.   Or, perhaps, he would lift himself to a sitting posture, blink at the fire for an unintelligent moment, throw a swift glance at his prostrate companion, and then cuddle down again with a grunt of sleepy content.

The youth sat in a forlorn heap until his friend the loud young soldier came, swinging two canteens by their light strings.   "Well, now, Henry, ol' boy," said the latter, "we'll have yeh fixed up in jest about a minnit."

He had the bustling ways of an amateur nurse. He fussed around the fire and stirred the sticks to brilliant exertions.   He made his patient drink largely from the canteen that contained the coffee. It was to the youth a delicious draught.   He tilted his head afar back and held the canteen long to his lips.   The cool mixture went caressingly down his blistered throat.   Having finished, he sighed with comfortable delight.

The loud young soldier watched his comrade with an air of satisfaction.   He later produced an extensive handkerchief from his pocket. He folded it into a manner of bandage, and soused water from the other canteen upon the middle of it. This crude arrangement he bound over the youth's head, tying the ends in a queer knot at the back of the neck.

"There," he said, moving off and surveying his deed, "yeh look like the devil, but I bet yeh feel better."

The youth contemplated his friend with grateful eyes. Upon his aching and swelling head the cold cloth was like a tender woman's hand.

"Yeh don't holler ner say nothin'," remarked his friend approvingly. "I know I'm a blacksmith at takin' keer 'a sick folks, an' yeh never squeaked. Yer a good un, Henry. Most 'a men would 'a' been in th' hospital long ago. A shot in th' head ain't foolin' business."

The youth made no reply, but began to fumble with the buttons of his jacket.

"Well, come now," continued his friend, "come on. I must put yeh t' bed, an' see that yeh git a good night's rest."

The other got carefully erect, and the loud young soldier led him among the sleeping forms lying in groups and rows. Presently he stooped and picked up his blankets. He spread the rubber one upon the ground, and placed the woollen one about the youth's shoulders.

"There now," he said, "lie down an git some sleep."

The youth, with his manner of dog-like obedience, got carefully down like a crone stooping. He stretched out with a murmur of relief and comfort. The ground felt like the softest couch.

But of a sudden he ejaculated, "Hol' on a minnit! Where you goin' t' sleep?"

His friend waved his hand impatiently. "Right down there by yeh."

"Well, but hol' on a minnit," continued the youth "What yeh goin' t' sleep in?   I've got your——"

The loud young soldier snarled, "Shet up an' go on t' sleep. Don't be makin' a damn' fool 'a yerself," he said severely.

After the reproof the youth said no more. An exquisite drowsiness had spread through him. The warm comfort of the blanket enveloped him and made a gentle languor. His head fell forward on his crooked arm, and his weighted lids went softly down over his eyes. Hearing a splatter of musketry from the distance, he wondered indifferently if those men sometimes slept. He gave a long sigh, snuggled down into his blanket, and in a moment was like his comrades.

CHAPTER XIV

WHEN the youth awoke it seemed to him that he
had been asleep for a thousand years, and he felt
sure that he opened his eyes upon an unexpected
world. Grey mists were slowly shifting before the
first efforts of the sun-rays. An impending splendour could be seen in the eastern sky. An icy dew
had chilled his face, and immediately upon arousing
he curled farther down into his blanket. He stared
for a while at the leaves overhead, moving in a
heraldic wind of the day.

The distance was splintering and blaring with the
noise of fighting. There was in the sound an expression of a deadly persistency, as if it had not
begun and was not to cease.

About him were the rows and groups of men that
he had dimly seen the previous night. They were
getting a last draught of sleep before the awakening.
The gaunt, careworn features and dusty figures were
made plain by this quaint light at the dawning, but
it dressed the skin of the men in corpse-like hues,
and made the tangled limbs appear pulseless and
dead. The youth started up with a little cry when
his eyes first swept over this motionless mass of
men, thick-spread upon the ground, pallid, and in

strange postures. His disordered mind interpreted the hall of the forest as a charnel place. He believed for an instant that he was in the house of the dead, and he did not dare to move lest these corpses start up, squalling and squawking. In a second, however, he achieved his proper mind. He swore a complicated oath at himself. He saw that this sombre picture was not a fact of the present, but a mere prophecy.

He heard then the noise of a fire crackling briskly in the cold air, and, turning his head, he saw his friend pottering busily about a small blaze. A few other figures moved in the fog, and he heard the hard cracking of axe-blows.

Suddenly there was a hollow rumble of drums. A distant bugle sang faintly. Similar sounds, varying in strength, came from near and far over the forest. The bugles called to each other like brazen gamecocks. The near thunder of the regimental drums rolled.

The body of men in the woods rustled. There was a general uplifting of heads. A murmuring of voices broke upon the air. In it there was much bass of grumbling oaths. Strange gods were addressed in condemnation of the early hours necessary to correct war. An officer's peremptory tenor rang out and quickened the stiffened movement of the men. The tangled limbs unravelled. The corpse-hued faces were hidden behind fists that twisted slowly in the eye-sockets.

The youth sat up and gave vent to an enormous yawn. "Thunder!" he remarked petulantly. He rubbed his eyes, and then putting up his hand felt carefully of the bandage over his wound. His friend, perceiving him to be awake, came from the fire. "Well, Henry, ol' man, how do yeh feel this mornin'?" he demanded.

The youth yawned again. Then he puckered his mouth to a little pucker. His head, in truth, felt precisely like a melon, and there was an unpleasant sensation at his stomach.

"O Lord, I feel pretty bad," he said.

"Thunder!" exclaimed the other. "I hoped ye'd feel all right this mornin'. Let's see th' bandage— I guess it's slipped." He began to tinker at the wound in rather a clumsy way until the youth exploded.

"Gosh-dern it!" he said, in sharp irritation; "you're the hangdest man I ever saw! You wear muffs on your hands. Why in good thunderation can't you be more easy? I'd rather you'd stand off an' throw guns at it. Now, go slow, an' don't act as if you was nailing down carpet."

He glared with insolent command at his friend, but the latter answered soothingly. "Well, well, come now, an' git some grub," he said. "Then, maybe, yeh'll feel better."

At the fireside the loud young soldier watched over his comrade's wants with tenderness and care. He was very busy marshalling the little black vagabonds of tin cups and pouring into them the steaming, iron coloured mixture from a small and sooty tin pail. He had some fresh meat, which he roasted hurriedly upon a stick. He sat down then and contemplated the youth's appetite with glee.

The youth took note of a remarkable change in his comrade since those days of camp life upon the river bank. He seemed no more to be continually regarding the proportions of his personal prowess. He was not furious at small words that pricked his conceits. He was no more a loud young soldier. There was about him now a fine reliance. He showed a quiet belief in his purposes and his abilities. And this inward confidence evidently enabled him to be indifferent to little words of other men aimed at him.

The youth reflected. He had been used to regarding his comrade as a blatant child with an audacity grown from his inexperience, thoughtless, headstrong, jealous, and filled with a tinsel courage —a swaggering babe accustomed to strut in his own door-yard. The youth wondered where had been born these new eyes; when his comrade had made the great discovery that there were many men who would refuse to be subjected by him. Apparently, the other had now climbed a peak of wisdom from which he could perceive himself as a very wee thing. And the youth saw that ever after it would be easier to live in his friend's neighbourhood.

His comrade balanced his ebony coffee-cup on his knee. "Well, Henry," he said, "what d'yeh think th' chances are? D'yeh think we'll wallop 'em?"

The youth considered for a moment. "Day-b'fore-yesterday," he finally replied, with boldness, "you would 'a' bet you'd lick the hull kit-an'-boodle all by yourself."

His friend looked a trifle amazed. "Would I?" he asked. He pondered. "Well, perhaps I would," he decided at last. He stared humbly at the fire.

The youth was quite disconcerted at this surprising reception of his remarks. "Oh no, you wouldn't either," he said, hastily trying to retrace.

But the other made a deprecating gesture. "Oh, yeh needn't mind, Henry," he said. "I believe I was a pretty big fool in those days." He spoke as after a lapse of years.

There was a little pause.

"All th' officers say we've got th' rebs in a pretty tight box," said the friend, clearing his throat in a commonplace way. "They all seem t' think we've got 'em jest where we want 'em."

"I don't know about that," the youth replied. "What I seen over on th' right makes me think it was th' other way about. From where I was, it looked as if we was gettin' a good poundin' yestirday."

"D' yeh think so?" inquired the friend. "I thought we handled 'em pretty rough yestirday."

"Not a bit," said the youth. "Why, lord, man, you didn't see nothing of the fight. Why!" Then a sudden thought came to him. "Oh! Jim Conklin's dead."

His friend started. "What? Is he? Jim Conklin?"

The youth spoke slowly. "Yes. He's dead. Shot in th' side."

"Yeh don't say so. Jim Conklin . . . poor cuss!"

All about them were other small fires, surrounded by men with their little black utensils. From one of these near came sudden, sharp voices in a row. It appeared that two light-footed soldiers had been teasing a huge, bearded man, causing him to spill coffee upon his blue knees. The man had gone into a rage and had sworn comprehensively. Stung by his language, his tormentors had immediately bristled at him with a great show of resenting unjust oaths. Possibly there was going to be a fight.

The friend arose and went over to them, making pacific motions with his arms. "Oh, here, now, boys, what's th' use?" he said. "We'll be at th' rebs in less'n an hour. What's th' good fightin' 'mong ourselves?"

One of the light-footed soldiers turned upon him, red-faced and violent. "Yeh needn't come around here with yer preachin'. I s'pose yeh don't approve 'a fightin' since Charley Morgan licked yeh; but I don't see what business this here is 'a yours or anybody else."

"Well, it ain't," said the friend mildly. "Still I hate t' see——"

There was a tangled argument.

"Well, he——" said the two, indicating their opponent with accusative forefingers.

The huge soldier was quite purple with rage. He pointed at the two soldiers with his great hand, extended claw-like. "Well, they——"

But during this argumentative time the desire to

deal blows seemed to pass, although they said much to each other. Finally, the friend returned to his old seat. In a short while the three antagonists could be seen together in an amiable bunch.

"Jimmie Rogers ses I'll have t' fight him after th' battle t'-day," announced the friend as he again seated himself. "He ses he don't allow no interferin' in his business. I hate t' see th' boys fightin' 'mong themselves."

The youth laughed. "Yer changed a good bit. Yeh ain't at all like yeh was. I remember when you an' that Irish feller——" He stopped and laughed again.

"No, I didn't use t' be that way," said his friend thoughtfully. "That's true 'nough."

"Well, I didn't mean——" began the youth.

The friend made another deprecatory gesture. "Oh, yeh needn't mind, Henry."

There was another little pause.

"Th' reg'ment lost over half th' men yestirday," remarked the friend eventually. "I thought 'a course they was all dead, but, laws, they kep' a-comin' back last night until it seems, after all, we didn't lose but a few. They'd been scattered all over, wanderin' around in th' woods, fightin' with other reg'ments, an' everything. Jest like you done."

"So?" said the youth.

CHAPTER XV

THE regiment was standing at order arms at the side
of a lane, waiting for the command to march, when
suddenly the youth remembered the little packet
enwrapped in a faded yellow envelope which the
loud young soldier with lugubrious words had in-
trusted to him. It made him start. He uttered
an exclamation and turned toward his comrade.

"Wilson!"

"What?"

His friend, at his side in the ranks, was thoughtfully staring down the road. From some cause his
expression was at that moment very meek. The
youth, regarding him with sidelong glances, felt
impelled to change his purpose. "Oh, nothing,"
he said.

His friend turned his head in some surprise.
"Why, what was yeh goin' t' say?"

"Oh, nothing," repeated the youth.

He resolved not to deal the little blow. It was
sufficient that the fact made him glad. It was not
necessary to knock his friend on the head with the
misguided packet.

He had been possessed of much fear of his friend,
for he saw how easily questionings could make holes

in his feelings. Lately, he had assured himself that the altered comrade would not tantalise him with a persistent curiosity, but he felt certain that during the first period of leisure his friend would ask him to relate his adventures of the previous day.

He now rejoiced in the possession of a small weapon, with which he could prostrate his comrade at the first signs of a cross-examination. He was master. It would now be he who could laugh and shoot the shafts of derision.

The friend had, in a weak hour, spoken with sobs of his own death. He had delivered a melancholy oration previous to his funeral, and had doubtless, in the packet of letters, presented various keepsakes to relatives. But he had not died, and thus he had delivered himself into the hands of the youth.

The latter felt immensely superior to his friend, but he inclined to condescension. He adopted toward him an air of patronising good-humour.

His self-pride was now entirely restored. In the shade of its flourishing growth he stood with braced and self-confident legs, and since nothing could now be discovered, he did not shrink from an encounter with the eyes of judges, and allowed no thoughts of his own to keep him from an attitude of manfulness. He had performed his mistakes in the dark, so he was still a man.

Indeed, when he remembered his fortunes of yesterday, and looked at them from a distance, he began to see something fine there. He had license to be pompous and veteran-like.

His panting agonies of the past he put out of his sight.

In the present, he declared to himself that it was only the doomed and the damned who roared with sincerity at circumstance. Few but they ever did it. A man with a full stomach and the respect of his fellows had no business to scold about anything that he might think to be wrong in the ways of the universe, or even with the ways of society. Let the unfortunates rail; the others may play marbles.

He did not give a great deal of thought to these battles that lay directly before him. It was not essential that he should plan his ways in regard to them. He had been taught that many obligations of a life were easily avoided. The lessons of yesterday had been that retribution was a laggard, and blind. With these facts before him, he did not deem it necessary that he should become feverish over the possibilities of the ensuing twenty-four hours. He could leave much to chance. Besides, a faith in himself had secretly blossomed. There was a little flower of confidence growing within him. He was now a man of experience. He had been out among the dragons, he said, and he assured himself that they were not so hideous as he had imagined them. Also they were inaccurate; they did not sting with precision. A stout heart often defied, and defying, escaped.

And furthermore, how could they kill him who was the chosen of gods and doomed to greatness?

He remembered how some of the men had run from the battle. As he recalled their terror-struck faces, he felt a scorn for them. They had surely been more fleet and more wild than was absolutely necessary. They were weak mortals. As for himself, he had fled with discretion and dignity.

He was aroused from this reverie by his friend, who, having hitched about nervously and blinked at the trees for a time, suddenly coughed in an introductory way, and spoke.

"Fleming!"

"What?"

The friend put his hand up to his mouth and coughed again. He fidgeted in his jacket.

"Well," he gulped at last, "I guess yeh might as well give me back them letters." Dark, prickling blood had flushed into his cheeks and brow.

"All right, Wilson," said the youth. He loosened two buttons of his coat, thrust in his hand, and brought forth the packet. As he extended it to his friend the latter's face was turned from him.

He had been slow in the act of producing the packet because during it he had been trying to invent a remarkable comment upon the affair. He could conjure nothing of sufficient point. He was compelled to allow his friend to escape unmolested with his packet. And for this he took unto himself considerable credit. It was a generous thing.

His friend at his side seemed suffering great shame. As he contemplated him, the youth felt his heart grow more strong and stout. He had never been compelled to blush in such manner for his acts; he was an individual of extraordinary virtues.

He reflected, with condescending pity: "Too bad! Too bad! The poor devil, it makes him feel tough!"

After this incident, and as he reviewed the battle pictures he had seen, he felt quite competent to return home and make the hearts of the people glow with stories of war. He could see himself in a room of warm tints telling tales to listeners. He could exhibit laurels. They were insignificant; still, in a district where laurels were infrequent, they might shine.

He saw his gaping audience picturing him as the central figure in blazing scenes. And he imagined the consternation and the ejaculations of his mother and the young lady at the seminary as they drank his recitals. Their vague feminine formula for beloved ones doing brave deeds on the field of battle without risk of life would be destroyed.

A SPUTTERING of musketry was always to be heard. Later, the cannon had entered the dispute. In the fog-filled air their voices made a thudding sound The reverberations were continued. This part of the world led a strange, battleful existence.

The youth's regiment was marched to relieve a command that had lain long in some damp trenches. The men took positions behind a curving line of rifle-pits that had been turned up, like a large furrow, along the line of woods. Before them was a level stretch, peopled with short, deformed stumps. From the woods beyond came the dull popping of the skirmishers and pickets, firing in the fog. From the right came the noise of a terrific fracas.

The men cuddled behind the small embankment, and sat in easy attitudes awaiting their turn. Many had their backs to the firing. The youth's friend lay down, buried his face in his arms, and almost instantly, it seemed, he was in a deep sleep.

The youth leaned his breast against the brown dirt, and peered over at the woods and up and down the line. Curtains of trees interfered with his ways of vision. He could see the low line of trenches but for a short distance. A few idle flags were perched on the dirt-hills.   Behind them were rows of dark bodies, with a few heads sticking curiously over the top.

Always the noise of skirmishers came from the woods on the front and left, and the din on the right had grown to frightful proportions.   The guns were roaring without an instant's pause for breath.   It seemed that the cannon had come from all parts, and were engaged in a stupendous wrangle.   It became impossible to make a sentence heard.

The youth wished to launch a joke—a quotation from newspapers.   He desired to say, "All quiet on the Rappahannock," but the guns refused to permit even a comment upon their uproar.   He never successfully concluded the sentence.   But at last the guns stopped, and among the men in the rifle-pits rumours again flew, like birds ; but they were now for the most part black creatures, who flapped their wings drearily near to the ground, and refused to rise on any wings of hope.   The men's faces grew doleful from the interpreting of omens.   Tales of hesitation and uncertainty on the part of those high in place and responsibility came to their ears.   Stories of disaster were borne into their minds with many proofs.   This din of musketry on the right, growing like a released genie of sound, expressed and emphasised the army's plight.

The men were disheartened, and began to mutter. They made gestures expressive of the sentence: "Ah, what more can we do ? "   And it could always be seen that they were bewildered by the alleged news, and could not fully comprehend a defeat.

Before the grey mists had been totally obliterated by the sun-rays, the regiment was marching in a spread column that was retiring carefully through the woods. The disordered, hurrying lines of the enemy could sometimes be seen down through the groves and little fields. They were yelling, shrill and exultant.

At this sight the youth forgot many personal matters, and became greatly enraged. He exploded in loud sentences. " B'jiminey, we're generaled by a lot 'a lunkheads."

" More than one feller has said that t'-day," observed a man.

His friend, recently aroused, was still very drowsy. He looked behind him until his mind took in the meaning of the movement. Then he sighed. " Oh, well, I s'pose we got licked," he remarked sadly.

The youth had a thought that it would not be handsome for him to freely condemn other men. He made an attempt to restrain himself, but the words upon his tongue were too bitter. He presently began a long and intricate denunciation of the commander of the forces.

" Mebbe it wa'n't all his fault—not all together. He did th' best he knowed. It's our luck t' git licked often," said his friend, in a weary tone. He was trudging along with stooped shoulders and shifting eyes, like a man who has been caned and kicked.

" Well, don't we fight like the devil ? Don't we do all that men can ?" demanded the youth loudly.

He was secretly dumfounded at this sentiment

when it came from his lips. For a moment his face lost its valour, and he looked guiltily about him. But no one questioned his right to deal in such words, and presently he recovered his air of courage. He went on to repeat a statement he had heard going from group to group at the camp that morning. "The brigadier said he never saw a new reg'ment fight the way we fought yestirday, didn't he? And we didn't do better than many another reg'ment, did we? Well, then, you can't say it's the army's fault, can you?"

In his reply, the friend's voice was stern. "'A course not," he said. "No man dare say we don't fight like th' devil. No man will ever dare say it. Th' boys fight like hell-roosters. But still—still, we don't have no luck."

"Well, then, if we fight like the devil an' don't ever whip, it must be the general's fault," said the youth grandly and decisively. "And I don't see any sense in fighting and fighting and fighting, yet always losing through some derned old lunkhead of a general."

A sarcastic man who was tramping at the youth's side, then spoke lazily. "Mebbe yeh think yeh fit th' hull battle yestirday, Fleming," he remarked.

The speech pierced the youth. Inwardly he was reduced to an abject pulp by these chance words. His legs quaked privately. He cast a frightened glance at the sarcastic man.

"Why, no," he hastened to say in a conciliating voice, "I don't think I fought the whole battle yesterday."

But the other seemed innocent of any deeper

meaning. Apparently he had no information. It was merely his habit. "Oh!" he replied, in the same tone of calm derision.

The youth, nevertheless, felt a threat. His mind shrank from going near to the danger, and thereafter he was silent. The significance of the sarcastic man's words took from him all loud moods that would make him appear prominent. He became suddenly a modest person.

There was low-toned talk among the troops. The officers were impatient and snappy, their countenances clouded with the tales of misfortune. The troops, sifting through the forest, were sullen. In the youth's company once a man's laugh rang out. A dozen soldiers turned their faces quickly toward him and frowned with vague displeasure.

The noise of firing dogged their footsteps. Sometimes it seemed to be driven a little way, but it always returned again with increased insolence. The men muttered and cursed, throwing black looks in its direction.

In a clear space the troops were at last halted. Regiments and brigades, broken and detached through their encounters with thickets, grew together again, and lines were faced toward the pursuing bark of the enemy's infantry.

This noise, following like the yellings of eager, metallic hounds, increased to a loud and joyous burst, and then, as the sun went serenely up the sky, throwing illuminating rays into the gloomy thickets, it broke forth into prolonged pealings. The woods began to crackle as if afire.

"Whoop-a-dadee," said a man, "here we are! Everybody fightin'. Blood an' destruction."

"I was willin' t' bet they'd attack as soon as th' sun got fairly up," savagely asserted the lieutenant who commanded the youth's company. He jerked without mercy at his little moustache. He strode to and fro with dark dignity in the rear of his men, who were lying down behind whatever protection they had collected.

A battery had trundled into position in the rear, and was thoughtfully shelling the distance. The regiment, unmolested as yet, awaited the moment when the grey shadows of the woods before them should be slashed by the lines of flame. There was much growling and swearing.

"Good Gawd," the youth grumbled, "we're always being chased around like rats! It makes me sick. Nobody seems to know where we go, or why we go. We just get fired around from pillar to post, and get licked here and get licked there, and nobody knows what it's done for. It makes a man feel like a damn' kitten in a bag. Now, I'd like to know what the eternal thunders we was marched into these woods for anyhow, unless it was to give the rebs a regular pot-shot at us. We came in here and got our legs all tangled up in these cussed briers, and then we begin to fight and the rebs had an easy time of it. Don't tell me its just luck! I know better. It's this derned old ——"

The friend seemed jaded, but he interrupted his comrade with a voice of calm confidence. "It'll turn out all right in th' end," he said.

"Oh, the devil it will! You always talk like a dog-hanged parson. Don't tell me! I know——"

At this time there was an interposition by the savage-minded lieutenant, who was obliged to vent some of his inward dissatisfaction upon his men. "You boys shut right up! There's no need 'a your wasting your breath in long-winded arguments about this an' that and th' other. You've been jawin' like a lot 'a old hens. All you've got t' do is to fight, and you'll get plenty 'a that t' do in about ten minutes. Less talkin' and more fightin' is what's best for you, boys. I never saw sech gabbling jackasses."

He paused, ready to pounce upon any man who might have the temerity to reply. No words being said, he resumed his dignified pacing.

"There's too much chin music and too little fightin' in this war, anyhow," he said to them, turning his head for a final remark.

The day had grown more white, until the sun shed his full radiance upon the thronged forest. A sort of a gust of battle came sweeping toward that part of the line where lay the youth's regiment. The front shifted a trifle to meet it squarely. There was a wait. In this part of the field there passed slowly the intense moments that precede the tempest.

A single rifle flashed in a thicket before the regiment. In an instant it was joined by many others. There was a mighty song of clashes and crashes that went sweeping through the woods. The guns in the rear, aroused and enraged by shells that had been thrown bur-like at them, suddenly involved themselves in a hideous altercation with another band of guns. The battle roar settled to a rolling thunder, which was a single, long explosion.

In the regiment there was a peculiar kind of hesitation denoted in the attitudes of the men. They were worn, exhausted, having slept but little and laboured much. They rolled their eyes toward the advancing battle as they stood awaiting the shock. Some shrank and flinched. They stood as men tied to stakes.

CHAPTER XVII

THIS advance of the enemy had seemed to the youth like a ruthless hunting. He began to fume with rage and exasperation. He beat his foot upon the ground, and scowled with hate at the swirling smoke that was approaching like a phantom flood. There was a maddening quality in this seeming resolution of the foe to give him no rest, to give him no time to sit down and think. Yesterday he had fought and had fled rapidly. There had been many adventures. For to-day he felt that he had earned opportunities for contemplative repose. He could have enjoyed portraying to uninitiated listeners various scenes at which he had been a witness, or ably discussing the processes of war with other proved men. Too, it was important that he should have time for physical recuperation. He was sore and stiff from his experiences. He had received his fill of all exertions, and he wished to rest.

But those other men seemed never to grow weary; they were fighting with their old speed. He had a wild hate for the relentless foe. Yesterday, when he had imagined the universe to be against him, he had hated it, little gods and big gods; to-day he hated the army of the foe with the same great hatred. He was not going to be badgered of his life, like a kitten chased by boys, he said. It was not well to drive men into final corners; at those moments they could all develop teeth and claws.

He leaned and spoke into his friend's ear. He menaced the woods with a gesture. "If they keep on chasing us, by Gawd, they'd better watch out. Can't stand *too* much."

The friend twisted his head and made a calm reply. "If they keep on a-chasin' us they'll drive us all inteh th' river."

The youth cried out savagely at this statement. He crouched behind a little tree, with his eyes burning hatefully, and his teeth set in a cur-like snarl. The awkward bandage was still about his head, and upon it, over his wound, there was a spot of dry blood. His hair was wondrously tousled, and some straggling, moving locks hung over the cloth of the bandage down toward his forehead. His jacket and shirt were open at the throat, and exposed his young bronzed neck. There could be seen spasmodic gulpings at his throat.

His fingers twined nervously about his rifle. He wished that it was an engine of annihilating power. He felt that he and his companions were being taunted and derided from sincere convictions that they were poor and puny. His knowledge of his inability to take vengeance for it made his rage into a dark and stormy spectre, that possessed him and made him dream of abominable cruelties. The tormentors were flies sucking insolently at his blood, and he thought that he would have given his life for a revenge of seeing their faces in pitiful plights.

The winds of battle had swept all about the regiment, until the one rifle, instantly followed by others, flashed in its front. A moment later the regiment roared forth its sudden and valiant retort. A dense wall of smoke settled slowly down. It was furiously slit and slashed by the knife-like fire from the rifles.

To the youth the fighters resembled animals tossed for a death-struggle into a dark pit. There was a sensation that he and his fellows, at bay, were pushing back, always pushing fierce onslaughts of creatures who were slippery. Their beams of crimson seemed to get no purchase upon the bodies of their foes; the latter seemed to evade them with ease, and come through, between, around, and about with unopposed skill.

When, in a dream, it occurred to the youth that his rifle was an impotent stick, he lost sense of everything but his hate, his desire to smash into pulp the glittering smile of victory which he could feel upon the faces of his enemies.

The blue smoke-swallowed line curled and writhed like a snake stepped upon. It swung its ends to and fro in an agony of fear and rage.

The youth was not conscious that he was erect upon his feet. He did not know the direction of the ground. Indeed, once he even lost the habit of balance, and fell heavily. He was up again immediately. One thought went through the chaos of his brain at the time. He wondered if he had fallen because he had been shot. But the suspicion flew away at once. He did not think more of it.

He had taken up a first position behind the little tree, with a direct determination to hold it against the world. He had not deemed it possible that his army could that day succeed, and from this he felt the ability to fight harder. But the throng had surged in all ways, until he lost directions and locations, save that he knew where lay the enemy.

The flames bit him, and the hot smoke broiled his skin. His rifle barrel grew so hot that ordinarily he could not have borne it upon his palms; but he kept on stuffing cartridges into it, and pounding them with his clanking, bending ramrod. If he aimed at some changing form through the smoke, he pulled his trigger with a fierce grunt, as if he were dealing a blow of the fist with all his strength.

When the enemy seemed falling back before him and his fellows, he went instantly forward, like a dog who, seeing his foes lagging, turns and insists upon being pursued. And when he was compelled to retire again, he did it slowly, sullenly, taking steps of wrathful despair.

Once he, in his intent hate, was almost alone, and was firing when all those near him had ceased. He was so engrossed in his occupation that he was not aware of a lull.

He was recalled by a hoarse laugh and a sentence that came to his ears in a voice of contempt and amazement. "Yeh infernal fool, don't yeh know enough t' quit when there ain't anything t' shoot at? Good Gawd!"

He turned then and, pausing with his rifle thrown half into position, looked at the blue line of his comrades. During this moment of leisure they seemed all to be engaged in staring with astonishment at him. They had become spectators. Turning to the front again he saw, under the lifted smoke, a deserted ground.

He looked bewildered for a moment. Then there appeared upon the glazed vacancy of his eyes a diamond point of intelligence. "Oh," he said, comprehending.

He returned to his comrades and threw himself upon the ground. He sprawled like a man who had been thrashed. His flesh seemed strangely on fire, and the sounds of the battle continued in his ears. He groped blindly for his canteen.

The lieutenant was crowing. He seemed drunk with fighting. He called out to the youth, "By heavens, if I had ten thousand wild cats like you, I could tear th' stomach outa this war in less'n a week!" He puffed out his chest with large dignity as he said it.

Some of the men muttered and looked at the youth in awestruck ways. It was plain that as he had gone on loading and firing and cursing without the proper intermission they had found time to regard him. And they now looked upon him as a war-devil.

The friend came staggering to him. There was

some fright and dismay in his voice. "Are yeh
all right, Fleming? Do yeh feel all right? There
ain't nothin' th' matter with yeh, Henry, is there?"

"No," said the youth with difficulty. His throat
seemed full of knobs and burs.

These incidents made the youth ponder. It was
revealed to him that he had been a barbarian, a
beast. He had fought like a pagan who defends
his religion. Regarding it, he saw that it was
fine, wild, and, in some ways, easy. He had been
a tremendous figure, no doubt. By this struggle
he had overcome obstacles which he had admitted
to be mountains. They had fallen like paper
peaks, and he was now what he called a hero.
And he had not been aware of the process. He
had slept, and, awakening, found himself a knight.

He lay and basked in the occasional stares of
his comrades. Their faces were varied in degrees
of blackness from the burned powder. Some were
utterly smudged. They were reeking with perspiration, and their breaths came hard and wheezing.
And from these soiled expanses they peered at him.

"Hot work! Hot work!" cried the lieutenant
deliriously. He walked up and down, restless and
eager. Sometimes his voice could be heard in a
wild, incomprehensible laugh.

When he had a particularly profound thought
upon the science of war he always unconsciously
addressed himself to the youth.

There was some grim rejoicing by the men. "By
thunder, I bet this army 'll never see another new
reg'ment like us!"

" You bet ! "

> " ' A dog, a woman, an' a walnut tree,
>   Th' more yeh beat 'em, th' better they be ! '

That's like us."

"Lost a piler men, they did. If an ol' woman swep' up th' woods she'd git a dustpanful."

"Yes, an' if she'll come around ag'in in 'bout an' hour she'll git a pile more."

The forest still bore its burden of clamour. From off under the trees came the rolling clatter of the musketry. Each distant thicket seemed a strange porcupine with quills of flame. A cloud of dark smoke, as from smouldering ruins, went up toward the sun, now bright and gay in the blue, enamelled sky.

CHAPTER XVIII

THE ragged line had respite for some minutes, but during its pause the struggle in the forest became magnified until the trees seemed to quiver from the firing, and the ground to shake from the rushing of the men. The voices of the cannon were mingled in a long and interminable row. It seemed difficult to live in such an atmosphere. The chests of the men strained for a bit of freshness, and their throats craved water.

There was one shot through the body, who raised a cry of bitter lamentation when came this lull. Perhaps he had been calling out during the fighting also, but at that time no one had heard him. But now the men turned at the woeful complaints of him upon the ground.

"Who is it? Who is it?"

"It's Jimmie Rogers. Jimmie Rogers."

When their eyes first encountered him there was a sudden halt, as if they feared to go near. He was thrashing about in the grass, twisting his shuddering body into many strange postures. He was screaming loudly. This instant's hesitation seemed to fill him with a tremendous fantastic contempt, and he damned them in shrieked sentences.

The youth's friend had a geographical illusion concerning a stream, and he obtained permission to go for some water. Immediately canteens were showered upon him. "Fill mine, will yeh?" "Bring me some, too." "And me, too." He departed, laden. The youth went with his friend, feeling a desire to throw his heated body into the stream and, soaking there, drink quarts.

They made a hurried search for the supposed stream, but did not find it. "No water here," said the youth. They turned without delay and began to retrace their steps.

From their position as they again faced toward the place of the fighting, they could of course comprehend a greater amount of the battle than when their visions had been blurred by the hurling smoke of the line. They could see dark stretches winding along the land, and on one cleared space there was a row of guns making grey clouds, which were filled with large flashes of orange-coloured flame. Over some foliage they could see the roof of a house. One window, glowing a deep murder red, shone squarely through the leaves. From the edifice a tall leaning tower of smoke went far into the sky.

Looking over their own troops, they saw mixed masses slowly getting into regular form. The sunlight made twinkling points of the bright steel. To the rear there was a glimpse of a distant roadway as it curved over a slope. It was crowded with retreating infantry. From all the interwoven forest arose the smoke and bluster of the battle. The air was always occupied by a blaring.

K

Near where they stood shells were flip-flapping and hooting. Occasional bullets buzzed in the air and spanged into tree trunks. Wounded men and other stragglers were slinking through the woods.

Looking down an aisle of the grove, the youth and his companion saw a jangling general and his staff almost ride upon a wounded man, who was crawling on his hands and knees. The general reined strongly at his charger's opened and foamy mouth, and guided it with dexterous horsemanship past the man. The latter scrambled in wild and torturing haste. His strength evidently failed him as he reached a place of safety. One of his arms suddenly weakened, and he fell, sliding over upon his back. He lay stretched out, breathing gently.

A moment later the small creaking cavalcade was directly in front of the two soldiers. Another officer, riding with the skilful abandon of a cowboy, galloped his horse to a position directly before the general. The two unnoticed foot-soldiers made a little show of going on, but they lingered near in the desire to overhear the conversation. Perhaps they thought some great inner historical things would be said.

The general, whom the boys knew as the commander of their division, looked at the other officer and spoke coolly, as if he were criticising his clothes. "Th' enemy's formin' over there for another charge," he said. "It'll be directed against Whiterside, an' I fear they'll break through there unless we work like thunder t' stop them."

The other swore at his restive horse, and then

cleared his throat. He made a gesture toward his cap. " It'll be hell t' pay stoppin' them," he said shortly.

"I presume so," remarked the general. Then he began to talk rapidly and in a lower tone. He frequently illustrated his words with a pointing finger. The two infantrymen could hear nothing until finally he asked, "What troops can you spare?"

The officer who rode like a cowboy reflected for an instant. "Well," he said, "I had to order in th' 12th to help th' 76th, an' I haven't really got any. But there's th' 304th. They fight like a lot 'a mule-drivers. I can spare them best of any."

The youth and his friend exchanged glances of astonishment.

The general spoke sharply. "Get 'em ready, then. I'll watch developments from here, an' send you word when t' start them. It'll happen in five minutes."

As the other officer tossed his fingers toward his cap and, wheeling his horse, started away, the general called out to him in a sober voice, "I don't believe many of your mule-drivers will get back."

The other shouted something in reply. He smiled.

With scared faces, the youth and his companion hurried back to the line.

These happenings had occupied an incredibly short time, yet the youth felt that in them he had been made aged. New eyes were given to him.

And the most startling thing was to learn suddenly that he was very insignificant. The officer spoke of the regiment as if he referred to a broom. Some part of the woods needed sweeping, perhaps, and he merely indicated a broom in a tone properly indifferent to its fate. It was war, no doubt, but it appeared strange.

As the two boys approached the line, the lieutenant perceived them and swelled with wrath. "Fleming—Wilson—how long does it take yeh to git water, anyhow?—where yeh been to?"

But his oration ceased as he saw their eyes, which were large with great tales. "We're goin' t' charge—we're goin' t' charge!" cried the youth's friend, hastening with his news.

"Charge?" said the lieutenant. "Charge? Well, b'Gawd! Now, this is real fightin'." Over his soiled countenance there went a boastful smile. "Charge? Well, b'Gawd!"

A little group of soldiers surrounded the two youths. "Are we, sure 'nough? Well, I'll be derned! Charge? What fer? What at? Wilson, you're lyin'."

"I hope to die," said the youth, pitching his tones to the key of angry remonstrance. "Sure as shooting, I tell you."

And his friend spoke in re-enforcement. "Not by a blame sight, he ain't lyin'. We heard 'em talkin'."

They caught sight of two mounted figures a short distance from them. One was the colonel of the regiment, and the other was the officer who had received orders from the commander of the division They were gesticulating at each other. The soldier pointing at them, interpreted the scene.

One man had a final objection: "How could yeh hear 'em talkin'?" But the men, for a large part, nodded, admitting that previously the two friends had spoken truth.

They settled back into reposeful attitudes with airs of having accepted the matter. And they mused upon it, with a hundred varieties of expression. It was an engrossing thing to think about. Many tightened their belts carefully and hitched at their trousers.

A moment later the officers began to bustle among the men, pushing them into a more compact mass and into a better alignment. They chased those that straggled, and fumed at a few men who seemed to show by their attitudes that they had decided to remain at that spot. They were like critical shepherds struggling with sheep.

Presently, the regiment seemed to draw itself up and heave a deep breath. None of the men's faces were mirrors of large thoughts. The soldiers were bended and stooped like sprinters before a signal. Many pairs of glinting eyes peered from the grimy faces toward the curtains of the deeper woods. They seemed to be engaged in deep calculations of time and distance.

They were surrounded by the noises of the monstrous altercation between the two armies. The world was fully interested in other matters. Apparently the regiment had its small affair to itself.

The youth, turning, shot a quick inquiring glance at his friend. The latter returned to him the same manner of look. They were the only ones who possessed an inner knowledge. "Mule-drivers—hell t' pay—don't believe many will get back." It was an ironical secret. Still, they saw no hesitation in each other's faces, and they nodded a mute and unprotesting assent when a shaggy man near them said in a meek voice, "We'll git swallowed."

CHAPTER XIX

The youth stared at the land in front of him. Its foliages now seemed to veil powers and horrors. He was unaware of the machinery of orders that started the charge, although from the corners of his eyes he saw an officer, who looked like a boy a-horseback, come galloping, waving his hat. Suddenly he felt a straining and heaving among the men. The line fell slowly forward like a toppling wall, and, with a convulsive gasp that was intended for a cheer, the regiment began its journey. The youth was pushed and jostled for a moment before he understood the movement at all, but directly he lunged ahead and began to run.

He fixed his eye upon a distant and prominent clump of trees where he had concluded the enemy were to be met, and he ran toward it as toward a goal. He had believed throughout that it was a mere question of getting over an unpleasant matter as quickly as possible, and he ran desperately, as if pursued for a murder. His face was drawn hard and tight with the stress of his endeavour. His eyes were fixed in a lurid glare. And with his soiled and disordered dress, his red and inflamed features surmounted by the dingy rag with its spot of blood, his wildly swinging rifle and banging accoutrements, he looked to be an insane soldier.

As the regiment swung from its position out into a cleared space the woods and thickets before it awakened. Yellow flames leaped toward it from many directions. The forest made a tremendous objection.

The line lurched straight for a moment. Then the right wing swung forward; it in turn was surpassed by the left. Afterward the centre careered to the front until the regiment was a wedge-shaped mass, but an instant later the opposition of the bushes, trees, and uneven places on the ground split the command and scattered it into detached clusters.

The youth, light-footed, was unconsciously in advance. His eyes still kept note of the clump of trees. From all places near it the clannish yell of the enemy could be heard. The little flames of rifles leaped from it. The song of the bullets was in the air, and shells snarled among the tree-tops. One tumbled directly into the middle of a hurrying group and exploded in crimson fury. There was an instant's spectacle of a man, almost over it, throwing up his hands to shield his eyes.

Other men, punched by bullets, fell in grotesque agonies. The regiment left a coherent trail of bodies. They had passed into a clearer atmosphere. There was an effect like a revelation in the new appearance of the landscape. Some men working madly at a battery were plain to them, and the opposing infantry's lines were defined by the grey walls and fringes of smoke.

It seemed to the youth that he saw everything. Each blade of the green grass was bold and clear. He thought that he was aware of every change in the thin, transparent vapour that floated idly in sheets. The brown or grey trunks of the trees showed each roughness of their surfaces. And the men of the regiment, with their starting eyes and sweating faces, running madly, or falling, as if thrown headlong, to queer, heaped-up corpses—all were comprehended. His mind took a mechanical but firm impression, so that afterward everything was pictured and explained to him, save why he himself was there.

But there was a frenzy made from this furious rush. The men, pitching forward insanely, had burst into cheerings, mob-like and barbaric, but tuned in strange keys that can arouse the dullard and the stoic. It made a mad enthusiasm that, it seemed, would be incapable of checking itself before granite and brass. There was the delirium that encounters despair and death, and is heedless and blind to the odds. It is a temporary but sublime absence of selfishness. And because it was of this order was the reason, perhaps, why the youth wondered, afterward, what reasons he could have had for being there.

Presently the straining pace ate up the energies of the men. As if by agreement, the leaders began to slacken their speed. The volleys directed against them had had a seeming wind-like effect. The regiment snorted and blew. Among some stolid trees it began to falter and hesitate. The men, staring intently, began to wait for some of the distant walls of smoke to move and disclose to them the scene. Since much of their strength and their breath had vanished, they returned to caution. They were become men again.

The youth had a vague belief that he had run miles, and he thought, in a way, that he was now in some new and unknown land.

The moment the regiment ceased its advance the protesting splutter of musketry became a steadied roar. Long and accurate fringes of smoke spread out. From the top of a small hill came level belchings of yellow flame that caused an inhuman whistling in the air.

The men, halted, had opportunity to see some of their comrades dropping with moans and shrieks. A few lay under foot, still or wailing. And now for an instant the men stood, their rifles slack in their hands, and watched the regiment dwindle. They appeared dazed and stupid. This spectacle seemed to paralyse them, overcome them with a fatal fascination. They stared woodenly at the sights, and, lowering their eyes, looked from face to face. It was a strange pause, and a strange silence.

Then, above the sounds of the outside commotion arose the roar of the lieutenant. He strode suddenly forth, his infantile features black with rage.

"Come on, yeh fools!" he bellowed. "Come on! Yeh can't stay here. Yeh must come on." He said more, but much of it could not be understood.

He started rapidly forward, with his head turned

toward the men. "Come on," he was shouting. The men stared with blank and yokel-like eyes at him. He was obliged to halt and retrace his steps. He stood then with his back to the enemy and delivered gigantic curses into the faces of the men. His body vibrated from the weight and force of his imprecations. And he could string oaths with the facility of a maiden who strings beads.

The friend of the youth aroused. Lurching suddenly forward and dropping to his knees, he fired an angry shot at the persistent woods. This action awakened the men. They huddled no more like sheep. They seemed suddenly to bethink them of their weapons, and at once commenced firing. Belaboured by their officers, they began to move forward. The regiment, involved like a cart involved in mud and muddle, started unevenly with many jolts and jerks. The men stopped now every few paces to fire and load, and in this manner moved slowly on from trees to trees.

The flaming opposition in their front grew with their advance until it seemed that all forward ways were barred by the thin leaping tongues, and off to the right an ominous demonstration could sometimes be dimly discerned. The smoke lately generated was in confusing clouds that made it difficult for the regiment to proceed with intelligence. As he passed through each curling mass the youth wondered what would confront him on the farther side.

The command went painfully forward until an open space interposed between them and the lurid lines. Here, crouching and cowering behind some trees, the men clung with desperation, as if threatened by a wave. They looked wild-eyed, and as if amazed at this furious disturbance they had stirred. In the storm there was an ironical expression of their importance. The faces of the men, too, showed a lack of a certain feeling of responsibility for being there. It was as if they had been driven. It was the dominant animal failing to remember in the supreme moments the forceful causes of various superficial qualities. The whole affair seemed incomprehensible to many of them.

As they halted thus the lieutenant again began to bellow profanely. Regardless of the vindictive threats of the bullets, he went about coaxing, berating, and bedamning. His lips, that were habitually in a soft and child-like curve, were now writhed into unholy contortions. He swore by all possible deities.

Once he grabbed the youth by the arm. "Come on, yeh lunkhead!" he roared. "Come on! We'll all git killed if we stay here. We've on'y got t' go across that lot. An' then"—the remainder of his idea disappeared in a blue haze of curses.

The youth stretched forth his arm. "Cross there?" His mouth was puckered in doubt and awe.

"Certainly. Jest 'cross th' lot! We can't stay here," screamed the lieutenant. He poked his face close to the youth and waved his bandaged hand. "Come on!" Presently he grappled with him as if for a wrestling bout. It was as if he planned to drag the youth by the ear on to the assault.

The private felt a sudden unspeakable indignation against his officer. He wrenched fiercely and shook him off.

"Come on yerself, then," he yelled. There was a bitter challenge in his voice.

They galloped together down the regimental front. The friend scrambled after them. In front of the colours the three men began to bawl, "Come on! come on!" They danced and gyrated like tortured savages.

The flag, obedient to these appeals, bended its glittering form and swept toward them. The men wavered in indecision for a moment, and then with a long, wailful cry the dilapidated regiment surged forward and began its new journey.

Over the field went the scurrying mass. It was a handful of men splattered into the faces of the enemy. Toward it instantly sprang the yellow tongues. A vast quantity of blue smoke hung before them. A mighty banging made ears value-less.

The youth ran like a madman to reach the woods before a bullet could discover him. He ducked his head low, like a football player. In his haste his eyes almost closed, and the scene was a wild blur. Pulsating saliva stood at the corners of his mouth.

Within him, as he hurled himself forward, was born a love, a despairing fondness for this flag which was near him. It was a creation of beauty and invulnerability. It was a goddess, radiant, that bended its form with an imperious gesture to him. It was a woman, red and white, hating and loving, that called him with the voice of his hopes. Because no harm could come to it he endowed it with power. He kept near, as if it could be a saver of lives, and an imploring cry went from his mind.

In the mad scramble he was aware that the colour-sergeant flinched suddenly, as if struck˜by a bludgeon. He faltered, and then became motionless, save for his quivering knees.

He made a spring and a clutch at the pole. At the same instant his friend grabbed it from the other side. They jerked at it, stout and furious, but the colour-sergeant was dead, and the corpse would not relinquish its trust. For a moment there was a grim encounter. The dead man, swinging with bended back, seemed to be obstinately tugging, in ludicrous and awful ways, for the possession of the flag.

It was past in an instant of time. They wrenched the flag furiously from the dead man, and, as they turned again, the corpse swayed forward with bowed head. One arm swung high, and the curved hand fell with heavy protest on the friend's unheeding shoulder.

CHAPTER XX

WHEN the two youths turned with the flag they saw that much of the regiment had crumbled away, and the dejected remnant was coming slowly back. The men, having hurled themselves in projectile fashion, had presently expended their forces. They slowly retreated, with their faces still toward the spluttering woods, and their hot rifles still replying to the din. Several officers were giving orders, their voices keyed to screams.

"Where in hell yeh goin'?" the lieutenant was asking in a sarcastic howl. And a red-bearded officer, whose voice of triple brass could plainly be heard, was commanding, "Shoot into 'em! Shoot into 'em, Gawd damn their souls!" There was a *mêlée* of screeches, in which the men were ordered to do conflicting and impossible things.

The youth and his friend had a small scuffle over the flag. "Give it t' me!" "No, let me keep it!" Each felt satisfied with the other's possession of it, but each felt bound to declare, by an offer to carry the emblem, his willingness to further risk himself. The youth roughly pushed his friend away.

The regiment fell back to the stolid trees. There it halted for a moment to blaze at some dark forms that had begun to steal upon its track. Presently it resumed its march again, curving among the tree trunks. By the time the depleted regiment had again reached the first open space they were receiving a fast and merciless fire. There seemed to be mobs all about them.

The greater part of the men, discouraged, their spirits worn by the turmoil, acted as if stunned. They accepted the pelting of the bullets with bowed and weary heads. It was of no purpose to strive against walls. It was of no use to batter themselves against granite. And from this consciousness that they had attempted to conquer an unconquerable thing there seemed to arise a feeling that they had been betrayed. They glowered with bent brows, but dangerously, upon some of the officers, more particularly upon the red-bearded one with the voice of triple brass.

However, the rear of the regiment was fringed with men, who continued to shoot irritably at the advancing foes. They seemed resolved to make every trouble. The youthful lieutenant was perhaps the last man in the disordered mass. His forgotten back was toward the enemy. He had been shot in the arm. It hung straight and rigid. Occasionally he would cease to remember it, and be about to emphasise an oath with a sweeping gesture. The multiplied pain caused him to swear with incredible power.

The youth went along with slipping, uncertain feet. He kept watchful eyes rearward. A scowl of mortification and rage was upon his face. He had thought of a fine revenge upon the officer who had referred to him and his fellows as mule-drivers. But he saw that it could not come to pass. His dreams had collapsed when the mule-drivers, dwindling rapidly, had wavered and hesitated on the little clearing, and then had recoiled. And now the retreat of the mule-drivers was a march of shame to him.

A dagger-pointed gaze from without his blackened face was held toward the enemy, but his greater hatred was riveted upon the man who, not knowing him, had called him a mule-driver.

When he knew that he and his comrades had failed to do anything in successful ways that might bring the little pangs of a kind of remorse upon the officer, the youth allowed the rage of the baffled to possess him. This cold officer upon a monument, who dropped epithets unconcernedly down, would be finer as a dead man, he thought. So grievous did he think it, that he could never possess the secret right to taunt truly in answer.

. He had pictured red letters of curious revenge. "We *are* mule-drivers, are we?" And now he was compelled to throw them away.

He presently wrapped his heart in the cloak of his pride and kept the flag erect. He harangued his fellows, pushing against their chests with his free hand. To those he knew well he made frantic appeals, beseeching them by name. Between him and the lieutenant, scolding and near to loosing his mind with rage, there was felt a subtle fellowship and equality. They supported each other in all manner of hoarse, howling protests.

*

L

But the regiment was a machine run down. The two men babbled at a forceless thing. The soldiers who had heart to go slowly were continually shaken in their resolves by a knowledge that comrades were slipping with speed back to the lines. It was difficult to think of reputation when others were thinking of skins. Wounded men were left crying on this black journey.

The smoke fringes and flames blustered always. The youth, peering once through a sudden rift in a cloud, saw a brown mass of troops, interwoven and magnified until they appeared to be thousands. A fierce-hued flag flashed before his vision.

Immediately, as if the uplifting of the smoke had been prearranged, the discovered troops burst into a rasping yell, and a hundred flames jetted toward the retreating band. A rolling grey cloud again interposed as the regiment doggedly replied. The youth had to depend again upon his misused ears, which were trembling and buzzing from the *mêlée* of musketry and yells.

The way seemed eternal. In the clouded haze men became panic-stricken with the thought that the regiment had lost its path, and was proceeding in a perilous direction. Once the men who headed the wild procession turned and came pushing back against their comrades, screaming that they were being fired upon from points which they had considered to be toward their own lines. At this cry a hysterical fear and dismay beset the troops. A soldier, who heretofore had been ambitious to make the regiment into a wise little band that would proceed calmly amid the huge-appearing difficulties, suddenly sank down and buried his face in his arms with an air of bowing to a doom. From another a shrill lamentation rang out filled with profane allusions to a general. Men ran hither and thither, seeking with their eyes roads of escape. With serene regularity, as if controlled by a schedule, bullets buffed into men.

The youth walked stolidly into the midst of the mob, and with his flag in his hands took a stand as if he expected an attempt to push him to the ground. He unconsciously assumed the attitude of the colourbearer in the fight of the preceding day. He passed over his brow a hand that trembled. His breath did not come freely. He was choking during this small wait for the crisis.

His friend came to him. "Well, Henry, I guess this is good-bye—John."

"Oh, shut up, you damned fool!" replied the youth, and he would not look at the other.

The officers laboured like politicians to beat the mass into a proper circle to face the menaces. The ground was uneven and torn. The men curled into depressions and fitted themselves snugly behind whatever would frustrate a bullet.

The youth noted with vague surprise that the lieutenant was standing mutely with his legs far apart, and his sword held in the manner of a cane. The youth wondered what had happened to his vocal organs that he no more cursed.

There was something curious in this little intent pause of the lieutenant. He was like a babe which, having wept its fill, raises its eyes and fixes upon a distant toy. He was engrossed in this contemplation, and the soft under-lip quivered from self-whispered words.

Some lazy and ignorant smoke curled slowly. The men, hiding from the bullets, waited anxiously for it to lift and disclose the plight of the regiment.

The silent ranks were suddenly thrilled by the eager voice of the youthful lieutenant bawling out, "Here they come! Right onto us, b'Gawd!" His further words were lost in a roar of wicked thunder from the men's rifles.

The youth's eyes had instantly turned in the direction indicated by the awakened and agitated lieutenant, and he had seen the haze of treachery disclosing a body of soldiers of the enemy. They were so near that he could see their features. There was a recognition as he looked at the types of faces. Also he perceived with dim amazement that their uniforms were rather gay in effect, being light grey, accented with a brilliant-hued facing. Too, the clothes seemed new.

These troops had apparently been going forward with caution, their rifles held in readiness, when the youthful lieutenant had discovered them, and their movement had been interrupted by the volley from the blue regiment. From the moment's glimpse, it was derived that they had been unaware of the proximity of their dark-suited foes, or had mistaken the direction. Almost instantly they were shut utterly from the youth's sight by the smoke from the energetic rifles of his companions He strained his vision to learn the accomplishment of the volley, but the smoke hung before him.

The two bodies of troops exchanged blows in the manner of a pair of boxers. The fast, angry firings went back and forth. The men in blue were intent with the despair of their circumstances, and they seized upon the revenge to be had at close range. Their thunder swelled loud and valiant. Their curving front bristled with flashes, and the place resounded with the clangour of their ramrods. The youth ducked and dodged for a time and achieved a few unsatisfactory views of the enemy. There appeared to be many of them, and they were replying swiftly. They seemed moving toward the blue regiment, step by step. He seated himself gloomily on the ground with his flag between his knees.

As he noted the vicious, wolf-like temper of his comrades he had a sweet thought that if the enemy was about to swallow the regimental broom as a large prisoner, it could at least have the consolation of going down with bristles forward.

But the blows of the antagonist began to grow more weak. Fewer bullets ripped the air, and finally, when the men slackened to learn of the fight, they could see only dark, floating smoke. The regiment lay still and gazed. Presently some chance whim came to the pestering blur, and it began to coil heavily away. The men saw a ground vacant of fighters. It would have been an empty stage if it were not for a few corpses that lay thrown and twisted into fantastic shapes upon the sward.

At sight of this tableau, many of the men in blue

sprang from behind their covers and made an ungainly dance of joy. Their eyes burned, and a hoarse cheer of elation broke from their dry lips.

It had begun to seem to them that events were trying to prove that they were impotent. These little battles had evidently endeavoured to demonstrate that the men could not fight well. When on the verge of submission to these opinions, the small duel had showed them that the proportions were not impossible, and by it they had revenged themselves upon their misgivings and upon the foe.

The impetus of enthusiasm was theirs again. They gazed about them with looks of uplifted pride, feeling new trust in the grim, always confident, weapons in their hands. And they were men.

CHAPTER XXI

PRESENTLY they knew that no firing threatened them. All ways seemed once more opened to them. The dusty blue lines of their friends were disclosed a short distance away. In the distance there were many colossal noises, but in all this part of the field there was a sudden stillness.

They perceived that they were free. The depleted band drew a long breath of relief and gathered itself into a bunch to complete its trip.

In this last length of journey the men began to show strange emotions. They hurried with nervous fear. Some who had been dark and unfaltering in the grimmest moments now could not conceal an anxiety that made them frantic. It was, perhaps, that they dreaded to be killed in insignificant ways after the times for proper military death had passed. Or, perhaps, they thought it would be too ironical to get killed at the portals of safety. With backward looks of perturbation they hastened.

As they approached their own lines there was some sarcasm exhibited on the part of a gaunt and bronzed regiment that lay resting in the shade of trees. Questions were wafted to them.

" Where th' hell yeh been ? "

"What yeh comin' back fer?"

"Why didn't yeh stay there?"

"Was it warm out there, sonny?"

"Goin' home now, boys?"

One shouted in taunting mimicry, "Oh, mother, come quick an' look at th' sodgers!"

There was no reply from the bruised and battered regiment, save that one man made broadcast challenges to fist fights and the red-bearded officer walked rather near and glared in great swashbuckler style at a tall captain in the other regiment. But the lieutenant suppressed the man who wished to fist fight, and the tall captain, flushing at the little fanfare of the red-bearded one, was obliged to look intently at some trees.

The youth's tender flesh was deeply stung by those remarks. From under his creased brows he glowered with hate at the mockers. He meditated upon a few revenges. Still, many in the regiment hung their heads in criminal fashion, so that it came to pass that the men trudged with sudden heaviness, as if they bore upon their bended shoulders the coffin of their honour. And the youthful lieutenant, recollecting himself, began to mutter softly in black curses.

They turned when they arrived at their old position to regard the ground over which they had charged.

The youth in this contemplation was smitten with a large astonishment. He discovered that the distances, as compared with the brilliant measurings of his mind, were trivial and ridiculous. The stolid trees, where much had taken place, seemed incredibly near. The time, too, now that he reflected, he saw to have been short. He wondered at the number of emotions and events that had been crowded into such little spaces. Elfin thoughts must have exaggerated and enlarged everything, he said.

It seemed, then, that there was bitter justice in the speeches of the gaunt and bronzed veterans. He veiled a glance of disdain at his fellows who strewed the ground, choking with dust, red from perspiration, misty-eyed, dishevelled.

They were gulping at their canteens, fierce to wring every mite of water from them, and they polished at their swollen and watery features with coat-sleeves and bunches of grass.

However, to the youth there was a considerable joy in musing upon his performances during the charge. He had had very little time previously in which to appreciate himself, so that there was now much satisfaction in quietly thinking of his actions. He recalled bits of colour that in the flurry had stamped themselves unawares upon his engaged senses.

As the regiment lay heaving from its hot exertions the officer who had named them as mule-drivers came galloping along the line. He had lost his cap. His tousled hair streamed wildly, and his face was dark with vexation and wrath. His temper was displayed with more clearness by the way in which he managed his horse. He jerked and wrenched savagely at his bridle, stopping the hard-breathing animal with a furious pull near the colonel of the regiment. He immediately exploded in reproaches which came unbidden to the ears of the men. They were suddenly alert, being always curious about black words between officers.

"Oh, thunder, MacChesnay, what an awful bull you made of this thing!" began the officer. He attempted low tones, but his indignation caused certain of the men to learn the sense of his words. "What an awful mess you made! Good Lord, man, you stopped about a hundred feet this side of a very pretty success! If your men had gone a hundred feet farther you would have made a great charge, but as it is—what a lot of mud-diggers you've got anyway!"

The men, listening with bated breath, now turned their curious eyes upon the colonel. They had a ragamuffin interest in this affair.

The colonel was seen to straighten his form and put one hand forth in oratorical fashion. He wore an injured air; it was as if a deacon had been accused of stealing. The men were wiggling in an ecstasy of excitement.

But of a sudden the colonel's manner changed from that of a deacon to that of a Frenchman. He shrugged his shoulders. "Oh, well, general, we went as far as we could," he said calmly.

"As far as you could? Did you, b'Gawd?" snorted the other. "Well, that wasn't very far, was it?" he added, with a glance of cold contempt into the other's eyes. "Not very far, I think. You were intended to make a diversion in favour of Whiterside. How well you succeeded your own ears can now tell you." He wheeled his horse and rode stiffly away.

The colonel, bidden to hear the jarring noises of an engagement in the woods to the left, broke out in vague damnations.

The lieutenant, who had listened with an air of impotent rage to the interview, spoke suddenly in firm and undaunted tones. "I don't care what a man is—whether he is a general or what—if he says th' boys didn't put up a good fight out there he's a damned fool."

"Lieutenant," began the colonel severely, "this is my own affair, and I'll trouble you——"

The lieutenant made an obedient gesture. "All right, colonel, all right," he said. He sat down with an air of being content with himself.

The news that the regiment had been reproached went along the line. For a time the men were bewildered by it. "Good thunder!" they ejaculated, staring at the vanishing form of the general. They conceived it to be a huge mistake.

Presently, however, they began to believe that in truth their efforts had been called light. The youth could see this conviction weigh upon the entire regiment until the men were like cuffed and cursed animals, but withal rebellious.

The friend, with a grievance in his eye, went to the youth. "I wonder what he does want," he said. "He must think we went out there an' played marbles! I never see sech a man!"

The youth developed a tranquil philosophy for

these moments of irritation. "Oh, well," he rejoined, "he probably didn't see nothing of it at
all and got mad as blazes, and concluded we were
a lot of sheep, just because we didn't do what he
wanted done. It's a pity old Grandpa Henderson
got killed yestirday—he'd have known that we did
our best and fought good. It's just our awful luck,
that's what."

"I should say so," replied the friend. He seemed
to be deeply wounded at an injustice. "I should
say we did have awful luck! There's no fun in
fightin' fer people when everything yeh do—no
matter what—ain't done right. I have a notion
t' stay behind next time an' let 'em take their ol'
charge an' go t' th' devil with it."

The youth spoke soothingly to his comrade.
"Well, we both did good. I'd like to see the
fool what'd say we both didn't do as good as we
could!"

"Of course we did," declared the friend stoutly.
"An' I'd break th' feller's neck if he was as big as
a church. But we're all right, anyhow, for I heard
one feller say that we two fit th' best in th' reg'ment,
an' they had a great argument 'bout it. Another
feller, 'a course, he had t' up an' say it was a lie
—he seen all what was goin' on an' he never seen
us from th' beginnin' t' th' end. An' a lot more
struck in an' ses it wasn't a lie—we did fight like
thunder, an' they give us quite a send-off. But
this is what I can't stand—these everlastin' ol'
soldiers, titterin' an laughin', an' then that general,
he's crazy."

The youth exclaimed with sudden exasperation, "He's a lunkhead! He makes me mad. I wish he'd come along next time. We'd show 'im what——"

He ceased because several men had come hurrying up. Their faces expressed a bringing of great news.

"O Flem, yeh jest oughta heard!" cried one eagerly.

"Heard what?" said the youth.

"Ye jest oughta heard!" repeated the other, and he arranged himself to tell his tidings. The others made an excited circle. "Well, sir, th' colonel met your lieutenant right by us—it was damnedest thing I ever heard—an' he ses: 'Ahem! ahem!' he ses. 'Mr. Hasbrouck!' he ses, 'by th' way, who was that lad what carried th' flag?' he ses. There, Flemin', what d' yeh think 'a that? 'Who was th' lad what carried th' flag?' he ses, an' th' lieutenant, he speaks up right away: 'That's Flemin', an' he's a jimhickey,' he ses, right away. What? I say he did. 'A jimhickey,' he ses— those 'r his words. He did, too. I say he did. If you kin tell this story better than I kin, go ahead an' tell it. Well, then, keep yer mouth shet. Th' lieutenant, he ses: 'He's a jimhickey,' an' th' colonel, he ses: 'Ahem! ahem! he is, indeed, a very good man t' have, ahem! He kep' th' flag 'way t' th' front. I saw 'im. He's a good un,' ses th' colonel. 'You bet,' ses th' lieutenant, 'he an' a feller named Wilson was at 'th' head 'a th' charge, an' howlin' like Indians all th' time,' he ses. 'Head 'a th' charge all th' time,' he ses. 'A feller named Wilson,' he ses.

There, Wilson, m' boy, put that in a letter an' send it hum t' yer mother, hay? 'A feller named Wilson,' he ses. An' th' colonel, he ses : 'Were they, indeed? Ahem! ahem! My sakes!' he ses. 'At th' head 'a th' reg'ment?' he ses. 'They were,' says th' lieutenant. 'My sakes!' ses th' colonel. He ses : 'Well, well, well,' he ses, 'those two babies?' 'They were,' ses th' lieutenant. 'Well, well,' ses th' colonel, 'they deserve t' be major-generals,' he ses. 'They deserve t' be major-generals.'"

The youth and his friend had said, "Huh!" "Yer lyin', Thompson." "Oh, go t' blazes!" "He never sed it." "Oh, what a lie!" "Huh!" But despite these youthful scoffings and embarrassments, they knew that their faces were deeply flushing from thrills of pleasure. They exchanged a secret glance of joy and congratulation.

They speedily forgot many things. The past held no pictures of error and disappointment. They were very happy, and their hearts swelled with grateful affection for the colonel and the youthful lieutenant.

WHEN the woods again began to pour forth the dark-hued masses of the enemy the youth felt serene self-confidence. He smiled briefly when he saw men dodge and duck at the long screechings of shells that were thrown in giant handfuls over them. He stood, erect and tranquil, watching the attack begin against a part of the line that made a blue curve along the side of an adjacent hill. His vision being unmolested by smoke from the rifles of his companions, he had opportunities to see parts of the hard fight. It was a relief to perceive at last from whence came some of these noises which had been roared into his ears.

Off a short way he saw two regiments fighting a little separate battle with two other regiments. It was in a cleared space, wearing a set-apart look. They were blazing as if upon a wager, giving and taking tremendous blows. The firings were incredibly fierce and rapid. These intent regiments apparently were oblivious of all larger purposes of war, and were slugging each other as if at a matched game.

In another direction he saw a magnificent brigade going with the evident intention of driving the enemy from a wood. They passed in out of sight, and presently there was a most awe-inspiring racket in the wood. The noise was unspeakable. Having stirred this prodigious uproar, and, apparently, finding it too prodigious, the brigade, after a little time, came marching airily out again with its fine formation in nowise disturbed. There were no traces of speed in its movements. The brigade was jaunty, and seemed to point a proud thumb at the yelling wood.

On a slope to the left there was a long row of guns, gruff and maddened, denouncing the enemy, who, down through the woods, were forming for another attack in the pitiless monotony of conflicts. The round red discharges from the guns made a crimson flare and a high, thick smoke. Occasional glimpses could be caught of groups of the toiling artillerymen. In the rear of this row of guns stood a house, calm and white, amid bursting shells. A congregation of horses, tied to a long railing, were tugging frenziedly at their bridles. Men were running hither and thither.

The detached battle between the four regiments lasted for some time. There chanced to be no interference, and they settled their dispute by themselves. They struck savagely and powerfully at each other for a period of minutes, and then the lighter-hued regiments faltered and drew back, leaving the dark-blue lines shouting. The youth could see the two flags shaking with laughter amid the smoke remnants.

Presently there was a stillness, pregnant with

meaning. The blue lines shifted and changed a trifle and stared expectantly at the silent woods and fields before them. The hush was solemn and church-like, save for a distant battery that, evidently unable to remain quiet, sent a faint rolling thunder over the ground. It irritated, like the noises of unimpressed boys. The men imagined that it would prevent their perched ears from hearing the first words of the new battle.

Of a sudden the guns on the slope roared out a message of warning. A spluttering sound had begun in the woods. It swelled with amazing speed to a profound clamour that involved the earth in noises. The splitting crashes swept along the lines until an interminable roar was developed. To those in the midst of it, it became a din fitted to the universe. It was the whirring and thumping of gigantic machinery, complications among the smaller stars. The youth's ears were filled up. They were incapable of hearing more.

On an incline over which a road wound he saw wild and desperate rushes of men perpetually backward and forward in riotous surges. These parts of the opposing armies were two long waves that pitched upon each other madly at dictated points. To and fro they swelled. Sometimes, one side by its yells and cheers would proclaim decisive blows, but a moment later the other side would be all yells and cheers. Once the youth saw a spray of light forms go in hound-like leaps toward the waving blue lines. There was much howling, and presently it went away with a vast mouthful of prisoners.

Again, he saw a blue wave dash with such thunderous force against a grey obstruction, that it seemed to clear the earth of it and leave nothing but trampled sod. And always in their swift and deadly rushes to and fro the men screamed and yelled like maniacs.

Particular pieces of fence or secure positions behind collections of trees were wrangled over, as gold thrones or pearl bedsteads. There were desperate lunges at these chosen spots seemingly every instant, and most of them were bandied like light toys between the contending forces. The youth could not tell from the battle-flags flying like crimson foam in many directions which colour of cloth was winning.

His emaciated regiment bustled forth with undiminished fierceness when its time came. When assaulted again by bullets, the men burst out in a barbaric cry of rage and pain. They bent their heads in aims of intent hatred behind the projected hammers of their guns. Their ramrods clanged loud with fury as their eager arms pounded the cartridges into the rifle barrels. The front of the regiment was a smoke-wall penetrated by the flashing points of yellow and red.

Wallowing in the fight, they were in an astonishingly short time resmudged. They surpassed in stain and dirt all their previous appearances. Moving to and fro with strained exertion, jabbering the while, they were, with their swaying bodies, black faces, and glowing eyes, like strange and ugly fiends jigging heavily in the smoke.

The lieutenant, returning from a tour after a bandage, produced from a hidden receptacle of his mind new and portentous oaths suited to the emergency. Strings of expletives he swung lash-like over the backs of his men, and it was evident that his previous efforts had in nowise impaired his resources.

The youth, still the bearer of the colours, did not feel his idleness. He was deeply absorbed as a spectator. The crash and swing of the great drama made him lean forward, intent-eyed, his face working in small contortions. Sometimes he prattled, words coming unconsciously from him in grotesque exclamations. He did not know that he breathed, that the flag hung silently over him, so absorbed was he.

A formidable line of the enemy came within dangerous range. They could be seen plainly—tall, gaunt men with excited faces running with long strides toward a wandering fence.

At sight of this danger the men suddenly ceased their cursing monotone. There was an instant of strained silence before they threw up their rifles and fired a plumping volley at the foes. There had been no order given; the men, upon recognising the menace, had immediately let drive their flock of bullets without waiting for word of command.

But the enemy were quick to gain the protection of the wandering line of fence. They slid down behind it with remarkable celerity, and from this position they began briskly to slice up the blue men.

These latter braced their energies for a great struggle. Often, white clinched teeth shone from the dusky faces. Many heads surged to and fro, floating upon a pale sea of smoke. Those behind the fence frequently shouted and yelped in taunts and gibe-like cries, but the regiment maintained a stressed silence. Perhaps at this new assault the men recalled the fact that they had been named mud - diggers, and it made their situation thrice bitter. They were breathlessly intent upon keeping the ground, and thrusting away the rejoicing body of the enemy. They fought swiftly, and with a despairing savageness denoted in their expressions.

The youth had resolved not to budge whatever should happen. Some arrows of scorn that had buried themselves in his heart had generated strange and unspeakable hatred. It was clear to him that his final and absolute revenge was to be achieved by his dead body lying, torn and gluttering, upon the field. This was to be a poignant retaliation upon the officer who had said " mule-drivers," and later " mud-diggers," for in all the wild graspings of his mind for a unit responsible for his sufferings and commotions he always seized upon the man who had dubbed him wrongly. And it was his idea, vaguely formulated, that his corpse would be for those eyes a great and salt reproach.

The regiment bled extravagantly. Grunting bundles of blue began to drop. The orderly sergeant of the youth's company was shot through the cheeks. Its supports being injured, his jaw hung afar down, disclosing in the wide cavern of his mouth a pulsing mass of blood and teeth. And with it all he made attempts to cry out. In his endeavour there was a dreadful earnestness, as if he conceived that one great shriek would make him well.

The youth saw him presently go rearward. His strength seemed in nowise impaired. He ran swiftly, casting wild glances for succour.

Others fell down about the feet of their companions. Some of the wounded crawled out and away, but many lay still, their bodies twisted into impossible shapes.

The youth looked once for his friend. He saw a vehement young man, powder-smeared and frowzled, whom he knew to be him. The lieutenant, also, was unscathed in his position at the rear. He had continued to curse, but it was now with the air of a man who was using his last box of oaths.

For the fire of the regiment had begun to wane and drip. The robust voice, that had come strangely from the thin ranks, was growing rapidly weak.

CHAPTER XXIII

THE colonel came running along back of the line. There were other officers following him. " We must charge 'm ! " they shouted. " We must charge 'm ! " they cried with resentful voices, as if anticipating a rebellion against this plan by the men.

The youth, upon hearing the shouts, began to study the distance between him and the enemy. He made vague calculations. He saw that to be firm soldiers they must go forward. It would be death to stay in the present place, and with all the circumstances to go backward would exalt too many others. Their hope was to push the galling foes away from the fence.

He expected that his companions, weary and stiffened, would have to be driven to this assault, but as he turned toward them he perceived with a certain surprise that they were giving quick and unqualified expressions of assent. There was an ominous, clanging overture to the charge when the shafts of the bayonets rattled upon the rifle barrels. At the yelled words of command the soldiers sprang forward in eager leaps. There was new and unexpected force in the movement of the regiment. A knowledge of its faded and jaded condition made the charge appear like a paroxysm, a display of the strength that comes before a final feebleness. The men scampered in insane fever of haste, racing as if to achieve a sudden success before an exhilarating fluid should leave them. It was a blind and despairing rush by the collection of men in dusty and tattered blue, over a green sward and under a sapphire sky, toward a fence, dimly outlined in smoke, from behind which spluttered the fierce rifles of enemies.

The youth kept the bright colours to the front. He was waving his free arm in furious circles, the while shrieking mad calls and appeals, urging on those that did not need to be urged, for it seemed that the mob of blue men hurling themselves on the dangerous group of rifles were again grown suddenly wild with an enthusiasm of unselfishness. From the many firings starting toward them, it looked as if they would merely succeed in making a great sprinkling of corpses on the grass between their former position and the fence. But they were in a state of frenzy, perhaps because of forgotten vanities, and it made an exhibition of sublime recklessness. There was no obvious questioning, nor figurings, nor diagrams. There was, apparently, no considered loopholes. It appeared that the swift wings of their desires would have shattered against the iron gates of the impossible.

He himself felt the daring spirit of a savage religion mad. He was capable of profound sacrifices, a tremendous death. He had no time for dissections, but he knew that he thought of the bullets only as things that could prevent him from reaching the place of his endeavour. There were subtle flashings of joy within him that thus should be his mind.

He strained all his strength. His eyesight was shaken and dazzled by the tension of thought and muscle. He did not see anything excepting the mist of smoke gashed by the little knives of fire, but he knew that in it lay the aged fence of a vanished farmer protecting the snuggled bodies of the grey men.

As he ran, a thought of the shock of contact gleamed in his mind. He expected a great concussion when the two bodies of troops crashed together. This became a part of his wild battle madness. He could feel the onward swing of the regiment about him, and he conceived of a thunderous, crushing blow, that would prostrate the resistance, and spread consternation and amazement for miles. The flying regiment was going to have a catapultian effect. This dream made him run faster among his comrades, who were giving vent to hoarse and frantic cheers.

But presently he could see that many of the men in grey did not intend to abide the blow. The smoke, rolling, disclosed men who ran, their faces still turned. These grew to a crowd, who retired stubbornly. Individuals wheeled frequently to send a bullet at the blue wave.

But at one part of the line there was a grim and obdurate group that made no movement. They were settled firmly down behind posts and rails. A flag, ruffled and fierce, waved over them, and their rifles dinned fiercely.

The blue whirl of men got very near, until it seemed that in truth there would be a close and frightful scuffle. There was an expressed disdain in the opposition of the little group that changed the meaning of the cheers of the men in blue. They became yells of wrath, directed, personal. The cries of the two parties were now in sound an interchange of scathing insults.

They in blue showed their teeth; their eyes shone all white. They launched themselves as at the throats of those who stood resisting. The space between dwindled to an insignificant distance.

The youth had centred the gaze of his soul upon that other flag. Its possession would be high pride. It would express bloody minglings, near blows. He had a gigantic hatred for those who made great difficulties and complications. They caused it to be as a craved treasure of mythology, hung amid tasks and contrivances of danger.

He plunged like a mad horse at it. He was resolved it should not escape if wild blows and darings of blows could seize it. His own emblem, quivering and aflare, was winging toward the other. It seemed there would shortly be an encounter of strange beaks and claws, as of eagles.

The swirling body of blue men came to a sudden halt at close and disastrous range, and roared a swift volley. The group in grey was split and broken by this fire, but its riddled body still fought The men in blue yelled again, and rushed in upon it

The youth, in his leapings, saw, as through a mist, a picture of four or five men stretched upon the ground, or writhing upon their knees with bowed heads, as if they had been stricken by bolts from the sky. Tottering among them was the rival colour-bearer, whom the youth saw had been bitten vitally by the bullets of the last formidable volley. He perceived this man fighting a last struggle, the struggle of one whose legs are grasped by demons. It was a ghastly battle. Over his face was the bleach of death, but set upon it was the dark and hard lines of desperate purpose. With this terrible grin of resolution he hugged his precious flag to him, and was stumbling and staggering in his design to go the way that led to safety for it.

But his wounds always made it seem that his feet were retarded, held, and he fought a grim fight, as with invisible ghouls fastened greedily upon his limbs. Those in advance of the scampering blue men, howling cheers, leaped at the fence. The despair of the lost was in his eyes as he glanced back at them.

The youth's friend went over the obstruction in a tumbling heap, and sprang at the flag as a panther at prey. He pulled at it, and, wrenching it free, swung up its red brilliancy with a mad cry of exultation, even as the colour-bearer, gasping, lurched over in a final throe, and, stiffening convulsively, turned his dead face to the ground. There was much blood upon the grass blades.

At the place of success there began more wild clamourings of cheers. The men gesticulated and

bellowed in an ecstacy.   When they spoke, it was as
if they considered their listener to be a mile away.
What hats and caps were left to them they often
slung high in the air.

At one part of the line four men had been swooped
upon, and they now sat as prisoners.   Some blue
men were about them in an eager and curious circle.
The soldiers had trapped strange birds, and there
was an examination.   A flurry of fast questions was
in the air.

One of the prisoners was nursing a superficial
wound in the foot.   He cuddled it, baby-wise, but
he looked up from it often to curse with an astonishing utter abandon straight at the noses of his captors.
He consigned them to red regions; he called upon
the pestilential wrath of strange gods.   And with
it all he was singularly free from recognition of the
finer points of the conduct of prisoners of war.   It
was as if a clumsy clod had trod upon his toe, and
he conceived it to be his privilege, his duty, to use
deep, resentful oaths.

Another, who was a boy in years, took his plight
with great calmness and apparent good-nature.   He
conversed with the men in blue, studying their faces
with his bright and keen eyes.   They spoke of
battles and conditions.   There was an acute interest
in all their faces during this exchange of view
points.   It seemed a great satisfaction to hear
voices from where all had been darkness and specu-
lation.

The third captive sat with a morose countenance.
He preserved a stoical and cold attitude.   To all

advances he made one reply without variation, " Ah, go t' hell ! "

The last of the four was always silent, and, for the most part, kept his face turned in unmolested directions. From the views the youth received he seemed to be in a state of absolute dejection. Shame was upon him, and with it profound regret that he was, perhaps, no more to be counted in the ranks of his fellows. The youth could detect no expression that would allow him to believe that the other was giving a thought to his narrowed future, the pictured dungeons, perhaps, and starvations and brutalities, liable to the imagination. All to be seen was shame for captivity, and regret for the right to antagonise.

After the men had celebrated sufficiently they settled down behind the old rail fence, on the opposite side to the one from which their foes had been driven. A few shot perfunctorily at distant marks.

There was some long grass. The youth nestled in it and rested, making a convenient rail support the flag. His friend, jubilant and glorified, holding his treasure with vanity, came to him there. They sat side by side and congratulated each other.

CHAPTER XXIV

THE roarings that had stretched in a long line of sound across the face of the forest began to grow intermittent and weaker. The stentorian speeches of the artillery continued in some distant encounter, but the crashes of the musketry had almost ceased. The youth and his friend of a sudden looked up, feeling a deadened form of distress at the waning of these noises, which had become a part of life. They could see changes going on among the troops. There were marchings this way and that way. A battery wheeled leisurely. On the crest of a small hill was the thick gleam of many departing muskets.

The youth arose. "Well, what now, I wonder?" he said. By his tone he seemed to be preparing to resent some new monstrosity in the way of dins and smashes. He shaded his eyes with his grimy hand and gazed over the field.

His friend also arose and stared. "I bet we're goin' t' git along out of this an' back over th' river," said he.

"Well, I swan!" said the youth.

They waited, watching. Within a little while the regiment received orders to retrace its way. The men got up grunting from the grass, regretting the

soft repose. They jerked their stiffened legs, and
stretched their arms over their heads. One man
swore as he rubbed his eyes. They all groaned "O
Lord!" They had as many objections to this change
as they would have had to a proposal for a new
battle.

They trampled slowly back over the field across
which they had run in a mad scamper.

The regiment marched until it had joined its
fellows. The reformed brigade, in column, aimed
through a wood at the road. Directly they were in
a mass of dust-covered troops, and were trudging
along in a way parallel to the enemy's lines as these
had been defined by the previous turmoil.

They passed within view of a stolid white house,
and saw in front of it groups of their comrades lying
in wait behind a neat breastwork. A row of guns
were booming at a distant enemy. Shells thrown
in reply were raising clouds of dust and splinters.
Horsemen dashed along the line of intrenchments.

At this point of its march the division curved
away from the field and went winding off in the
direction of the river. When the significance of this
movement had impressed itself upon the youth he
turned his head and looked over his shoulder toward
the trampled and débris - strewed ground. He
breathed a breath of new satisfaction. He finally
nudged his friend. "Well, it's all over," he said to
him.

His friend gazed backward. "B'Gawd, it is," he
assented. They mused.

For a time the youth was obliged to reflect in a

puzzled and uncertain way. His mind was undergoing a subtle change. It took moments for it to cast off its battleful ways and resume its accustomed course of thought. Gradually his brain emerged from the clogged clouds, and at last he was enabled to more closely comprehend himself and circumstance.

He understood then that the existence of shot and counter-shot was in the past. He had dwelt in a land of strange, squalling upheavals and had come forth. He had been where there was red of blood and black of passion, and he was escaped. His first thoughts were given to rejoicings at this fact.

Later, he began to study his deeds, his failures, and his achievements. Thus, fresh from scenes where many of his usual machines of reflection had been idle, from where he had proceeded sheep-like, he struggled to marshal all his acts.

At last they marched before him clearly. From this present view-point he was enabled to look upon them in spectator fashion and to criticise them with some correctness, for his new condition had already defeated certain sympathies.

Regarding his procession of memory he felt gleeful and unregretting, for in it his public deeds were paraded in great and shining prominence. Those performances which had been witnessed by his fellows marched now in wide purple and gold having various deflections. They went gaily with music. It was pleasure to watch these things. He spent delightful minutes viewing the gilded images of memory.

He saw that he was good. He recalled with a

thrill of joy the respectful comments of his fellows upon his conduct.

Nevertheless, the ghost of his flight from the first engagement appeared to him and danced. There were small shoutings in his brain about these matters. For a moment he blushed, and the light of his soul flickered with shame.

A spectre of reproach came to him. There loomed the dogging memory of the tattered soldier —he who, gored by bullets and faint for blood, had fretted concerning an imagined wound in another; he who had loaned his last of strength and intellect for the tall soldier; he who, blind with weariness and pain, had been deserted in the field.

For an instant a wretched chill of sweat was upon him at the thought that he might be detected in the thing. As he stood persistently before his vision, he gave vent to a cry of sharp irritation and agony.

His friend turned. "What's the matter, Henry?" he demanded. The youth's reply was an outburst of crimson oaths.

As he marched along the little branch-hung roadway among his prattling companions this vision of cruelty brooded over him. It clung near him always and darkened his view of these deeds in purple and gold. Whichever way his thoughts turned, they were followed by the sombre phantom of the desertion in the fields. He looked stealthily at his companions, feeling sure that they must discern in his face evidences of this pursuit. But they were plodding in ragged array, discussing with quick tongues the accomplishments of the late battle.

"Oh, if a man should come up an' ask me, I'd say we got a dum good lickin'."

"Lickin'—in yer eye! We ain't licked, sonny. We're goin' down here aways, swing aroun', an' come in behint 'em."

"Oh, hush, with your comin' in behint 'em. I've seen all 'a that I wanta. Don't tell me about comin' in behint——"

"Bill Smithers, he ses he'd rather been in ten hundred battles than been in that heluva hospital. He ses they got shootin' in th' night-time, an' shells dropped plum among 'em in th' hospital. He ses sech hollerin' he never see."

"Hasbrouck? He's th' best off'cer in this here reg'ment. He's a whale."

"Didn't I tell yeh we'd come aroun' in behint em? Didn't I tell yeh so? We——"

"Oh, shet yeh mouth!"

For a time this pursuing recollection of the tattered man took all elation from the youth's veins. He saw his vivid error, and he was afraid that it would stand before him all his life. He took no share in the chatter of his comrades, nor did he look at them or know them, save when he felt sudden suspicion that they were seeing his thoughts and scrutinising each detail of the scene with the tattered soldier.

Yet gradually he mustered force to put the sin at a distance. And at last his eyes seemed to open to some new ways. He found that he could look back upon the brass and bombast of his earlier gospels and see them truly. He was gleeful when he discovered that he now despised them.

*

.. With this conviction came a store of assurance. He felt a quiet manhood, non-assertive, but of sturdy and strong blood. He knew that he would no more quail before his guides wherever they should point. He had been to touch the great death, and found that, after all, it was but the great death. He was a man.

So it came to pass that as he trudged from the place of blood and wrath his soul changed. He came from hot ploughshares to prospects of clover tranquilly, and it was as if hot ploughshares were not. Scars faded as flowers.

It rained. The procession of weary soldiers became a bedraggled train, despondent and muttering, marching with churning effort in a trough of liquid brown mud under a low, wretched sky. Yet the youth smiled, for he saw that the world was a world for him, though many discovered it to be made of oaths and walking-sticks. He had rid himself of the red sickness of battle. The sultry nightmare was in the past. He had been an animal blistered and sweating in the heat and pain of war. He turned now with a lover's thirst to images of tranquil skies, fresh meadows, cool brooks—an existence of soft and eternal peace.

Over the river a golden ray of sun came through the hosts of leaden rain-clouds.

The Little Regiment

The Little Regiment

I

THE fog made the clothes of the men of the column in the roadway seem of a luminous quality. It imparted to the heavy infantry over-coats a new colour, a kind of blue which was so pale that a regiment might have been merely a long, low shadow in the mist. However, a muttering, one part grumble, three parts joke, hovered in the air above the thick ranks, and blended in an undertoned roar, which was the voice of the column.

The town on the southern shore of the little river loomed spectrally, a faint etching upon the grey cloud-masses which were shifting with oily languor. A long row of guns upon the northern bank had been pitiless in their hatred, but a little battered belfry could be dimly seen still pointing with invincible resolution toward the heavens.

The enclouded air vibrated with noises made by hidden colossal things. The infantry tramplings, the heavy rumbling of the artillery, made the earth speak of gigantic preparation. Guns on distant heights thundered from time to time with sudden, nervous roar, as if unable to endure in silence a knowledge of hostile troops massing, other guns going to position. These sounds, near and remote, defined an immense battle-ground, described the tremendous width of the stage of the prospective drama. The voices of the guns, slightly casual, unexcited in their challenges and warnings, could not destroy the unutterable eloquence of the word in the air, a meaning of impending struggle which made the breath halt at the lips.

The column in the roadway was ankle-deep in mud. The men swore piously at the rain which drizzled upon them, compelling them to stand always very erect in fear of the drops that would sweep in under their coat-collars. The fog was as cold as wet cloths. The men stuffed their hands deep in their pockets, and huddled their muskets in their arms. The machinery of orders had rooted these soldiers deeply into the mud, precisely as almighty nature roots mullein stalks.

They listened and speculated when a tumult of fighting came from the dim town across the river. When the noise lulled for a time they resumed their descriptions of the mud and graphically exaggerated the number of hours they had been kept waiting. The general commanding their division rode along the ranks, and they cheered admiringly, affectionately, crying out to him gleeful prophecies of the coming battle. Each man scanned him with a peculiarly keen personal interest, and afterward spoke of him with unquestioning devotion and confidence, narrating anecdotes which were mainly untrue.

When the jokers lifted the shrill voices which invariably belonged to them, flinging witticisms at their comrades, a loud laugh would sweep from rank to rank, and soldiers who had not heard would lean forward and demand repetition. When were borne past them some wounded men with grey and blood-smeared faces, and eyes that rolled in that helpless beseeching for assistance from the sky which comes with supreme pain, the soldiers in the mud watched intently, and from time to time asked of the bearers an account of the affair. Frequently they bragged of their corps, their division, their brigade, their regiment. Anon they referred to the mud and the cold drizzle. Upon this threshold of a wild scene of death they, in short, defied the proportion of events with that splendour of heedlessness which belongs only to veterans.

"Like a lot of wooden soldiers," swore Billie Dempster, moving his feet in the thick mass, and casting a vindictive glance indefinitely: "standing in the mud for a hundred years."

"Oh, shut up!" murmured his brother Dan. The manner of his words implied that this fraternal voice near him was an indescribable bore.

"Why should I shut up?" demanded Billie.

"Because you're a fool," cried Dan, taking no time to debate it; "the biggest fool in the regiment."

There was but one man between them, and he was habituated. These insults from brother to brother had swept across his chest, flown past his face, many times during two long campaigns. Upon this occasion he simply grinned first at one, then at the other.

The way of these brothers was not an unknown topic in regimental gossip. They had enlisted simultaneously, with each sneering loudly at the other for doing it. They left their little town, and went forward with the flag, exchanging protestations of undying suspicion. In the camp life they so openly despised each other that, when entertaining quarrels were lacking, their companions often contrived situations calculated to bring forth display of this fraternal dislike.

Both were large-limbed, strong young men, and often fought with friends in camp unless one was near to interfere with the other. This latter happened rather frequently, because Dan, preposterously willing for any manner of combat, had a very great horror of seeing Billie in a fight; and Billie, almost odiously ready himself, simply refused to see Dan stripped to his shirt and with his fists aloft. This sat queerly upon them, and made them the objects of plots.

When Dan jumped through a ring of eager

soldiers and dragged forth his raving brother by the arm, a thing often predicted would almost come to pass. When Billie performed the same office for Dan, the prediction would again miss fulfilment by an inch. But indeed they never fought together, although they were perpetually upon the verge.

They expressed longing for such conflict. As a matter of truth, they had at one time made full arrangement for it, but even with the encouragement and interest of half of the regiment they somehow failed to achieve collision.

If Dan became a victim of police duty, no jeering was so destructive to the feelings as Billie's comment. If Billie got a call to appear at the headquarters, none would so genially prophesy his complete undoing as Dan. Small misfortunes to one were, in truth, invariably greeted with hilarity by the other, who seemed to see in them great re-enforcement of his opinion.

As soldiers, they expressed each for each a scorn intense and blasting. After a certain battle, Billie was promoted to corporal. When Dan was told of it, he seemed smitten dumb with astonishment and patriotic indignation. He stared in silence, while the dark blood rushed to Billie's forehead, and he shifted his weight from foot to foot. Dan at last found his tongue, and said: "Well, I'm durned!" If he had heard that an army mule had been appointed to the post of corps commander, his tone could not have had more derision in it. Afterward, he adopted a fervid insubordination, an almost religious reluctance to obey the new corporal's orders, which came near to developing the desired strife.

It is here finally to be recorded also that Dan, most ferociously profane in speech, very rarely swore in the presence of his brother; and that Billie, whose oaths came from his lips with the grace of falling pebbles, was seldom known to express himself in this manner when near his brother Dan.

At last the afternoon contained a suggestion of evening. Metallic cries rang suddenly from end to end of the column. They inspired at once a quick, business-like adjustment. The long thing stirred in the mud. The men had hushed, and were looking across the river. A moment later the shadowy mass of pale blue figures was moving steadily toward the stream. There could be heard from the town a clash of swift fighting and cheering. The noise of the shooting coming through the heavy air had its sharpness taken from it, and sounded in thuds.

There was a halt upon the bank above the pontoons. When the column went winding down the incline, and streamed out upon the bridge, the fog had faded to a great degree, and in the clearer dusk the guns on a distant ridge were enabled to perceive the crossing. The long whirling outcries of the shells came

into the air above the men.   An occasional solid
shot struck the surface of the river, and dashed
into view a sudden vertical jet.   The distance
was subtly illuminated by the lightning from the
deep-booming guns.   One by one the batteries on
the northern shore aroused, the innumerable guns
bellowing in angry oration at the distant ridge.
The rolling thunder crashed and reverberated as
a wild surf sounds on a still night, and to this
music the column marched across the pontoons.

The waters of the grim river curled away in a
smile from the ends of the great boats, and slid
swiftly beneath the planking.   The dark, riddled
walls of the town upreared before the troops, and
from a region hidden by these hammered and
tumbled houses came incessantly the yells and
firings of a prolonged and close skirmish.

When Dan had called his brother a fool, his
voice had been so decisive, so brightly assured,
that many men had laughed, considering it to
be great humour under the circumstances.   The
incident happened to rankle deep in Billie.   It
was not any strange thing that his brother had
called him a fool.   In fact, he often called him
a fool with exactly the same amount of cheerful
and prompt conviction, and before large audiences,
too.   Billie wondered in his own mind why he
took such profound offence in this case; but, at
any rate, as he slid down the bank and on to the
bridge with his regiment, he was searching his
knowledge for something that would pierce Dan's

blithesome spirit. But he could contrive nothing at this time, and his impotency made the glance which he was once able to give his brother still more malignant.

The guns far and near were roaring a fearful and grand introduction for this column which was marching upon the stage of death. Billie felt it, but only in a numb way. His heart was cased in that curious dissonant metal which covers a man's emotions at such times. The terrible voices from the hills told him that in this wide conflict his life was an insignificant fact, and that his death would be an insignificant fact. They portended the whirlwind to which he would be as necessary as a butterfly's waved. wing. The solemnity, the sadness of it came near enough to make him wonder why he was neither solemn nor sad. When his mind vaguely adjusted events according to their importance to him, it appeared that the uppermost thing was the fact that upon the eve of battle, and before many comrades, his brother had called him a fool.

Dan was in a particularly happy mood. "Hurray! Look at 'em shoot," he said, when the long witches' croon of the shells came into the air. It enraged Billie when he felt the little thorn in him, and saw at the same time that his brother had completely forgotten it.

The column went from the bridge into more mud. At this southern end there was a chaos of hoarse directions and commands. Darkness was coming upon the earth, and regiments were being hurried up the slippery bank. As Billie floundered in the black mud, amid the swearing, sliding crowd, he suddenly resolved that, in the absence of other means of hurting Dan, he would avoid looking at him, refrain from speaking to him, pay absolutely no heed to his existence; and this done skilfully would, he imagined, soon reduce his brother to a poignant sensitiveness.

At the top of the bank the column again halted and rearranged itself, as a man after a climb rearranges his clothing. Presently the great steel-backed brigade, an infinitely graceful thing in the rhythm and ease of its veteran movement, swung up a little narrow, slanting street.

Evening had come so swiftly that the fighting on the remote borders of the town was indicated by thin flashes of flame. Some building was on fire, and its reflection upon the clouds was an oval of delicate pink.

II

All demeanour of rural serenity had been wrenched violently from the little town by the guns and by the waves of men which had surged through it. The hand of war laid upon this village had in an instant changed it to a thing of remnants. It resembled the place of a monstrous shaking of the earth itself. The windows, now mere unsightly holes, made the tumbled and blackened dwellings seem skeletons. Doors lay splintered to fragments. Chimneys had flung their bricks everywhere. The artillery fire had not neglected the rows of gentle shade-trees which had lined the streets. Branches and heavy trunks cluttered the mud in driftwood tangles, while a few shattered forms had contrived to remain dejectedly, mournfully upright. They expressed an innocence, a helplessness, which perforce created a pity for their happening into this caldron of battle. Furthermore, there was under foot a vast collection of odd things reminiscent of the charge, the fight, the retreat. There were boxes and barrels filled with earth, behind which riflemen had lain snugly, and in these little trenches were the dead in blue with the dead in grey, the poses eloquent of the struggles for possession of the town, until the history of the whole conflict was written plainly in the streets.

And yet the spirit of this little city, its quaint individuality, poised in the air above the ruins, defying the guns, the sweeping volleys; holding in contempt those avaricious blazes which had attacked many dwellings. The hard earthen sidewalks proclaimed the games that had been played there during long lazy days, in the careful shadows of the trees. "General Merchandise," in faint letters upon a long board, had to be read with a slanted glance, for the sign dangled by one end; but the porch of the old store was a palpable legend of wide-hatted men, smoking.

This subtle essence, this soul of the life that had been, brushed like invisible wings the thoughts of the men in the swift columns that came up from the river.

In the darkness a loud and endless humming arose from the great blue crowds bivouacked in the streets. From time to time a sharp spatter of firing from far picket lines entered this bass chorus. The smell from the smouldering ruins floated on the cold night breeze.

Dan, seated ruefully upon the doorstep of a shot-pierced house, was proclaiming the campaign badly managed. Orders had been issued forbidding camp-fires.

Suddenly he ceased his oration, and scanning the group of his comrades, said: "Where's Billie? Do you know?"

"Gone on picket."

"Get out! Has he?" said Dan. "No business to go on picket. Why don't some of them other corporals take their turn?"

A bearded private was smoking his pipe of confiscated tobacco, seated comfortably upon a horse-hair trunk which he had dragged from the house. He observed: " *Was* his turn."

"No such thing," cried Dan. He and the man on the horse-hair trunk held discussion in which Dan stoutly maintained that if his brother had been sent on picket it was an injustice. He ceased his argument when another soldier, upon whose arms could faintly be seen the two stripes of a corporal, entered the circle. "Humph," said Dan, "where you been?"

The corporal made no answer. Presently Dan said: "Billie, where you been?"

His brother did not seem to hear these inquiries. He glanced at the house which towered above them, and remarked casually to the man on the horse-hair trunk: "Funny, ain't it? After the pelting this town got, you'd think there wouldn't be one brick left on another."

"Oh," said Dan, glowering at his brother's back. "Getting mighty smart, ain't you?"

The absence of camp-fires allowed the evening to make apparent its quality of faint silver light in which the blue clothes of the throng became black, and the faces became white expanses, void of expression. There was considerable excitement a short distance from the group around the doorstep. A soldier had chanced upon a hoop-skirt, and arrayed in it he was performing a dance amid the applause of his companions. Billie and a greater part of the men immediately poured over there to witness the exhibition.

"What's the matter with Billie?" demanded Dan of the man upon the horse-hair trunk.

"How do I know?" rejoined the other in mild resentment. He arose and walked away. When he returned he said briefly, in a weather-wise tone, that it would rain during the night.

Dan took a seat upon one end of the horse-hair trunk. He was facing the crowd around the dancer, which in its hilarity swung this way and that way. At times he imagined that he could recognise his brother's face.

He and the man on the other end of the trunk thoughtfully talked of the army's position. To their minds, infantry and artillery were in a most precarious jumble in the streets of the town; but they did not grow nervous over it, for they were used to having the army appear in a precarious jumble to their minds. They had learned to accept such puzzling situations as a consequence of their position in the ranks, and were now usually in possession of a simple but perfectly immovable faith that somebody understood the jumble. Even if they had been convinced that the army was a headless monster, they would merely have nodded with the veteran's singular cynicism. It was none of their business as soldiers. Their duty was to grab sleep and food when occasion permitted, and cheerfully fight wherever their feet were planted until more orders came. This was a task sufficiently absorbing.

They spoke of other corps, and this talk being confidential, their voices dropped to tones of awe. "The Ninth" — "The First" — "The Fifth" — "The Sixth" — "The Third" — the simple numerals rang with eloquence, each having a meaning which was to float through many years as no intangible arithmetical mist, but as pregnant with individuality as the names of cities.

Of their own corps they spoke with a deep veneration, an idolatry, a supreme confidence which apparently would not blanch to see it match against everything.

It was as if their respect for other corps was due partly to a wonder that organisations not blessed with their own famous numeral could take such an interest in war. They could prove that their division was the best in the corps, and that their brigade was the best in the division. And their regiment—it was plain that no fortune of life was equal to the chance which caused a man to be born, so to speak, into this command, the keystone of the defending arch.

At times Dan covered with insults the character of a vague, unnamed general to whose petulance and busy-body spirit he ascribed the order which made hot coffee impossible.

Dan said that victory was certain in the coming battle. The other man seemed rather dubious. He remarked upon the fortified line of hills, which had impressed him even from the other side of the river. "Shucks," said Dan. "Why, we——" He pictured a splendid overflowing of these hills by the sea of men in blue. During the period of this conversation Dan's glance searched the merry throng about the dancer. Above the babble of voices in the street a

far-away thunder could sometimes be heard—
evidently from the very edge of the horizon—
the boom-boom of restless guns.

III

Ultimately the night deepened to the tone of
black velvet. The outlines of the fireless camp
were like the faint drawings upon ancient tapestry.
The glint of a rifle, the shine of a button, might
have been of threads of silver and gold sewn upon
the fabric of the night. There was little presented
to the vision, but to a sense more subtle there
was discernible in the atmosphere something like
a pulse; a mystic beating which would have
told a stranger of the presence of a giant thing—
the slumbering mass of regiments and batteries.

With fires forbidden, the floor of a dry old
kitchen was thought to be a good exchange for
the cold earth of December, even if a shell had
exploded in it, and knocked it so out of shape
that when a man lay curled in his blanket his
last waking thought was likely to be of the wall
that bellied out above him, as if strongly anxious
to topple upon the score of soldiers.

Billie looked at the bricks ever about to descend
in a shower upon his face, listened to the indus-
trious pickets plying their rifles on the border of
the town, imagined some measure of the din of
the coming battle, thought of Dan and Dan's

chagrin, and rolling over in his blanket went to sleep with satisfaction.

At an unknown hour he was aroused by the creaking of boards. Lifting himself upon his elbow, he saw a sergeant prowling among the sleeping forms. The sergeant carried a candle in an old brass candlestick. He would have resembled some old farmer on an unusual midnight tour if it were not for the significance of his gleaming buttons and striped sleeves.

Billie blinked stupidly at the light until his mind returned from the journeys of slumber. The sergeant stooped among the unconscious soldiers, holding the candle close, and peering into each face.

"Hello, Haines," said Billie. "Relief?"

"Hello, Billie," said the sergeant. "Special duty."

"Dan got to go?"

"Jameson, Hunter, McCormack, D. Dempster. Yes. Where is he?"

"Over there by the winder," said Billie, gesturing. "What is it for, Haines?"

"You don't think I know, do you?" demanded the sergeant. He began to pipe sharply but cheerily at men upon the floor. "Come, Mac, get up here. Here's a special for you. Wake up, Jameson. Come along, Dannie, me boy."

Each man at once took this call to duty as a personal affront. They pulled themselves out of their blankets, rubbed their eyes, and swore

at whoever was responsible. "Them's orders,'
cried the sergeant. "Come! Get out of here."
An undetailed head with dishevelled hair thrust
out from a blanket, and a sleepy voice said : "Shut
up, Haines, and go home."

When the detail clanked out of the kitchen,
all but one of the remaining men seemed to be
again asleep. Billie, leaning on his elbow, was
gazing into darkness. When the footsteps died
to silence, he curled himself into his blanket.

At the first cool lavender lights of daybreak
he aroused again, and scanned his recumbent
companions. Seeing a wakeful one he asked: "Is
Dan back yet ? "

The man said : " Hain't seen 'im."

Billie put both hands behind his head, and
scowled into the air. " Can't see the use of these
cussed details in the night-time," he muttered in
his most unreasonable tones. "Darn nuisances.
Why can't they——" He grumbled at length and
graphically.

When Dan entered with the squad, however,
Billie was convincingly asleep.

IV

The regiment trotted in double time along the
street, and the colonel seemed to quarrel over
the right of way with many artillery officers.
Batteries were waiting in the mud, and the men

of them, exasperated by the bustle of this ambitious infantry, shook their fists from saddle and caisson, exchanging all manner of taunts and jests. The slanted guns continued to look reflectively at the ground.

On the outskirts of the crumbled town a fringe of blue figures were firing into the fog. The regiment swung out into skirmish lines, and the fringe of blue figures departed, turning their backs and going joyfully around the flank.

The bullets began a low moan off toward a ridge which loomed faintly in the heavy mist. When the swift crescendo had reached its climax, the missiles zipped just overhead, as if piercing an invisible curtain. A battery on the hill was crashing with such tumult that it was as if the guns had quarrelled and had fallen pell-mell and snarling upon each other. The shells howled on their journey toward the town. From short-range distance there came a spatter of musketry, sweeping along an invisible line, and making faint sheets of orange light.

Some in the new skirmish lines were beginning to fire at various shadows discerned in the vapour, forms of men suddenly revealed by some humour of the laggard masses of clouds. The crackle of musketry began to dominate the purring of the hostile bullets. Dan, in the front rank, held his rifle poised, and looked into the fog keenly, coldly, with the air of a sportsman. His nerves were so steady that it was as if they had been drawn from his body, leaving him merely a muscular machine; but his numb heart was somehow beating to the pealing march of the fight.

The waving skirmish line went backward and forward, ran this way and that way. Men got lost in the fog, and men were found again. Once they got too close to the formidable ridge, and the thing burst out as if repulsing a general attack. Once another blue regiment was apprehended on the very edge of firing into them. Once a friendly battery began an elaborate and scientific process of extermination. Always as busy as brokers, the men slid here and there over the plain, fighting their foes, escaping from their friends, leaving a history of many movements in the wet yellow turf, cursing the atmosphere, blazing away every time they could identify the enemy.

In one mystic changing of the fog, as if the fingers of spirits were drawing aside these draperies, a small group of the grey skirmishers, silent, statuesque, were suddenly disclosed to Dan and those about him. So vivid and near were they that there was something uncanny in the revelation.

There might have been a second of mutual staring. Then each rifle in each group was at the shoulder. As Dan's glance flashed along the barrel of his weapon, the figure of a man suddenly loomed as if the musket had been a telescope. The short black beard, the slouch hat, the pose of the man as he sighted to shoot, made a quick picture in Dan's mind. The same moment, it would seem, he pulled his own trigger, and the man, smitten, lurched forward, while his exploding rifle made a slanting crimson streak in the air, and the slouch hat fell before the body. The billows of the fog, governed·by singular impulses, rolled between.

"You got that feller sure enough," said a comrade to Dan. Dan looked at him absent-mindedly.

V

When the next morning calmly displayed another fog, the men of the regiment exchanged eloquent comments; but they did not abuse it at length, because the streets of the town now contained enough galloping aides to make three troops of cavalry, and they knew that they had come to the verge of the great fight.

Dan conversed with the man who had once possessed a horse-hair trunk; but they did not mention the line of hills which had furnished them in more careless moments with an agreeable topic. They avoided it now as condemned men do the subject of death, and yet the thought of it stayed in their eyes as they looked at each other and talked gravely of other things.

The expectant regiment heaved a long sigh of relief when the sharp call: "Fall in," repeated indefinitely, arose in the streets. It was inevitable that a bloody battle was to be fought, and they wanted to get it off their minds. They were, however, doomed again to spend a long period planted firmly in the mud. They craned their necks, and wondered where some of the other regiments were going.

At last the mists rolled carelessly away. Nature made at this time all provisions to enable foes to see each other, and immediately the roar of guns resounded from every hill. The endless cracking of the skirmishers swelled to rolling crashes of musketry. Shells screamed with panther-like noises at the houses. Dan looked at the man of the horse-hair trunk, and the man said: "Well, here she comes!"

The tenor voices of younger officers and the deep and hoarse voices of the older ones rang in the streets. These cries pricked like spurs. The masses of men vibrated from the suddenness with which they were plunged into the situation of troops about to fight. That the orders were long-expected did not concern the emotion.

Simultaneous movement was imparted to all these thick bodies of men and horses that lay in the town. Regiment after regiment swung rapidly into the streets that faced the sinister ridge.

This exodus was theatrical. The little sober-hued village had been like the cloak which disguises the king of drama. It was now put aside, and an army, splendid thing of steel and blue, stood forth in the sunlight.

Even the soldiers in the heavy columns drew deep breaths at the sight, more majestic than they had dreamed. The heights of the enemy's position were crowded with men who resembled people come to witness some mighty pageant. But as the column moved steadily to their positions, the guns, matter-of-fact warriors, doubled their number, and shells burst with red thrilling tumult on the crowded plain. One came into the ranks of the regiment, and after the smoke and the wrath of it had faded, leaving motionless figures, every one stormed according to the limits of his vocabulary, for veterans detest being killed when they are not busy.

The regiment sometimes looked sideways at its brigade companions composed of men who had never been in battle; but no frozen blood could withstand the heat of the splendour of this army before the eyes on the plain, these lines so long that the flanks were little streaks, this mass of men of one intention. The recruits carried themselves heedlessly. At the rear was an idle battery, and three artillerymen in a foolish row on a caisson nudged each other and grinned at the recruits. "You'll catch it pretty soon," they called out. They were impersonally gleeful, as if they themselves were not also likely to catch it pretty soon. But with this picture of an army in their hearts, the new men perhaps felt the devotion which the drops may feel for the wave; they were of its power and glory; they smiled jauntily at the foolish row of gunners, and told them to go to blazes.

The column trotted across some little bridges, and spread quickly into lines of battle. Before them was a bit of plain, and back of the plain was the ridge. There was no time left for considerations. The men were staring at the plain, mightily wondering how it would feel to be out there, when a brigade in advance yelled and charged. The hill was all grey smoke and fire-points.

That fierce elation in the terrors of war, catching a man's heart and making it burn with such ardour that he becomes capable of dying, flashed in the faces of the men like coloured lights, and made them resemble leashed animals, eager, ferocious, daunting at nothing. The line was really in its first leap before the wild, hoarse crying of the orders.

The greed for close quarters, which is the emotion of a bayonet charge, came then into the minds of the men and developed until it was a madness. The field, with its faded grass of a Southern winter, seemed to this fury miles in width.

High, slow-moving masses of smoke, with an odour of burning cotton, engulfed the line until the men might have been swimmers. Before them the ridge, the shore of this grey sea, was outlined, crossed, and recrossed by sheets of flame.   The howl of the battle arose to the noise of innumerable wind demons.

The line, galloping, scrambling, plunging like a herd of wounded horses, went over a field that was sown with corpses, the records of other charges.

Directly in front of the black-faced, whooping Dan, carousing in this onward sweep like a new kind of fiend, a wounded man appeared, raising his shattered body, and staring at this rush of men down upon him.   It seemed to occur to him that he was to be trampled; he made a desperate, piteous effort to escape; then finally huddled in a waiting heap.   Dan and the soldier near him widened the interval between them without looking down, without appearing to heed the wounded man.   This little clump of blue seemed to reel past them as boulders reel past a train.

Bursting through a smoke-wave, the scampering, unformed bunches came upon the wreck of the brigade that had preceded them, a floundering mass stopped afar from the hill by the swirling volleys.

It was as if a necromancer had suddenly shown them a picture of the fate which awaited them; but the line with muscular spasm hurled itself over this wreckage and onward, until men were stumbling amid the relics of other assaults, the point where the fire from the ridge consumed.

The men, panting, perspiring, with crazed faces, tried to push against it; but it was as if they had come to a wall. The wave halted, shuddered in an agony from the quick struggle of its two desires, then toppled, and broke into a fragmentary thing which has no name.

Veterans could now at last be distinguished from recruits. The new regiments were instantly gone, lost, scattered, as if they never had been. But the sweeping failure of the [charge, the battle, could not make the veterans forget their business. With a last throe, the band of maniacs drew itself up and blazed a volley at the hill, insignificant to those iron entrenchments, but nevertheless expressing that singular final despair which enables men coolly to defy the walls of a city of death.

After this episode the men renamed their command. They called it the Little Regiment.

VI

"I seen Dan shoot a feller yesterday. Yes, sir. I'm sure it was him that done it. And maybe he thinks about that feller now, and wonders if *he* tumbled down just about the same way. Them things come up in a man's mind."

Bivouac fires upon the sidewalks, in the streets, in the yards, threw high their wavering reflections, which examined, like slim, red fingers, the dingy, scarred walls and the piles of tumbled brick. The droning of voices again arose from great blue crowds.

The odour of frying bacon, the fragrance from countless little coffee-pails floated among the ruins. The rifles, stacked in the shadows, emitted flashes of steely light. Wherever a flag lay horizontally from one stack to another was the bed of an eagle which had led men into the mystic smoke.

The men about a particular fire were engaged in holding in check their jovial spirits. They moved whispering around the blaze, although they looked at it with a certain fine contentment, like labourers after a day's hard work.

There was one who sat apart. They did not address him save in tones suddenly changed. They did not regard him directly, but always in little sidelong glances.

At last a soldier from a distant fire came into this circle of light. He studied for a time the man who sat apart. Then he hesitatingly stepped closer, and said: "Got any news, Dan?"

"No," said Dan.

The new-comer shifted his feet. He looked at the fire, at the sky, at the other men, at Dan. His face expressed a curious despair; his tongue was plainly in rebellion. Finally, however, he contrived to say: "Well, there's some chance yet, Dan. Lots of the wounded are still lying out there, you know. There's some chance yet."

"Yes," said Dan.

The soldier shifted his feet again, and looked miserably into the air. After another struggle he said: "Well, there's some chance yet, Dan." He moved hastily away.

One of the men of the squad, perhaps encouraged by this example, now approached the still figure. "No news yet, hey?" he said, after coughing behind his hand.

"No," said Dan.

"Well," said the man, "I've been thinking of how he was fretting about you the night you went on special duty. You recollect? Well, sir, I was surprised. He couldn't say enough about it. I swan, I don't believe he slep' a wink after you left, but just lay awake cussing special duty and worrying. I was surprised. But there he lay cussing. He——"

Dan made a curious sound, as if a stone had wedged in his throat. He said: "Shut up, will you?"

Afterward the men would not allow this moody contemplation of the fire to be interrupted.

"Oh, let him alone, can't you?"

"Come away from there, Casey!"

"Say, can't you leave him be?"

They moved with reverence about the immovable figure, with its countenance of mask-like invulnerability.

VII

After the red round eye of the sun had stared long at the little plain and its burden, darkness, a sable mercy, came heavily upon it, and the wan hands of the dead were no longer seen in strange frozen gestures.

The heights in front of the plain shone with tiny camp-fires, and from the town in the rear, small shimmerings ascended from the blazes of the bivouac. The plain was a black expanse upon which, from time to time, dots of light, lanterns, floated slowly here and there. These fields were long steeped in grim mystery.

Suddenly, upon one dark spot, there was a resurrection. A strange thing had been groaning there, prostrate. Then it suddenly dragged itself to a sitting posture, and became a man.

The man stared stupidly for a moment at the lights on the hill, then turned and contemplated the faint colouring over the town. For some moments he remained thus, staring with dull eyes, his face unemotional, wooden.

Finally he looked around him at the corpses dimly to be seen. No change flashed into his face upon viewing these men. They seemed to suggest merely that his information concerning himself was not too complete. He ran his fingers over his arms and chest, bearing always the air of an idiot upon a bench at an almshouse door.

Finding no wound in his arms nor in his chest, he raised his hand to his head, and the fingers came away with some dark liquid upon them. Holding these fingers close to his eyes, he scanned them in the same stupid fashion, while his body gently swayed.

The soldier rolled his eyes again toward the town. When he arose, his clothing peeled from the frozen ground like wet paper. Hearing the sound of it, he seemed to see reason for deliberation. He paused and looked at the ground, then at his trousers, then at the ground.

Finally he went slowly off toward the faint reflection, holding his hands palm outward before him, and walking in the manner of a blind man.

VIII

The immovable Dan again sat unaddressed in the midst of comrades, who did not joke aloud. The dampness of the usual morning fog seemed to make the little camp-fires furious.

Suddenly a cry arose in the streets, a shout of amazement and delight. The men making breakfast at the fire looked up quickly. They broke forth in clamorous exclamation: "Well! Of all things! Dan! Dan! Look who's coming! Oh, Dan!"

Dan the silent raised his eyes and saw a man, with a bandage of the size of a helmet about his head, receiving a furious demonstration from the company. He was shaking hands, and explaining, and haranguing to a high degree.

Dan started. His face of bronze flushed to his temples. He seemed about to leap from the ground, but then suddenly he sank back, and resumed his impassive gazing.

The men were in a flurry. They looked from one to the other. "Dan! Look! See who's coming!" some cried again. "Dan! Look!"

He scowled at last, and moved his shoulders sullenly. "Well, don't I know it?"

But they could not be convinced that his eyes were in service. "Dan, why can't you look! See who's coming!"

He made a gesture then of irritation and rage. "Curse it! Don't I know it?"

The man with a bandage of the size of a helmet moved forward, always shaking hands and explaining. At times his glance wandered to Dan, who saw with his eyes riveted.

After a series of shiftings, it occurred naturally that the man with the bandage was very near to the man who saw the flames. He paused, and there was a little silence. Finally he said: "Hello, Dan."

"Hello, Billie."

Three Miraculous Soldiers

Three Miraculous Soldiers

I

THE girl was in the front room on the second floor, peering through the blinds. It was the "best room." There was a very new rag carpet on the floor. The edges of it had been dyed with alternate stripes of red and green. Upon the wooden mantel there were two little puffy figures in clay—a shepherd and a shepherdess probably. A triangle of pink and white wool hung carefully over the edge of this shelf. Upon the bureau there was nothing at all save a spread newspaper, with edges folded to make it into a mat. The quilts and sheets had been removed from the bed and were stacked upon a chair. The pillows and the great feather mattress were muffled and tumbled until they resembled great dumplings. The picture of a man terribly leaden in complexion hung in an oval frame on one white wall and steadily confronted the bureau.

From between the slats of the blinds she had a view of the road as it wended across the meadow

229

to the woods, and again where it reappeared crossing the hill, half a mile away. It lay yellow and warm in the summer sunshine. From the long grasses of the meadow came the rhythmic click of the insects. Occasional frogs in the hidden brook made a peculiar chug-chug sound, as if somebody throttled them. The leaves of the wood swung in gentle winds. Through the dark-green branches of the pines that grew in the front yard could be seen the mountains, far to the south-east, and inexpressibly blue.

Mary's eyes were fastened upon the little streak of road that appeared on the distant hill. Her face was flushed with excitement, and the hand which stretched in a strained pose on the sill trembled because of the nervous shaking of the wrist. The pines whisked their green needles with a soft, hissing sound against the house.

At last the girl turned from the window and went to the head of the stairs. " Well, I just know they're coming, anyhow," she cried argumentatively to the depths.

A voice from below called to her angrily : " They ain't. We've never seen one yet. They never come into this neighbourhood. You just come down here and 'tend to your work insteader watching for soldiers."

" Well, ma, I just know they're coming."

A voice retorted with the shrillness and mechanical violence of occasional housewives.

The girl swished her skirts defiantly and returned to the window.

Upon the yellow streak of road that lay across the hillside there now was a handful of black dots—horsemen. A cloud of dust floated away. The girl flew to the head of the stairs and whirled down into the kitchen.

"They're coming! They're coming!"

It was as if she had cried "Fire!" Her mother had been peeling potatoes while seated comfortably at the table. She sprang to her feet. "No—it can't be — how you know it's them — where?" The stubby knife fell from her hand, and two or three curls of potato skin dropped from her apron to the floor.

The girl turned and dashed upstairs. Her mother followed, gasping for breath, and yet contriving to fill the air with questions, reproach, and remonstrance. The girl was already at the window, eagerly pointing. "There! There! See 'em! See 'em!"

Rushing to the window, the mother scanned for an instant the road on the hill. She crouched back with a groan. "It's them, sure as the world! It's them!" She waved her hands in despairing gestures.

The black dots vanished into the wood. The girl at the window was quivering and her eyes were shining like water when the sun flashes. "Hush! They're in the woods! They'll be here directly." She bent down and intently watched the green archway whence the road emerged. "Hush! I hear 'em coming," she swiftly whispered to her mother, for the elder woman had dropped dolefully upon the mattress and was sobbing. And, indeed, the girl could hear the quick, dull trample of horses. She stepped aside with sudden apprehension, but she bent her head forward in order to still scan the road.

"Here they are!"

There was something very theatrical in the sudden appearance of these men to the eyes of the girl. It was as if a scene had been shifted. The forest suddenly disclosed them — a dozen brown-faced troopers in blue—galloping.

"Oh, look!" breathed the girl. Her mouth was puckered into an expression of strange fascination, as if she had expected to see the troopers change into demons and gloat at her. She was at last looking upon those curious beings who rode down from the North—those men of legend and colossal tale—they who were possessed of such marvellous hallucinations.

The little troop rode in silence. At its head was a youthful fellow with some dim yellow stripes upon his arm. In his right hand he held his carbine, slanting upward, with the stock resting upon his knee. He was absorbed in a scrutiny of the country before him.

At the heels of the sergeant the rest of the squad rode in thin column, with creak of leather and tinkle of steel and tin.   The girl scanned the faces of the horsemen, seeming astonished vaguely to find them of the type she knew.

The lad at the head of the troop comprehended the house and its environments in two glances. He did not check the long, swinging stride of his horse.   The troopers glanced for a moment like casual tourists, and then returned to their study of the region in front.   The heavy thudding of the hoofs became a small noise.   The dust, hanging in sheets, slowly sank.

The sobs of the woman on the bed took form in words which, while strong in their note of calamity, yet expressed a querulous mental reaching for some near thing to blame.   "And it'll be lucky fer us if we ain't both butchered in our sleep—plundering and running off horses —old Santo's gone—you see if he ain't—plundering——"

"But, ma," said the girl, perplexed and terrified in the same moment, "they've gone."

"Oh, but they'll come back!" cried the mother, without pausing her wail.   "They'll come back— trust them for that—running off horses.   O John, John! why did you, why did you?"   She suddenly lifted herself and sat rigid, staring at her daughter. "Mary," she said in tragic whisper, "the kitchen door isn't locked!"   Already she was bended forward to listen, her mouth agape, her eyes fixed upon her daughter.

"Mother," faltered the girl.

Her mother again whispered, "The kitchen door isn't locked."

Motionless and mute they stared into each other's eyes.

At last the girl quavered, "We better — we better go and lock it." The mother nodded. Hanging arm in arm they stole across the floor toward the head of the stairs. A board of the floor creaked. They halted and exchanged a look of dumb agony.

At last they reached the head of the stairs. From the kitchen came the bass humming of the kettle and frequent sputterings and cracklings from the fire. These sounds were sinister. The mother and the girl stood incapable of movement. "There's somebody down there!" whispered the elder woman.

Finally, the girl made a gesture of resolution. She twisted her arm from her mother's hands and went two steps downward. She addressed the kitchen: "Who's there?" Her tone was intended to be dauntless. It rang so dramatically in the silence that a sudden new panic seized them as if the suspected presence in the kitchen had cried out to them. But the girl ventured again: "Is there anybody there?" No reply was made save by the kettle and the fire.

With a stealthy tread the girl continued her journey. As she neared the last step the fire crackled explosively and the girl screamed. But the mystic presence had not swept around the corner to grab her, so she dropped to a seat on the step and laughed. "It was—was only the —the fire," she said, stammering hysterically.

Then she arose with sudden fortitude and cried: "Why, there isn't anybody there! I know there isn't." She marched down into the kitchen. In her face was dread, as if she half expected to confront something, but the room was empty. She cried joyously: There's nobody here! Come on down, ma." She ran to the kitchen door and locked it.

The mother came down to the kitchen. "Oh, dear, what a fright I've had! It's given me the sick headache. I know it has."

"Oh, ma," said the girl.

"I know it has—I know it. Oh, if your father was only here! He'd settle those Yankees mighty quick—he'd settle 'em! Two poor helpless women——"

"Why, ma, what makes you act so? The Yankees haven't——"

"Oh, they'll be back—they'll be back. Two poor helpless women! Your father and your uncle Asa and Bill off galavanting around and fighting when they ought to be protecting their home! That's the kind of men they are. Didn't I say to your father just before he left——"

"Ma," said the girl, coming suddenly from the window, "the barn door is open. I wonder if they took old Santo?"

"Oh, of course they have—of course——Mary

I don't see what we are going to do—I don't see what we are going to do."

The girl said, "Ma, I'm going to see if they took old Santo."

"Mary," cried the mother, "don't you dare!"

"But think of poor old Sant, ma."

"Never you mind old Santo. We're lucky to be safe ourselves, I tell you. Never mind old Santo. Don't you dare to go out there, Mary— Mary!"

The girl had unlocked the door and stepped out upon the porch. The mother cried in despair, "Mary!"

"Why, there isn't anybody out here," the girl called in response. She stood for a moment with a curious smile upon her face as of gleeful satisfaction at her daring.

The breeze was waving the boughs of the apple trees. A rooster with an air importantly courteous was conducting three hens upon a foraging tour. On the hillside at the rear of the grey old barn the red leaves of a creeper flamed amid the summer foliage. High in the sky clouds rolled toward the north. The girl swung impulsively from the little stoop and ran toward the barn.

The great door was open, and the carved peg which usually performed the office of a catch lay on the ground. The girl could not see into the barn because of the heavy shadows. She paused in a listening attitude and heard a horse munching placidly. She gave a cry of delight and sprang across the threshold. Then she suddenly shrank back and gasped. She had confronted three men in grey seated upon the floor with their legs stretched out and their backs against Santo's manger. Their dust-covered countenances were expanded in grins.

II

As Mary sprang backward and screamed, one of the calm men in grey, still grinning, announced, "I knowed you'd holler." Sitting there comfortably the three surveyed her with amusement.

Mary caught her breath, throwing her hand up to her throat. "Oh!" she said, "you—you frightened me!"

"We're sorry, lady, but couldn't help it no way," cheerfully responded another. "I knowed you'd holler when I seen you coming yere, but I raikoned we couldn't help it no way. We hain't a-troubling this yere barn, I don't guess. We been doing some mighty tall sleeping yere. We done woke when them Yanks loped past."

"Where did you come from? Did—did you escape from the—the Yankees?" The girl still stammered and trembled.

The three soldiers laughed. "No, m'm. No, m'm. They never cotch us. We was in a muss down the road yere about two mile. And Bill

yere they gin it to him in the arm, kehplunk.
And they pasted me thar, too. Curious. And
Sim yere, he didn't get nothing, but they chased
us all quite a little piece, and we done lose track
of our boys."

"Was it—was it those who passed here just
now? Did they chase you?"

The men in grey laughed again. "What—
them? No, indeedee! There was a mighty big
swarm of Yanks and a mighty big swarm of
our boys, too. What—that little passel? No,
m'm."

She became calm enough to scan them more
attentively. They were much begrimed and
very dusty. Their grey clothes were tattered.
Splashed mud had dried upon them in reddish
spots. It appeared, too, that the men had not
shaved in many days. In the hats there was a
singular diversity. One soldier wore the little
blue cap of the Northern infantry, with corps
emblem and regimental number; one wore a
great slouch hat with a wide hole in the crown;
and the other wore no hat at all. The left sleeve
of one man and the right sleeve of another had
been slit, and the arms were neatly bandaged with
clean cloths. "These hain't no more than two
little cuts," explained one. "We stopped up
yere to Mis' Leavitts—she said her name was—
and she bind them for us. Bill yere, he had
the thirst come on him. And the fever too.
We——"

"Did you ever see my father in the army?" asked Mary. "John Hinckson—his name is."

The three soldiers grinned again, but they replied kindly: "No, m'm. No, m'm, we hain't never. What is he—in the cavalry?"

"No," said the girl. "He and my uncle Asa and my cousin—his name is Bill Parker—they are all with Longstreet—they call him."

"Oh," said the soldiers. "Longstreet? Oh, they're a good smart ways from yere. 'Way off up nawtheast. There hain't nothing but cavalry down yere. They're in the infantry, probably."

"We haven't heard anything from them for days and days," said Mary.

"Oh, they're all right in the infantry," said one man, to be consoling. "The infantry don't do much fighting. They go bellering out in a big swarm and only a few of 'em get hurt. But if they was in the cavalry—the cavalry——"

Mary interrupted him without intention. "Are you hungry?" she asked.

The soldiers looked at each other, struck by some sudden and singular shame. They hung their heads. "No, m'm," replied one at last.

Santo, in his stall, was tranquilly chewing and chewing. Sometimes he looked benevolently over at them. He was an old horse, and there was something about his eyes and his forelock which created the impression that he wore spectacles. Mary went and patted his nose. "Well, if you are hungry, I can get you something," she told the men. "Or you might come to the house."

"We wouldn't dast go to the house," said one. "That passel of Yanks was only a scouting crowd, most like. Just an advance. More coming, likely."

"Well, I can bring you something," cried the girl eagerly. "Won't you let me bring you something?"

"Well," said a soldier with embarrassment, "we hain't had much. If you could bring us a little snack-like—just a snack—we'd——"

Without waiting for him to cease, the girl turned toward the door. But before she had reached it she stopped abruptly. "Listen!" she whispered. Her form was bent forward, her head turned and lowered, her hand extended toward the men, in a command for silence.

They could faintly hear the thudding of many hoofs, the clank of arms, and frequent calling voices.

"By cracky, it's the Yanks!" The soldiers scrambled to their feet and came toward the door. "I knowed that first crowd was only an advance."

The girl and the three men peered from the shadows of the barn. The view of the road was intersected by tree trunks and a little henhouse. However, they could see many horsemen streaming down the road. The horsemen were in blue. "Oh, hide—hide—hide!" cried the girl, with a sob in her voice.

"Wait a minute," whispered a grey soldier excitedly. "Maybe they're going along by. No, by thunder, they hain't! They're halting. Scoot, boys!"

They made a noiseless dash into the dark end of the barn. The girl, standing by the door, heard them break forth an instant later in clamorous whispers. "Where'll we hide? Where'll we hide? There hain't a place to hide!" The girl turned and glanced wildly about the barn. It seemed true. The stock of hay had grown low under Santo's endless munching, and from occasional levyings by passing troopers in grey. The poles of the mow were barely covered, save in one corner where there was a little bunch.

The girl espied the great feed-box. She ran to it and lifted the lid. "Here! here!" she called. "Get in here."

They had been tearing noiselessly around the rear part of the barn. At her low call they came and plunged at the box. They did not all get in at the same moment without a good deal of a tangle. The wounded men gasped and muttered, but they at last were flopped down on the layer of feed which covered the bottom. Swiftly and softly the girl lowered the lid and then turned like a flash toward the door.

No one appeared there, so she went close to survey the situation. The troopers had dismounted, and stood in silence by their horses.

A grey-bearded man, whose red cheeks and nose
shone vividly above the whiskers, was strolling
about with two or three others. They wore
double-breasted coats, and faded yellow sashes
were wound under their black leather sword-
belts. The grey-bearded soldier was apparently
giving orders, pointing here and there.

Mary tiptoed to the feed-box. "They've all
got off their horses," she said to it. A finger
projected from a knot-hole near the top, and said
to her very plainly, "Come closer." She obeyed,
and then a muffled voice could be heard: "Scoot
for the house, lady, and if we don't see you again,
why, much obliged for what you done."

"Good-bye," she said to the feed-box.

She made two attempts to walk dauntlessly
from the barn, but each time she faltered and
failed just before she reached the point where she
could have been seen by the blue-coated troopers.
At last, however, she made a sort of a rush forward and went out into the bright sunshine.

The group of men in double-breasted coats
wheeled in her direction at the instant. The
grey-bearded officer forgot to lower his arm which
had been stretched forth in giving an order.

She felt that her feet were touching the
ground in a most unnatural manner. Her bearing, she believed, was suddenly grown awkward
and ungainly. Upon her face she thought that
this sentence was plainly written: "There are
three men hidden in the feed-box."

The grey-bearded soldier came toward her. She stopped; she seemed about to run away. But the soldier doffed his little blue cap and looked amiable. "You live here, I presume?" he said.

"Yes," she answered.

"Well, we are obliged to camp here for the night, and as we've got two wounded men with us I don't suppose you'd mind if we put them in the barn."

"In—in the barn?"

He became aware that she was agitated. He smiled assuringly. "You needn't be frightened. We won't hurt anything around here. You'll all be safe enough."

The girl balanced on one foot and swung the other to and fro in the grass. She was looking down at it. "But—but I don't think ma would like it if—if you took the barn."

The old officer laughed. "Wouldn't she?" said he. "That's so. Maybe she wouldn't." He reflected for a time and then decided cheerfully: "Well, we will have to go ask her, anyhow. Where is she? In the house?"

"Yes," replied the girl, "she's in the house. She—she'll be scared to death when she sees you!"

"Well, you go and ask her then," said the soldier, always wearing a benign smile. "You go ask her and then come and tell me."

When the girl pushed open the door and

entered the kitchen, she found it empty. "Ma!" she called softly. There was no answer. The kettle still was humming its low song. The knife and the curl of potato-skin lay on the floor.

She went to her mother's room and entered timidly. The new, lonely aspect of the house shook her nerves. Upon the bed was a confusion of coverings. "Ma!" called the girl, quaking in fear that her mother was not there to reply. But there was a sudden turmoil of the quilts, and her mother's head was thrust forth. "Mary!" she cried, in what seemed to be a supreme astonishment, "I thought—I thought——"

"Oh, ma," blurted the girl, "there's over a thousand Yankees in the yard, and I've hidden three of our men in the feed-box!"

The elder woman, however, upon the appearance of her daughter had begun to thrash hysterically about on the bed and wail.

"Ma!" the girl exclaimed, "and now they want to use the barn—and our men in the feed-box! What shall I do, ma? What shall I do?"

Her mother did not seem to hear, so absorbed was she in her grievous flounderings and tears. "Ma!" appealed the girl. "Ma!"

For a moment Mary stood silently debating, her lips apart, her eyes fixed. Then she went to the kitchen window and peeked.

The old officer and the others were staring up the road. She went to another window in order to get a proper view of the road, and saw that they were gazing at a small body of horsemen approaching at a trot and raising much dust. Presently she recognised them as the squad that had passed the house earlier, for the young man with the dim yellow chevron still rode at their head.   An unarmed horseman in grey was receiving their close attention.

As they came very near to the house she darted to the first window again. The grey-bearded officer was smiling a fine broad smile of satisfaction. "So you got him?" he called out. The young sergeant sprang from his horse and his brown hand moved in a salute. The girl could not hear his reply. She saw the unarmed horseman in grey stroking a very black moustache and looking about him coolly and with an interested air.   He appeared so indifferent that she did not understand he was a prisoner until she heard the grey-beard call out: "Well, put him in the barn. He'll be safe there, I guess." A party of troopers moved with the prisoner toward the barn.

The girl made a sudden gesture of horror, remembering the three men in the feed-box.

III

The busy troopers in blue scurried about the long lines of stamping horses. Men crooked their

backs and perspired in order to rub with cloths
or bunches of grass these slim equine legs,
upon whose splendid machinery they depended
so greatly. The lips of the horses were still
wet and frothy from the steel bars which had
wrenched at their mouths all day. Over their
backs and about their noses sped the talk of the
men.

"Moind where yer plug is steppin', Finerty!
Keep 'im aff me!"

"An ould elephant! He shtrides like a school-
house."

"Bill's little mar'—she was plum beat when she
come in with Crawford's crowd."

"Crawford's the hardest-ridin' cavalryman in
the army. An' he don't use up a horse, neither
—much. They stay fresh when the others are
most a-droppin'."

"Finerty, will yeh moind that cow a yours?"

Amid a bustle of gossip and banter, the horses
retained their air of solemn rumination, twisting
their lower jaws from side to side and sometimes
rubbing noses dreamfully.

Over in front of the barn three troopers sat
talking comfortably. Their carbines were leaned
against the wall. At their side and outlined in
the black of the open door stood a sentry, his
weapon resting in the hollow of his arm. Four
horses, saddled and accoutred, were conferring
with their heads close together. The four bridle-
reins were flung over a post.

Upon the calm green of the land, typical in every way of peace, the hues of war brought thither by the troops shone strangely. Mary, gazing curiously, did not feel that she was contemplating a familiar scene. It was no longer the home acres. The new blue, steel, and faded yellow thoroughly dominated the old green and brown. She could hear the voices of the men, and it seemed from their tone that they had camped there for years. Everything with them was usual. They had taken possession of the landscape in such a way that even the old marks appeared strange and formidable to the girl.

Mary had intended to go and tell the commander in blue that her mother did not wish his men to use the barn at all, but she paused when she heard him speak to the sergeant. She thought she perceived then that it mattered little to him what her mother wished, and that an objection by her or by anybody would be futile. She saw the soldiers conduct the prisoner in grey into the barn, and for a long time she watched the three chatting guards and the pondering sentry. Upon her mind in desolate weight was the recollection of the three men in the feed-box.

It seemed to her that in a case of this description it was her duty to be a heroine. In all the stories she had read when at boarding-school in Pennsylvania, the girl characters, confronted with such difficulties, invariably did hair-breadth things. True, they were usually bent upon rescuing and recovering their lovers, and neither the calm man in grey, nor any of the three in the feed-box, was lover of hers, but then a real heroine would not pause over this minor question. Plainly a heroine would take measures to rescue the four men. If she did not at least make the attempt, she would be false to those carefully constructed ideals which were the accumulation of years of dreaming.

But the situation puzzled her. There was the barn with only one door, and with four armed troopers in front of this door, one of them with his back to the rest of the world, engaged, no doubt, in a steadfast contemplation of the calm man, and incidentally, of the feed-box. She knew, too, that even if she should open the kitchen door, three heads, and perhaps four, would turn casually in her direction. Their ears were real ears.

Heroines, she knew, conducted these matters with infinite precision and despatch. They severed the hero's bonds, cried a dramatic sentence, and stood between him and his enemies until he had run far enough away. She saw well, however, that even should she achieve all things up to the point where she might take glorious stand between the escaping and the pursuers, those grim troopers in blue would not pause. They would run around her, make a circuit. One by one she saw the gorgeous contrivances and expedients of fiction fall before the

plain, homely difficulties of this situation.   They
were of no service.   Sadly, ruefully, she thought
of the calm man and of the contents of the feed-
box.

The sum of her invention was that she could
sally forth to the commander of the blue cavalry,
and confessing to him that there were three of
her friends and his enemies secreted in the feed-
box, pray him to let them depart unmolested.
But she was beginning to believe the old grey-
beard to be a bear.   It was hardly probable that
he would give this plan his support.   It was
more probable that he and some of his men
would at once descend upon the feed-box and
confiscate her three friends.   The difficulty with
her idea was that she could not learn its value
without trying it, and then in case of failure it
would be too late for remedies and other plans.
She reflected that war made men very unreasonable.

All that she could do was to stand at the
window and mournfully regard the barn.   She
admitted this to herself with a sense of deep
humiliation.   She was not, then, made of that
fine stuff, that mental satin, which enabled some
other beings to be of such mighty service to the
distressed.   She was defeated by a barn with
one door, by four men with eight eyes and eight
ears—trivialities that would not impede the real
heroine.

The vivid white light of broad day began

slowly to fade. Tones of grey came upon the fields, and the shadows were of lead. In this more sombre atmosphere the fires built by the troops down in the far end of the orchard grew more brilliant, becoming spots of crimson colour in the dark grove.

The girl heard a fretting voice from her mother's room. "Mary!" She hastily obeyed the call. She perceived that she had quite forgotten her mother's existence in this time of excitement.

The elder woman still lay upon the bed. Her face was flushed and perspiration stood amid new wrinkles upon her forehead. Weaving wild glances from side to side, she began to whimper. "Oh, I'm just sick—I'm just sick! Have those men gone yet? Have they gone?"

The girl smoothed a pillow carefully for her mother's head. "No, ma. They're here yet. But they haven't hurt anything—it doesn't seem. Will I get you something to eat?"

Her mother gestured her away with the impatience of the ill. "No—no—just don't bother me. My head is splitting, and you know very well that nothing can be done for me when I get one of these spells. It's trouble—that's what makes them. When are those men going? Look here, don't you go 'way. You stick close to the house now."

"I'll stay right here," said the girl. She sat in the gloom and listened to her mother's incessant moaning. When she attempted to move, her mother cried out at her. When she desired to ask if she might try to alleviate the pain, she was interrupted shortly. Somehow her sitting in passive silence within hearing of this illness seemed to contribute to her mother's relief. She assumed a posture of submission. Sometimes her mother projected questions concerning the local condition, and although she laboured to be graphic and at the same time soothing, un-alarming, her form of reply was always displeasing to the sick woman, and brought forth ejaculations of angry impatience.

Eventually the woman slept in the manner of one worn from terrible labour. The girl went slowly and softly to the kitchen. When she looked from the window, she saw the four soldiers still at the barn door. In the west, the sky was yellow. Some tree-trunks intersecting it appeared black as streaks of ink. Soldiers hovered in blue clouds about the bright splendour of the fires in the orchard. There were glimmers of steel.

The girl sat in the new gloom of the kitchen and watched. The soldiers lit a lantern and hung it in the barn. Its rays made the form of the sentry seem gigantic. Horses whinnied from the orchard. There was a low hum of human voices. Sometimes small detachments of troopers rode past the front of the house. The girl heard the abrupt calls of sentries. She fetched some food and ate it from her hand, standing by the window. She was so afraid that something would occur that she barely left her post for an instant.

A picture of the interior of the barn hung vividly in her mind. She recalled the knot-holes in the boards at the rear, but she admitted that the prisoners could not escape through them. She remembered some inadequacies of the roof, but these also counted for nothing. When confronting the problem, she felt her ambitions, her ideals tumbling headlong like cottages of straw.

Once she felt that she had decided to reconnoitre at any rate. It was night; the lantern at the barn and the camp fires made everything without their circle into masses of heavy mystic blackness. She took two steps toward the door. But there she paused. Innumerable possibilities of danger had assailed her mind. She returned to the window and stood wavering. At last, she went swiftly to the door, opened it, and slid noiselessly into the darkness.

For a moment she regarded the shadows. Down in the orchard the camp fires of the troops appeared precisely like a great painting, all in reds upon a black cloth. The voices of the troopers still hummed. The girl started slowly off in the opposite direction. Her eyes were fixed in a stare; she studied the darkness in front for a moment, before she ventured upon a forward step. Unconsciously, her throat was arranged for a sudden shrill scream. High in the tree-branches she could hear the voice of the wind, a melody of the night, low and sad, the plaint of an endless, incommunicable sorrow. Her own distress, the plight of the men in grey—·these near matters as well as all she had known or imagined of grief — everything was expressed in this soft mourning of the wind in the trees. At first she felt like weeping. This sound told her of human impotency and doom. Then later the trees and the wind breathed strength to her, sang of sacrifice, of dauntless effort, of hard carven faces that did not blanch when Duty came at midnight or at noon.

She turned often to scan the shadowy figures that moved from time to time in the light at the barn door. Once she trod upon a stick, and it flopped, crackling in the intolerable manner of all sticks. At this noise, however, the guards at the barn made no sign. Finally, she was where she could see the knot-holes in the rear of the structure gleaming like pieces of metal from the effect of the light within. Scarcely breathing in her excitement she glided close and applied an eye to a knot-hole. She had barely achieved one glance at the interior before she sprang back shuddering.

For the unconscious and cheerful sentry at the door was swearing away in flaming sentences, heaping one gorgeous oath upon another, making a conflagration of his description of his troop-horse.

"Why," he was declaring to the calm prisoner in grey, "you ain't got a horse in your hull —— army that can run forty rod with that there little mar'!"

As in the outer darkness Mary cautiously returned to the knot-hole, the three guards in front suddenly called in low tones: "S-s-s-h!" "Quit, Pete; here comes the lieutenant." The sentry had apparently been about to resume his declamation, but at these warnings he suddenly posed in a soldierly manner.

A tall and lean officer with a smooth face entered the barn. The sentry saluted primly. The officer flashed a comprehensive glance about him. "Everything all right?"

"All right, sir."

This officer had eyes like the points of stilettos. The lines from his nose to the corners of his mouth were deep, and gave him a slightly disagreeable aspect, but somewhere in his face there was a quality of singular thoughtfulness, as of the absorbed student dealing in generalities, which was utterly in opposition to the rapacious keenness of the eyes which saw everything.

Suddenly he lifted a long finger and pointed. "What's that?"

"That? That's a feed-box, I suppose."

"What's in it?"

"I don't know. I——"

"You ought to know," said the officer sharply. He walked over to the feed-box and flung up the lid. With a sweeping gesture he reached down and scooped a handful of feed. " You ought to know what's in everything when you have prisoners in your care," he added, scowling.

During the time of this incident, the girl had nearly swooned. Her hands searched weakly over the boards for something to which to cling. With the pallor of the dying she had watched the downward sweep of the officer's arm, which after all had only brought forth a handful of feed. The result was a stupefaction of her mind. She was astonished out of her senses at this spectacle of three large men metamorphosed into a handful of feed.

IV

It is perhaps a singular thing that this absence of the three men from the feed-box at the time of the sharp lieutenant's investigation should terrify the girl more than it should joy her. That for which she had prayed had come to pass. Apparently the escape of these men in the face of every improbability had been granted her, but her dominating emotion was fright. The feed-box was a mystic and terrible machine, like some dark magician's trap. She felt it almost possible that she should see the three weird men floating spectrally away through the air. She glanced with swift apprehension behind her, and when the dazzle from the lantern's light had left her eyes, saw only the dim hillside stretched in solemn silence.

The interior of the barn possessed for her another fascination because it was now uncanny. It contained that extraordinary feed-box. When she peeped again at the knot-hole, the calm, grey prisoner was seated upon the feed-box, thumping it with his dangling, careless heels as if it were in nowise his conception of a remarkable feed-box. The sentry also stood facing it. His carbine he held in the hollow of his arm. His legs were spread apart, and he mused. From without came the low mumble of the three other troopers. The sharp lieutenant had vanished.

The trembling yellow light of the lantern caused the figures of the men to cast monstrous wavering shadows. There were spaces of gloom which shrouded ordinary things in impressive garb. The roof presented an inscrutable blackness, save where small rifts in the shingles glowed phosphorescently. Frequently old Santo put down a thunderous hoof. The heels of the prisoner made a sound like the booming of a wild kind of drum. When the men moved their heads, their eyes shone with ghoulish whiteness, and their complexions were always waxen and unreal. And there was that profoundly strange feed-box, imperturbable with its burden of fantastic mystery.

Suddenly from down near her feet the girl heard a crunching sound, a sort of a nibbling, as if some silent and very discreet terrier was at work upon the turf. She faltered back; here was no doubt another grotesque detail of this most unnatural episode. She did not run, because physically she was in the power of these events. Her feet chained her to the ground in submission to this march of terror after terror. As she stared at the spot from which this sound seemed to come, there floated through her mind a vague, sweet vision—a vision of her safe little room, in which at this hour she usually was sleeping.

The scratching continued faintly and with frequent pauses, as if the terrier was then listening. When the girl first removed her eyes from the knot-hole the scene appeared of one velvet blackness; then gradually objects loomed with a dim lustre. She could see now where the tops of the trees joined the sky and the form of the barn was before her dyed in heavy purple. She was ever about to shriek, but no sound came from her constricted throat. She gazed at the ground with the expression of countenance of one who watches the sinister-moving grass where a serpent approaches.

Dimly she saw a piece of sod wrenched free and drawn under the great foundation-beam of the barn. Once she imagined that she saw human hands, not outlined at all, but sufficient,

*

in colour, form, or movement to make subtle
suggestion.

Then suddenly a thought that illuminated the
entire situation flashed in her mind like a light.
The three men, late of the feed-box, were beneath
the floor of the barn and were now scraping their
way under this beam. She did not consider for
a moment how they could come there. They
were marvellous creatures. The supernatural was
to be expected of them. She no longer trembled,
for she was possessed upon this instant of the
most unchangeable species of conviction. The
evidence before her amounted to no evidence at
all, but nevertheless her opinion grew in an
instant from an irresponsible acorn to a rooted
and immovable tree. It was as if she was on
a jury.

She stooped down hastily and scanned the
ground. There she indeed saw a pair of hands
hauling at the dirt where the sod had been dis-
placed. Softly, in a whisper like a breath, she
said, " Hey ! "

The dim hands were drawn hastily under the
barn. The girl reflected for a moment. Then she
stooped and whispered : " Hey ! It's me ! "

After a time there was a resumption of the
digging. The ghostly hands began once more
their cautious mining. She waited. In hollow reverberations from the interior of the barn came
the frequent sounds of old Santo's lazy movements. The sentry conversed with the prisoner.

At last the girl saw a head thrust slowly from under the beam. She perceived the face of one of the miraculous soldiers from the feed-box. A pair of eyes glintered and wavered, then finally settled upon her, a pale statue of a girl. The eyes became lit with a kind of humorous greeting. An arm gestured at her.

Stooping, she breathed, "All right." The man drew himself silently back under the beam. A moment later the pair of hands resumed their cautious task. Ultimately the head and arms of the man were thrust strangely from the earth. He was lying on his back. The girl thought of the dirt in his hair. Wriggling slowly and pushing at the beam above him he forced his way out of the curious little passage. He twisted his body and raised himself upon his hands. He grinned at the girl and drew his feet carefully from under the beam. When he at last stood erect beside her, he at once began mechanically to brush the dirt from his clothes with his hands. In the barn the sentry and his prisoner were evidently engaged in an argument.

The girl and the first miraculous soldier signalled warily. It seemed that they feared that their arms would make noises in passing through the air. Their lips moved, conveying dim meanings.

In this sign-language the girl described the situation in the barn. With guarded motions, she told him of the importance of absolute stillness. He nodded, and then in the same manner he told her of his two companions under the barn floor. He informed her again of their wounded state, and wagged his head to express his despair. He contorted his face, to tell how sore were their arms; and jabbed the air mournfully, to express their remote geographical position.

This signalling was interrupted by the sound of a body being dragged or dragging itself with slow, swishing sound under the barn. The sound was too loud for safety. They rushed to the hole and began to semaphore until a shaggy head appeared with rolling eyes and quick grin.

With frantic downward motions of their arms they suppressed this grin and with it the swishing noise. In dramatic pantomime they informed this head of the terrible consequences of so much noise. The head nodded, and painfully, but with extreme care, the second man pushed and pulled himself from the hole.

In a faint whisper the first man said, " Where's Sim ? "

The second man made low reply : " He's right here." He motioned reassuringly toward the hole.

When the third head appeared, a soft smile of glee came upon each face, and the mute group exchanged expressive glances.

When they all stood together, free from this tragic barn, they breathed a long sigh that was contemporaneous with another smile and another exchange of glances.

One of the men tiptoed to a knot-hole and peered into the barn. The sentry was at that moment speaking. "Yes, we know 'em all. There isn't a house in this region that we don't know who is in it most of the time. We collar 'em once in a while—like we did you. Now, that house out yonder, we——"

The man suddenly left the knot-hole and returned to the others. Upon his face, dimly discerned, there was an indication that he had made an astonishing discovery. The others questioned him with their eyes, but he simply waved an arm to express his inability to speak at that spot. He led them back toward the hill, prowling carefully. At a safe distance from the barn he halted, and as they grouped eagerly about him, he exploded in an intense undertone: "Why, that—that's Cap'n Sawyer they got in yonder."

"Cap'n Sawyer!" incredulously whispered the other men.

But the girl had something to ask. "How did you get out of that feed-box?" He smiled. "Well, when you put us in there, we was just in a minute when we allowed it wasn't a mighty safe place, and we allowed we'd get out. And we did. We skedaddled 'round and 'round until it 'peared like we was going to get cotched, and then we flung ourselves down in the cow-stalls where it's low-like—just dirt floor—and then we just naturally went a-whooping under the barn floor when the Yanks come. And we didn't know

Cap'n Sawyer by his voice nohow. We heard 'im discoursing, and we allowed it was a mighty pert man, but we didn't know that it was him. No, m'm."

These three men, so recently from a situation of peril, seemed suddenly to have dropped all thought of it. They stood with sad faces looking at the barn. They seemed to be making no plans at all to reach a place of more complete safety. They were halted and stupefied by some unknown calamity.

"How do you raikon they cotch him, Sim?" one whispered mournfully.

"I don't know," replied another in the same tone.

Another with a low snarl expressed in two words his opinion of the methods of Fate: "Oh, hell!"

The three men started then as if simultaneously stung, and gazed at the young girl who stood silently near them. The man who had sworn began to make agitated apology: "Pardon, miss! 'Pon my soul, I clean forgot you was by. 'Deed, and I wouldn't swear like that if I had knowed. 'Deed, I wouldn't."

The girl did not seem to hear him. She was staring at the barn. Suddenly she turned and whispered, "Who is he?"

"He's Cap'n Sawyer, m'm," they told her sorrowfully. "He's our own cap'n. He's been in command of us yere since a long time. He's got folks about yere. Raikon they cotch him while he was a-visiting."

She was still for a time, and then, awed, she said: "Will they—will they hang him?"

"No, m'm. Oh no, m'm. Don't raikon no such thing. No, m'm."

The group became absorbed in a contemplation of the barn. For a time no one moved nor spoke. At last the girl was aroused by slight sounds, and turning, she perceived that the three men who had so recently escaped from the barn were now advancing toward it.

V

The girl, waiting in the darkness, expected to hear the sudden crash and uproar of a fight as soon as the three creeping men should reach the barn. She reflected in an agony upon the swift disaster that would befall any enterprise so desperate. She had an impulse to beg them to come away. The grass rustled in silken movements as she sped toward the barn.

When she arrived, however, she gazed about her bewildered. The men were gone. She searched with her eyes, trying to detect some moving thing, but she could see nothing.

Left alone again, she began to be afraid of the night. The great stretches of darkness could hide crawling dangers. From sheer desire to see a human, she was obliged to peep again at the knot-hole. The sentry had apparently wearied of talking. Instead, he was reflecting. The prisoner still sat on the feed-box, moodily staring at the floor. The girl felt in one way that she was looking at a ghastly group in wax. She started when the old horse put down an echoing hoof. She wished the men would speak; their silence re - enforced the strange aspect. They might have been two dead men.

The girl felt impelled to look at the corner of the interior where were the cow-stalls. There was no light there save the appearance of peculiar grey haze which marked the track of the dimming rays of the lantern. All else was sombre shadow. At last she saw something move there. It might have been as small as a rat, or it might have been a part of something as large as a man. At any rate, it proclaimed that something in that spot was alive. At one time she saw it plainly, and at other times it vanished, because her fixture of gaze caused her occasionally to greatly tangle and blur those peculiar shadows and faint lights. At last, however, she perceived a human head. It was monstrously dishevelled and wild. It moved slowly forward until its glance could fall upon the prisoner and then upon the sentry. The wandering rays caused the eyes to glitter like silver. The girl's heart pounded so that she put her hand over it.

The sentry and the prisoner remained immovably waxen, and over in the gloom the head thrust from the floor watched them with its silver eyes.

Finally, the prisoner slipped from the feed-box, and raising his arms, yawned at great length. "Oh, well," he remarked, "you boys will get a good licking if you fool around here much longer. That's some satisfaction, anyhow, even if you did bag me. You'll get a good walloping." He reflected for a moment, and decided: "I'm sort of willing to be captured if you fellows only get a d——d good licking for being so smart."

The sentry looked up and smiled a superior smile. "Licking, hey? Nixey!" He winked exasperatingly at the prisoner. "You fellows are not fast enough, my boy. Why didn't you lick us at ——? and at ——? and at ——?" He named some of the great battles.

To this the captive officer blurted in angry astonishment: "Why, we did!"

The sentry winked again in profound irony. "Yes, I know you did. Of course. You whipped us, didn't you? Fine kind of whipping that was! Why, we——"

He suddenly ceased, smitten mute by a sound that broke the stillness of the night. It was the sharp crack of a distant shot that made wild echoes among the hills. It was instantly followed by the hoarse cry of a human voice, a far-away yell of warning, singing of surprise, peril, fear of death. A moment later there was a distant, fierce spattering of shots.   The sentry and the prisoner stood facing each other, their lips apart, listening.

The orchard at that instant awoke to sudden tumult.   There were the thud and scramble and scamper of feet, the mellow, swift clash of arms, men's voices in question, oath, command, hurried and unhurried, resolute and frantic.   A horse sped along the road at a raging gallop.   A loud voice shouted, "What is it, Ferguson?"   Another voice yelled something incoherent.   There was a sharp, discordant chorus of command.   An uproarious volley suddenly rang from the orchard. The prisoner in grey moved from his intent, listening attitude.   Instantly the eyes of the sentry blazed, and he said with a new and terrible sternness: "Stand where you are!"

The prisoner trembled in his excitement. Expressions of delight and triumph bubbled to his lips.   "A surprise, by Gawd! Now—now, you'll see!"

The sentry stolidly swung his carbine to his shoulder.   He sighted carefully along the barrel until it pointed at the prisoner's head, about at his nose.   "Well, I've got you, anyhow. Remember that!   Don't move!"

The prisoner could not keep his arms from nervously gesturing.   "I won't; but——"

"And shut your mouth!"

The three comrades of the sentry flung themselves into view.   "Pete—devil of a row!—can you——"

"I've got him," said the sentry calmly and without moving. It was as if the barrel of the carbine rested on piers of stone. The three comrades turned and plunged into the darkness.

In the orchard it seemed as if two gigantic animals were engaged in a mad, floundering encounter, snarling, howling in a whirling chaos of noise and motion. In the barn the prisoner and his guard faced each other in silence.

As for the girl at the knot-hole, the sky had fallen at the beginning of this clamour. She would not have been astonished to see the stars swinging from their abodes, and the vegetation, the barn, all blow away. It was the end of everything, the grand universal murder. When two of the three miraculous soldiers who formed the original feed-box corps emerged in detail from the hole under the beam, and slid away into the darkness, she did no more than glance at them.

Suddenly she recollected the head with silver eyes. She started forward and again applied her eyes to the knot-hole. Even with the din resounding from the orchard, from up the road and down the road, from the heavens and from the deep earth, the central fascination was this mystic head. There, to her, was the dark god of the tragedy.

The prisoner in grey at this moment burst into a laugh that was no more than a hysterical gurgle. "Well, you can't hold that gun out for ever! Pretty soon you'll have to lower it."

The sentry's voice sounded slightly muffled, for his cheek was pressed against the weapon. " I won't be tired for some time yet."

The girl saw the head slowly rise, the eyes fixed upon the sentry's face. A tall, black figure slunk across the cow-stalls and vanished back of old Santo's quarters. She knew what was to come to pass. She knew this grim thing was upon a terrible mission, and that it would reappear again at the head of the little passage between Santo's stall and the wall, almost at the sentry's elbow; and yet when she saw a faint indication as of a form crouching there, a scream from an utterly new alarm almost escaped her.

The sentry's arms, after all, were not of granite. He moved restively. At last he spoke in his even, unchanging tone: " Well, I guess you'll have to climb into that feed-box. Step back and lift the lid."

" Why, you don't mean——"

" Step back !"

The girl felt a cry of warning arising to her lips as she gazed at this sentry. She noted every detail of his facial expression. She saw, moreover, his mass of brown hair bunching disgracefully about his ears, his clear eyes lit now with a hard, cold light, his forehead puckered in a mighty scowl, the ring upon the third finger

of the left hand. "Oh, they won't kill him!
Surely they won't kill him!"   The noise of
the fight in the orchard was the loud music,
the thunder and lightning, the rioting of the
tempest which people love during the critical
scene of a tragedy.

When the prisoner moved back in reluctant
obedience, he faced for an instant the entrance
of the little passage, and what he saw there
must have been written swiftly, graphically in
his eyes.   And the sentry read it and knew then
that he was upon the threshold of his death.   In
a fraction of time, certain information went from
the grim thing in the passage to the prisoner,
and from the prisoner to the sentry.   But at
that instant the black formidable figure arose,
towered, and made its leap.   A new shadow flashed
across the floor when the blow was struck.

As for the girl at the knot-hole, when she
returned to sense she found herself standing with
clenched hands and screaming with her might.

As if her reason had again departed from
her, she ran around the barn, in at the door,
and flung herself sobbing beside the body of
the soldier in blue.

The uproar of the fight became at last coherent, inasmuch as one party was giving shouts
of supreme exultation.   The firing no longer
sounded in crashes; it was now expressed in
spiteful crackles, the last words of the combat,
spoken with feminine vindictiveness.

Presently there was a thud of flying feet. A grimy, panting, red-faced mob of troopers in blue plunged into the barn, became instantly frozen to attitudes of amazement and rage, and then roared in one great chorus: "He's gone!"

The girl who knelt beside the body upon the floor turned toward them her lamenting eyes and cried: "He's not dead, is he? He can't be dead?"

They thronged forward. The sharp lieutenant who had been so particular about the feed-box knelt by the side of the girl, and laid his head against the chest of the prostrate soldier. "Why, no," he said, rising and looking at the man. "He's all right. Some of you boys throw some water on him."

"Are you sure?" demanded the girl feverishly.

"Of course! He'll be better after awhile."

"Oh!" said she softly, and then looked down at the sentry. She started to arise, and the lieutenant reached down and hoisted rather awkwardly at her arm.

"Don't you worry about him. He's all right."

She turned her face with its curving lips and shining eyes once more toward the unconscious soldier upon the floor. The troopers made a lane to the door, the lieutenant bowed, the girl vanished.

"Queer," said a young officer. "Girl very clearly worst kind of rebel, and yet she falls to weeping and wailing like mad over one of her enemies. Be around in the morning with all sorts of doctoring—you see if she ain't. Queer."

The sharp lieutenant shrugged his shoulders. After reflection he shrugged his shoulders again. He said: "War changes many things; but it doesn't change everything, thank God!"

A Mystery of Heroism

s

A Mystery of Heroism

THE dark uniforms of the men were so coated with dust from the incessant wrestling of the two armies that the regiment almost seemed a part of the clay bank which shielded them from the shells. On the top of the hill a battery was arguing in tremendous roars with some other guns, and to the eye of the infantry, the artillery-men, the guns, the caissons, the horses, were distinctly outlined upon the blue sky. When a piece was fired, a red streak as round as a log flashed low in the heavens, like a monstrous bolt of lightning. The men of the battery wore white duck trousers, which somehow emphasised their legs: and when they ran and crowded in little groups at the bidding of the shouting officers, it was more impressive than usual to the infantry.

Fred Collins, of A Company, was saying: "Thunder, I wisht I had a drink. Ain't there any water round here?" Then, somebody yelled: "There goes th' bugler!"

As the eyes of half the regiment swept in one machine-like movement, there was an instant's picture of a horse in a great convulsive leap of a death-wound and a rider leaning back with a crooked arm and spread fingers before his face. On the ground was the crimson terror of an exploding shell, with fibres of flame that seemed like lances. A glittering bugle swung clear of the rider's back as fell headlong the horse and the man. In the air was an odour as from a conflagration.

Sometimes they of the infantry looked down at a fair little meadow which spread at their feet. Its long, green grass was rippling gently in a breeze. Beyond it was the grey form of a house half torn to pieces by shells and by the busy axes of soldiers who had pursued firewood. The line of an old fence was now dimly marked by long weeds and by an occasional post. A shell had blown the well-house to fragments. Little lines of grey smoke ribboning upward from some embers indicated the place where had stood the barn.

From beyond a curtain of green woods there came the sound of some stupendous scuffle, as if two animals of the size of islands were fighting. At a distance there were occasional appearances of swift-moving men, horses, batteries, flags, and, with the crashing of infantry volleys were heard, often, wild and frenzied cheers. In the midst of it all Smith and Ferguson, two privates of A Company, were engaged in a heated discussion, which involved the greatest questions of the national existence.

The battery on the hill presently engaged in a frightful duel. The white legs of the gunners scampered this way and that way, and the officers redoubled their shouts. The guns, with their demeanours of stolidity and courage, were typical of something infinitely self-possessed in this clamour of death that swirled around the hill.

One of a "swing" team was suddenly smitten quivering to the ground, and his maddened brethren dragged his torn body in their struggle to escape from this turmoil and danger. A young soldier astride one of the leaders swore and fumed in his saddle, and furiously jerked at the bridle. An officer screamed out an order so violently that his voice broke and ended the sentence in a falsetto shriek.

The leading company of the infantry regiment was somewhat exposed, and the colonel ordered it moved more fully under the shelter of the hill. There was the clank of steel against steel.

A lieutenant of the battery rode down and passed them, holding his right arm carefully in his left hand. And it was as if this arm was not at all a part of him, but belonged to another man. His sober and reflective charger went slowly. The officer's face was grimy and perspiring, and his uniform was tousled as if he had been in direct grapple with an enemy. He smiled grimly when the men stared at him. He turned his horse toward the meadow.

Collins, of A Company, said : " I wisht I had a drink. I bet there's water in that there ol' well yonder ! "

" Yes ; but how you goin' to git it ? "

For the little meadow which intervened was now suffering a terrible onslaught of shells. Its green and beautiful calm had vanished utterly. Brown earth was being flung in monstrous handfuls. And there was a massacre of the young blades of grass. They were being torn, burned, obliterated. Some curious fortune of the battle had made this gentle little meadow the object of the red hate of the shells, and each one as it exploded seemed like an imprecation in the face of a maiden.

The wounded officer who was riding across this expanse said to himself : " Why, they couldn't shoot any harder if the whole army was massed here ! "

A shell struck the grey ruins of the house, and as, after the roar, the shattered wall fell in fragments, there was a noise which resembled the flapping of shutters during a wild gale of winter. Indeed, the infantry paused in the shelter of the bank appeared as men standing upon a shore contemplating a madness of the sea. The angel of calamity had under its glance the battery upon the hill. Fewer white-legged men laboured about the guns. A shell had smitten one of the pieces, and after the flare, the smoke, the dust, the wrath of this blow were gone, it was possible to see white legs stretched horizontally upon the ground. And at that interval to the rear, where it is the business of battery horses to stand with their noses to the fight awaiting the command to drag their guns out of the destruction, or into it, or wheresoever these incomprehensible humans demanded with whip and spur—in this line of passive and dumb spectators, whose fluttering hearts yet would not let them forget the iron laws of man's control of them—in this rank of brute-soldiers there had been relentless and hideous carnage. From the ruck of bleeding and prostrate horses, the men of the infantry could see one animal raising its stricken body with its fore legs, and turning its nose with mystic and profound eloquence toward the sky.

Some comrades joked Collins about his thirst. "Well, if yeh want a drink so bad, why don't yeh go git it?"

"Well, I will in a minnet, if yeh don't shut up!"

A lieutenant of artillery floundered his horse straight down the hill with as little concern as if it were level ground. As he galloped past the colonel of the infantry, he threw up his hand in swift salute. "We've got to get out of that," he roared angrily. He was a black-bearded officer, and his eyes, which resembled beads, sparkled like those of an insane man. His jumping horse sped along the column of infantry.

The fat major, standing carélessly with his sword held horizontally behind him and with his legs far apart, looked after the receding horseman and laughed. "He wants to get back with orders pretty quick, or there'll be no batt'ry left," he observed.

The wise young captain of the second company hazarded to the lieutenant-colonel that the enemy's infantry would probably soon attack the hill, and the lieutenant-colonel snubbed him.

A private in one of the rear companies looked out over the meadow, and then turned to a companion and said, "Look there, Jim!" It was the wounded officer from the battery, who some time before had started to ride across the meadow, supporting his right arm carefully with his left hand. This man had encountered a shell apparently at a time when no one perceived him, and he could now be seen lying face downward with a stirruped foot stretched across the body of his dead horse. A leg of the charger extended slantingly upward precisely as stiff as a stake. Around this motionless pair the shells still howled.

There was a quarrel in A Company. Collins was shaking his fist in the faces of some laughing comrades. "Dern yeh! I ain't afraid t' go. If yeh say much, I will go!"

"Of course, yeh will! You'll run through that there medder, won't yeh?"

Collins said, in a terrible voice : " You see now ! "
At this ominous threat his comrades broke into
renewed jeers.

Collins gave them a dark scowl, and went to
find his captain. The latter was conversing with
the colonel of the regiment.

" Captain," said Collins, saluting and standing
at attention—in those days all trousers bagged
at the knees—" Captain, I wan't t' get permission
to go git some water from that there well over
yonder ! "

The colonel and the captain swung about
simultaneously and stared across the meadow.
The captain laughed. " You must be pretty
thirsty, Collins ? "

" Yes, sir, I am."

" Well—ah," said the captain. After a moment,
he asked, " Can't you wait ? "

" No, sir."

The colonel was watching Collins's face. " Look
here, my lad," he said, in a pious sort of a voice—
" Look here, my lad "—Collins was not a lad—
" don't you think that's taking pretty big risks for
a little drink of water."

" I dunno," said Collins uncomfortably. Some
of the resentment toward his companions, which
perhaps had forced him into this affair, was beginning to fade. " I dunno wether 'tis."

The colonel and the captain contemplated him
for a time.

" Well," said the captain finally.

"Well," said the colonel, "if you want to go, why, go."

Collins saluted. "Much obliged t' yeh."

As he moved away the colonel called after him. "Take some of the other boys' canteens with you an' hurry back now."

"Yes, sir, I will."

The colonel and the captain looked at each othei then, for it had suddenly occurred that they could not for the life of them tell whether Collins wanted to go or whether he did not.

They turned to regard Collins, and as they perceived him surrounded by gesticulating comrades, the colonel said: "Well, by thunder! I guess he's going."

Collins appeared as a man dreaming. In the midst of the questions, the advice, the warnings, all the excited talk of his company mates, he maintained a curious silence.

They were very busy in preparing him for his ordeal. When they inspected him carefully, it was somewhat like the examination that grooms give a horse before a race; and they were amazed, staggered by the whole affair. Their astonishment found vent in strange repetitions.

"Are yeh sure a-goin'?" they demanded again and again.

"Certainly I am," cried Collins at last furiously.

He strode sullenly away from them. He was swinging five or six canteens by their cords. It seemed that his cap would not remain firmly on his head, and often he reached and pulled it down over his brow.

There was a general movement in the compact column. The long animal-like thing moved slightly. Its four hundred eyes were turned upon the figure of Collins.

"Well, sir, if that ain't th' derndest thing! I never thought Fred Collins had the blood in him for that kind of business."

"What's he goin' to do, anyhow?"

"He's goin' to that well there after water."

"We ain't dyin' of thirst, are we? That's foolishness."

"Well, somebody put him up to it, an' he's doin' it."

"Say, he must be a desperate cuss."

When Collins faced the meadow and walked away from the regiment, he was vaguely conscious that a chasm, the deep valley of all prides, was suddenly between him and his comrades. It was provisional, but the provision was that he return as a victor. He had blindly been led by quaint emotions, and laid himself under an obligation to walk squarely up to the face of death.

But he was not sure that he wished to make a retraction, even if he could do so without shame. As a matter of truth, he was sure of very little. He was mainly surprised.

It seemed to him supernaturally strange that he had allowed his mind to manœuvre his body into such a situation. He understood that it might be called dramatically great.

However, he had no full appreciation of anything, excepting that he was actually conscious of being dazed. He could feel his dulled mind groping after the form and colour of this incident. He wondered why he did not feel some keen agony of fear cutting his sense like a knife. He wondered at this, because human expression had said loudly for centuries that men should feel afraid of certain things, and that all men who did not feel this fear were phenomena—heroes.

He was, then, a hero. He suffered that disappointment which we would all have if we discovered that we were ourselves capable of those deeds which we most admire in history and legend. This, then, was a hero. After all, heroes were not much.

No, it could not be true. He was not a hero. Heroes had no shames in their lives, and, as for him, he remembered borrowing fifteen dollars from a friend and promising to pay it back the next day, and then avoiding that friend for ten months. When at home his mother had aroused him for the early labour of his life on the farm, it had often been his fashion to be irritable, childish, diabolical; and his mother had died since he had come to the war.

He saw that, in this matter of the well, the canteens, the shells, he was an intruder in the land of fine deeds.

He was now about thirty paces from his comrades. The regiment had just turned its many faces toward him.

From the forest of terrific noises there suddenly emerged a little uneven line of men. They fired fiercely and rapidly at distant foliage on which appeared little puffs of white smoke. The spatter of skirmish firing was added to the thunder of the guns on the hill. The little line of men ran forward. A colour-sergeant fell flat with his flag as if he had slipped on ice. There was hoarse cheering from this distant field.

Collins suddenly felt that two demon fingers were pressed into his ears. He could see nothing but flying arrows, flaming red. He lurched from the shock of this explosion, but he made a mad rush for the house, which he viewed as a man submerged to the neck in a boiling surf might view the shore. In the air, little pieces of shell howled and the earthquake explosions drove him insane with the menace of their roar. As he ran the canteens knocked together with a rhythmical tinkling.

As he neared the house, each detail of the scene became vivid to him. He was aware of some bricks of the vanished chimney lying on the sod. There was a door which hung by one hinge.

Rifle bullets called forth by the insistent skirmishers came from the far-off bank of foliage. They mingled with the shells and the pieces of shells until the air was torn in all directions by hootings, yells, howls. The sky was full of fiends who directed all their wild rage at his head.

When he came to the well, he flung himself face downward and peered into its darkness. There were furtive silver glintings some feet from the surface. He grabbed one of the canteens, and, unfastening its cap, swung it down by the cord. The water flowed slowly in with an indolent gurgle.

And now as he lay with his face turned away he was suddenly smitten with the terror. It came upon his heart like the grasp of claws. All the power faded from his muscles. For an instant he was no more than a dead man.

The canteen filled with a maddening slowness, in the manner of all bottles. Presently he recovered his strength and addressed a screaming oath to it. He leaned over until it seemed as if he intended to try to push water into it with his hands. His eyes as he gazed down into the well shone like two pieces of metal, and in their expression was a great appeal and a great curse. The stupid water derided him.

There was the blaring thunder of a shell. Crimson light shone through the swift-boiling smoke, and made a pink reflection on part of the wall of the well. Collins jerked out his arm and canteen with the same motion that a man would use in withdrawing his head from a furnace.

He scrambled erect and glared and hesitated. On the ground near him lay the old well bucket with a length of rusty chain. He lowered it swiftly into the well. The bucket struck the water and then, turning lazily over, sank. When, with hand reaching tremblingly over hand, he hauled it out, it knocked often against the walls of the well and spilled some of its contents.

. In running with a filled bucket, a man can adopt but one kind of gait. So through this terrible field, over which screamed practical angels of death, Collins ran in the manner of a farmer chased out of a dairy by a bull.

His face went staring white with anticipation—anticipation of a blow that would whirl him around and down. He would fall as he had seen other men fall, the life knocked out of them so suddenly that their knees were no more quick to touch the ground than their heads. He saw the long blue line of the regiment, but his comrades were standing looking at him from the edge of an impossible star. He was aware of some deep wheel-ruts and hoof-prints in the sod beneath his feet.

The artillery officer who had fallen in this meadow had been making groans in the teeth of the tempest of sound. These futile cries, wrenched from him by his agony, were heard only by shells, bullets. When wild-eyed Collins came running, this officer raised himself. His face contorted and blanched from pain, he was about to utter some great beseeching cry. But suddenly his face straightened and he called:

"Say, young man, give me a drink of water, will you?"

Collins had no room amid his emotions for surprise. He was mad from the threats of destruction.

"I can't!" he screamed, and in his reply was a full description of his quaking apprehension. His cap was gone and his hair was riotous. His clothes made it appear that he had been dragged over the ground by the heels. He ran on.

The officer's head sank down, and one elbow crooked. His foot in its brass-bound stirrup still stretched over the body of his horse, and the other leg was under the steed.

But Collins turned. He came dashing back. His face had now turned grey, and in his eyes was all terror. "Here it is! here it is!"

The officer was as a man gone in drink. His arm bent like a twig. His head drooped as if his neck were of willow. He was sinking to the ground, to lie face downward.

Collins grabbed him by the shoulder. "Here it is. Here's your drink. Turn over. Turn over, man, for God's sake!"

With Collins hauling at his shoulder, the officer twisted his body and fell with his face turned toward that region where lived the unspeakable noises of the swirling missiles. There was the faintest shadow of a smile on his lips as he looked at Collins. He gave a sigh, a little primitive breath like that from a child.

Collins tried to hold the bucket steadily, but his shaking hands caused the water to splash all over the face of the dying man. Then he jerked it away and ran on.

The regiment gave him a welcoming roar. The grimed faces were wrinkled in laughter.

His captain waved the bucket away. "Give it to the men!"

The two genial, skylarking young lieutenants were the first to gain possession of it. They played over it in their fashion.

When one tried to drink the other teasingly knocked his elbow. "Don't, Billie! You'll make me spill it," said the one. The other laughed.

Suddenly there was an oath, the thud of wood on the ground, and a swift murmur of astonishment among the ranks. The two lieutenants glared at each other. The bucket lay on the ground empty.

An Indiana Campaign

An Indiana Campaign

I

WHEN the able-bodied citizens of the village
formed a company and marched away to the war,
Major Tom Boldin assumed in a manner the
burden of the village cares. Everybody ran to
him when they felt obliged to discuss their
affairs. The sorrows of the town were dragged
before him. His little bench at the sunny side
of Migglesville tavern became a sort of an open
court where people came to speak resentfully of
their grievances. He accepted his position and
struggled manfully under the load. It behoved
him, as a man who had seen the sky red over
the quaint, low cities of Mexico, and the compact Northern bayonets gleaming on the narrow
roads.

One warm summer day the major sat asleep on
his little bench. There was a lull in the tempest
of discussion which usually enveloped him. His
cane, by use of which he could make the most
tremendous and impressive gestures, reposed

beside him. His hat lay upon the bench, and his old bald head had swung far forward until his nose actually touched the first button of his waistcoat.

The sparrows wrangled desperately in the road, defying perspiration. Once a team went jangling and creaking past, raising a yellow blur of dust before the soft tones of the field and sky. In the long grass of the meadow across the road the insects chirped and clacked eternally.

Suddenly a frouzy-headed boy appeared in the roadway, his bare feet pattering rapidly. He was extremely excited. He gave a shrill whoop as he discovered the sleeping major and rushed toward him. He created a terrific panic among some chickens who had been scratching intently near the major's feet. They clamoured in an insanity of fear, and rushed hither and thither seeking a way of escape, whereas in reality all ways lay plainly open to them.

This tumult caused the major to arouse with a sudden little jump of amazement and apprehension. He rubbed his eyes and gazed about him. Meanwhile, some clever chicken had discovered a passage to safety, and led the flock into the garden, where they squawked in sustained alarm.

Panting from his run and choked with terror, the little boy stood before the major, struggling with a tale that was ever upon the tip of his tongue.

" Major—now—major——"

The old man, roused from a delicious slumber,

glared impatiently at the little boy. ' Come, come! What's th' matter with yeh?" he demanded. "What's th' matter? Don't stand there shaking! Speak up!"

"Lots is th' matter!" the little boy shouted valiantly, with a courage born of the importance of his tale. "My ma's chickens 'uz all stole, an' —now—he's over in th' woods!"

"Who is? Who is over in the woods? Go ahead!"

"Now—th' rebel is!"

"What?" roared the major.

"Th' rebel!" cried the little boy, with the last of his breath.

The major pounced from his bench in tempestuous excitement. He seized the little boy by the collar and gave him a great jerk. "Where? Are yeh sure? Who saw 'im? How long ago? Where is he now? Did you see 'im?"

The little boy, frightened at the major's fury, began to sob. After a moment he managed to stammer: "He—now—he's in the woods. I saw 'im. He looks uglier'n anythin'."

The major released his hold upon the boy, and pausing for a time, indulged in a glorious dream. Then he said: "By thunder! we'll ketch th' cuss. You wait here," he told the boy, "and don't say a word t' anybody. Do you hear?"

The boy, still weeping, nodded, and the major hurriedly entered the inn. He took down from its pegs an awkward smooth-bore rifle and carefully examined the enormous percussion cap that was fitted over the nipple. Mistrusting the cap, he removed it and replaced it with a new one. He scrutinised the gun keenly, as if he could judge in this manner of the condition of the load. All his movements were deliberate and deadly.

When he arrived upon the porch of the tavern he beheld the yard filled with people. Peter Witheby, sooty-faced and grinning, was in the van. He looked at the major. "Well?" he said.

"Well?" returned the major, bridling.

"Well, what's 'che got?" said old Peter.

"'Got?' Got a rebel over in th' woods!" roared the major.

At this sentence the women and boys, who had gathered eagerly about him, gave vent to startled cries. The women had come from adjacent houses, but the little boys represented the entire village. They had miraculously heard the first whisper of rumour, and they performed wonders in getting to the spot. They clustered around the important figure of the major and gazed in silent awe. The women, however, burst forth. At the word "rebel," which represented to them all terrible things, they deluged the major with questions which were obviously unanswerable.

He shook them off with violent impatience. Meanwhile Peter Witheby was trying to force exasperating interrogations through the tumult to the major's ears. "What? No! Yes! How d' I know?" the maddened veteran snarled as he struggled with his friends. "No! Yes! What? How in thunder d' I know?" Upon the steps of the tavern the landlady sat, weeping forlornly.

At last the major burst through the crowd, and went to the roadway. There, as they all streamed after him, he turned and faced them. "Now, look a' here, I don't know any more about this than you do," he told them forcibly. "All that I know is that there's a rebel over in Smith's woods, an' all I know is that I'm agoin' after 'im."

"But hol' on a minnet," said old Peter. "How do yeh know he's a rebel?"

"I know he is!" cried the major. "Don't yeh think I know what a rebel is?"

Then, with a gesture of disdain at the babbling crowd, he marched determinedly away, his rifle held in the hollow of his arm. At this heroic moment a new clamour arose, half admiration, half dismay. Old Peter hobbled after the major, continually repeating, "Hol' on a minnet."

The little boy who had given the alarm was the centre of a throng of lads who gazed with envy and awe, discovering in him a new quality. He held forth to them eloquently. The women stared after the figure of the major and old Peter, his pursuer. Jerozel Bronson, a half-witted lad who comprehended nothing save an occasional genial word, leaned against the fence and grinned like a skull. The major and the pursuer passed out of view around the turn in the road where the great maples lazily shook the dust that lay on their leaves.

For a moment the little group of women listened intently as if they expected to hear a sudden shot and cries from the distance. They looked at each other, their lips a little way apart. The trees sighed softly in the heat of the summer sun. The insects in the meadow continued their monotonous humming, and, somewhere, a hen had been stricken with fear and was cackling loudly.

Finally, Mrs. Goodwin said: "Well, I'm goin' up to th' turn a' th' road, anyhow." Mrs. Willets and Mrs. Joe Peterson, her particular friends, cried out at this temerity, but she said: "Well, I'm goin', anyhow."

She called Bronson. "Come on, Jerozel. You're a man, an' if he should chase us, why, you mus' pitch inteh 'im. Hey?"

Bronson always obeyed everybody. He grinned an assent, and went with her down the road.

A little boy attempted to follow them, but a shrill scream from his mother made him halt.

The remaining women stood motionless, their eyes fixed upon Mrs. Goodwin and Jerozel. Then at last one gave a laugh of triumph at her conquest of caution and fear, and cried: "Well, I'm goin' too!"

Another instantly said, "So am I." There

began a general movement. Some of the little boys had already ventured a hundred feet away from the main body, and at this unanimous advance they spread out ahead in little groups. Some recounted terrible stories of rebel ferocity. Their eyes were large with excitement. The whole thing, with its possible dangers, had for them a delicious element. Johnnie Peterson, who could whip any boy present, explained what he would do in case the enemy should happen to pounce out at him.

The familiar scene suddenly assumed a new aspect. The field of corn, which met the road upon the left, was no longer a mere field of corn. It was a darkly mystic place whose recesses could contain all manner of dangers. The long green leaves, waving in the breeze, rustled from the passing of men. In the song of the insects there were now omens, threats.

There was a warning in the enamel blue of the sky, in the stretch of yellow road, in the very atmosphere. Above the tops of the corn loomed the distant foliage of Smith's woods, curtaining the silent action of a tragedy whose horrors they imagined.

The women and the little boys came to a halt, overwhelmed by the impressiveness of the landscape. They waited silently.

Mrs. Goodwin suddenly said: "I'm goin' back." The others, who all wished to return, cried at once disdainfully:

" Well, go back, if yeh want to ! "

A cricket at the roadside exploded suddenly in his shrill song, and a woman, who had been standing near, shrieked in startled terror. An electric movement went through the group of women. They jumped and gave vent to sudden screams. With the fears still upon their agitated faces, they turned to berate the one who had shrieked. "My! what a goose you are, Sallie! Why, it took my breath away. Goodness sakes don't holler like that again ! "

II.

" Hol' on a minnet !" Peter Witheby was crying to the major, as the latter, full of the importance and dignity of his position as protector of Migglesville, paced forward swiftly. The veteran already felt upon his brow a wreath formed of the flowers of gratitude, and as he strode he was absorbed in planning a calm and self-contained manner of wearing it. "Hol' on a minnet ! " piped old Peter in the rear.

At last the major, aroused from his dream of triumph, turned about wrathfully. "Well, what ? "

"Now, look a' here," said Peter. "What 'che goin' t' do ? "

The major, with a gesture of supreme exasperation, wheeled again and went on. When he arrived at the cornfield he halted and waited for Peter. He had suddenly felt that indefinable menace in the landscape.

"Well?" demanded Peter, panting.

The major's eyes wavered a trifle. "Well," he repeated—" well, I'm goin' in there an' bring out that there rebel."

They both paused and studied the gently swaying masses of corn, and behind them the looming woods, sinister with possible secrets.

"Well," said old Peter.

The major moved uneasily and put his hand to his brow. Peter waited in obvious expectation.

The major crossed through the grass at the roadside and climbed the fence. He put both legs over the topmost rail and then sat perched there, facing the woods. Once he turned his head and asked, "What?"

"I hain't said anythin'," answered Peter.

The major clambered down from the fence and went slowly into the corn, his gun held in readiness. Peter stood in the road.

Presently the major returned and said, in a cautious whisper: "If yeh hear anythin', you come a-runnin', will yeh?"

"Well, I hain't got no gun nor nuthin'," said Peter, in the same low tone; "what good 'ud I do?"

"Well, yeh might come along with me an' watch," said the major. "Four eyes is better'n two."

"If I had a gun——" began Peter.

"Oh, yeh don't need no gun," interrupted the major, waving his hand. "All I'm afraid of is that I won't find 'im. My eyes ain't so good as they was."

"Well——"

"Come along," whispered the major. "Yeh hain't afraid, are yeh?"

"No, but——"

"Well, come along, then. What's th' matter with yeh?"

Peter climbed the fence. He paused on the top rail and took a prolonged stare at the inscrutable woods. When he joined the major in the cornfield he said, with a touch of anger:

"Well, you got the gun. Remember that. If he comes for me, I hain't got a blame thing!"

"Shucks!" answered the major. "He ain't agoin' t' come for yeh."

The two then began a wary journey through the corn. One by one the long aisles between the rows appeared. As they glanced along each of them it seemed as if some gruesome thing had just previously vacated it. Old Peter halted once and whispered: "Say, look a' here; supposin'—supposin'——"

"Supposin' what?" demanded the major.

"Supposin'——" said Peter. "Well, remember you got th' gun, an' I hain't got anythin'."

"Thunder!" said the major.

When they got to where the stalks were very

short because of the shade cast by the trees of the wood, they halted again. The leaves were gently swishing in the breeze. Before them stretched the mystic green wall of the forest, and there seemed to be in it eyes which followed each of their movements.

Peter at last said, "I don't believe there's anybody in there."

"Yes, there is, too," said the major. "I'll bet anythin' he's in there."

"How d' yeh know?" asked Peter. "I'll bet he ain't within a mile o' here."

The major suddenly ejaculated, "Listen!"

They bent forward, scarce breathing, their mouths agape, their eyes glinting. Finally, the major turned his head. "Did yeh hear that?" he said hoarsely.

"No," said Peter in a low voice. "What was it?"

The major listened for a moment. Then he turned again. "I thought I heerd somebody holler!" he explained cautiously.

They both bent forward and listened once more. Peter, in the intentness of his attitude, lost his balance, and was obliged to lift his foot hastily and with noise. "S-s-sh!" hissed the major.

After a minute Peter spoke quite loudly: "Oh, shucks! I don't believe yeh heerd anythin'."

The major made a frantic downward gesture with his hand. "Shet up, will yeh!" he said in an angry undertone.

Peter became silent for a moment, but presently he said again: "Oh, yeh didn't hear anythin'."

The major turned to glare at his companion in despair and wrath.

"What's th' matter with yeh? Can't -yeh shet up?"

·"Oh, this here ain't no use. If you're goin' in after 'im, why don't yeh go in after 'im?"

"Well, gimme time, can't yeh?" said the major in a growl. And, as if to add more to this reproach, he climbed the fence that compassed the woods, looking resentfully back at his companion.

"Well," said Peter, when the major paused.

The major stepped down upon the thick carpet of brown leaves that stretched under the trees. He turned then to whisper: "You wait here, will yeh?" His face was red with determination.

"Well, hol' on a minnet!" said Peter. "You —I—we'd better——"

No," said the major. "You wait here."

He went stealthily into the thickets. Peter watched him until he grew to be a vague, slow-moving shadow. From time to time he could hear the leaves crackle and twigs snap under the major's awkward tread. Peter, intent, breathless, waited for the peal of sudden tragedy. Finally, the woods grew silent in a solemn and impressive hush that caused Peter to feel the thumping of his heart. He began to look about him to make sure that nothing should spring upon him from the sombre shadows. He scrutinised this cool gloom before him, and at times he thought he could perceive the moving of swift silent shapes. He concluded that he had better go back and try to muster some assistance to the major.

As Peter came through the corn, the women in the road caught sight of the glittering figure and screamed. Many of them began to run. The little boys, with all their valour, scurried away in clouds. Mrs. Joe Peterson, however, cast a glance over her shoulders as she, with her skirts gathered up, was running as best she could. She instantly stopped and, in tones of deepest scorn, called out to the others, "Why, it's on'y Pete Witheby!" They came faltering back then, those who had been naturally swiftest in the race avoiding the eyes of those whose limbs had enabled them to flee a short distance.

Peter came rapidly, appreciating the glances of vivid interest in the eyes of the women. To their lightning-like questions, which hit all sides of the episode, he opposed a new tranquillity, gained from his sudden ascent in importance. He made no answer to their clamour. When he had reached the top of the fence he called out commandingly: "Here you, Johnnie, you and George, run an' git my gun! It's hangin' on th' pegs over th' bench in th' shop."

At this terrible sentence, a shuddering cry broke from the women. The boys named sped down the road, accompanied by a retinue of envious companions.

Peter swung his legs over the rail and faced the woods again. He twisted his head once to say: "Keep still, can't yeh? Quit scufflin' aroun'!" They could see by his manner that this was a supreme moment. The group became motionless and still. Later, Peter turned to say, "S-s-sh!" to a restless boy, and the air with which he said it smote them all with awe.

The little boys who had gone after the gun came pattering along hurriedly, the weapon borne in the midst of them. Each was anxious to share in the honour. The one who had been delegated to bring it was bullying and directing his comrades.

Peter said, "S-s-sh!" He took the gun and poised it in readiness to sweep the cornfield. He scowled at the boys and whispered angrily: "Why didn't yeh bring th' powder-horn an' th' thing with th' bullets in? I told yeh t' bring 'em. I'll send somebody else next time."

"Yeh didn't tell us!" cried the two boys shrilly.

"S-s-sh! Quit yeh noise," said Peter, with a violent gesture.

However, this reproof enabled other boys to recover that peace of mind which they had lost when seeing their friends loaded with honours.

The women had cautiously approached the fence, and, from time to time, whispered feverish questions; but Peter repulsed them savagely, with an air of being infinitely bothered by their interference in his intent watch. They were forced to listen again in silence to the weird and prophetic chanting of the insects and the mystic silken rustling of the corn.

At last the thud of hurrying feet in the soft soil of the field came to their ears. A dark form sped toward them. A wave of a mighty fear swept over the group, and the screams of the women came hoarsely from their choked throats. Peter swung madly from his perch, and turned to use the fence as a rampart.

But it was the major. His face was inflamed and his eyes were glaring. He clutched his rifle by the middle and swung it wildly. He was bounding at a great speed for his fat, short body.

"It's all right! it's all right!" he began to yell some distance away. "It's all right! It's on'y ol' Milt' Jacoby!"

When he arrived at the top of the fence he paused, and mopped his brow.

"What?" they thundered, in an agony of sudden, unreasoning disappointment.

Mrs. Joe Peterson, who was a distant connection of Milton Jacoby, thought to forestall any damage to her social position by saying at once disdainfully, "Drunk, I s'pose!"

"Yep," said the major, still on the fence, and

mopping his brow. "Drunk as a fool. Thunder! I was surprised. I—I—thought it was a rebel, sure."

The thoughts of all these women wavered for a time. They were at a loss for precise expression of their emotion. At last, however, they hurled this superior sentence at the major:

"Well, yeh might have known."

A Grey Sleeve

A Grey Sleeve

I

"It looks as if it might rain this afternoon," remarked the lieutenant of artillery.

"So it does," the infantry captain assented. He glanced casually at the sky. When his eyes had lowered to the green-shadowed landscape before him, he said fretfully: "I wish those fellows out yonder would quit pelting at us. They've been at it since noon."

At the edge of a grove of maples, across wide fields, there occasionally appeared little puffs of smoke of a dull hue in this gloom of sky which expressed an impending rain. The long wave of blue and steel in the field moved uneasily at the eternal barking of the far-away sharpshooters, and the men, leaning upon their rifles, stared at the grove of maples. Once a private turned to borrow some tobacco from a comrade in the rear rank, but, with his hand still stretched out, he continued to twist his head and glance at the distant trees. He was afraid the enemy would shoot him at a time when he was not looking.

Suddenly the artillery officer said : " See what's coming ! "

Along the rear of the brigade of infantry a column of cavalry was sweeping at a hard gallop. A lieutenant, riding some yards to the right of the column, bawled furiously at the four troopers just at the rear of the colours. They had lost distance and made a little gap, but at the shouts of the lieutenant they urged their horses forward. The bugler, careering along behind the captain of the troop, fought and tugged like a wrestler to keep his frantic animal from bolting far ahead of the column.

On the springy turf the innumerable hoofs thundered in a swift storm of sound. In the brown faces of the troopers their eyes were set like bits of flashing steel.

The long line of the infantry regiments standing at ease underwent a sudden movement at the rush of the passing squadron. The foot soldiers turned their heads to gaze at the torrent of horses and men.

The yellow folds of the flag fluttered back in silken, shuddering waves, as if it were a reluctant thing. Occasionally a giant spring of a charger would rear the firm and sturdy figure of a soldier suddenly head and shoulders above his comrades. Over the noise of the scudding hoofs could be heard the creaking of leather trappings, the jingle and clank of steel, and the tense, low-toned commands or appeals of the men to their horses; and the horses were mad with the headlong sweep of this movement. Powerful under jaws bent back and straightened, so that the bits were clamped as rigidly as vices upon the teeth, and glistening necks arched in desperate resistance to the hands at the bridles. Swinging their heads in rage at the granite laws of their lives, which compelled even their angers and their ardours to chosen directions and chosen faces, their flight was as a flight of harnessed demons.

The captain's bay kept its pace at the head of the squadron with the lithe bounds of a thoroughbred, and this horse was proud as a chief at the roaring trample of his fellows behind him. The captain's glance was calmly upon the grove of maples whence the sharpshooters of the enemy had been picking at the blue line. He seemed to be reflecting. He stolidly rose and fell with the plunges of his horse in all the indifference of a deacon's figure seated plumply in church. And it occurred to many of the watching infantry to wonder why this officer could remain imperturbable and reflective when his squadron was thundering and swarming behind him like the rushing of a flood.

The column swung in a sabre-curve toward a break in a fence, and dashed into a roadway. Once a little plank bridge was encountered, and the sound of the hoofs upon it was like the long roll of many drums. An old captain in the infantry turned to his first lieutenant and made a remark, which was a compound of bitter disparagement of cavalry in general and soldierly admiration of this particular troop.

Suddenly the bugle sounded, and the column halted with a jolting upheaval amid sharp, brief cries. A moment later the men had tumbled from their horses, and, carbines in hand, were running in a swarm toward the grove of maples. In the road one of every four of the troopers was standing with braced legs, and pulling and hauling at the bridles of four frenzied horses.

The captain was running awkwardly in his boots. He held his sabre low, so that the point often threatened to catch in the turf. His yellow hair ruffled out from under his faded cap. "Go in hard now!" he roared, in a voice of hoarse fury. His face was violently red.

The troopers threw themselves upon the grove like wolves upon a great animal. Along the whole front of woods there was the dry crackling of musketry, with bitter, swift flashes and smoke that writhed like stung phantoms. The troopers yelled shrilly and spanged bullets low into the foliage.

For a moment, when near the woods, the line almost halted. The men struggled and fought for a time like swimmers encountering a powerful current. Then with a supreme effort they went on again. They dashed madly at the grove, whose foliage from the high light of the field was as inscrutable as a wall.

Then suddenly each detail of the calm trees became apparent, and with a few more frantic leaps the men were in the cool gloom of the woods. There was a heavy odour as from burned paper. Wisps of grey smoke wound upward. The men halted and, grimy, perspiring, and puffing, they searched the recesses of the woods with eager, fierce glances. Figures could be seen flitting afar off. A dozen carbines rattled at them in an angry volley.

During this pause the captain strode along the line, his face lit with a broad smile of contentment. " When he sends this crowd to do anything, I guess he'll find we do it pretty sharp," he said to the grinning lieutenant.

" Say, they didn't stand that rush a minute, did they ? " said the subaltern. Both officers were profoundly dusty in their uniforms, and their faces were soiled like those of two urchins.

Out in the grass behind them were three tumbled and silent forms.

Presently the line moved forward again. The men went from tree to tree like hunters stalking game. Some at the left of the line fired occasionally, and those at the right gazed curiously in that direction. The men still breathed heavily from their scramble across the field.

Of a sudden a trooper halted and said: " Hello!

there's a house!" Every one paused. The men turned to look at their leader.

The captain stretched his neck and swung his head from side to side. "By George, it is a house!" he said.

Through the wealth of leaves there vaguely loomed the form of a large white house. These troopers, brown-faced from many days of campaigning, each feature of them telling of their placid confidence and courage, were stopped abruptly by the appearance of this house. There was some subtle suggestion—some tale of an unknown thing—which watched them from they knew not what part of it.

A rail fence girded a wide lawn of tangled grass. Seven pines stood along a drive-way which led from two distant posts of a vanished gate. The blue-clothed troopers moved forward until they stood at the fence peering over it.

The captain put one hand on the top rail and seemed to be about to climb the fence, when suddenly he hesitated, and said in a low voice: "Watson, what do you think of it?"

The lieutenant stared at the house. "Derned if I know!" he replied.

The captain pondered. It happened that the whole company had turned a gaze of profound awe and doubt upon this edifice which confronted them. The men were very silent.

At last the captain swore and said: "We are certainly a pack of fools. Derned old deserted house halting a company of Union cavalry, and making us gape like babies!"

"Yes, but there's something—something——" insisted the subaltern in a half stammer.

"Well, if there's 'something—something' in there, I'll get it out," said the captain. "Send Sharpe clean around to the other side with about twelve men, so we will sure bag your 'something —something,' and I'll take a few of the boys and find out what's in the d——d old thing!"

He chose the nearest eight men for his "storming party," as the lieutenant called it. After he had waited some minutes for the others to get into position, he said "Come ahead" to his eight men, and climbed the fence.

The brighter light of the tangled lawn made him suddenly feel tremendously apparent, and he wondered if there could be some mystic thing in the house which was regarding this approach. His men trudged silently at his back. They stared at the windows and lost themselves in deep speculations as to the probability of there being, perhaps, eyes behind the blinds—malignant eyes, piercing eyes.

Suddenly a corporal in the party gave vent to a startled exclamation, and half threw his carbine into position. The captain turned quickly, and the corporal said: "I saw an arm move the blinds—an arm with a grey sleeve!"

"Don't be a fool, Jones, now," said the captain sharply.

"I swear t'——" began the corporal, but the captain silenced him.

When they arrived at the front of the house, the troopers paused, while the captain went softly up the front steps. He stood· before the large front door and studied it. Some crickets chirped in the long grass, and the nearest pine could be heard in its endless sighs. One of the privates moved uneasily, and his foot crunched the gravel. Suddenly the captain swore angrily and kicked the door with a loud crash. It flew open.

II

The bright lights of the day flashed into the old house when the captain angrily kicked open the door. He was aware of a wide hallway, carpeted with matting and extending deep into the dwelling. There was also an old walnut hat-rack and a little marble-topped table with a vase and two books upon it. Farther back was a great, venerable fireplace containing dreary ashes.

But directly in front of the captain was a young girl. The flying open of the door had obviously been an utter astonishment to her, and she remained transfixed there in the middle of the floor, staring at the captain with wide eyes.

She was like a child caught at the time of a raid upon the cake. She wavered to and fro upon her feet, and held her hands behind her. There were two little points of terror in her eyes, as she gazed up at the young captain in dusty blue, with his reddish, bronze complexion, his yellow hair, his bright sabre held threateningly.

These two remained motionless and silent, simply staring at each other for some moments.

The captain felt his rage fade out of him and leave his mind limp. He had been violently angry, because this house had made him feel hesitant, wary. He did not like to be wary. He liked to feel confident, sure. So he had kicked the door open, and had been prepared to march in like a soldier of wrath.

But now he began, for one thing, to wonder if his uniform was so dusty and old in appearance. Moreover, he had a feeling that his face was covered with a compound of dust, grime, and perspiration. He took a step forward and said: "I didn't mean to frighten you." But his voice was coarse from his battle-howling. It seemed to him to have hempen fibres in it.

The girl's breath came in little, quick gasps, and she looked at him as she would have looked at a serpent.

"I didn't mean to frighten you," he said again.

The girl, still with her hands behind her, began to back away.

"Is there any one else in the house?" he went on, while slowly following her. "I don't wish to disturb you, but we had a fight with some rebel skirmishers in the woods, and I thought maybe some of them might have come in here. In fact, I was pretty sure of it. Are there any of them here?"

The girl looked at him and said, "No!" He wondered why extreme agitation made the eyes of some women so limpid and bright.

"Who is here besides yourself?"

By this time his pursuit had driven her to the end of the hall, and she remained there with her back to the wall and her hands still behind her. When she answered this question, she did not look at him but down at the floor. She cleared her voice and then said: "There is no one here."

"No one?"

She lifted her eyes to him in that appeal that the human being must make even to falling trees, crashing boulders, the sea in a storm, and said, "No, no, there is no one here." He could plainly see her tremble.

Of a sudden he bethought him that she continually kept her hands behind her. As he recalled her air when first discovered, he remembered she appeared precisely as a child detected at one of the crimes of childhood. Moreover, she had always backed away from him. He thought now that she was concealing something which was an evidence of the presence of the enemy in the house.

"What are you holding behind you?" he said suddenly.

She gave a little quick moan, as if some grim hand had throttled her.

"What are you holding behind you ?"

"Oh, nothing—please. I am not holding anything behind me; indeed I'm not."

"Very well. Hold your hands out in front of you, then."

"Oh, indeed, I'm not holding anything behind me. Indeed I'm not."

"Well," he began. Then he paused, and remained for a moment dubious. Finally, he laughed. "Well, I shall have my men search the house, anyhow. I'm sorry to trouble you, but I feel sure that there is some one here whom we want." He turned to the corporal, who with the other men was gaping quietly in at the door, and said : "Jones, go through the house."

As for himself, he remained planted in front of the girl, for she evidently did not dare to move and allow him to see what she held so carefully behind her back. So she was his prisoner.

The men rummaged around on the ground floor of the house. Sometimes the captain called to them, "Try that closet," "Is there any cellar ?" But they found no one, and at last they went trooping toward the stairs which led to the second floor.

But at this movement on the part of the men the girl uttered a cry—a cry of such fright and appeal that the men paused. "Oh, don't go up there! Please don't go up there!—ple—ease! There is no one there! Indeed—indeed there is not! Oh, ple—ease!"

"Go on, Jones," said the captain calmly.

The obedient corporal made a preliminary step, and the girl bounded toward the stairs with another cry.

As she passed him, the captain caught sight of that which she had concealed behind her back, and which she had forgotten in this supreme moment. It was a pistol.

She ran to the first step, and standing there, faced the men, one hand extended with perpendicular palm, and the other holding the pistol at her side. "Oh, please, don't go up there! Nobody is there—indeed, there is not! P-l-e-a-s-e!" Then suddenly she sank swiftly down upon the step, and, huddling forlornly, began to weep in the agony and with the convulsive tremors of an infant. The pistol fell from her fingers and rattled down to the floor.

The astonished troopers looked at their astonished captain. There was a short silence.

Finally, the captain stooped and picked up the pistol. It was a heavy weapon of the army pattern. He ascertained that it was empty.

He leaned toward the shaking girl, and said gently: "Will you tell me what you were going to do with this pistol?"

He had to repeat the question a number of times, but at last a muffled voice said, "Nothing."

"Nothing!" He insisted quietly upon a further answer. At the tender tones of the captain's voice, the phlegmatic corporal turned and winked gravely at the man next to him.

"Won't you tell me?"

The girl shook her head.

"Please tell me!"

The silent privates were moving their feet uneasily and wondering how long they were to wait.

The captain said: "Please, won't you tell me?"

Then this girl's voice began in stricken tones half coherent, and amid violent sobbing: "It was grandpa's. He—he—he said he was going to shoot anybody who came in here—he didn't care if there were thousands of 'em. And—and I know he would, and I was afraid they'd kill him. And so—and—so I stole away his pistol—and I was going to hide it when you—you—you kicked open the door."

The men straightened up and looked at each other. The girl began to weep again.

The captain mopped his brow. He peered down at the girl. He mopped his brow again. Suddenly he said: "Ah, don't cry like that."

He moved restlessly and looked down at his boots. He mopped his brow again.

Then he gripped the corporal by the arm and dragged him some yards back from the others. "Jones," he said, in an intensely earnest voice, "will you tell me what in the devil I am going to do?"

The corporal's countenance became illuminated with satisfaction at being thus requested to advise his superior officer. He adopted an air of great thought, and finally said: "Well, of course, the feller with the grey sleeve must be upstairs, and we must get past the girl and up there somehow. Suppose I take her by the arm and lead her——"

"What!" interrupted the captain from between his clinched teeth. As he turned away from the corporal, he said fiercely over his shoulder: "You touch that girl and I'll split your skull!"

III

The corporal looked after his captain with an expression of mingled amazement, grief, and philosophy. He seemed to be saying to himself that there unfortunately were times, after all, when one could not rely upon the most reliable of men. When he returned to the group he found the captain bending over the girl and saying: "Why is it that you don't want us to search upstairs?"

The girl's head was buried in her crossed arms. Locks of her hair had escaped from their fastenings, and these fell upon her shoulder.

"Won't you tell me?"

The corporal here winked again at the man next to him.

"Because," the girl moaned—"because—there isn't anybody up there."

The captain at last said timidly: "Well, I'm afraid—I'm afraid we'll have to——"

The girl sprang to her feet again, and implored him with her hands. She looked deep into his eyes with her glance, which was at this time like that of the fawn when it says to the hunter, "Have mercy upon me!"

These two stood regarding each other. The captain's foot was on the bottom step, but he seemed to be shrinking. He wore an air of being deeply wretched and ashamed. There was a silence.

Suddenly the corporal said in a quick, low tone: "Look out, captain!"

All turned their eyes swiftly toward the head of the stairs. There had appeared there a youth in a grey uniform. He stood looking coolly down at them. No word was said by the troopers. The girl gave vent to a little wail of desolation, "O Harry!"

He began slowly to descend the stairs. His right arm was in a white sling, and there were some fresh blood-stains upon the cloth. His face was rigid and deathly pale, but his eyes flashed like lights. The girl was again moaning in an utterly dreary fashion, as the youth came slowly down toward the silent men in blue.

Six steps from the bottom of the flight he halted and said: " I reckon it's me you're looking for."

The troopers had crowded forward a trifle and, posed in lithe, nervous attitudes, were watching him like cats. The captain remained unmoved. At the youth's question he merely nodded his head and said, "Yes."

The young man in grey looked down at the girl, and then, in the same even tone which now, however, seemed to vibrate with suppressed fury, he said: " And is that any reason why you should insult my sister ? "

At this sentence, the girl intervened, desperately, between the young man in grey and the officer in blue. "Oh, don't, Harry, don't! He was good to me! He was good to me, Harry— indeed he was!"

The youth came on in his quiet, erect fashion, until the girl could have touched either of the men with her hand, for the captain still remained with his foot upon the first step. She continually repeated: "O Harry! O Harry!"

The youth in grey manœuvred to glare into the captain's face, first over one shoulder of the girl and then over the other. In a voice that rang like metal, he said: "You are armed and unwounded, while I have no weapons and am wounded; but——"

The captain had stepped back and sheathed his sabre. The eyes of these two men were gleaming fire, but otherwise the captain's countenance was imperturbable. He said: "You are mistaken. You have no reason to——"

"You lie!"

All save the captain and the youth in grey started in an electric movement. These two words crackled in the air like shattered glass. There was a breathless silence.

The captain cleared his throat. His look at the youth contained a quality of singular and terrible ferocity, but he said in his stolid tone: "I don't suppose you mean what you say now."

Upon his arm he had felt the pressure of some unconscious little fingers. The girl was leaning against the wall as if she no longer knew how to keep her balance, but those fingers—he held his arm very still. She murmured: "O Harry, don't! He was good to me—indeed he was!"

The corporal had come forward until he in a measure confronted the youth in grey, for he saw those fingers upon the captain's arm, and he knew that sometimes very strong men were not able to move hand nor foot under such conditions.

The youth had suddenly seemed to become weak. He breathed heavily and clung to the rail. He was glaring at the captain, and apparently summoning all his will power to combat his weakness. The corporal addressed him with profound straightforwardness: "Don't you be a derned fool!" The youth turned toward him

30 fiercely that the corporal threw up a knee and an elbow like a boy who expects to be cuffed.

The girl pleaded with the captain. " You won't hurt him, will you? He don't know what he's saying. He's wounded, you know. Please don't mind him!"

" I won't touch him," said the captain, with rather extraordinary earnestness; "don't you worry about him at all. I won't touch him!"

Then he looked at her, and the girl suddenly withdrew her fingers from his arm.

The corporal contemplated the top of the stairs, and remarked without surprise: " There's another of 'em coming!"

An old man was clambering down the stairs with much speed. He waved a cane wildly. "Get out of my house, you thieves! Get out! I won't have you cross my threshold! Get out!" He mumbled and wagged his head in an old man's fury. It was plainly his intention to assault them.

And so it occurred that a young girl became engaged in protecting a stalwart captain, fully armed, and with eight grim troopers at his back, from the attack of an old man with a walking-stick!

A blush passed over the temples and brow of the captain, and he looked particularly savage and weary. Despite the girl's efforts, he suddenly faced the old man.

"Look here," he said distinctly, "we came in because we had been fighting in the woods yonder, and we concluded that some of the enemy were in this house, especially when we saw a grey sleeve at the window. But this young man is wounded, and I have nothing to say to him. I will even take it for granted that there are no others like him upstairs. We will go away, leaving your d——d old house just as we found it! And we are no more thieves and rascals than you are!"

The old man simply roared: "I haven't got a cow nor a pig nor a chicken on the place! Your soldiers have stolen everything they could carry away. They have torn down half my fences for firewood. This afternoon some of your accursed bullets even broke my window panes!"

The girl had been faltering: "Grandpa! O grandpa!"

The captain looked at the girl. She returned his glance from the shadow of the old man's shoulder. After studying her face a moment, he said: "Well, we will go now." He strode toward the door, and his men clanked docilely after him.

At this time there was the sound of harsh cries and rushing footsteps from without. The door flew open, and a whirlwind composed of blue-coated troopers came in with a swoop. It was headed by the lieutenant. "Oh, here you are!" he cried, catching his breath. "We thought——Oh, look at the girl!"

The captain said intensely: "Shut up, you fool!"

The men settled to a halt with a clash and a bang. There could be heard the dulled sound of many hoofs outside of the house.

"Did you order up the horses?" inquired the captain.

"Yes. We thought——"

"Well, then, let's get out of here," interrupted the captain morosely.

The men began to filter out into the open air. The youth in grey had been hanging dismally to the railing of the stairway. He now was climbing slowly up to the second floor. The old man was addressing himself directly to the serene corporal.

"Not a chicken on the place!" he cried.

"Well, I didn't take your chickens, did I?"

"No, maybe you didn't, but——"

The captain crossed the hall and stood before the girl in rather a culprit's fashion. "You are not angry at me, are you?" he asked timidly.

"No," she said. She hesitated a moment, and then suddenly held out her hand. "You were good to me—and I'm—much obliged."

The captain took her hand, and then he blushed, for he found himself unable to formulate a sentence that applied in any way to the situation.

She did not seem to heed that hand for a time.

He loosened his grasp presently, for he was ashamed to hold it so long without saying anything clever. At last, with an air of charging an intrenched brigade, he contrived to say: "I would rather do anything than frighten or trouble you."

His brow was warmly perspiring. He had a sense of being hideous in his dusty uniform and with his grimy face.

She said, "Oh, I'm so glad it was you instead of somebody who might have—might have hurt brother Harry and grandpa!"

He told her, "I wouldn't have hurt 'em for anything!"

There was a little silence.

"Well, good-bye!" he said at last.

"Good-bye!"

He walked toward the door past the old man, who was scolding at the vanishing figure of the corporal. The captain looked back. She had remained there watching him.

At the bugle's order, the troopers standing beside their horses swung briskly into the saddle. The lieutenant said to the first sergeant:

"Williams, did they ever meet before?"

"Hanged if I know!"

"Well, say——"

The captain saw a curtain move at one of the windows. He cantered from his position at the head of the column and steered his horse between two flower-beds.

"Well, good-bye!"

The squadron trampled slowly past.

"Good-bye!"

They shook hands.

He evidently had something enormously important to say to her, but it seems that he could not manage it. He struggled heroically. The bay charger, with his great mystically solemn eyes, looked around the corner of his shoulder at the girl.

The captain studied a pine tree. The girl inspected the grass beneath the window. The captain said hoarsely: "I don't suppose—I don't suppose—I'll ever see you again!"

She looked at him affrightedly and shrank back from the window. He seemed to have woefully expected a reception of this kind for his question. He gave her instantly a glance of appeal.

She said: "Why, no, I don't suppose you will."

"Never?"

"Why, no, 'tain't possible. You—you are a —Yankee!"

"Oh, I know it, but——" Eventually he continued: "Well, some day, you know, when there's no more fighting, we might——" He observed that she had again withdrawn suddenly into the shadow, so he said: "Well, good-bye!"

When he held her fingers she bowed her head, and he saw a pink blush steal over the curves of her cheek and neck.

"Am I never going to see you again ?"

She made no reply.

"Never ?" he repeated.

After a long time, he bent over to hear a faint reply: "Sometimes—when there are no troops in the neighbourhood—grandpa don't mind if I —walk over as far as that old oak tree yonder —in the afternoons."

It appeared that the captain's grip was very strong, for she uttered an exclamation and looked at her fingers as if she expected to find them mere fragments.   He rode away.

The bay horse leaped a flower-bed.   They were almost to the drive, when the girl uttered a panic-stricken cry.

The captain wheeled his horse violently, and upon his return journey went straight through a flower-bed.

The girl had clasped her hands.   She beseeched him wildly with her eyes.   "Oh, please, don't believe it !   I never walk to the old oak tree.   Indeed I don't !   I never—never—never walk there."

The bridle drooped on the bay charger's neck. The captain's figure seemed limp.   With an expression of profound dejection and gloom he stared off at where the leaden sky met the dark green line of the woods.   The long-impending rain began to fall with a mournful patter, drop and drop.   There was a silence.

At last a low voice said, "Well—I might—sometimes I might—perhaps—but only once in a great while—I might walk to the old tree—in the afternoons."

The Veteran

The Veteran

OUT of the low window could be seen three hickory trees placed irregularly in a meadow that was resplendent in spring-time green. Farther away, the old, dismal belfry of the village church loomed over the pines. A horse, meditating in the shade of one of the hickories, lazily swished his tail. The warm sunshine made an oblong of vivid yellow on the floor of the grocery.

"Could you see the whites of their eyes?" said the man, who was seated on a soap box.

"Nothing of the kind," replied old Henry warmly. "Just a lot of flitting figures, and I let go at where they 'peared to be the thickest. Bang!"

"Mr. Fleming," said the grocer—his deferential voice expressed somehow the old man's exact social weight—"Mr. Fleming, you never was frightened much in them battles, was you?"

The veteran looked down and grinned. Observing his manner, the entire group tittered. "Well, I guess I was," he answered finally. "Pretty well scared, sometimes. Why, in my first battle I thought the sky was falling down. I thought the world was coming to an end. You bet I was scared."

Every one laughed. Perhaps it seemed strange and rather wonderful to them that a man should admit the thing, and in the tone of their laughter there was probably more admiration than if old Fleming had declared that he had always been a lion. Moreover, they knew that he had ranked as an orderly sergeant, and so their opinion of his heroism was fixed. None, to be sure, knew how an orderly sergeant ranked, but then it was understood to be somewhere just shy of a major-general's stars. So, when old Henry admitted that he had been frightened, there was a laugh.

"The trouble was," said the old man, "I thought they were all shooting at me. Yes, sir, I thought every man in the other army was aiming at me in particular, and only me. And it seemed so darned unreasonable, you know. I wanted to explain to 'em what an almighty good fellow I was, because I thought then they might quit all trying to hit me. But I couldn't explain, and they kept on being unreasonable—blim!—blam! bang! So I run!"

Two little triangles of wrinkles appeared at the corners of his eyes. Evidently he appreciated some comedy in this recital. Down near his feet, however, little Jim, his grandson, was visibly horror-stricken. His hands were clasped nervously, and his eyes were wide with astonishment at this terrible scandal, his most magnificent grandfather telling such a thing.

"That was at Chancellorsville. Of course, afterward I got kind of used to it. A man does. Lots of men, though, seem to feel all right from the start. I did, as soon as I 'got on to it,' as they say now; but at first I was pretty well flustered. Now, there was young Jim Conklin, old Si Conklin's son—that used to keep the tannery—you none of you recollect him—well, he went into it from the start just as if he was born to it. But with me it was different. I had to get used to it."

When little Jim walked with his grandfather he was in the habit of skipping along on the stone pavement, in front of the three stores and the hotel of the town, and betting that he could avoid the cracks. But upon this day he walked soberly, with his hand gripping two of his grandfather's fingers. Sometimes he kicked abstractedly at dandelions that curved over the walk. Any one could see that he was much troubled.

"There's Sickles's colt over in the medder, Jimmie," said the old man. "Don't you wish you owned one like him?"

"Um," said the boy, with a strange lack of interest. He continued his reflections. Then finally he ventured: "Grandpa—now—was that true what you was telling those men?"

"What?" asked the grandfather. "What was I telling them?"

"Oh, about your running."

"Why, yes, that was true enough, Jimmie. It was my first fight, and there was an awful lot of noise, you know."

Jimmie seemed dazed that this idol, of its own will, should so totter. His stout boyish idealism was injured.

Presently the grandfather said: "Sickles's colt is going for a drink. Don't you wish you owned Sickles's colt, Jimmie?"

The boy merely answered: "He ain't as nice as our'n." He lapsed then into another moody silence.

.   .   .   .   .   .

One of the hired men, a Swede, desired to drive to the county seat for purposes of his own. The old man loaned a horse and an unwashed buggy. It appeared later that one of the purposes of the Swede was to get drunk.

After quelling some boisterous frolic of the farm hands and boys in the garret, the old man had that night gone peacefully to sleep, when he was aroused by clamouring at the kitchen door. He grabbed his trousers, and they waved out behind as he dashed forward. He could hear the voice of the Swede, screaming and blubbering. He pushed the wooden button, and, as the door flew open, the Swede, a maniac, stumbled inward, chattering, weeping, still screaming: "De barn fire! Fire! Fire! De barn fire! Fire! Fire! Fire!"

There was a swift and indescribable change in the old man. His face ceased instantly to be a face; it became a mask, a grey thing, with horror written about the mouth and eyes. He hoarsely shouted at the foot of the little rickety stairs, and immediately, it seemed, there came down an avalanche of men. No one knew that during this time the old lady had been standing in her night-clothes at the bedroom door, yelling: "What's th' matter? What's th' matter? What's th' matter?"

When they dashed toward the barn it presented to their eyes its usual appearance, solemn, rather mystic in the black night. The Swede's lantern was overturned at a point some yards in front of the barn doors. It contained a wild little conflagration of its own, and even in their excitement some of those who ran felt a gentle secondary vibration of the thrifty part of their minds at sight of this overturned lantern. Under ordinary circumstances it would have been a calamity.

But the cattle in the barn were trampling, trampling, trampling, and above this noise could be heard a humming like the song of innumerable bees. The old man hurled aside the great doors, and a yellow flame leaped out at one corner and sped and wavered frantically up the old grey wall. It was glad, terrible, this single flame, like the wild banner of deadly and triumphant foes.

The motley crowd from the garret had come with all the pails of the farm. They flung themselves upon the well. It was a leisurely old machine, long dwelling in indolence. It was in the habit of giving out water with a sort of reluctance. The men stormed at it, cursed it; but it continued to allow the buckets to be filled only after the wheezy windlass had howled many protests at the mad-handed men.

With his opened knife in his hand old Fleming himself had gone headlong into the barn, where the stifling smoke swirled with the air currents, and where could be heard in its fulness the terrible chorus of the flames, laden with tones of hate and death, a hymn of wonderful ferocity.

He flung a blanket over an old mare's head, cut the halter close to the manger, led the mare to the door, and fairly kicked her out to safety. He returned with the same blanket, and rescued one of the work horses. He took five horses out, and then came out himself, with his clothes bravely on fire. He had no whiskers, and very little hair on his head. They soused five pailfuls of water on him. His eldest son made a clean miss with the sixth pailful, because the old man had turned and was running down the decline and around to the basement of the barn, where were the stanchions of the cows. Some one noticed at the time that he ran very lamely, as if one of the frenzied horses had smashed his hip.

The cows, with their heads held in the heavy

stanchions, had thrown themselves, strangled themselves, tangled themselves—done everything which the ingenuity of their exuberant fear could suggest to them.

Here, as at the well, the same thing happened to every man save one. Their hands went mad. They became incapable of everything save the power to rush into dangerous situations.

The old man released the cow nearest the door, and she, blind drunk with terror, crashed into the Swede. The Swede had been running to and fro babbling. He carried an empty milk-pail, to which he clung with an unconscious, fierce enthusiasm. He shrieked like one lost as he went under the cow's hoofs, and the milk-pail, rolling across the floor, made a flash of silver in the gloom.

Old Fleming took a fork, beat off the cow, and dragged the paralysed Swede to the open air. When they had rescued all the cows save one, which had so fastened herself that she could not be moved an inch, they returned to the front of the barn, and stood sadly, breathing like men who had reached the final point of human effort.

Many people had come running. Some one had even gone to the church, and now, from the distance, rang the tocsin note of the old bell. There was a long flare of crimson on the sky, which made remote people speculate as to the whereabouts of the fire.

The long flames sang their drumming chorus

in voices of the heaviest bass. The wind whirled clouds of smoke and cinders into the faces of the spectators. The form of the old barn was outlined in black amid these masses of orange-hued flames.

And then came this Swede again, crying as one who is the weapon of the sinister fates: "De colts! De colts! You have forgot de colts!"

Old Fleming staggered. It was true: they had forgotten the two colts in the box-stalls at the back of the barn. "Boys," he said, "I must try to get 'em out." They clamoured about him then, afraid for him, afraid of what they should see. Then they talked wildly each to each. "Why, it's sure death!" "He would never get out!" "Why, it's suicide for a man to go in there!" Old Fleming stared absent-mindedly at the open doors. "The poor little things!" he said. He rushed into the barn.

When the roof fell in, a great funnel of smoke swarmed toward the sky, as if the old man's mighty spirit, released from its body—a little bottle — had swelled like the genie of fable. The smoke was tinted rose-hue from the flames, and perhaps the unutterable midnights of the universe will have no power to daunt the colour of this soul.

Printed by Ballantyne, Hanson & Co.
Edinburgh & London

Art.

AN ALMANAC OF TWELVE SPORTS FOR 1898. By William Nicholson. Twelve Coloured Plates, each illustrating a sport for the month. With accompanying Rhymes by RUDYARD KIPLING. 4to. *Popular Edition*, Lithographed, price 2s. 6d. *Library Edition*, on Japanese Vellum, all sold. *Edition de Luxe* (Limited). Hand-coloured and signed bv the Artist. In Vellum Portfolio. Price £12 12. net.

AN ALPHABET. By William Nicholson. Twenty-six Coloured Plates, each illustrating a letter of the Alphabet. 4to. *Popular Edition*, Lithographed, all sold *Library Edition*, on Dutch Hand-made Paper, mounted on brown paper and bound in cloth, gilt edges. Price 12s. 6d. net. *Eaition de Luxe* (Limited). Hand-coloured and signed by the Artist. In Vellum Portfolio. Price £21 net.

PORTRAITS BY MR. NICHOLSON. HER MAJESTY THE QUEEN, MADAME SARAH BERNHARDT, LORD ROBERTS MR. WHISTLER, MR. RUDYARD KIPLING, MR. CECIL RHODES, and PRINCE BISMARCK. Mounted on card for framing, price 2s. 6d.each[net.
. A few copies of each Portrait printed from the Original Woodblocks, Hand-coloured, and signed by the Artist, are still obtainable. Price £2 2s. each net.

A HISTORY OF DANCING: From the Earliest Ages to Our Own Times. From the French of Gaston Vuillier. With 20 Plates in Photogravure and 409 Illustrations in the Text. 4to., cloth, price 36s. net., or full Vellum, gilt top, 50s. net.
. Also 35 copies printed on Japanese Vellum (containing three additional plates), with a duplicate set of the Plates on India paper for framing. Each copy numbered and signed, price £12 12s. net.

MEISSONIER: His Life, and His Art. By Vallery C. O. Greard. Translated by LADY MARY LOYD and FLORENCE SIMMONDS. 4to., with 38 full-page plates and 200 text illustrations, price £1 16s. net.

ANTONIO ALLEGRI DA CORREGGIO: His Life, His Friends, and His Time By Dr. Corrado Ricci. Translated by Florence Simmonds. 4to, with 37 plates and 190 text illustrations, price £2 2s. net; also a limited edition on Japanese Vellum, with duplicates of the Photogravure plates on India paper; price £12 12s. net.

MASTERPIECES OF GREEK SCULPTURE. A Series of Essays on the History of Art. By Adolf Furtwangler. Edited by E. Sellers. 4to, with 19 full-page and 200 text Illustrations, price £3 3s. *net.*
Also an Edition de Luxe limited to 50 copies on Japanese Vellum, in Two Volumes, £10 10s. *net.*

REMBRANDT: Seventeen of his Masterpieces from the Collection of his Pictures in the Cassel Gallery. Reproduced in Photogravure by the Berlin Photographic Company. With an Essay by Frederick Wedmore. In large portfolio 27½ inches by 20 inches.
Fourteen of the first twenty-five impressions numbered and signed, Twenty Guineas net, the set. After impressions Twelve Guineas net, per set.

REMBRANDT: His Life, His Work, and His Time. By Emile Michel, Member of the Institute of France. Translated by Florence Simmonds. Edited and Prefaced by Frederick Wedmore. Second Edition In Two Volumes, with 76 plates and 250 text illustrations, price £2 2s. *net.*
. A few copies of the EDITION DE LUXE of the FIRST EDITION (printed on Japanese vellum with India proof duplicates of the photogravures), are still on sale, price £12 12s. net.

A CATALOGUE OF THE ACCADEMIA DELLE BELLE ARTI AT VENICE. With Biographical Notices of the Painters and Reproductions of some of their Works. Edited by E. M. KEARY. Crown 8vo, cloth, 2s. 6d. net.; paper, 2s. net.

A CATALOGUE OF THE MUSEO DEL PRADO AT MADRID. Edited by E. LAWSON. Crown 8vo., cloth. 3s. net.; paper, 2s. 6d. net.

BEAUTY AND ART. By Aldam Heaton. Crown 8vo., with hand-painted title page, 6s.

ANIMAL SYMBOLISM IN ECCLESIASTICAL ARCHITECTURE. By E P. Evans. With a Bibliography and 78 Illustrations, crown 8vo. 9s.

Travel and Adventure.

THE INDIAN FRONTIER CAMPAIGN. An account of the Mohmund and Tirah Expedition 1897. By Lionel James. 8vo., Illustrated, 7s. 6d.

ROMANTIC INDIA. By Andre Chevrillon. Demy 8vo., 7s. 6d. *net*.

WITH THE ZHOB FIELD FORCE, 1890. By Captain Crawford McFall, K.O.Y.L.I. Demy 8vo, with Illustrations, price 18s.

COREA; or, Cho-sen, The Land of the Morning Calm. By A. Henry Savage-Landor. With Seven Full-page Plates and over Thirty Text Illustrations. Demy 8vo, cloth, price 18s.

UNDER THE DRAGON FLAG. My Experiences in the Chino-Japanese War. By James Allan. Crown 8vo., 2s.

MY FOURTH TOUR IN WESTERN AUSTRALIA. By Albert F. Calvert, F.R.G.S. 4to., with many Illustrations and Photographs, price 21s. net.

THE NEW AFRICA. A Journey up the Chobe and down the Okovanga Rivers. By Aurel Schulz, M.D., and August Hammar, C.E. Demy 8vo., with original illustrations, 28s.

ACTUAL AFRICA, or, The Coming Continent. A Tour of Exploration. By Frank Vincent, Author of "The Land of the White Elephant." With Map and over 100 Illustrations, demy 8vo, cloth, price 24s.

THE LAND OF THE MUSKEG. By H. Somers Somerset. With a Preface by A. Hungerford Pollen. In One Volume, demy 8vo, with Maps and 110 Illustrations, price 14s. *Net*.

CUBA, IN WARTIME. By Richard Harding Davis. With numerous Illustrations by Frederic Remington. Crown 8vo., 3s. 6d.

IN THE TRACK OF THE SUN. Readings from the Diary of a Globe-Trotter. By Frederick Diodati Thompson. In One Volume, 4to. With many Illustrations by Mr Harry Fenn and from Photographs, price 25s.

THE OUTGOING TURK. Impressions of a Journey through the Western Balkans. By H. C. Thomson. Demy 8vo., with original illustrations, 14s. net.

TIMBUCTOO THE MYSTERIOUS. By Felix Dubois. With 153 Illustrations, and 11 Maps and Plans. Demy 8vo., 12s. 6d.

THE WORKERS, AN EXPERIMENT IN REALITY. By Walter A. Wyckoff. Illustrated. Crown 8vo., 3s. 6d.

Illustrated Books and Books for Presents.

THE CASTLES OF ENGLAND; Their Story and Structure. By Sir James Mackenzie, Bart. With 40 photogravure and other plates, 58 text illustrations, and 70 plans. In two volumes, imperial 8vo., £3 3s. net.

DRIVING FOR PLEASURE; or, The Harness Stable and Its Appointments. By Francis T. Underhill. 4to., with 125 Illustrations, 28s. net.

THE POCKET IBSEN. A Collection of some of the Master's best known Dramas, condensed, revised, and slightly rearranged for the benefit of the Earnest Student. By F. Anstey. Reprinted with Illustrations, by permission from *Punch*. With a new Frontispiece, by Bernard Partridge. A New Edition, 16mo, cloth, 3s. 6d., paper 2s. 6d.

Illustrated Books and Books for Presents.—*Continued.*

FROM WISDOM COURT. By Henry Seton Merriman and Stephen Graham Tallentyre. Crown 8vo, with 30 Illustrations by E. Courboin, price 3s. 6d. cloth; or 2s. picture boards.

THE OLD MAIDS' CLUB. By I. Zangwill, Author of "Children of the Ghetto," &c. Crown 8vo, illustrated by F. H. Townsend, price 3s. 6d. cloth; or 2s. picture boards.

WOMAN—THROUGH A MAN'S EYEGLASS. By Malcolm C. Salaman. Crown 8vo, with Illustrations by Dudley Hardy, price 3s. 6d. cloth; or 2s. picture boards.

THE PINERO BIRTHDAY BOOK. Selected and arranged by MYRA HAMILTON, 16mo, with a portrait, 2s. 6d.

THE SPINSTER'S SCRIP. As compiled by Cecil Raynor. Narrow foolscap, limp cloth, price 2s. 6d.

STORIES OF GOLF. Collected by William Knight and T. T. Oliphant. With Rhymes on Golf by various hands; also Shakespeare on Golf, &c. *Enlarged Edition.* Fcap. 8vo, price 2s. 6d.

THE ROSE: A Treatise on the Cultivation, History, Family Characteristics, &c., of the Various Groups of Roses. With Accurate Description of the Varieties now Generally Grown. By H. B. Ellwanger. With an Introduction by George H. Ellwanger. 12mo, price 5s.

THE GARDEN'S STORY; or Pleasures and Trials of an Amateur Gardener. By G. H. Ellwanger. With an Introduction by the Rev. C. Wolley Dod. 12mo, with Illustrations, price 5s.

GIRLS AND WOMEN. By E. Chester. Pott 8vo, price 2s. 6d., or gilt extra, 3s. 6d.

A BATTLE AND A BOY. By Blanche Willis Howard. Crown 8vo, cloth gilt. With 39 Illustrations by A MacNiell-Barbour. Price 6s.

THE ATTACK ON THE MILL. By Emile Zola. In One Volume. 4to, With Twenty-four Illustrations, and Five exquisitely printed Coloured Plates, from original drawings by E. Courboin. Price 5s.

LITTLE JOHANNES. By F. Van Eeden. Translated from the Dutch by Clara Bell. With an Introduction by Andrew Lang. 16mo. Price 3s. *net.*

Handbooks for Tourists.

NOTES FOR THE NILE. Together with a Metrical Rendering of the Hymns of Ancient Egypt and of the Precepts of Ptahhotep (the oldest book in the world). By Hardwicke D. Rawnsley, M.A. 16mo, cloth, 5s.

THE CANADIAN GUIDE-BOOK. Part I. The Tourist's and Sportsman's Guide to Eastern Canada and Newfoundland, including full descriptions of Routes, Cities, Points of Interest, Summer Resorts, Fishing Places, &c., In Eastern Ontario, The Muskoka District, The St. Lawrence Region, The Lake St. John Country, The Maritime Provinces, Prince Edward Island, and Newfoundland. With an Appendix giving Fish and Game Laws, and Official Lists of Trout and Salmon Rivers and their Lessees. By Charles G. D. Roberts, Professor of English Literature in King's College, Windsor, N.S. Crown 8vo, limp cloth, with Maps and many Illustrations, price 6s.

Handbooks for Tourists. *Continued.*

THE CANADIAN GUIDE BOOK. Part II. **Western Canada.** Including the Peninsula and Northern Regions of Ontario, the Canadian Shores of the Great Lakes, the Lake of the Woods Region, Manitoba and "The Great North-West," The Canadian Rocky Mountains and National Park, British Columbia, and Vancouver Island. **By Ernest Ingersoll.** Crown 8vo, limp cloth, with Maps and many Illustrations, price 6s.

THE GUIDE-BOOK TO ALASKA AND THE NORTH-WEST COAST. including the Shores of Washington, British Columbia, South-Eastern Alaska, the Aleutian and the Seal Islands, the Behring and the Arctic Coasts. **By E. R. Scidmore.** Crown 8vo limp cloth, with Maps and many Illustrations, price 6s.

Essays and Criticism.

THE FOREIGNER IN THE FARMYARD. By Ernest E. Williams. Author of "Made in Germany." Crown 8vo., 2s. 6d.

"MADE IN GERMANY." By Ernest Edwin Williams. Crown 8vo., Cloth, 2s. 6d.; paper covers, 1s.

ANIMA POETÆ. A Selection from the unpublished Note Books of Samuel Taylor Coleridge. Edited by E. H. Colerdge. Crown 8vo, price 7s. 6d.

ESSAYS. By Arthur Christopher Benson. Crown 8vo, buckram, price 7s. 6d.

WILLIAM SHAKESPEARE. A Critical Study. By George Brandes. Translated from the Danish by William Archer and Diana White. In Two Volumes, Demy 8vo., 24s. *net.*

THE WORKS OF LORD BYRON. Edited by W. E. Henley. In Twelve Volumes, Crown 8vo., 5s. net. each. Volume I., Letters 1803-1814, ready.
. Also 150 sets on Van Gelder's hand made paper £6 6s. net.

CORRECTED IMPRESSIONS. By George Saintsbury. In One Volume. Crown 8vo, price 7s. 6d.

CRITICAL KIT-KATS. By Edmund Gosse. Crown 8vo., Buckram, gilt top, 7s. 6d.

GOSSIP IN A LIBRARY. By Edmund Gosse. Third Edition. Crown 8vo, buckram, gilt top, price 7s. 6d.
. A Limited Edition on Large Paper, 25s. net.

QUESTIONS AT ISSUE. Essays. By Edmund Gosse. Crown 8vo, buckram, gilt top, price 7s. 6d.
. A Limited Edition on Large Paper, 25s. net.

SEVENTEENTH CENTURY STUDIES. A Contribution to the History of English Poetry. By Edmund Gosse. A New Edition. Crown 8vo. buckram, gilt top, 7s. 6d.

GENIUS AND DEGENERATION. A Psychological Study. By Dr. W. Hirsch. Demy 8vo, price 17s. net.

THE NON-RELIGION OF THE FUTURE. By Marie Jean Guyau. Demy 8vo., price 17s. net.

THE COMING TERROR. And other Essays and Letters. By Robert Buchanan. Second Edition. Demy 8vo, price 12s. 6d.

Essays and Criticism. *Continued.*

THE GENTLE ART OF MAKING ENEMIES. As pleasingly exemplified in many instances, wherein the serious ones of this earth, carefully exasperated, have been prettily spurred on to indiscretions and unseemliness, while overcome by an undue sense of right. **By J. McNeill Whistler.** A New Edition. *(In preparation.*

MANNERS, CUSTOMS, AND OBSERVANCES: Their Origin and Signification. By Leopold Wagner. In One Volume, Crown 8vo price 6s.

THE POSTHUMOUS WORKS OF THOMAS DE QUINCEY. Edited with Introduction and Notes from the Author's Original MSS., by ALEXANDER H. JAPP, LL.D., F.R.S.E., &c. Crown 8vo, price 6s. each.

I. **Suspiria de Profundis.** With other Essays.—II. **Conversation and Coleridge.** With other Essays.

THE PROSE WORKS OF HEINRICH HEINE. Translated by CHARLES GODFREY LELAND, M.A.. F.R.L.S. (Hans Breitmann). In Eight Volumes, Crown 8vo, cloth, 5s. per volume. Cabinet Edition, boxed, price £2 10s. the set. Large Paper Edition, limited to 50 Numbered Copies, price £6 net. the set.

I. **Florentine Nights, &c.**—II., III. **Pictures of Travel.**—IV. **The Salon.**—V., VI. **Germany.**—VII., VIII. **French Affairs.**

A COMMENTARY ON THE WORKS OF HENRIK IBSEN. By Hjalmar Hjorth Boyesen. Crown 8vo, price 7s. 6d. *net.*

AMERICA AND THE AMERICANS. From a French Point of View. Crown 8vo., 3s. 6d.

Biography and History.

NEW LETTERS OF NAPOLEON I. Omitted from the collection published under the auspices of Napoleon III. Translated by **Lady Mary Loyd.** Demy 8vo., with frontispiece, 15s. net.

PETER THE GREAT. By **K. Waliszewski.** Translated by **Lady Mary Loyd.** 8vo. With Portrait, 6s.

MARYSIENKA, MARIE DE LA GRANGE D'ARQUIEN. QUEEN OF POLAND AND WIFE OF SOBIESKI. By **K. Waliszewski.** Translated by Lady MARY LOYD. With Portrait. *(In preparation.*

CATHERINE SFORZA. A Study. By Count Pasolini. Adapted from Italian by PAUL SYLVESTER. Demy 8vo., with many Illustrations. *(In preparation.*

THE PAGET PAPERS. Diplomatic and other Correspondence of **The Rt. Hon. Sir Arthur Paget, G.C.B., 1794—1807.** Edited by **The Rt. Hon. Sir Augustus Paget, G.C.B.** (Late H.M. Ambassador at Vienna). With notes by Mrs. J. R. Green. In Two Volumes. Demy 8vo, with Portraits. 32s. net.

CARDINAL MANNING. By **Francis de Pressense.** Crown 8vo., cloth, price 5s.

BROTHER AND SISTER. A Memoir and the Letters of Ernest and Henriette Renan. Translated by **Lady Mary Loyd.** Demy 8vo, with Two Portraits, price 14s.

Biography and History.—*Continued.*

THE PALMY DAYS OF NANCE OLDFIELD. By Edward Robins. In One Volume, 8vo., with 12 Illustrations.   *(In preparation.*

CHARLES GOUNOD. Autobiographical Reminiscences with Family Letters and Notes on Music. Translated by the Hon. W. Hely Hutchinson. Demy 8vo, with a Portrait, price 10s. 6d.

THE LIFE OF NELSON. By Robert Southey. A New Edition. Edited by David Hannay. Crown 8vo, gilt, with two Portraits, 6s.

ROBERT EARL NUGENT.' A Memoir. By Claud Nugent. Demy 8vo, with Portraits.   *(In preparation.*

LETTERS OF SAMUEL TAYLOR COLERIDGE. Edited by Ernest Hartley Coleridge. With Portraits and Illustrations. In Two Volumes demy 8vo, price 32s.

DE QUINCEY MEMORIALS. Being Letters and other Records here first Published, with Communications from Coleridge, The Wordsworths, Hannah More, Professor Wilson, and others. Edited with Introduction, Notes, and Narrative, by Alexander H. Japp, LL.D., F.R.S.E. In Two Volumes, demy 8vo, cloth, with Portraits, price 30s. net.

MEMOIRS OF THE PRINCE DE JOINVILLE. Translated from the French by Lady Mary Loyd. With 78 Illustrations from drawings by the Author. 8vo, price 6s.

ALFRED, LORD TENNYSON. A Study of His Life and Work. By Arthur Waugh, B.A., Oxon. With Twenty Illustrations from Photographs specially taken for this Work, Five Portraits, and Facsimile of Tennyson's MS. Fourth Edition. 8vo, price 6s.

MEMOIRS. By Charles Godfrey Leland (Hans Breitmann). Second Edition. In One Volume, 8vo, with Portrait, price 7s. 6d.

VILLIERS DE L'ISLE ADAM: His Life and Works. From the French of Vicomte Robert du Pontavice de Heussey. By Lady Mary Loyd. Crown 8vo, with Portrait and Facsimile, price 10s. 6d.

RECOLLECTIONS OF MIDDLE LIFE. By Francisque Sarcey. Translated by E. L. Carey. In One Volume, 8vo, with Portrait, price 10s. 6d.

PRINCE BISMARCK. An Historical Biography. By Charles Lowe, M.A. Crown 8vo, with Portraits, price 6s.

ALEXANDER III. OF RUSSIA. By Charles Lowe, M.A. Crown 8vo, with Portrait, price 6s.

THE FAMILY LIFE OF HEINRICH HEINE. Illustrated by one hundred and twenty-two hitherto unpublished letters addressed by him to different members of his family. Edited by his nephew, Baron Ludwig Von Embden, and translated by Charles Godfrey Leland. In One Volume, 8vo, with Four Portraits, price 6s.

RECOLLECTIONS OF COUNT LEO TOLSTOY. Together with a Letter to the Women of France on the "Kreutzer Sonata." By C. A. Behrs. Translated from the Russian by C. E. Turner, English Lecturer in the University of St. Petersburg. In One Volume, 8vo, with Portrait, price 6s.

THE LIFE OF HENRIK IBSEN. By Henrik Jæger. Translated by Clara Bell. With the Verse done into English from the Norwegian Original by Edmund Gosse. Crown 8vo, price 6s.

EDMOND AND JULES DE GONCOURT. Letters and Leaves from their Journals. Selected. In Two Volumes, 8vo., with Eight Portraits, 32s.

𝔅iography and 𝔥istory. *Continued.*

THE LIFE OF JUDGE JEFFREYS. By H. B. Irving, M.A., Oxon. 8vo., with Three Portraits and a Facsimile. Price 12s. 6d. net.

TWENTY-FIVE YEARS IN THE SECRET SERVICE. The Recollections of a Spy. By Major Henry Le Caron. With New Preface. 8vo, boards, price 2s. 6d., or cloth, 3s. 6d.

. The Library Edition, with Portraits and Facsimiles, 8vo, 14s., is still on sale.

THE NATURALIST OF THE SEA-SHORE. The Life of Philip Henry Gosse. By his son, Edmund Gosse, Hon. M.A., Trinity College, Cambridge. With a Portrait. 8vo., price 6s.

LETTERS OF A COUNTRY VICAR. From the French of M. Guyau. Crown 8vo., cloth, 5s.

LETTERS OF A BARITONE. By Francis Walker. In One Volume, small crown 8vo, 5s.

THE LOVE LETTERS OF MR. H. AND MISS R. 1775-1779. Edited by Gilbert Burgess. Small crown 8vo., 5s.

STUDIES IN FRANKNESS. By Charles Whibley. Crown 8vo., with Frontispiece, price 7s. 6d.

A BOOK OF SCOUNDRELS. By Charles Whibley. Crown 8vo, with Frontispiece. 7s. 6d.

QUEEN JOANNA I. OF NAPLES, SICILY, AND JERUSALEM : Countess of Provence, Forcalquier, and Piedmont. An Essay on her Times. By St. Clair Baddeley. 8vo., with numerous Illustrations, 16s.

CHARLES III. OF NAPLES AND URBAN VI. ; also Cecco D'Ascoli, Poet. Astrologer, Physician. Two Historical Essays. By St. Clair Baddeley. 8vo., with Illustrations, 10s. 6d.

ROBERT THE WISE AND HIS HEIRS, 1278-1352. By St. Clair Baddeley. 8vo., with Illustrations, 21s.

THE WOMEN OF HOMER. By Walter Copland Perry. With 22 Illustrations, 8vo., price 6s.

KRUPP'S STEEL WORKS. By Prof. F. C. G. Muller. With 88 Illustrations. Authorised Translation. 4to., 25s. *net.*

THE GENESIS OF THE UNITED STATES. A Narrative of the Movement in England, 1605-1616, which resulted in the Plantation of North America by Englishmen, disclosing the Contest between England and Spain for the Possession of the Soil now occupied by the United States of America; set forth through a series of Historical Manuscripts now first printed, together with a Re-issue of Rare Contemporaneous Tracts, accompanied by Bibliographical Memoranda, Notes, and Brief Biographies. Collected, Arranged, and Edited by Alexander Brown, F.R.H.S. In two volumes, royal 8vo, buckram, with 100 Portraits, Maps, and Plans, price £3 13s. 6d. net.

DENMARK : its History, Topography, Language, Literature, Fine Arts, Social Life, and Finance. Edited by H. Weitemeyer. Demy 8vo, cloth, with Map, price 12s. 6d.

. *Dedicated, by permission, to H.R.H. the Princess of Wales.*

𝔅iography and 𝔥istory. *Continued.*

SPANISH PROTESTANTS IN THE SIXTEENTH CENTURY. Compiled from the German of C. A. Wilkens by Rachel Challice. With an Introduction by the Late Most Rev. Lord Plunket, D.D., Archbishop of Dublin, and Preface by the Rev. Canon Fleming, B.D. Crown 8vo., 4s. 6d. *net.*

STUDIES IN DIPLOMACY. From the French of Count Benedetti, French Ambassador at the Court of Berlin. 8vo, cloth, with Portrait, price 10s. 6d.

AN AMBASSADOR OF THE VANQUISHED. Viscount Elie De Gontaut—Biron's Mission to Berlin, 1871—1877. From His Diaries and Memoranda. By the Duke De Broglie. Translated with Notes by Albert D. Vandam, Author of "An Englishman in Paris." 8vo, 10s. 6d.

MY PARIS NOTE-BOOK. By the Author of "An Englishman in Paris." Second Edition, 8vo, price 6s.

THE REALM OF THE HABSBURGS. By Sidney Whitman, Author of "Imperial Germany." In One Volume, crown 8vo, price 7s. 6d.

IMPERIAL GERMANY. A Critical Study of Fact and Character. By Sidney Whitman. New Edition, Revised and Enlarged. Crown 8vo, price, cloth, 2s. 6d.; paper, 2s.

THE LITTLE MANX NATION. (Lectures delivered at the Royal Institution, 1891). By Hall Caine. Crown 8vo, price, cloth, 3s. 6d.; paper, 2s. 6d.

ISRAEL AMONG THE NATIONS. By Anatole Leroy-Beaulieu. Translated from the French. In One Volume, 8vo, price 7s. 6d.

THE NEW EXODUS. A Study of Israel in Russia. By Harold Frederic. Demy 8vo, Illustrated, price 16s.

THE JEW AT HOME. Impressions of a Summer and Autumn spent with Him in Austria and Russia. By Joseph Pennell. 4to, with Illustrations by the Author, price 5s.

THE LABOUR MOVEMENT IN AMERICA. By Richard T. Ely, Ph.D., Associate in Political Economy, Johns Hopkins University. Crown 8vo, price 5s.

AS OTHERS SAW HIM. A Retrospect, A.D. 54. In One Volume crown 8vo, gilt top, 6s.

𝔓oetry.

THE WORKS OF LORD BYRON. Edited by W. E. Henley. In Twelve Volumes, Crown 8vo., 5s. each. *(In Preparation.*

POEMS FROM THE DIVAN OF HAFIZ. Translated from the Persian by Gertrude Lowthian Bell. Small crown 8vo., price 6s.

A SELECTION FROM THE POEMS OF WILFRID SCAWEN BLUNT. With an Introduction by W. E. Henley. Crown 8vo., price 6s.

THE BLACK RIDERS, and other Lines. By Stephen Crane. 16mo, leather gilt, 3s. net.

FIRDAUSI IN EXILE, and other Poems. By Edmund Gosse. Fcap 8vo., with Frontispiece, price 3s. 6d. *net.*

ON VIOL AND FLUTE. By Edmund Gosse. Fcap 8vo., with Frontispiece, price 3s. 6d. *net.*

Poetry. *Continued.*

IN RUSSET AND SILVER: Poems. By Edmund Gosse, Author of "Gossip in a Library," &c. F'cap, price 3s. 6d. net.

IN CAP AND GOWN: Three Centuries of Cambridge Wit. Edited by Charles Whibley. Third Edition. With Frontispiece. Crown 8vo., 3s. 6d. *net.*

THE POETRY OF PATHOS AND DELIGHT. From the works of Coventry Patmore. Passages selected by Alice Meynell. Fcap 8vo, with a Portrait, price 5s.

A CENTURY OF GERMAN LYRICS. Selected, Arranged, and Translated by KATE FREILIGRATH KROEKER. Fcap. 8vo, price 3s. 6d.

LOVE SONGS OF ENGLISH POETS. 1500–1800. With Notes by RALPH H. CAINE. Fcap. 8vo, rough edges, price 3s. 6d.
   . Large Paper Edition, limited to 100 Copies, 10s. 6d. net.

IDYLLS OF WOMANHOOD. By C. Amy Dawson. Fcap. 8vo, gilt top, price 5s.

TENNYSON'S GRAVE. By St. Clair Baddeley. 8vo, paper, price 1s.

IVY AND PASSION FLOWER: Poems. By Gerard Bendall, Author of "Estelle," &c., &c. 12mo, cloth, price 3s. 6d.

VERSES. By Gertrude Hall. 12mo, cloth, price 3s. 6d.

The Drama.

CYRANO DE BERGERAC: A Play in Five Acts. By Edmond Rostand. Authorised Translation, prepared with the help of the Author. Small 4to., price 5s.

THE PLAYS OF W. E. HENLEY AND R. L. STEVENSON. DEACON BRODIE. BEAU AUSTIN. ADMIRAL GUINEA. MACAIRE. In one volume, crown 8vo, cloth. An edition of 250 copies only, 10s. 6d. net. Also separately. 16mo., cloth, 2s. 6d.; paper, 1s. 6d. each.

THE PLAYS OF HENRIK IBSEN. THE MASTER BUILDER. HEDDA GABLER. LITTLE EYOLF. JOHN GABRIEL BORKMAN. Small 4to., cloth, 5s., paper, 1s. 6d. each.

BRAND: A Dramatic Poem in Five Acts. By Henrik Ibsen. Translated in the original metres, with an Introduction and Notes, by C. H. Herford. Small 4to, cloth, 7s. 6d.

THE PLAYS OF GERHART HAUPTMANN. HANNELE. Small 4to, cloth, with Portrait, 5s. LONELY LIVES, THE WEAVERS. (*In preparation.*) 16mo., cloth, 2s. 6d., paper, 1s. 6d. each.

THE PRINCESSE MALEINE: A Drama in Five Acts. (Translated by Gerard Harry), and THE INTRUDER : A Drama in One Act. By Maurice Maeterlinck. With an Introduction by Hall Caine, and a Portrait of the Author. Small 4to, cloth, 5s.

THE FRUITS OF ENLIGHTENMENT: A Comedy in Four Acts. By Count Lyof Tolstoy. Translated from the Russian by E. J. Dillon. With Introduction by A. W. Pinero. Small 4to, with Portrait, 5s.

KING ERIK. A Tragedy. By Edmund Gosse. A Re-issue with a Critical Introduction by Mr. Theodore Watts. Fcap. 8vo, boards, 5s. net.

HYPATIA. A Play in Four Acts. Founded on Charles Kingsley's Novel. By G. Stuart Ogilvie. With Frontispiece by J. D. Batten. Crown 8vo, cloth, printed in Red and Black, 2s. 6d. net.

The Drama.
Continued.

THE PIPER OF HAMELIN. A Fantastic Opera in Two Acts By Robert Buchanan. With Illustrations by Hugh Thomson. 4to, cloth, 2s. 6d. net.

THE DRAMA: Addresses. By Henry Irving. With Portrait by J. McN. Whistler. Second Edition. Fcap. 8vo, 3s. 6d.

SOME INTERESTING FALLACIES OF THE MODERN STAGE. An Address delivered to the Playgoers' Club at St. James's Hall, on Sunday, 6th December, 1891. By HERBERT BEERBOHM TREE. Crown 8vo, sewed, 6d. net.

THE PLAYS OF ARTHUR W. PINERO.
THE TIMES. THE PROFLIGATE.   THE CABINET MINISTER. THE HOBBY HORSE. LADY BOUNTIFUL. THE MAGISTRATE. DANDY DICK. SWEET LAVENDER. THE SCHOOLMISTRESS. THE WEAKER SEX. THE AMAZONS. THE NOTORIOUS Mrs. EBBSMITH. THE BENEFIT OF THE DOUBT. THE SECOND Mrs. TANQUERAY. THE PRINCESS AND THE BUTTERFLY.
16mo., paper covers, 1s. 6d.; or cloth, 2s. 6d. each.

Law.

A SHORT TREATISE ON BELGIAN LAW AND LEGAL PROCEDURE. From a practical standpoint for the guidance of British Traders, Patentees, and Bankers, and British Residents in Belgium. By Gaston de Leval. Fcap., 8vo., paper 1s. 6d.

PRISONERS ON OATH, PRESENT AND FUTURE. By Sir Herbert Stephen, Bart. 8vo., boards, 1s. *net.*

THE ARBITRATOR'S MANUAL. Under the London Chamber of Arbitration. Being a Practical Treatise on the Power and Duties of an Arbitrator, with the Rules and Procedure of the Court of Arbitration, and the Forms. By Joseph Seymour Salaman, Author of "Trade Marks," &c. Fcap. 8vo, 3s. 6d.

Science and Education.

MOVEMENT. Translated from the French of E. MAREY. By Eric Pritchard, M.A., M.B. (Oxon.) In One Volume, Crown 8vo, with 170 Illustrations chiefly from instantaneous photographs. Price 7s. 6d.

LUMEN. By Camille Flammarion. Authorised Translation from the French by A. A. M. and R. M.. With portions of the last chapter written specially for this edition. Crown 8vo., 3s. 6d.

THE STORY OF THE GREEKS. By H. A. Guerber. Crown 8vo., with Illustrations. 3s. 6d.

THE STORY OF THE ROMANS. By H. A. Guerber. Crown 8vo.

THE SPEECH OF MONKEYS. By Professor R. L. Garner. Crown 8vo. 7s. 6d.

ARABIC AUTHORS: A Manual of Arabian History and Literature. By F. F. Arbuthnot, M.R.A.S., Author of "Early Ideas," "Persian Portraits," &c. 8vo, cloth, 5s.

Science and Education.—*Continued.*

EVOLUTIONAL ETHICS AND ANIMAL PSYCHOLOGY. By E. P. Evans. Crown, 8vo., 9s.

HEINEMANN'S SCIENTIFIC HANDBOOKS.

THE BIOLOGICAL PROBLEM OF TO-DAY: PREFORMATION or EPIGENESIS. By Dr. Oscar Hertwig, translated by P. Chalmers Mitchell, M.A. Crown 8vo., cloth, 3s. 6d.

MANUAL OF BACTERIOLOGY. By A. B. Griffiths, Ph.D., F.R.S. (Edin.), F.C.S. Crown 8vo, cloth, Illustrated. 7s. 6d.

MANUAL OF ASSAYING GOLD, SILVER, COPPER, TIN, AND LEAD ORES. By Walter Lee Brown, B.Sc. Revised, Corrected and considerably Enlarged, and with chapters on the Assaying of Fuels, Iron and Zinc Ores, &c. By A. B. Griffiths, Ph.D., F.R.S. (Edin.), F.C.S. New Edition. Crown 8vo, cloth, Illustrated, price 7s. 6d.

GEODESY By J. Howard Gore. Crown 8vo, cloth, Illustrated, 5s.

THE PHYSICAL PROPERTIES OF GASES. By Arthur L. Kimball, of the Johns Hopkins University. Crown 8vo, cloth, Illustrated, 5s.

HEAT AS A FORM OF ENERGY. By Professor R. H. Thurston, of Cornell University. Crown 8vo, cloth, Illustrated, 5s.

LITERATURES OF THE WORLD.

Edited by EDMUND GOSSE.

A Series of Short Histories of the Ancient and Modern Literatures of the World. Each volume will treat an entire literature, and will aim at giving a uniform impression of its development, history, and character, and its relation to previous and to contemporary work.

Each Volume Large Crown 8vo., Cloth, 6s.

A HISTORY OF ANCIENT GREEK LITERATURE. By Gilbert Murray, M.A., Professor of Greek in the University of Glasgow.

A HISTORY OF FRENCH LITERATURE. By Edward Dowden, D.C.L., LL.D., Professor of English Literature at the University of Dublin.

A HISTORY OF MODERN ENGLISH LITERATURE. By Edmund Gosse, Hon. M.A., of Trinity College, Cambridge.

A HISTORY OF ITALIAN LITERATURE. By Richard Garnett, C.B., LL.D., Keeper of Printed Books in the British Museum.

Science and Education.—*Continued.*

LITERATURES OF THE WORLD.

The following volumes are also arranged for:

SPANISH LITERATURE. By J. Fitzmaurice-Kelly, Corresponding Member of the Spanish Academy.

JAPANESE LITERATURE. By W. G. Aston, M.A., C.M.G., Late Acting Secretary at the British Legation at Tokio.

MODERN SCANDINAVIAN LITERATURE. By Dr. George Brandes, of Copenhagen.

SANSCRIT LITERATURE. By A. A. Macdonell, M.A., Deputy Boden professor of Sanscrit at the University of Oxford.

HUNGARIAN LITERATURE. By Dr. Zoltan Beothy, Professor of Hungarian Literature at the Univereity of Budapest, and Secretary of the Kisfaludy Society.

AMERICAN LITERATURE. By Professor Moses Coit Tyler.

GERMAN LITERATURE. By Dr. C. H. Herford, Professor of English Literature in the University of Wales.

LATIN LITERATURE. By Dr. A. W. Verrall, Fellow and Senior Tutor of Trinity College, Cambridge.

BOHEMIAN LITERATURE. By Francis Count Lutzow.

Volumes dealing with RUSSIAN, ARABIC, DUTCH, MODERN GREEK, *and other Literatures will follow in due course.*

THE GREAT EDUCATORS.

A Series of Volumes by Eminent Writers, presenting in their entirety "A Biographical History of Education."

Each subject will form a complete volume, crown 8vo, 5s.
Now ready.

ARISTOTLE, and the Ancient Educational Ideals. By Thomas Davidson, M.A., L.L.D.

LOYOLA, and the Educational System of the Jesuits. By Rev. Thomas Hughes. S.J.

ALCUIN, and the Rise of the Christian Schools. By Professor Andrew F. West, Ph.D.

FROEBEL, and Education by Self-Activity. By H. Courthope Bowen, M.A.

ABELARD, and the Origin and Early History of Universities. By Jules Gabriel Compayre, Professor in the Faculty of Toulouse.

HERBART and the HERBARTIANS. By Charles de Garmo, Ph.D.

THOMAS and MATTHEW ARNOLD, and their Influence on English Education. By Sir J. G. Fitch, M.A., LL.D., formerly Her Majesty's Inspector of Training Colleges.

HORACE MANN, and the Common School Revival in the United States. By B. A. Hinsdale. Ph.D., LL.D.

ROUSSEAU; and Education according to Nature. By Thomas Davidson, M.A.

In preparation

PESTALOZZI, or the Friend and Student of Children.

London: **WM. HEINEMANN, 21, Bedford Street, W.C.**

The Pioneer Series.

Price per Volume in the Colonies and India, Cloth, 3s. 6d.
Paper Covers, 3s.

arles Allen	*Papier Mache*
s. Oscar Beringer ...	*The New Virtue*
Cahan	*Yekl*
Colmore	*Love for a Key*
G. Compton	*Her Own Devices*
phen Crane	*The Red Badge of Courage*
phen Crane	*The Little Regiment*
s. Montague Crackanthorpe ...	*Milly's Story (The New Moon)*
s. Henry Dudeney ...	*A Man with a Maid*
Hamilton	*Across an Ulster Bog*
ert Hichens	*The Green Carnation*
lie E. Holdsworth ...	*Joanna Traill, Spinster*
J. Locke	*The Demagogue and Lady Phayre*
Marsh	*Mrs. Musgrave and her Husband*
rmol Monk	*An Altar of Earth*
vin Pugh	*A Street in Suburbia*
E. Raimond	*George Mandeville's Husband*
E. Raimond	*The New Moon*
rence Alma Tadema ...	*The Wings of Icarus*
n Upward	*One of God's Dilemmas*

Other Volumes in Preparation.

Heinemann's International Library.

Cloth, 3s. 6d.; Paper Covers, 2s. 6d.

Bjornstjerne Bjornson ...	*In God's Way*
Bjornstjerne Bjornson ...	*The Heritage of the Kurts*
Louis Couperus	*Footsteps of Fate*
Gemma Ferruggia... ...	*Woman's Folly*
Karl Emil Franzos ..	*The Chief Justice*
Rudolf Golm	*The Old Adam and the New Eve.*
Ivan Gontcharoff	*A Common Story*
J. G. Jacobsen	*Siren Voices (Niels Lyhne)*
Joseph Ignatius Kraszewski	*The Jew*
Jonas Lie	*The Commodore's Daughters*
Jonas Lie	*Niobe*
Guy de Maupassant	*Pierre and Jean*
Don Armando Palacio-Valdes ..	*Froth*
Don Armando Palacio-Valdes	*The Grandee*
Baron Alexander Von Roberts	*Lou*
Matilde Serao	*Fantasy*
Matilde Serao	*Farewell Love*
Count Leo Tolstoy ...	*Work while ye have the Light*
Juan Valera...	*Pepita Jimenez*
Juan Valera...	*Dona Luz*
Ivan Vazoff...	*Under the Yoke*